Forgetting Tomorrow

Nightmares Through Time, Volume 1

Jerry Evanoff

Published by Jerry Evanoff, 2019.

FORGETTING TOMORROW

First edition. July 4, 2019.

Written by Jerry Evanoff.

Please consider joining my mailing list.

You'll receive an occasional newsletter where I'll share personal stories about myself, how I write and other things about me.

I'll also be giving away FREEBIES, short stories, novellas and anything else in the series I plan on writing. Do you have a character you like? If so, drop me an email and if there's enough interest, I'll throw a short story out there about that character...for FREE!

Details on joining the mailing list are at the end of the book.

For my mom. There was no way I could have or would have done this without her

Prologue

Peter, 2017

Peter stretched out across the bed, his arms and legs flailing in all directions. The weight of the blankets made him sweat, and he flung them off his body. But the room was cool, and the air chilled the beads of perspiration on his skin. His body shivered, forcing him to push his legs under the blankets. The mattress, although it was nearly brand new, felt lumpy. The pillows were flat and hard, making his head slope at an odd angle. That was why he couldn't sleep. Yes, that's what it had to be.

No, that's not it, he thought.

He knew the real reason. He didn't want to allow the words to fall from his lips, but he couldn't stop his own thoughts.

The nightmares are coming again.

He refused to close his eyes. If he did, the nightmares would return, filling his mind with death and destruction.

For the fourth straight night, Peter lay exhausted but afraid to sleep. His eyes drifted closed. He jerked them open to avoid the nightmares. As time went by, they became worse —whereas before his dreams had been pleasant, and sleep a welcome escape from daily boredom.

A few months ago, when the dreams had begun, they had not been nightmares. They had been what dreams should be.

They had been enjoyable. He would go to bed early. In each dream, *she* had revealed more of herself, her amusing little quirks, her likes and dislikes. Each day she had surprised him with some new peculiarity that wasn't there the day before. And he had taken advantage of that. He had kept diligent notes of their conversations and studied the notebook every night. Their second first meeting had been amazing, and they had become the closest of friends.

But these nightmares were different. They were horrific. She was there, and each time he lost her. His friends were there, and he lost them too. He wanted it all to stop. He knew how to make it stop, but he couldn't bring himself to do it. It had taken way too long for him to develop the machine to just toss it away like a broken iPhone. He had a new life. There had to be another way.

Too bad you can't stay up all night, every night. Imagine how much you could get done.

He didn't always like his thoughts. They were truthful, sarcastic and sometimes downright mean.

He couldn't fight sleep anymore. His eyelids gave in.

Hey! Wake up!

Maybe his thoughts were working on his side. He rolled his tired body off the mattress, stood and paced. But eventually, like the three previous nights, he lay back down. His eyes slowly closed. As hard as he tried, he couldn't stop them.

She was there. They were all there, and it all happened again. They all died.

Chapter 1

Peter, 1873

Looking at the three aces in his hand, then at the man across the table staring back at him, Peter felt a small bead of sweat forming at the top of his forehead. He already knew he was winning, and all that remained was to figure out how to get the maximum amount of money from his opponent.

The much larger man opposite him seemed to have been in more than one gunfight that morning. His dark, receding hairline matched a small black mustache perched under his crooked nose. His face and hands matched his dirty white shirt, and a black bow tie accented the black jacket he was wearing. The outline of a pistol was visible against his side, and Peter caught a glimpse of it each time the man pushed chips into the pot. Was that how he intimidated other players?

This must be what passes for business casual these days, Peter thought as he eyed the stranger.

Their eyes met, and Peter held his gaze.

He's staring right at you. He's bluffing. Show no fear.

The bead of sweat slowly glided along Peter's forehead and rested on the bridge of his nose. He didn't touch it.

He wasted many a lonely Saturday night at home watching reruns of the World Series of Poker, guessing what each player was holding. Spotting tells was second nature to him. The man across from him was holding two pair. His betting pattern gave it away.

Before Peter sat down at the poker table, he had spent a few hours at the bar, sipping from a beer mug while watching players face the man who crushed anyone who dared challenge him. Peter had studied him. He had begun to know the man's every facial expression and gesture. It hadn't been long before he was easily predicting each hand the man held before he put his cards on the table.

Full house, he had thought to himself at one point. He had been right.

Bluffing. Right again.

"Come on boy, I'm tired of waiting. Fold or call," the man said, snapping Peter back into the moment. The bead of sweat now hung off the top of his nose.

He didn't dare wipe it off.

The smell of cigarette smoke and humans in need of a shower was heavy. It would have been smarter to pick a time in history with air conditioning and indoor showers, but Peter liked it there. It was peaceful. Most of the time. Right now, he just wanted to finish this hand, collect his winnings and get out in one piece.

The man banged his fist on the table. "Let's go!" he said, a little more loudly.

The hair on the back of Peter's neck rose, and his right leg shook. He finally wiped the bead of sweat from his nose. The customers watching the contest stood and crowded around the players. A spectator next to Peter leaned in and whispered, "You better not be cheating kid. Jack hates cheaters."

Without looking back, Peter let out a nervous sound intended as a laugh, although it came out more like a groan. There was no question what his move was. He pushed his chips to the center of the table. Jack gave a big, toothless grin and flung his cards down.

"Two pair, kings and tens," he said.

"Three of a kind," Peter squeaked in a quiet voice that surprised even him.

Get the money and get out. Don't make eye contact. Just go.

He reached out but was too late. Jack jumped, flipped the table and went for his pistol.

"Shit," Peter mouthed.

Peter shot out of his chair and ran behind the bar, hoping for cover. Jack wasted no time firing in his direction. Pieces of wood splintered in front of Peter as he felt the wind from the bullets speeding past him. There was sharp pain above his eyes. A stray piece of wood had ricocheted and caught him in the forehead. He ran the back of his hand across it, pushing a couple of splinters deeper into his skin.

Next time sit near the door.

He was at the top of the staircase when he finally looked back to see where Jack had gone. Peter didn't see him, but he spotted his backpack lying on the ground under the flipped table.

"You're a goddamn cheat!" Jack yelled.

He finally emerged from behind the bar, still shooting in every direction. It was a wonder no one else was hit. Everyone on Jack's side of the bar heard the shots and reacted as if a shootout were a nightly occurrence. They sunk to the floor with the same energy as if they had dropped their money under the table and were reaching for it. Half of them groaned while others made sure nothing happened to their beer as they waited for Jack to run past them. It was just another Saturday night for them, and very unlike a typical Monday morning for Peter.

Jack shot wildly in his direction. Turning around wasn't an option, but without his backpack, Peter wasn't getting home. Another bullet buzzed by his head, forcing him to take cover in the hallway. The first open door he got to was occupied by a man and a woman. He was dressed; she wasn't. Peter went to the window, paused for a split second and looked back at the empty doorway. Jack would be there any second.

I built this thing to escape my boring life. I guess I succeeded.

A thin stream of blood mixed with sweat dripped into his eyes. He wiped it away and looked out the window. A giant pile of hay lay on the ground below him.

"Not quite as far as the Sky Jump at the Stratosphere," he said to the woman as he climbed onto the window, "but it will have to do."

Peter jumped.

"Which way did the kid go?" Jack yelled loudly enough for Peter to hear.

In the city where Peter had lived his whole life, bales of hay weren't exactly crowding the street corners, but his landing was softer than he imagined. He stood and dusted himself off just as Jack appeared at the window. Peter rushed around the corner of the building to the front. He pushed through the swiveling doors and ran inside. It was a risk, but without his backpack, he was trapped there forever—and much as he loved the peaceful life of Clayborne, Montana in 1873, Columbus, Ohio in 2017 was his real home. Sure, it was boring—but sitting in an office all day was smarter than running from crazy drunk cowboys with guns. And it paid better.

He dove behind the overturned table, scooped the part of his winnings that had not yet been looted by the crowd and grabbed his backpack. Jack, who had decided not to jump, came running downstairs. He saw Peter and fired again.

How many bullets did guns hold in 1873? Aren't these things called six-shooters for a reason?

A bullet caught Peter's shoulder, almost knocking him off his feet. He braced for the pain, but it didn't come. The bullet must have lodged itself in something inside the backpack. He prayed it wasn't the machine.

He ran to his mare, and in one fluid motion, he was in the saddle, ready to go. The first time he had come here, a few months ago, one of the things he had immediately done was learn how to ride. He gave Roscoe a swift kick, and the animal sped off, leaving everyone in a cloud of dust. Everyone except Jack, and a couple of his men, who mounted their horses and gave chase.

It was a basic Wild West small town. There were saloons, stores, a sheriff's office and a place to hold trials. There was absolutely no color unless dirt and dust were colors. Peter could have been in a black-and-white television show, and it would have looked the same. He rode past the last building on what seemed to be a road, or at least the strip of land most likely to be used by horses. He looked back again.

Holy shit, he stopped shooting. Maybe that clown car of a gun finally ran out of bullets.

But Jack and his men were getting closer, and Peter was going to lose this fight if he didn't escape soon. He grabbed the rein, made a hard right and pulled off the dirt road next to a cluster of pine trees.

"Don't worry girl. I'll be back for you in like sixty seconds. You won't even miss me," he said to his mare as he tied her to a tree.

On his second trip here, he had bought a small house with a barn. But to fit into and live the Old West experience, he had needed a horse. He had searched all day and eventually found her. She was all black and of medium height. He had practiced the art of mounting her for hours.

Take a couple of steps, use your momentum to jump, throw a leg over her and hold on.

He had called her Roscoe because mounting her all in one move made him feel like the Bo Duke of the Old West.

He looked behind him again. Jack and his men had also stopped.

"Why did they stop?" Peter asked Roscoe as he pulled the backpack off his shoulder.

Does he think I'm going to turn and mount an attack?

He reached into his backpack, pulled out his bracelet and strapped it to his wrist. Everything looked intact, which meant something else inside the bag had saved his life.

"I'll be back before you know I'm gone," he told Roscoe.

He pushed a few buttons on his cell phone and disappeared.

Chapter 2

Peter, 2017

P eter appeared next to his bed.

"Seven thirty-four a.m. Only took me four minutes to wake up and want to get away from here," he said to Buddy, his white cairn terrier. "Back to this life, I guess."

A dark cloud of dust filled the room as he pulled his shirt over his head. Buddy let out a few sneezes, ran to the other end of the bed and ducked under the covers. Flinching as the shirt rubbed across his forehead, Peter noticed a pattern of blood snaking along its front.

"Oh dammit, Buddy, I really liked this shirt."

Buddy didn't seem to care. Peter could only see his backside, still sticking out from under the blanket.

He pushed the curtains and cracked the window open. Buddy burrowed the rest of his body under the blankets as cold air rushed in, helping to push the dust out. The morning light revealed small dots of blood on the carpet next to the bed. Peter's attempt at dabbing the shirt over cheap white material did not go well.

"Well, that was clearly the wrong approach. I'm terrible at being an adult."

Peter grabbed a second washcloth from the sink and stepped into the shower. Pushing it against his forehead stopped the bleeding for a few minutes, enabling him to run through the rest of his routine. The one difference this morning was to put a Band-Aid across the cut. He threw on his shoes and walked toward the stairs. As he placed a foot on the first step, he paused.

The headlights were back.

In the library parking lot across from Peter's house, the same car from the previous morning faced forward as if staring at his front door, waiting to light him up when he stepped outside.

Yesterday it was no big deal, but two days in a row?

Inside the car, the light from a cell phone appeared, showing the outline of a man's face looking at the house. Peter froze. Their eyes met. He recoiled and nearly tripped over the top step as he hurried down the stairs.

Maybe someone is just returning books. For the second straight day. Without getting out of his car.

He ate his cereal slowly, cautiously, lifting each spoon only to pause long enough for the contents to fall back into the bowl. At each successful bite, Peter's eyes darted to the curtains, then to the door, then back again. The thought of the stranger still held center stage in his head.

Who was he, and why was he there? The man didn't even react when their eyes had met. He had just stared.

Peter grabbed his bag, made sure the machine was still intact, found his keys and stood at the unopened front door. Heart pounding and legs shaking, he took hold of the doorknob.

"Okay Buddy, here goes nothing," he said. "Be good. I'll be back later."

With a deep breath and his head down, he slowly stepped outside.

Sure, good thought. You're not looking at him, and therefore he's not looking at you. Maybe if you throw a blanket over him, he'll fall asleep.

Peter peeked over his glasses.

He's looking at you.

The stabbing pain in his head returned. His eyes went straight to the sidewalk as he walked faster. Again, beads of sweat formed on his forehead, causing one side of the Band-Aid to come unstuck. It didn't matter. *Just get to the car.*

Push through the pain. It will go away.

But would it? It was the same stabbing pain he felt during the nightmares. The nightmares. They were coming back to him. Were things about to change? *Is this when it starts?*

He yanked the car door shut, sending a burst of sound echoing through the silence of an early February morning. *Did this get the man's attention?* He could feel the light from the headlights in his rearview mirror. But they grew smaller as Peter drove away.

"Okay, good," he said, relieved the man didn't follow. "Maybe not yet."

Chapter 3

Peter, 2017

Once safe inside his office, Peter dropped the backpack onto his desk and fell into the old, lumpy, brown office chair he had occupied since his first day. He reclined, swung his feet onto his desk and took a deep breath. It was the first time all morning he had managed to breathe.

"Maybe you weren't such a good idea after all," he said to the machine still tucked in his backpack.

He turned on his laptop and worked through the morning ritual he had practiced since his second day. First, a quick check of the security cameras. He scanned each one of them and, for like the thousandth straight night, nothing happened.

We're a software company. We make 99 cent apps. Our company secrets aren't exactly anything earth shattering.

Only one help-desk ticket, and no surprise to anyone, it was from Anna.

He stretched one more time, yawned and looked out into the main office. From his spot in the back left corner of the building, he could see a large open area with four rows of cubicles stretching to either side. All MPH employees were lucky enough to receive their own private workspace. Privacy, in this case, meant a four-foot wall surrounding an L-shaped desk tucked into the corner of the cubicle. Each desk had two monitors connected to a tower on the floor, a standard keyboard and a boring, black, two-button mouse.

Marketing had its own row of cubicles running along the windows on the left side of the building. Anna's desk was just out of view from Peter's office; he couldn't see it unless he stood on his tiptoes and bent his neck into an awkward position. *Not that you haven't tried about a hundred times.*

Peter was one of the lucky few non-managers to have an office—but only because he was the IT Hardware Tech, and his boss forced him to share a space with a large rack of servers housing every line of code, marketing image and application MPH had used in its ten years of existence. His office was the last one in a row that included his supervisor, the software developer managers and two sales managers.

He shared his back wall with another row of offices, reachable from a hallway where most of the company's bigwigs, including the three co-owners, the controller and two human resources managers spent most of their day. Tinted windows kept the sun from getting inside and mixed with the dreary lighting. It was sometimes hard to tell if you were inside the building or outside during a cloudy Columbus day.

Come on, he thought, *let's take the walk.*

First, the snack machine. He grabbed two Cokes, a bag of BBQ potato chips, filled an empty mug with coffee and made his way to Anna's desk. It was always hit or miss whether she'd be there when he took his walk, but he liked the thought of her sitting down to find the steaming cup he had left, and of her smile as she briefly thought about him.

As he set it down, an image formed in his mind. It was one of his more repetitive scenarios. He would roll over in bed and give her a quick kiss on the forehead before heading down to turn on the coffeemaker as he passed by. After just a few minutes, she would stir—finally surrendering to the smell and coming downstairs to start her day. Their day.

"Good morning, Peter," someone yelled from behind, pulling him back into the real world.

"Yes, yes, it is," he muttered.

He spun around to return the sentiment, but the unknown voice disappeared into an office. Further along, he bumped into Max and Alison as they walked in together, much like they did every morning. He handed Max a Coke.

Tall. Good Looking. Athletic. And a total computer nerd. Way to break that stereotype.

"Morning, dude," Max said, turning his attention away from Alison. "Carson's Bar for lunch later and text Zach. Tell him to come along. Haven't seen that guy since he got canned! How's he doing?"

"He likes it there better than here. Says it's an easier job." Peter said.

"Great! Can't want to see him."

It was nice to be part of the cool kids' group even if tagging along with Zach was what had gotten him included.

"I'm in for lunch too!" Alison said, taking her place in the cube next to Max.

Of course you are, Ali. If Max is in, so are you. Could you two be more obvious?

Peter handed her a Coke.

"Thanks!" she said as she stood to greet Peter.

She was a few inches taller than he, and just as athletic as Max.

"This company should start a softball team," Peter muttered to himself.

You can't catch.

Next was Padma, but her cube was empty. Peter checked his watch.

"Where's Padma?" he asked.

"Not sure yet. She's been late the last couple of days," Alison said. "She better watch herself, the boss doesn't like it when you can't seem to get here on time."

Peter tossed the bag of chips on Padma's desk.

Gotta take care of the people who take care of you.

His pace quickened as he moved past the last row of offices. Staff people. They were nice most of the time, but they wore ties. The only time people wearing ties talked to Peter was when they needed something.

He circled back to the snack machine to get one last Coke for himself. His coworkers weren't alone in their need for morning caffeine.

Feeling safe back in his office, he opened his running list of things to do. A normal day included installing software on his coworkers' computers, testing and fixing errors and general maintenance of printers spread throughout the building. He also monitored the help desk and watched for tickets coming in. And if there was nothing else to do, he volunteered to test apps for the developers, to give them a fresh set of eyes on their creations.

He set the Coke down and promptly bumped it with his elbow as he reached for his mouse. It tumbled to the floor and rolled under his desk.

"Oh, Goddammit," Peter muttered as he dropped to his hands and knees and crawled. "You'd think I'd be able to come in and have a normal—"

"Hey, good morning," Anna said behind him with a chuckle. "When you're done playing down there, come help me."

Peter left the Coke and caught up with her on the way to her desk. As he walked behind her, he watched her ponytail swing back and forth over a peach sweater. She had once told him that whenever she was lazy in the morning, she would just go with a ponytail. It was his favorite. He reached out to grab a stray strand of brown hair stuck to the sweater, halfway down her back. He stopped himself, though, rethinking the idea of physical contact. They stepped through the entryway to her cubicle and sat down.

"What did you spill on it this time?" Peter asked.

"Nothing, I swear. It's just slow."

"It's a brand-new computer. I gave it to you like six weeks ago. What are you doing to these things?"

"Here, you drive." She stood and moved away from her chair.

As they passed in front of each other, close enough to barely be able to slide a piece a paper between their bodies, she paused and touched his forehead, pushing the Band-Aid back into place. He looked into her eyes.

Don't look away.

Peter flinched and looked past her.

Wimp.

"What happened to your head?" she asked.

"Oh yeah." Peter chuckled as he sat down. "Apparently I forgot to dry my feet this morning after I got out of the shower. I took one step into the hallway, hit the tile floor, and down I went. Scraped my head against the closet door. It could have been worse, I guess."

Nice one. The dumber you sound in a lie, the more believable it is.

"Well, that was pretty stupid of you," she said with a smile.

"Looks like something happened with the settings," he said, changing the subject. "I'm trying to restore them, but they aren't saving. I don't understand."

He tried a few more times to change the settings, but each time they reverted. Before he even hit the "Apply" button to save them, they changed. It was as if someone was moving another mouse attached to the same computer.

"What is happening here?" Peter wondered, checking the back of the computer.

"Try restarting," Anna said. "That's what I always do."

It was as good a suggestion as any. He rebooted and sat back as the computer went silent. Seconds later, the fan started, and the boot process began. But as quickly as it had started, the monitor went black and hazy.

"What is that?" Anna asked. She moved closer to Peter for a better view. "No, wait, who is that?"

The reflection of a woman appeared in the center of the screen and slowly grew larger. Was someone walking behind them? Peter checked over his shoulder, yet no one was there. The apparition wasn't completely clear; it was as if the dial on a camera hadn't been turned all the way, keeping the woman just out of focus. She seemed to be wearing a nurse's outfit, but not like any nurse Peter had seen recently. She was more like something he had seen on one of his dad's favorite black-and-white TV shows. Her mouth was moving, though no words were coming from it. Peter reached for the speakers and turned them up to an eerie silence.

"Peter," Anna said, "I think she's saying your name."

They both moved forward to get a closer look. Anna put her arm around his shoulder and leaned against him. For the second time that morning, he stopped breathing, and his heart tried to leap out of his chest. Her cheek brushed against his. He turned his head slightly to say something and caught a whiff of her hair. Everything happening on the screen was now an afterthought as he worked out what to do next.

Jesus, dude, take a breath and focus.

"Do you have some kind of screensaver or something on this thing?" he stammered.

"You're the one who sets up my computer," she whispered. "I've had a lot of issues, but I've never seen this before. Maybe I'm being haunted."

The specter slowly raised one arm and extended a finger toward the pair. In unison, they slid their chairs backward. Anna kept her body against his.

The image disappeared as the sound of the computer continuing its login ritual boomed through her speakers. Peter lurched forward and turned the volume back down.

"What do you suppose that was?" Anna asked.

"Maybe you have some kind of virus. Let me run a few checks while we're here," Peter said, happy that he now had a reason to sit with her a little longer, even if that reason was a strange apparition in her monitor.

"A virus that points to you and mouths your name?"

"We're doing lunch later if you want to come along," he said, ignoring her question.

"Great, I'm in. Who's 'we'?"

"Looks like it's Max and Alison and us. Max wants me to text Zach."

"Oh God, he has to come? I can't stand him," she said. "I guess I'll still come, but I'm not sitting beside him."

It's never good when your future wife hates your best friend.

"Okay, great," Peter said.

Her expression drooped as she looked over his shoulder. Her boss, Albert Peterson, was approaching, carrying a stack of paperwork in one hand and his daily chocolate doughnut in the other. He stopped at Anna's desk, set the paperwork in her inbox and eyed Peter sitting in her chair.

He couldn't even put down the doughnut to come out here.

"Miss Symons, Mr. Cardona, I trust you enjoyed your weekend?" Peterson said, his chins jiggling as he looked from Anna to Peter.

"Yes, sir," she said with obvious disdain. Obvious to some people, but Peterson never caught on. He'd have had to care about people to feel anything.

"Well actually, sir," Peter said, "I did. I went out and saw—"

"That's lovely, Peter. Now please get Miss Symons taken care of so she can get some work done." Peterson waddled away with his hand in the air.

"I'm not sure why he asked," Peter said.

"He's an idiot," Anna said.

"It doesn't appear to be a virus." Peter turned his attention to the computer. "Just let me know if something like that happens again."

Back at his desk, Peter spent the rest of the morning testing apps for the programmers and clock watching. It would have been so easy to shut the office door, lock it, pull out the machine and go west, but as he touched the Band-Aid on his forehead, he thought better of it.

Maybe take a little break.

At about the time the clock reached noon, Max popped his head in.

"Hey!" Max said a little too loudly, startling Peter. "Come on, it's lunchtime."

LIKE MOST BUILDINGS in the city, Carson's had recently gone through some renovations, and half the restaurant area was still under construction. It was darker than usual, with most of the light coming from the wall of televisions, all of them showing sports on different channels. The bartender led them to a high table at the far end of the bar, where Zach was already waiting with a cup of coffee before him.

"How's the new job been treating you?" Max asked as he pulled out a chair next to Alison's.

"It's a piece of cake there," Zach said. "We have twice as many developers as you guys."

"Dude, I still can't believe you got fired," Max said.

"Yeah, no shit. One stupid bug in my program and I'm not even sure how it happened. I tried to tell them I didn't do it, but no one would listen."

"That's all it was?" Max asked. "One bug in an app? No one ever puts anything out that is perfect the first time. Why did you get fired for it?"

"Yeah, one bug and they hung me out to dry."

"It *did* cost us something like fifty-eight thousand dollars and a longtime client," Anna whispered as she stared at the televisions.

"They knew you didn't do it on purpose," Alison said. "They just needed someone to blame to try and keep the client. They even helped you move on. Classy move, if you ask me."

"They made me the bad guy!" Zach exclaimed. "I'm not the bad guy. It wasn't my fault. Someone framed me."

"Probably aliens," Anna said, her voice filled with anger. She turned toward him. "We lost the customer because of you."

"Yeah and they ended up leaving you guys and coming to where I'm at now. They would shit a brick if they knew I was handling their app again!"

"Come on, it's old news," Peter said, trying to diffuse the conversation. "Besides, it all worked out for everyone."

"I wouldn't be caught dead at your place again. They could have kept me, but they needed a scapegoat."

"They hired this girl named Padma to replace you. She's quiet, keeps to herself," Alison said as the waitress put her lunch in front of her—a grilled cheese sandwich with a large plate of fries she shared with Max. Alison moved her chair closer to his.

Peter glanced at Anna, who already was looking his way. He knew what she was thinking.

They should just get a room.

"What do you think she does for a living?" Max said to Alison, changing the conversation and nodding toward a woman sitting alone on the other side of the bar. She was wearing a dark business-casual suit, holding a cell phone to one ear and paperwork covered the table in front of her.

"Jesus Christ," Zach said, "did she open her briefcase and dump it on the table?"

"This again?" Ali asked. "Okay, I'll play. She looks like she could be a spy. She's probably watching people as they eat, maybe even one of us."

"She's not watching me!" Zach yelled, causing the woman to raise her head.

"A spy?" Max said. "You're terrible at this. She's obviously a lawyer who—"

Anna turned her attention away from the banter at the table and back to the television, where sports highlights were being shown.

"Hey, we're over here," Peter whispered to her. He kicked at her feet under the table. "You're not even paying attention."

"Sorry, I missed last night's game and wanted to see how they scored. Plus him," she whispered as she tilted her head slightly toward Zach.

"It was Kaminov," Peter said. "He scored twice within the last five minutes to put them ahead. It was exciting. Too bad you missed it. They play again tonight, going for a nice little winning streak."

"Yeah, I won't be missing two nights in a row. Where you plan on watching?"

"Sitting on my butt on my couch, most likely with a puppy in my lap, just like always."

"Let's meet back here around seven. We'll watch together."

"Sure. Yeah," he said, surprised by her request.

"Great!" she said, turning her attention back to the highlights.

Peter pushed the rest of his lunch around the plate, taking an occasional bite. Those words bounced around his head.

We'll watch together.

What did she mean by that? Two friends hanging out? They'd hung out before, although usually for work-related stuff. She'd even been to his house once but again, it had been to pick up something for work. This was different. This was not a work thing. This was a total non-work thing. This was two people getting together to watch something they both had an interest in. Possibly even sitting on the same side of a booth.

Wait. Was this an actual date? It was almost like a movie, except it was a hockey game at a restaurant instead of a dark theater. And without dinner first. It was no different than if he and Zach went to the bar to watch basketball, or if he stopped by his dad's house to watch the football game. Maybe none of her friends liked hockey. *I like hockey, and we're friends, so that makes sense. Not a date.*

IN HIS OFFICE ONCE more, Peter sat and stared at his computer. His help-desk screen was open, but at the moment, there were no outstanding issues in the queue.

"Come on, something break. Give me some kind of emergency," Peter said as he tried to come up with ways to make the day go faster.

But there was no emergency. It was a routine Monday. He helped the developers with testing and put out small fires if they popped up. His eyes kept moving to the clock.

2:15.

2:36.

3:01.

Come on, hurry 4:00!

His mind wasn't settled. It continued to spin.

Maybe she does have a thing for me? She's always hanging around my office. And when I'm not here, she's texting to see how I'm doing.

The clock finally hit 4:00. Anna stopped by to say good night, same as she did each day. He looked up and smiled. At least he thought it was a smile. The reflection in his office window showed a giant toothy grin.

"Hey, show up at six instead, we'll grab something to eat first," she said.

"Sounds good, it's a date!"

Oh no, not the D-word.

He didn't mean to say it. But it had been on his mind all day, and it forced its way out. Stupid Freud. Maybe she didn't hear, but seconds later she appeared in his doorway.

"Yup," she said and walked away.

Chapter 4

Peter, 2017

"Sorry, Buddy," Peter said as he tripped over his puppy on the way up the stairs. "I'm in a hurry, got a date tonight!"

After he showered, he stared into his closet. The only Columbus Blue Jackets shirt he owned was a free one he had received after signing up for a credit card, but it was nowhere to be found.

"Must be in the laundry," he told Buddy.

At one edge of the closet hung a collection of shirts with buttons and a collar. Half were white and the other half black. This made up the 'dress up' corner of his closet.

"What do you think, Buddy? Funeral or wedding?"

If this works out, you're gonna have to get a new wardrobe before the second date.

He chose wedding, grabbed a pair of black shoes and was ready. He checked the clock. It wasn't even five yet.

Great, now you have an hour to kill.

He sat down at his laptop and opened his usual Monday-evening plans, a chat room. He slid the Dream Machine, a virtual reality headset, over his head and on to his shoulders. As it slid past his eyes, a new world opened before him. He was no longer sitting in the desk chair in his living room; instead, he had been transported to a sidewalk at a motel so close to the highway he could imagine the feeling of the wind from the trucks hitting him as they zoomed by. Chirping birds, two of them apparently yelling at each other, occupied the trees on each side of the motel. He looked into the driveway. It was large and empty, and there didn't seem to be any kind of exit ramp or road from the highway leading to the parking lot.

Did tassemari just drop a motel in the middle of nowhere?

He turned toward the motel and was standing in front of a large wooden door with the room number 3A just above the peephole. He blindly reached for the keyboard and mouse sitting on the desk and used them to control his movements. As he pushed the mouse forward, his virtual reality hand moved, leaving a slight tail of pixels behind it, and grabbed the doorknob. He rotated the mouse against the top of the desk, and although he couldn't feel the cool metal of the doorknob, his virtual hand turned it. The door slowly opened, and he leaned his head slightly forward, making his virtual body move through the doorway.

"Hey all," he said, announcing his presence. "What happened to our Sims world? It was my favorite. This is boring."

"Yeah, this is shitty, right?" a voice from the bed yelled to Peter. "We're about to talk time travel, something futuristic, fun and world-changing and tass put us in a hotel room that looks like something out of the middle of Nowhere, Texas, in 1962."

Peter took a seat next to the large man sprawled out on the bed. He went by Sudo Brownlock, a username Peter always liked. It was more creative than his own, VanBurenBoy, which most people assumed he had stolen from an old television show.

"No kidding. I'd hate to run a black light over this place," Peter said to Sudo Brownlock, who dressed his avatar in a tuxedo with a black bow tie and a cane. "Looking good, Sudo. You going to a virtual wedding later?"

"No, but I can't stay long. I'm meeting a woman from another chat room to watch some black-and-white noir."

"Which one, this time?" Peter asked.

"*Double Indemnity*, one of my favorites. I'm hoping I can turn her into a fan."

"Well, the British accent makes you seem classier," Peter laughed. "And the tux *actually* looks good with the hat."

Sudo Brownlock completed all his ensembles with the same brown Stetson. It was the one rule tassemari enforced. Back when she had created GROUP, she wanted to allow members to be creative with their avatar, but there needed to be a way to identify each other. So you could change your outfit as much as you wanted, yet something must stay constant. Actual name tags were too boring, and that constant identified you.

"Always gotta match the trademark," he said.

"At least you stopped grossing us out with the yellow banana hammock and hat combination. That wasn't a pretty sight, even for an avatar," a female voice said from the doorway.

"Oh, elfGlimmer, we both know you never looked at the hat."

"Hey, VanBurenBoy," she said as she sat down beside Sudo Brownlock. "How come you never change yours? Are you this boring in real life?"

Peter never did anything fancy with his avatar. It wore a pair of faded blue jeans, a white t-shirt mostly hidden under a black overcoat and his signature black sunglasses. If you can't be cool in the real world, at least pretend to be cool in the pretend world.

"I keep telling tass one of these days she ought to give us a strip club. At least give us something to look at while we're doing these updates," Sudo Brownlock said.

"Speak for yourself, ya big perv," marymary said. She was sitting at a small brown desk next to the window. Her constant was a red skirt, and today she was Strawberry Shortcake.

"It would be fun to design a room," elfGlimmer said in her soft, high-pitched voice. Her avatar was a 1960s flower child complete with a headband made of tiny fake sunflowers, oversized round glasses and a long dress full of bright colors. She always wore that outfit but changed the color scheme before each Monday meeting.

"Nah, I'll keep taking care of things around here," tassemari said as she appeared in the room. Her avatar spun, allowing her to scan her latest creation. "This is perfect."

Niven and his ever-changing avatar came in next. It was always something related to a superhero. "If you let that asshole do it, our scenarios would change about every ten minutes," he said.

"Kiss my ass!" Sudo Brownlock shot back.

One by one, members filtered in. Johan, followed by lightninggirl, took a seat on the edge of the bed. Ricka Daigr was next and stood near the bathroom door.

"Looks like we're all here except Rome." tassemari brought everyone to order. "Anyone have anything new to report?

VanBurenBoy, you were working on something. Any progress?"

"Not yet," Peter said. Almost a year after he made time travel work, he still wasn't ready to admit it to anyone. "The only thing I've worked out so far is how to electrocute myself. Poor Buddy won't come near me."

"Be careful, sweetie. You need to be around if one of us manages to work this out," marymary said.

"How about you, Niven. Any hardware updates?" tassemari asked.

"No, I'm still working on getting all the equipment I need for my testing together."

"I thought I had something here," Johan said, "but it turns out you can't build a time machine out of wood. I have hope for my next model, though."

"Stop messing around Johan," tassemari said. "Anyone have anything else?"

"I'm almost out of ideas on the research front, so yesterday I watched *Back to the Future* again. It didn't help." Ricka chuckled. "Seriously, I'm out of ideas. Someone else want to take over research? VanBurenBoy, you want to do it?"

"Sorry Ricka, I'm a hardware guy."

"I'll take it over," lightninggirl said. "I'm tired of reading about history, anyway. Someone else figure out the most interesting time period to visit." Sometimes it was a strain to hear her.

"I think I may have something here," Sudo Brownlock said.

"Christ, Sudo, why didn't you speak up? You should have gone first!" tassemari said.

"I was testing a small machine I built and—"

A bright light pin holed through the front door. Slowly it grew into a circle until the image of a woman shined through. She was dressed as a nurse, and Peter recognized her.

"Not again," Peter muttered.

"Who the hell is that?" Sudo Brownlock shouted. Each of the avatars spun their bodies, turning toward her.

"Oh, no, I shouldn't be here," the nurse said, looking at VanBurenBoy's avatar. She floated backward and faded through the door.

"Shit. We're supposed to be secure!" tassemari shouted. Her avatar moved to the front door and faded in and out, signaling she was switching between virtual reality and the real world.

"tass, what was—" Sudo Brownlock began.

"Are we not secure?" marymary asked. She disappeared from the room before waiting for an answer. Ricka Daigr followed.

"VanBurenBoy, did you say, 'not again'? You've seen her before?" Sudo Brownlock yelled. His British accent faded, and his booming voice overpowered the room.

"No, I don't know her. And sorry, y'all, with that excitement, I'm outta here for the evening. I have a date."

"What? With who?" elfGlimmer said.

"You're off the market?" lightninggirl asked.

tassemari flickered again, and the scene changed from a hotel room to the default scene for the chat software: a large, gray, empty warehouse.

"Everyone out. I need to figure this out. We can't have strangers popping in whenever," she said in a stern teacher-like voice as if she were scolding everyone for talking during a test.

Peter signed out of GROUP, pulled the Dream Machine from his head and left.

Chapter 5

Peter, 2017

The man's car was still there. It was parked between two SUVs at the back of the library parking lot. He was sitting inside, but his attention was no longer on Peter. He was reading a book, probably something he had checked out.

"Maybe I overthought things this morning," Peter muttered as he hit the door-lock button on his keys. He stole a quick glance at the car. The man continued to stare at a page in his thick hardcover, apparently more interested in the words than in what was happening outside his car. "Maybe he's lying to his wife or something. He's telling her he's working, but instead, he comes here to sit and read."

Yeah, or maybe he's one of those new undercover library cops watching for some massive book-related scandal going down any day now.

Either way, Peter didn't have time to care. His mind focused only on Anna, who was meeting him downtown. That's all that mattered.

He pulled into the parking lot at Carson's and reached into the back seat, where the machine sat safely inside his backpack. He paused.

"Do I take it?"

After he had agonized over it all day, she had confirmed it was a date. The backpack hadn't left his side since the first time the machine had worked successfully. He would feel strange and unsafe without it. Would she ask why he had brought it? If she did, would he tell her? No, he wouldn't tell her. He would keep it a surprise in case the night went well. Imagine where the second date could be. Or *when* it could be.

He stepped onto the sidewalk in front of the entrance. His mind was racing.

You should tell her. No one can ever give her a second date like you can. You can take her anywhere you want. Find out where she wants to go. But don't ask. Be subtle, work it into the conversation.

"Nope, not even going to mention it," he muttered.

"Mention what?" she asked.

"Huh?" Peter flinched. He turned and saw her. Her smile wiped away all the stress and worry clouding his brain. "Oh, nothing. Sorry, I was in my own little world, and you snuck up on me."

"Why are you standing outside?" she asked. "It's freezing."

She grabbed his hand and pulled him through the front doors.

ONCE INSIDE, THE HOSTESS led them to a booth in a dimly lit section of the bar. Multiple flat screen TVs hung over their shoulders, blasting highlights from the previous night's game. Jerseys hung on the wall, not only from Ohio State but many of the colleges in Ohio and the professional teams from Cleveland and Cincinnati. Sitting on the table beside the tray of condiments was a small silver vase with six white flowers. One flower was hanging limp. Peter reached over and tried to arrange it with the others, but it broke off in his hand. He crumpled it and dropped it under the table.

Anna took the seat across from him. He sat up straight, repeatedly crossing and uncrossing his feet below his chair. Shoving his hands under the table, he cracked his knuckles, trying to muffle the loud popping sound. Thankfully, Anna was watching the TV over his shoulder and didn't witness his slight emotional breakdown.

"How about that?" she said, pointing to the screen. "Nine and one over their last ten. That's their best stretch for as long as I've been watching."

Relax. She started with sports. You know sports.

"I didn't realize you were this big of a fan." Peter thought back to the Blue Jackets decals scattered among the family pictures hanging on her cubicle walls.

"Yeah, when I was younger, my dad used to take us to games all the time. It started out as a fun way to hang out with him and watch his favorite team lose until..." She trailed off.

Peter nodded. She had mentioned her father a few times in the past but never revealed the details of his disappearance. He remembered a time one evening when his curiosity had grabbed hold of him and wouldn't let go.

It had been an afternoon at work. He had sat in the cubicle, chatting with her as she hung a few pictures of her family on the walls. One picture had caught his eye. It was Anna, her two sisters, and her mom and dad standing outside the arena. Anna and her dad had painted their faces to match the Blue Jackets colors, and the smiles on their faces dwarfed everyone else.

Later, at home, Peter pushed his dinner plate to the side and powered on his laptop. He opened a search window, put his fingers on the keyboard and paused.

"I don't even know his name," he said aloud to no one.

Buddy's ears perked up at the sound of Peter's voice.

He started with the only name he knew, Anna Symons. Thousands of results populated the screen.

"Anna Symons Ohio," he said as he typed, trying to narrow down the search.

Peter scanned through the list of results looking for any keyword that would reveal her father's name. He added "disappeared" to the end of the search and tried again.

Inside the first three results, he saw the name Petros. Each was an article about a man who had disappeared from the side of a road in 2006. The police had found his wife's broken-down car outside the city and assumed he'd wandered off looking for help. He hadn't been seen since, and there were no clues or leads. The case had quickly gone cold.

Peter changed his search to "Petros Symons Ohio," but the results were almost all copies of the same article reprinted in multiple newspapers around the state. As he scrolled through, looking for something different, a link to an obituary from a 1965 edition of the *Columbus Dispatch* stood out.

"Why is his name there?" Peter asked Buddy, who was now asleep—having grown unimpressed with Peter's detective skills.

"Come on," he said after clicking the link, "you have to be a subscriber?"

Pushing his chair back, he turned toward Buddy, now lying on the couch under the living room window. When Peter's eyes moved to the window, an idea formed.

"Despite what you may believe, Buddy, not everything is on the internet," he said. "Be good. I'll be back in a little while."

He ran across the street to the library and sat down in front of the microfilm reader.

"Did I just travel back in time?" he whispered as he looked at the monstrosity in front of him. It made his first computer seem small and compact like he could have shoved it into his pocket. There was a set of reels similar to a movie projector's on each side; the film attached to them, and a large magnifying glass pointed at the center of the tray. Resting over the platform was the bulk of the machine: a large monitor to view the contents of the film that made Peter appreciate the invention of the flat screen.

He stared at the dials on the front of the monitor, pushed a few buttons—but nothing happened. There was no instruction manual.

"Excuse me," he said to the woman behind the information desk. She looked a few days past her retirement.

"What date are you looking for, honey?" she asked in a raspy voice. Peter assumed he'd caught her between one of her many cigarette breaks.

"1965?"

She shuffled over and dropped a metal case on the table next to him with a clang like she had knocked over a suit of armor. Taking the cartridge marked *Columbus Dispatch*, 1965, she attached it to the reels and turned on the light for the magnifying glass. Like a seasoned guitar player's, the fingers of one hand tapped the buttons on the tray while the other's turned the dial, keeping every word in focus as the film moved across the monitor at a consistent slow speed.

Peter watched her hands dance and looked up at her. "Can you maybe do that again, but a little slower?"

She groaned and started over. One by one, she clicked each button, allowing Peter to see how it affected the movement of the film. "With this button, it will move back, and with this one, it moves forward. Do you see what I'm doing? And here's how you focus."

When she finally had enough of him, she turned toward her desk.

Peter shot her a sarcastic smile. "Thank you."

"Kids today..." she said, still in earshot.

He skimmed through the obituaries looking for Petros' name. About an hour in, and tired of turning the dial, he found what he was looking for.

It was an obituary for a woman named Linda Dixon. She had fallen into a coma after being struck by lightning and died three months later. She had been survived by her parents, George and Mary and her fiancé, Petros Symons.

Peter's chair screeched against the floor as he pushed back from the microfilm. "Petros Symons? The same one? I wonder if Anna knows."

"Keep it down honey," the raspy voice said behind him.

Ignoring the woman's warning, he had continued his search; but there had been nothing else about the accident. He'd walked home with more questions than answers.

"...but I kept going to games," Anna continued, pulling Peter back to the reality of their first date. "I tried to get my sisters to go with me, but they didn't embrace hockey like I did. It was one of my only connections to him. I would sit alone and scour the crowd. I wasn't even paying attention to the game. Maybe he was there in disguise, and whatever reason caused him to leave, he still took the chance to see a hockey game whenever he could.

"I never saw him, and eventually, something happened that I didn't expect. I turned into this rabid fan who watched every game. It was a shocking transformation!" She chuckled as she shook her head. "My friends hung pictures of boy bands on their bedroom walls, but my posters were of hockey players. They weren't much of a team back then, but lately, it's much more fun being a fan."

"I've become somewhat of a bandwagon fan," Peter said. "When they are good, I pay attention, and when they aren't, I watch the box scores and wait until they become good again."

His feet stopped shaking, and his shoulders relaxed. This was like every conversation they'd been having for years. She kept one eye on a television at all times but hadn't missed a beat. Her ability to multitask the date was very impressive. Peter was the same way in most conversations, except at this moment, his multitasking included paying attention to what she said as he kept his mouth from saying what his brain was thinking.

What do you think we should name our kids?

"...so when I was younger, I really didn't know what I wanted to do with my life. I enjoyed spending a lot of time by myself. I read a lot, and over time I started to—GOALLLLLLLL!" She threw her hands above her head and cheered.

Peter's eyes widened as he leaned back in his seat. He looked up at her hands and flung his own hands into the air, joining her celebration. "Woo-hoo!" he yelled, frantically looking around and trying to figure out what had just happened.

"You're gonna have to learn to pay attention to both me and the game at the same time!" she said while giving him a high five. "You and that world of yours. I need to see what's inside it."

She leaned forward. "Tell me something about yourself. Something you haven't told me yet."

Peter rifled through his memory, looking for something she didn't know and cautiously reminding himself that he wasn't ready to mention time travel.

"Well, you already know my dad worked a lot and wasn't around much while I was growing up, so he tried to make up for it by buying me things. He bought me my first computer, and at the time I didn't know what it was."

"Right, you've told me that. He was a good guy, never home, did his best, sad Peter, blah blah blah. Come on, get to the good stuff," Anna said with a laugh.

"Okay, when I was about fourteen, I needed parts to improve that computer. It was nice, but my dad knew less about computers than I did."

Peter paused, questioning whether he would finish. He took a deep breath.

"Well, it was about that time I taught myself how to shoplift."

Silence. He studied her face.

She would have made a great poker player.

Maybe that should have stayed in his past, at least until he took her to see Stonehenge being built or to dinner with the Lincolns, followed by *Romeo and Juliet* on opening night.

"See, now that's a good secret." She grinned. "What did you steal?"

"It was mostly parts for my computer. They were small and easy to stuff into my pockets."

"Did you ever get caught?" she asked.

"No, the first time was a small computer shop, owned by just one guy who bought and sold parts. I went in looking for a new hard drive. He had a bunch on a shelf, and when he went into the back to look to see what else he had, I shoved one in my coat. I wasn't even planning on doing it when I walked in.

"The trick was to only do it from places where there were no cameras and no security in the packaging of the items," he continued, "but there weren't many places like that around, and I couldn't go back to the places I had already stolen from."

"You don't still do it by any chance, do you? This meal could be pricey."

"No, it was a phase. It only lasted a few months. I felt guilty and stopped."

She smirked. "And also, you ran out of places to steal from."

Peter nodded and smiled. "Well, yeah. That, too."

"Okay," she said, "I have one for you. Not a single person knows this, so you're sworn to secrecy."

"I promise," he said.

"You remember the day I popped into your office, pulled the door shut and showed you the comic books I was working on?"

"Yeah."

"The next day, I sent them to a few publishers to look at, and since then, I've received three positive responses. I don't know what will come of it, but I don't think I would have sent them if not for your encouragement. Thank you for that."

"They were fun to read." He shifted in his seat and turned away from her. He was bubbling over inside, about to burst. She trusted him. He gave her courage she couldn't find on her own. That was a good sign.

Stop looking for signs, dummy. She's here with you. This was her idea!

The next couple of hours flew by as they continued to watch the game and talk like they had known each other forever.

"Hey, we're winning by three goals. Let's get out of here. There's a place I want to show you," Anna said.

"How can I drive?" Peter asked as he opened the passenger door for her. "You won't tell me where we're going."

"I'll guide you."

She slid into the passenger seat and buckled her belt as Peter took the driver's seat. She directed him onto the highway, and after a few miles, they exited into a residential area.

"This is exciting," she said, bouncing in the seat next to him. "Turn left here."

"But it's a dead end," Peter pointed out.

"Yep," she said, nodding her head in agreement.

"Okay," he whispered. His eyes narrowed as he scanned the area for clues to where they might be going.

They ended up on a long winding road where houses lined each side of the street. It was mostly dark, except for the occasional light from someone's front porch offering Peter a peek at the neighborhood. Each house was exactly the same as if some contractor had taken the empty street and built house after house using the same set of plans. They were two-story homes with a two-car garage on one side, and a large front porch protected by shrubbery with perfect landscaping in front. The road was wide, with two lanes but for a few spots where parked cars caused Peter to slow down and maneuver around some narrow spots.

"Almost there." Anna smiled, glanced at him and back to the road.

At least she's not rubbing her hands together like an evil mad scientist.

"Where are you taking—?"

Sudden headlights in the rearview mirror silenced him. He moved forward in the seat and held the steering wheel more tightly, keeping one eye on the road and the other on his pursuer. Up ahead, someone was working on a car in the driveway of one of the cookie-cutter houses, using a floodlight to get a better view of what was under the hood. Rising from the engine, the man shouted to the young boy in the driver's seat. The engine roared, and a plume of white smoke erupted from the exhaust. Both were oblivious to Peter and Anna or the car that followed them, but the light from the driveway was enough to show Peter a glimpse of the car behind them. It was brown and looked like the same model as the one from the library. A chill ran down his spine.

"Okay, drive to the end. You'll see a dirt road. Pull onto it, follow the path, and I'll tell you when to stop," Anna told him, unaware of the potential danger behind them.

"What was that?" he asked, only hearing part of what she'd said. The rearview mirror was holding most of his attention.

"Just go until you get to the end and then keep going," she said. "Trust me. You'll love it!"

The car pulled so close to Peter that the headlights disappeared.

Is he going to hit us? What do I do?

But the man decided for him. Just before he touched Peter's bumper, he slowed down and turned into the driveway of one of the houses. He drove all the way to the garage and turned off the ignition. Peter let out a breath and patted his chest, trying to calm his heart. He eased back in the seat as they rounded another curve.

"There it is," Anna said, still oblivious to what had just happened and Peter's concern. She pointed to a wooded area ahead.

Peter carefully guided the car off the main road onto a path. Over the years, trees made their home here except for this path, carved by the tall grasses growing. Over time, the path had turned into hard clay that would turn into a muddy mess after the lightest rain.

The light and the sound from the city disappeared, and Peter's headlights were the only thing showing the way. He drove straight until the path led him around a sharp curve to the right. He looked over at Anna, who was smiling and nodding her head. She raised a hand and pointed.

"Right there," she said. "Keep going."

At the end of the path, it was as if they were leaving a tunnel. The lights of the city slowly opened to them. He stopped the car at the foot of a small cliff. She jumped out before he turned off the ignition.

"Let's go!" she yelled as she jogged away.

He ran after her, the cold February air stinging his cheeks. When he finally caught up, she was standing in front of a solitary park bench at the foot of the cliff. She sat down and patted the seat beside her, motioning him to sit. Once down, Peter finally got a full look at the landscape. It was mostly dark, with pockets of light throughout as if someone had misted white paint over a large black canvas.

"Okay, see that house right there?" she turned and pointed through an opening in the trees behind them. "That's where I grew up."

He looked at her, at the smile on her face. Everything she had gone through as a child, thousands of memories running through her mind at once—he could see all of them in that smile. He had seen it every day as he fixed her computer, or at the times when they stood together in the cafeteria, recounting something that had happened over the weekend. And especially the time when she had walked into his office and pulled the door shut to tell him about a talent for drawing that no one else knew about. She had had that same smile. Now he understood where it came from.

"At night," she continued, "I would walk over here and draw. There was never anyone else around, and I loved the view."

"You can see so much of the city from here," Peter said. "It's a lot of energy, but calm at the same time. It's amazing."

"You should see it when it's really snowing hard, and everything is a sparkly white."

They sat in silence for a few moments, taking in the city. On cue, a light snow began to fall.

She planned that.

She moved closer to him, slid her arm under his and rested her head on his shoulder.

"It was always a great place to sit and draw," she whispered. "It's quiet, and I think the beauty of it made things easier for me. It was like my muse."

Peter put his arm around her and pulled her closer. All the anxiety that had built up in him like water filling a bathtub fell away at that moment as if someone had pulled the drain plug.

"One time I was writing, and my mom walked over," she continued. "She would sometimes bring me a snack if I sat out here long enough. I tried to hide my drawings from her, but I think she saw them. I wanted to keep them private. I really didn't think I was any good."

She lifted her head and looked up at him, now only inches away. He could feel the heat from her breath as she spoke, "How come I had to ask you out first?"

The question caught him by surprise. "Well, you know, I wasn't sure what you'd say. I guess I was waiting for a sign. Plus, I was afraid it would ruin—"

She stared at his mouth as he spoke and paused, then tilted her head to one side, took hold of his waist and leaned in. The realization of what was about to happen hit Peter like a ton of bricks. He inhaled hard as her lips touched his. They were soft and smelled of cherry Chapstick, his new favorite scent. She pulled away and returned her head back to his shoulder.

"How's that for a sign?" she asked.

Peter exhaled. He licked at his lower lip, tasting the Chapstick that had stayed with him.

"Yeah, that's um, that's good. That was definitely a sign."

He tightened his arm around her, pulled her close and sat quietly. The snow was falling harder now.

"You're shivering," she said.

Peter noted the goosebumps that just recently formed on his arms. "It's not from the snow."

"We should probably go," she said. "Neither of us is dressed to be sitting out here in this cold."

"Yeah, I should have worn something heavier than this jacket," Peter said with a laugh on the way back to the car.

"What do you want to do next?" Anna said as she closed the car door. "Maybe a movie?"

"Sure, what should we see? I'm not even sure what's playing," he said. The lights of the city behind them disappeared as he drove along the path toward the street.

"I can check." She reached for her phone.

He drove the car back onto the street and rounded the first curve.

"Got it," she said.

As she rattled off a list of movies, his eyes moved to the car that had followed them in. The minute Peter looked at it, its headlights turned on. The interior light was on as well, and Peter could not only see the man behind the wheel, he recognized him. The man pulled the car into the street and blocked both lanes.

"Oh no," Peter whispered.

"What's he doing?" Anna asked.

An older, seemingly broken man stumbled from the car and stood behind his open door. They could see his large grizzled face, dirty blonde mullet and matching blonde mustache, soaked with blood on one side from the open gash on his cheek. He wore a torn-up denim jacket over a ripped black t-shirt. He reached down to his side, lifted a small pistol and pointed it toward them.

"Stop," he mouthed.

Peter pressed hard on the brakes. They lurched forward as the car came to an immediate stop.

"Peter? What is happening?"

"I don't know but let's not stick around to see."

He yanked the steering wheel to the left and mashed his foot into the accelerator, driving the car onto the sidewalk. The engine roared, spraying a burst of white smoke from Peter's tailpipe that engulfed the man. Peter turned the steering wheel left again, just missing a telephone pole, as he made his way through a white fence and into a yard. Throwing grass and dirt in his wake, he pulled the steering wheel to the right and crashed the car through another section of fence, over the curb and back onto the road. Two loud pops cracked behind them. The bullets ripped through the back window, tossing glass into the back seat.

"Shit, someone knows," Peter mumbled.

He looked over at Anna. She had gone pale. She was holding tightly to the door handle with her right hand, her left hand gripping the seat, her knuckles turning white. Her head was on a swivel, twisting from Peter to behind them to the road in front. He reached over, wrapping his hand around the back of her neck and pushing her head down toward the center console.

"Keep your head down!" Peter yelled.

"Who knows what?" She ignored his request, raised her head and looked around.

He grabbed his phone and pressed his 1873 preset, but it immediately switched back to Home. He pressed 1873 again, and again it reverted.

"What the hell phone?" he said, shaking it. "It's a Goddamn chore lately, every time I want to go back."

"Go back where?" she yelled, still getting no answer.

Peter stared down at his phone. He pressed 1873 once more, and this time it appeared to stay. Anna's shoulder crashed into his as she grabbed the wheel and pulled it hard to the right. Peter jumped in his seat and looked up. The parked car she had just avoided zoomed past his window. His tires slammed into the curb on the other side of the street, and again they were on the sidewalk. He dropped his phone between his legs and clamped onto the steering wheel with both hands, guiding the car back onto the street. Anna slid back into her seat and lowered her head. He checked his rearview. The man was back in his car and gaining ground. Suddenly, the headlights in the mirror faded into darkness. The ghostly image of a woman appeared. She was sitting alone in the back seat. It was the same nurse that had haunted Peter throughout the day.

He glanced over his shoulder, but the backseat was empty. Through the rear window, headlights blinded him. The man was still there. Peter turned back to the rearview mirror. The nurse was waving her arms madly as if she were trying to get someone's attention across a crowded room. Her thumb and pinky pressed against her head. He scrambled to grab the phone from his lap and checked the display. It had switched back to Home.

"What the hell is going on?" Peter shrieked.

He pushed the 1873 preset and looked into the rearview mirror. A glowing red ring formed around the woman. It outlined her entire body as tears streamed down her cheeks. She became transparent, dropped her chin to her chest, shook her head and faded away. Peter snapped his eyes closed, and when he opened them, the headlights were back, right on their bumper. He violently shoved the rearview mirror out of position, making a loud cracking noise as he nearly broke it off the hinge.

Anna's head shot back up. "What did you see?"

"I can't explain now but I..." The man smashed his car into them spinning Peter's car 180 degrees bringing it to a stop. He pulled his car next to them.

Anna turned and looked out her window. The man looked at her and smiled, revealing a black hole where two front teeth should have been. His puffy eyes set deep into his head, hiding in the dark, swollen bags that surrounded them. There was something in those eyes, something evil, something that looked forward to the violence he was about to cause. His large smile opened the gash on his cheek, a thin stream of blood falling from it. Everything went silent as they locked eyes.

Slowly he lifted the gun and tapped the barrel on his window. Anna screamed. A piercing scream that filled the car, piercing Peter's brain. He stomped on the accelerator, propelling the car toward the dead-end road.

"Listen—when I stop," he screamed over the roar of the engine, "we're gonna to jump out and run as fast as we can to your bench!"

"What is going on?" she shouted back.

"I'll tell you. No, I'll show you everything. But first, I need you just to trust me. I stop, we jump out and meet at the bench." Peter said.

There was only one escape. Only one place they could be safe.

"Do you trust me?" he asked.

There was a brief silence before she nodded her head.

Holding the steering wheel with one hand, Peter reached into the back seat with the other and grabbed his bag. He pulled the machine out and connected one side to his wrist. Buddy had traveled back with him many times, but this would be the first time with another human.

Hopefully, it works the same way.

The car dove off the main road and onto the path. They lunged forward. Peter could feel the bruise forming on his chest as he hit the steering wheel hard, nearly knocking the wind out of his lungs. Anna cried out in pain as she grabbed her neck with both hands. He rounded the corner between the narrow line of trees, and the city lights shined more brightly as he approached the cliff. With both feet, he smashed on the brake pedal and the car skidded to a stop. Anna jumped out, sprinted to the bench and ducked behind the seat. Peter bolted from the car, grabbing his phone and the bag on the way. Crouching next to her, he strapped the other side of the machine to her wrist.

The man rounded the curve and stopped his car. He stumbled out and limped toward them, staring intently at the machine strapped to each of them. In the past, when someone saw Peter's machine, they assumed it was a simple pair of handcuffs, but bulkier. No one had ever questioned why he had them, but this man knew exactly what he was seeing.

Peter checked his phone one last time. It still said 1873.

"Don't do it, kid," the grizzled old man slurred. He hobbled toward them, nearly falling over several times until he finally balanced himself by holding onto the hood of Peter's car.

"You wanted a peek inside my world," Peter whispered to Anna. He pressed the button, and they disappeared, leaving the man behind.

Chapter 6

Nelson, 1987

As I stood with my parents on our front porch, I struggled to keep a straight face. I knew what was about to happen. They knew I knew what was about to happen, but no one acknowledged it. Everyone played their part.

"Nelson, your gift is waiting inside. You go first," Mom whispered. She put her hand on my shoulder and gave it a slight squeeze. That was strange. She'd never done that before.

Every birthday I remembered had been the same. Mom called my school and told them I was sick. She made my dad take a rare day off work, and the three of us went to the restaurant of my choice for lunch. After that, we went to the toy store where I could pick any one thing I wanted.

On my twelfth birthday, I tested my dad's "any one thing" rule by picking the most expensive item I could find. It was a go-cart, and the two times I drove it were a blast. It's since been abandoned in the back of the garage with half the original tank of gas still inside, yet his "any one thing" rule still applied. This year I'd picked a Nintendo. The birthday boy is by far the easiest part to play.

Dad, who carried the same detached look on his face, opened the door and pushed me inside.

"Surprise!"

The collective yell from the crowd was louder than previous years, but I chalked that up to most of my classmates finally hitting puberty.

"Thanks everyone," I said. "I appreciate you all coming. Now anyone who didn't bring gifts, get out!"

A laugh rose from the crowd. A few of them pretended to leave. But they knew me well enough to know I was joking.

"Dude, this house is awesome," Jeff, one of my best friends, said. "You guys are so rich. What does your dad do?"

"We're not rich," I said. "I'm not even sure what he does. Some systems-manager type thing? It's too confusing to explain, and he stopped halfway through the first attempt."

"Let's go, everyone!" Dad yelled to the crowd. "Pick a room and get into the clothes your parents brought you. Let's get outside before it gets too dark."

"I guess it's big," I said, turning back to Jeff who went to change out of his school uniform.

"Is it big?" I continued, muttering to myself. "I never really thought about it. It's always just been our house. I mean, we *do* have a vestibule. I didn't even know vestibule was a word until I heard Mom say it. 'Your grandmother is here. She's in the vestibule.' None of my other friends ever talked about their vestibule."

I turned to head outside with the others and was face to face with someone I didn't know.

"Why do you keep saying 'vestibule'?" She asked.

"Sorry. I didn't realize anyone could hear me. We haven't met yet, right? You just moved here?"

"A couple of weeks ago," she said. "My mom invited me here. She's trying to force me to make friends as quickly as possible."

"I'm Nelson." I stretched my hand.

"Nice to meet you, Nelson. I'm Sarah."

She took my hand and pulled me closer.

"To be honest, though," she whispered. "I think she wants to get in good with your parents."

"Why?"

"Every time we move somewhere new, my mom will find the richest person in town and do what she can to become their best friend."

"Really?" I said.

"Yeah, she's awful. You know how she met her last husband?"

"At her debutante ball, like my mom?"

"She was behind him at the ATM." She ignored my feeble attempt at humor. "He left his receipt in the machine. She saw his balance and made it her mission to find him."

"Really?"

"She called my second dad," Sarah said. "He used to be a cop. He ran the man's plates, and she immediately knew everything about him. It was quite impressive. Three months later, I'm on daddy number four!"

"You still have a hold of my hand," I said.

"Yeah, I know, let's see what's going on outside."

She pulled me along the hallway and out the back door. One step down and she halted. I collided with her shoulder, almost knocking her down the rest of the stairs.

"Oh yeah, you're not rich," she said, scanning the backyard. "What is all this?"

"Last year I told my mom about this new thing called paintball. I saw it in a magazine. She told my dad about it, and three weeks later, this appeared."

Sarah surveyed the backyard. Along the left side were small buildings normally found on a farm. There was a chicken coop, a milk house, two small sheds and a large red barn next to a pigsty. On the other side was a two-car garage and a large swimming pool. Behind all of it was a small forest.

"He built you a farm with no animals so you can play the most amazing paintball game?"

"Yeah. My friends come over all the time and play, even when we're not here."

"So, this is what it's like to have an awesome dad," she remarked.

"He's not really that awesome," I said. "He just writes the checks. It's just another way to keep me out of his hair during those rare moments when he's home."

A few guys from the football team took control. We usually played teams, but that day, one of them suggested something different. He called it battle-royale style. Everyone for themselves and the last one standing won.

"Just like WrestleMania!" Bryan Belton yelled.

Each member of the offensive line formed a circle around Bryan as if their coach had just blown his whistle. One at a time, he ran toward them, jumped in the air and bumped chests.

"East High School Football rules!" they yelled during each collision.

The choreography was perfect. Did they *actually* spend time during practice making sure they executed this routine exactly right every single time? I loved the challenge of going against the jocks. For them, it was about speed and strength. While there was no doubt they were faster and stronger than me, I beat them with brains every time.

The experienced players crowded my dad, who was standing next to the garage. He opened a cabinet and handed each of them a paintball gun and a mask. They wasted no time filling their hoppers with paintballs, strapping the extra paintball containers to their belt and putting on their masks. Small groups formed and players worked out their battle strategy. It quickly became obvious that "everyone for themselves" might not necessarily mean "everyone for themselves."

Dad gathered the rookies, including Sarah, and took them through a tutorial. He showed them how to load their guns, aim and shoot. It was a safe bet none of them would last long, so I concentrated on the veterans. They would be my main competition. I also looked for Steve Gladwin, my best friend and rival. He was by himself sizing up our opponents. Since my dad had built this field, we'd battled almost every night. We knew each other's style better than anyone else.

After the tutorial ended, each player checked in with me. I entered their names into the laptop that controlled a giant outdoor movie screen attached to the house. During our games, it doubled as a scoreboard. Everyone started in the ALIVE column. Once they were shot, they moved their name to the DEAD column. Since the field was so big, it was nice to have a scoreboard you could see from anywhere.

Once we were ready, my dad blew an air horn. As if someone had kicked a hornet's nest, we scattered in all directions searching out that perfect first hiding spot to keep from quickly being killed. Some, including Steve, sprinted into the woods, while others barricaded themselves inside buildings. I looked for Sarah, but she fell in with two boys who hurried her inside the barn. The urge to shoot them overwhelmed me. I ran behind the barn, jumped across a small ditch that separated our yard from the field and dropped to my stomach in the tall grass. With my finger on the trigger, I took aim at the barn door waiting for either of them to emerge.

My dad, who was now manning the laptop, blew the air horn again, signaling to us that the game had started.

The immediate sound of compressed air pushing a little ball of paint through a narrow tube exploded throughout the backyard like popcorn in a microwave. Most of the rookies died first. I glanced at the scoreboard. Names moved from ALIVE to DEAD in rapid succession.

I never moved until there were five people left, regardless of how many started the game. No point running out and risk getting killed by someone I didn't see. I lay still in the damp grass, keeping my eyes moving from the scoreboard to the field to the barn door. From my spot, I could see most of the woods and the backs of each building. Water from the ground soaked through my coat and into my shirt. I was shivering, although it might have been nerves and not the wind that whipped under me each time. I shifted to keep my legs from cramping.

Patience, Nelson. That's the key to winning. You don't have to get the most kills, just the last one.

More names ticked off. Fourteen left alive, now eleven. Now seven and three of them were in that barn. My heart was beating so hard, it felt as if it would burst through my chest and pound itself into the ground. My finger caressed the trigger. I wanted to shoot someone. I took deep, consistent breaths, counting to four on each inhale, holding it, then counting to four as I exhaled. I've used this technique several times when struggling to fall asleep. The rhythmic breathing calmed me.

A barrage of shots rang out inside the barn. I jerked my head toward the door and waited. Seconds went by before the door finally opened. I held my breath. Todd Colton walked out first, head down, with a large yellow paint spot on his chest. Ryan Cartwright followed close behind him, yellow paint covering his shoulder.

She got them both. Not bad for a newbie.

I checked the scoreboard again. In the ALIVE column under my name were Sean Prescott and Dan Rogers—the two football players who decided on battle royale—my best friend Steve and Sarah.

Out of the corner of my eye, I saw Sean moving along the ditch I'd jumped. He wasn't sneaking or crawling or trying to hide at all. He was casually walking along as if he were taking a late-night stroll along the beach. He probably didn't realize it, but if he kept going, he would gain a perfect position behind me. I couldn't let the guy whose best subject in high school was lunch get the best of me.

I sprang to my feet, the grass and leaves crackling beneath them. Sean turned toward me and squatted, trying to make his six-foot four-inch frame smaller. He pulled the trigger before he lifted his gun, and purple paint exploded on the ground in front of him. He looked at me and chuckled. I bolted toward him at full speed, flailing my arms and shooting wildly. His eyes grew wide as he stumbled, nearly tripping over his own feet.

He regained his balance, turned and sprinted into the woods. I chased him along a path my dad had carved out a few years back, which split the woods in half. He was almost close enough to shoot, but he unexpectedly turned and fired at me first. I tried to stop, but my foot caught a wet spot in the dirt, and I tumbled to the ground. I landed on my back with a thud, knocking the wind from my lungs.

"This is why I don't play sports," I muttered.

I rolled over and saw Sean. He glared at me. The embarrassment in his eyes turned to determination. We weren't playing a game anymore. We were two people who wanted to kill each other. He took two steps my way, but I raised my gun and fired. Red paint exploded a few feet short of him. They weren't kills, but they bought me time. My lungs ached with each breath, but I pushed through and fought my way to my feet. This had to end now. I didn't want to run anymore. He took a step toward me, but I wasn't budging. No way. *I'm not afraid of you.* I raised my gun and pointed it at him like I was Babe Ruth calling my shot.

"Come at me," I whispered. "I dare you."

He grinned—a big toothy grin. Did he hear me? He dropped his arms to each side and puffed his chest out. Was he giving me a target?

Like a flash, he turned and was running again, this time more slowly. Was he trying to get killed?

"Come on," I said as I jogged after him.

We rounded a small curve and cut across a stream. Sean looked away from the path at something ahead of him. I followed his line of sight in time to see Dan duck and then squat behind a tree stump, unable to hide his big offensive lineman legs poking out on either side.

My dad's voice popped into my head: *Always watch for traps.*

Just as he reached Dan, Sean dove off the other side of the path. He rolled down a short hill next to a stream. The trap was complete. At least they were trying something different instead of their usual over-aggressive steamroller style. They put some thought into it. Impressive. Except they forgot whose brain they were trying to fool.

As soon as I was close enough, I stopped short of the tree stump, jumped off the path, and before Dan realized it, I was behind him. I pulled the trigger twice. His camouflage jacket turned a crimson red as the second shot followed the first to the center of his back.

My dad's voice continued to haunt me. *Only a coward shoots someone in the back.*

Hearing the shots, Sean emerged and raised his gun at Dan. Was he *actually* going to shoot Dan after they'd worked together to knock me out? I dove to the ground behind Dan, who was still kneeling, putting all two hundred and eighty pounds of him between Sean and myself. Sean shot twice, hitting Dan in the shoulder as he turned to look at me.

A good old-fashioned double cross. I smirked.

"Dude, I'm already dead," Dan said, flinging his mask to the ground.

Seizing my opportunity, I leaned out and pulled the trigger. The first shot hit Sean in the neck, just below his mask. He grabbed his throat and staggered back. I pulled the trigger again. Red paint exploded against the mask. He toppled down the hill.

"Oh shit," Dan yelled. He scrambled to his feet and ran to the foot of the hill. "You okay?"

"Man, screw this game!" Sean yelled. He yanked off his mask and sulked away.

The only thing I loved more than putting them in their place was taking out Steve, and he was still out there, stalking me. I ducked behind a large tree just in case he was ready to take the shot. He'd probably seen the whole thing. I needed a place to regroup and make with a plan. And I needed to find Sarah.

I exited the woods and snuck behind the swimming pool. The sun began to set, offering more hiding spots; places in the shadows that hadn't existed when the game started. If Steve was looking to snipe me, this would be his best chance. I crept around the circular pool toward the garage, watching for any movement. I stopped and listened. But there was nothing. The garage was just a few feet away. I held my breath, closed my eyes and took three steps. When I opened them, I was there, safely in front of the garage with no shots fired. What was he waiting for?

Pinning my back against the garage door, I took small steps until I reached the other side. I checked the scoreboard. Under my name in the ALIVE column were just two names, Sarah and Steve. It was a short run to the barn, but if I made it safely, I would have all the cover I needed to regroup and reposition. And Sarah might still be inside. I peered around the corner, inspecting each tree. No movement. The only sound I could hear was my heartbeat, and it pounded so hard I was sure it would give away my position.

"Here we go," I whispered.

I took a deep breath. Using the garage door as leverage, I pushed off and sprinted to the barn. Once I reached it, I ran around the other side. The window next to me offered a view of the woods through the inside of the barn and out a window on the other side. I examined each tree. I was ready to give up. Maybe Steve was out and didn't tell my dad. Maybe he was hiding in a building, waiting for me to open the door. Maybe he was...

Movement. A shadow deep in the woods was slowly moving toward me. He must have been watching me the whole time. I scanned the inside of the barn, looking for a spot to make my final stand. There was a loft that would give me the high ground, a great view of the door and a clear view out each window, but getting caught with no way to make a quick escape was not an ideal strategy.

Along the barn's back wall sat my dad's favorite part of the paintball field, his fleet. He drove hundreds of miles in all directions looking for antique tractors. At two different estate sales, he bought a 1966 green John Deere with large yellow tires and a 1975 International 766 in bright red. Next to them sat a 1966 Farmall 660. It was a combination of orange and rusty. The first two had small front tires with large rear tires keeping them low to the ground, but the four large tires on the Farmall raised the body so high I could walk under it without bending over. The last one was his favorite: a 1946 BF Avery in bright red he'd bought from eBay for $4,000. He even made signs and hung them above each one showing the year, model, the value and a short description of each as if this was a small tractor museum. I'd seen him trap unlucky business associates out there at the end of meetings and bore them with fake back stories about each one.

I was ready to give up on the barn as a place to make my final stand when movement near the Avery caught my eye. Tucked against the wall next to the large, red, back tire sat Sarah. She saw me and raised her gun. I put my hands up.

"Not going to shoot," I mouthed.

She lowered her gun and waved me inside.

I made my way around to the front door, keeping an eye out for Steve. I pushed it open and stepped inside.

"Since it's your birthday, I decided not to kill you," she whispered. "At least not yet."

"Well, happy birthday to me."

"Is this fun? I'm not quite ready to call this fun."

"I like doing this," I said as I squeezed myself between her and the wall. "It's like exercise for my brain. It teaches me how to calm myself and work out puzzles."

"Calm?" she asked. "My heart is about to burst out of my chest. Have you shot anyone?"

"A couple, what about you?"

"Nope, not one. As soon as the horn blew, I came running in here. Two guys followed me in, but they shot each other. I decided hiding was my best move."

"Yeah, probably the best strategy," I said.

"How many are left?"

"Just three of us."

"I could have shot you," she said, "and made it to the final two."

I laughed. She was right. And she should have. I lost focus, and a newbie could have taken me out. Steve would easily shoot her, win, and he would never let me live it down. I adjusted my mask, pulling it below my eyes, and looked away.

"I could have shot you too," I muttered.

"Well, one of us will have to die before this thing is over."

She was right about that as well. There can only be one winner. I didn't want to shoot her but winning is the only outcome that makes sense. The first time I invited friends for a paintball game, my dad sat me down and gave me the speech. It was the same speech he gave me whenever I tried anything competitive.

"Everything you do in your childhood prepares you for life as an adult, Nelson. You're not out there to make friends or congratulate someone on their good game as they hoist the trophy. It's your trophy, and you do whatever it takes to get it. There are two types of people in this world, winners and losers. Never be a loser."

An idea materialized in my head. I could use Sarah as bait. It wasn't gentlemanly at all. Mom always told me that chivalry was king, but my dad was right, losing wasn't an option. She could draw Steve out and push him right into my lap. But first, he would have to shoot her. It would work.

"I have an idea. Let's join forces and take Steve out," I said.

I explained my plan, leaving out the part where she was the bait. She agreed immediately, most likely because she wanted the game to end so we could go inside where it was warm. And there was cake. I stood first, held my hand out and helped her to her feet. I checked the window. Steve planted himself against the closest tree about twenty-five feet away. I pointed out his location and took one step. She put her hand out and stopped. "What are you doing?" I whispered.

She moved closer. My body tensed. What was happening? She put one hand on my shoulder. With the other, she reached out and straightened my mask.

"You'll probably want to be able to see."

"Thanks," I said, hoping the mask hid my flushed cheeks.

We weaved through the fleet of rusty tractors and snuck out the door. I directed her to the far back corner of the barn.

"He's behind that tree. Randomly fire that way. If you hit him, that would be great, but if not, you should be able to push him right into my lap. I'll shoot him, and we'll figure out who wins after that."

She fired short bursts toward Steve. An explosion of blue paint around him followed each pop from her gun. While he focused his attention on keeping the splatter from hitting him, I crept along the back of the barn. I paused at the corner and waited. Another burst of paint sailed toward him. I dropped to my hands and knees and crawled to the next building, the chicken coop.

From my position, I could see the small cluster of trees at the front of the woods where Steve was hiding. He would have to decide to either go back into the woods or sprint to the barn while avoiding Sarah's shots. He looked at the scoreboard and froze. There were three names. I think he expected to see two. He glanced around, his head on a swivel, no doubt looking for that third person. *He doesn't know who is firing at him, and he doesn't know where I am.* Perfect.

Sarah continued to fire her gun in a steady five-shot burst, splattering the trees around Steve. She was pushing him my way, just like I planned. He planted his back against a large maple tree and waited for another burst. The fifth paintball exploded so close to his cheek he must have gotten splattered. Out of options, he sprinted to the barn and crashed into the wall on the opposite side.

There, he was left with two options. He could take her head-on or try to surprise her from behind. He would probably win if he went at her, but he might not know which one of us he'd be facing. If he thought it was me, it was a bad move. We both knew I was quicker and a better shot. His only option was to sneak behind her, which sent him my way.

I steadied my breathing again. One. Two. Three. Four. I waited. The field went eerily silent as most everyone went inside to escape the chill. One. Two. Three. Four. Sarah stepped around the corner of the barn and disappeared on the other side. Had she seen something?

I rose to my knees and waited. I steadied my gun and aimed it at the front corner of the barn. Sarah reappeared, looked my way and shrugged.

"Keep shooting," I mouthed.

She raised her gun and fired again, breaking the silence. I dropped to my squatting position and waited. One. Two. Three. Four. He had to come this way. My body shivered as the wind picked up.

One. Two. Three. My eyes darted to the front corner of the barn. The barrel of Steve's gun appeared first. He held it out in front of him, ready to shoot, as he crept along the wall. When he reached the back corner, he peeked around it. He saw Sarah standing with her back to him. He gave a satisfied, smug grin as he raised his gun. Was this how he looked whenever he shot me?

This is it. He shoots her. I take him out, and it's game over. It was a perfect plan. I had opened the chess board, arranged the pieces and seen three moves ahead of everyone else.

Will she realize I used her as bait? She'll surely understand I saw him coming and didn't shoot until after he shot her. Am I a jerk? Will she ever talk to me again?

"Steve," I whispered.

He straightened and looked over his shoulder. I twisted my face into the same smug look and aimed at his chest. *Always go for the chest, center mass, hard to miss.* I squeezed the trigger. The paint exploded on contact, spreading in a pattern that looked like something abstract hanging in my dad's office. He was dead. Sarah heard the shot and turned.

"We won!" I jumped to my feet and ran toward her. I didn't expect to be happy splitting my win, and I was sure my dad would have a talk with me about it later.

"Never settle for second place," he would say.

She walked toward me, a big smile on her face, ready to celebrate our win. A few yards away, she stopped. Her eyes narrowed as her wide smile faded to a smirk. She fired twice. The first shot buzzed past my waist. The second found its target: my right leg.

"I win," she said, winking at me.

I looked at the blue splotch on my pants, my mouth hanging wide open. No wonder she'd agreed to the plan so quickly, she had been looking one move ahead of me.

"This wasn't part of the plan," I said.

"Just like I said in there," she said, pointing to the barn, "there can only be one winner. Besides, you tried to use me as bait."

Defeated by my feelings. My dad would not like that either. After changing out of our paint-sprayed clothes, we joined everyone else in the dining room. While Mom served cake and ice cream, I opened my gifts. Most of my friends brought me cards with cash inside, but there were a few things I wanted, so in the weeks leading to my birthday I had dropped a few hints.

Kelly Norton, a girl in my class, bought me a dark-gray sweater. We had been walking through the mall on our way to the arcade a few weeks before, and I'd seen it hanging in a storefront.

"I really like that," I'd said to her, "but with my birthday coming, it's better not to buy anything right now."

Another boy, Mark Watson, gave me the final ten cards I needed to complete my 1985 Topps Baseball card set. The previous weekend, I'd slipped him the list while we discussed what sets we still hadn't finished.

When Steve handed me a giant wrapped box, I stared at him in confusion. I told him I'd be getting a Nintendo for my birthday, and *The Legend of Zelda* looked fun. Had he not understood?

"Um, thanks," I said.

I tore off the paper and opened the box. Inside was a smaller box, also wrapped. Inside that one was an even smaller one. When I finally got to the last one, I opened it to see *Zelda*.

"Thanks," I said with a laugh.

Sometimes I felt bad manipulating my friends, but it was so easy. I preferred to think I was helping them. They probably didn't know what to get me, so I made it easy.

AFTER CAKE AND ICE cream, it was getting late. Little by little parents stopped by to take their kids home. Sarah was the last to go. I grabbed my coat and walked with her the three blocks to her house. The evening grew dark and cloudy. A full moon tried unsuccessfully to peek out, and a cold wind hit us head-on. I pulled my hood, covering my ears and neck and buried my hands in my pockets.

"I'm glad my mom invited me," she said. "Your parents throw a fun party."

"Yeah, my mom has some serious party skills," I said.

"And I won the game."

"I let you win."

She turned to face me. Her hat and scarf covered most of her face. Only her brown eyes and perfect nose stuck out.

"No, you didn't," she said.

Movement behind her caught my eye.

"Is that your mom?"

Sarah turned. Her mom was standing in a window, making no attempt to hide. Instead, she waved and gave a thumbs up.

"Be sure to tell her you made a new friend," I said. "She'll be happy."

"Yeah, she'll like that."

"See you tomorrow in school?"

"Absolutely," she said as she walked toward her front door.
I watched her go inside before I turned to go home.

THE FINAL PART OF THE birthday was something Mom
came up with on her own. I'm not sure when it started, but she
liked to end the day with a gift for me, something she picked
out herself. It stayed hidden until the last person left and it was
just the three of us. Although most of the time, it became the
two of us, as my dad usually excused himself to his home office
to get a little work done. I guess making up the work hours
missed that day was more important than making up the son
hours missed.

I sat at the table and waited.

"You're staying?" I asked as my dad emerged with mom
behind him. He was holding a small box, wrapped in a plain
white paper with a thin red bow around it.

"Yes, Nelson," he said. His voice was cold and monotone.
He set the box in front of me. "Happy birthday, son."

"Happy birthday, baby!" Mom said, nearly cutting him off.
Her voice trembled.

I lifted it. It felt empty. I held it next to my ear and shook
it. Silence.

"An empty box?"

I unwrapped it and lifted the lid. Nestled in the center
was a folded piece of paper. It was a check made out to me,
dated June 1, 1990. Two and a half years from now. The dollar
amount was blank.

My dad sat stoically like a statue as he spoke, "Son, you're almost an adult. You'll be out on your own soon but let's be honest, you're still a child."

How would you know? You're never around.

"Gee. Thanks, dad," I said.

Mom stood. She wouldn't look at me as she walked around the table. Giving my shoulder a squeeze, she sniffed, wiped her eyes and disappeared into the kitchen.

"You've been living under our roof for sixteen years, and you haven't had to do any growing up. You haven't had to work hard or experience any kind of failure. These are things you need to go through to become a man."

I glanced toward the kitchen, but pots and pans clanging were the only proof she was still within earshot. I tilted my head and stared at the doorway. Was she crying? Why wasn't she coming back? I looked at the check. What was this?

"Nelson!"

I turned back to my dad. He never raised his voice.

He continued, "When you graduate, you're leaving this house."

"Yeah, dad. I assumed I wouldn't be living here forever. Maybe I'll go to college or get a job or something. I don't know. I haven't really thought about it much. But eventually, I'll get my own place."

"There's no 'eventually' Nelson."

"What?"

"After you graduate high school, you're moving out."

"Where will I go?"

"Take that check, hang on to it, and when you're ready to enter college, use it. Write a number in there that will pay for everything you *need* to get your degree. And I'm emphasizing *need*. It's not for fun. It's not to keep buying these toys." He pointed toward the pile of gifts. "It will pay for your classes, books, housing and anything else you need. Make sure you're ready to enter the real world. And I'll even make you a deal: You don't have to work your first two years. Give yourself enough money to study with no interruptions while you figure things out."

For my entire life, this man had done one, and only one thing for me. He had handed over the money. That was the extent of his parenting. He never took me fishing or to a baseball game. We never even played catch in the front yard. And now his grand gesture was to do what he was best at, sign a check. How was this even parenting?

"Nelson, look at me," my dad said. He straightened up in his chair and looked directly at me. "I'm putting you in complete control of your future, and I'm giving you the tools you need to get started. Work harder than you ever have and come out the other side a man. A man who can survive on his own."

"What if I don't want to go to college?"

"You have two years to figure that out. But if you don't go to college, I'll take that check back, and your mom can buy you another video game or something else you'll play with a couple of times before tossing it aside. And you're still moving out on your own after you graduate high school."

I grabbed the check and pushed it into my pocket.

"Are we clear?" he asked.

"Is this real?" I said. "Where's my real gift? Mom's looking for it now, right?"

"This is real, Nelson. I have been discussing it with her for a couple of years now. We agreed this was the best thing for you."

More like you *agreed.*

"You've gotten everything you've ever wanted in life, and you haven't shown me anything—"

"You're never here!" I yelled.

"You haven't shown me anything that proves you can go out and get it on your own," he said, ignoring me as usual. "This is a good thing, son. Trust me."

He stood. His shoulders went back, and his chest thrust out as if he were waiting for me to applaud his great parenting. Another check written and signed. How could I be surprised? That had been his M.O. for as long as I'd known him. He patted my head and repeated. "It's a good thing."

I pushed his hand away and spun toward him. Heat rushed through my body. "Good thing? What if I'm homeless and starving at twenty-three? Will you help me then?"

Pots and pans crashed against the floor in the kitchen.

He remained calm. "If you work hard in school, find something you like and can succeed at it, we won't need to cross that bridge."

That was the last time I ever spoke to my dad.

Chapter 7

Peter, 1873

Peter opened his eyes. Still kneeling, he scanned his surroundings.

"A guest bedroom?" Peter muttered. "That's rare."

A window on the back wall let in enough sunlight to give him an idea of where they appeared. He saw a bed, a small night table and a large wooden bench against a bare wall under the window. Where a door would normally be, a blanket hung, giving privacy to anyone who used the room.

In the Old West, the guest room was usually separated from the main room by a breezeway and served as additional storage. It gave friends and family a place to sleep if there wasn't enough space in the main room. Peter's house also had a guest room, but a few days after he'd moved in, he converted it into a master bedroom. This was not his bedroom.

Something had happened.

Anna squatted next to him, also in the same position she had been in when Peter pushed the button. She stared at him. Her face was pale, her eyes wide as she tried to wrap her mind around what just happened. She reached out, put her hand on his shoulder and squeezed. It was enough to throw him off balance. He fell forward, smashing both knees onto the dirt floor.

Dirt floor?

He stifled a groan and moved to a seated position leaning against the bed. Anna moved next to him. He opened his mouth to say something, but she pushed her finger against his lips, keeping him quiet. Voices from another part of the house caught his attention.

Where are we?

He grabbed his phone and checked the display. The date was right, but they shouldn't have appeared here. Something didn't add up. When he looked at Anna, she looked as confused as he felt. He thrust the phone into her face.

"May third, 1873?" she said, reading the display. She pushed his arm to the side. "What?"

The unmistakable smell of sawdust mixed with the different shades of brown wooden furniture confirmed they were in the right time, but this was not his home. Struggling to find the right words, he pointed at his phone and shook his head. "I don't know."

"I don't underst..." Anna trailed off. Her head whipped toward the doorway. A voice on the other side grew louder. Peter tucked the phone into his pocket. His body tensed as the confusion turned to fear.

"Someone's coming," Anna whispered.

He unhooked the machine from her wrist, dropped it into his bag and pointed toward the front of the bed. Anna fell to her hands and knees and crawled. She reached the front and continued around to the other side. Peter followed close behind her. His hands trembled. He put most of the weight on his arms, trying to keep his aching knees from bouncing off the floor.

Made of a small wooden frame with six short wooden stubby legs, four on each corner and two along the sides for maximum support, the bed was only a foot off the floor. A small night table between the bed and the wall left a narrow space, tight, but just enough for Anna to squeeze into. She dropped to her stomach and slid under the bed.

A man's spurs rattled. He's getting closer. Peter put his head down, closed his eyes and propelled himself into the spot Anna had just vacated.

"I'm checking!" the man yelled. He pushed the green army blanket at the doorway aside.

Peter flattened himself on the floor next to Anna.

"I don't know what you *think* you heard." The man's deep, powerful voice echoed throughout the room.

Peter covered his mouth and held his breath. He could see the man's black cowboy boots, with denim pants tucked into them, as he took a step inside the room.

"I told you there was nothing here!" the man said, letting go of the blanket. The rattle of his spurs faded as he joined the rest of the voices in the main room.

Anna stood, stretched her arms high to the ceiling and collapsed onto the bed. Peter emerged next. He recognized the exhaustion on her face. Over time, he had grown used to what traveling through time did to you, physically. Hopefully, she would too.

"What the hell just happened?" she asked.

"We, um...we're in 1873," Peter replied.

She tilted her head, pressed her lips together. "No, seriously, where are we?"

"I'll explain later. Right now, we need to get out of this house."

Peter crept to the doorway and peeled the blanket back far enough to see into the breezeway. Anna pressed against him and peered over his shoulder, trying to get a glimpse of what waited for them. Most breezeways were open on both sides, which allowed the wind to move through. On warm nights, families gathered there, since it was the coolest area in the house. Unfortunately, this breezeway only had small openings at the top of each side, similar to Peter's car when he cracked the windows at work on a hot day to keep it from turning into an oven.

There goes the easy escape route.

They stepped into the breezeway. A row of denim and cotton pants along with red plaid shirts, both large and small, hung on the first clothesline, to take advantage of the warm air blowing through. Next to it, another row of clothes hung, mostly wool drawers, bloomer pants, socks, two dresses and a red flannel petticoat. Peter and Anna weaved their way through the hanging laundry and paused on each side of the opening that led into the main room. A large fireplace dominated the center. Through small openings on each side, Peter saw a family sitting at a table, preparing for a meal.

"Jimmy," the man with the powerful voice said, "bring the firewood inside first thing then tend to the animals. Take your brother and sister with you. And don't let me catch you playing in the wheelbarrow until you finish your chores."

He was as large as his voice was powerful. Above the denim pants, he wore a white-collared, long-sleeved shirt with a dark vest. His bushy brown mustache and beard hid the bottom half of his grizzled, sunburnt face.

A woman spoke next. She was standing next to the fireplace, hidden from Peter's view. "I'm taking Jenny into town to get supplies. After we get back, I'm going to teach her how to make soap."

"Thomas and William should be here anytime," the man said. "We'll be in the field most of the day."

Peter examined the rest of the room. Two beds occupied most of the space in the corner closest to where he was hiding with Anna. Shelves hung above the beds holding clothes, towels and other items usually found in a modern bathroom. The bottom shelf held three pictures, each one of a different child, and a Bible.

Their only other escape, the front door, was on the other side of the room. Against the wall next to it were two wooden chairs. Facing the chairs was a small bright red Victorian-style couch, which seemed out of place compared to the brown wooden furniture in the rest of the room. Had a rich relative left it to them? Maybe it had fallen off a train, and they were in the right place at the right time to snatch it.

"What do we do?" Anna whispered.

Peter motioned toward the front door, about ten feet away. A latchstring hung through either side of a hole where a doorknob would be, which meant an unlocked door. They should be able to get there and outside before anyone could react.

"We have to run for it," Peter said. "On three, we go."

He braced himself, the pain in his knees fading. Most of the family sat at the table, including the man whose voice they'd heard while hiding under the bed. His back was to Peter and Anna. A loud knock on the door startled everyone. Peter dropped the blanket. They flattened themselves against the walls just inside the breezeway. The door opened, and two men entered.

"Uncle Thomas!" the youngest boy yelled. His bare feet stomped against the dirt floor as he ran into the main room to greet his uncle. The man sitting at the table followed the little boy into the room.

Peter peered through a thin crack between the doorway and the blanket. Both arrivals were tall, one a few inches taller than the other. They looked alike, possibly brothers. Each wore wool grey pants, blue shirts and suspenders.

"Harlow," Thomas, the taller of the two, said to the man in the house as he pried the little boy off his leg. His voice was flat and monotonous, and he didn't make eye contact with Harlow.

"Thomas. William." Harlow's lower lip twitched as he welcomed them. He offered his hand. The other men shook it, but they were quick, cold handshakes.

A chill ran down Peter's spine.

This is probably not a safe place to be right now. There's a history with these men, something recent, and whatever it is, it's not good.

"Ma'am, nice to see you this morning," William said.

"Good morning boys," she said. "Thank you for helping us today. This is the wrong time of the year to be shorthanded."

"Sorry to hear about your brother," William said, his attention now on Harlow.

"I'm sure you are, William. Thank you," Harlow said. "We're hoping he's out before the harvest. Sit, we have a big breakfast ready."

Chairs scraped across the hard-packed dirt as each man found a seat. Harlow took his place at the head of the table with the two young boys on one side and Jenny on the other. All three children sat close to their father. Thomas and William sat across from each other at the foot of the table, near the woman. Peter assumed she was Harlow's wife. Peter and Anna moved to the edge of the doorway. They lifted a small piece of the blanket and peeked out, looking for the right time to run.

"We need a distraction," Peter whispered.

"Everyone," Harlow said. On cue, the members of his family bowed their heads and joined hands.

That works.

"Ready?" Peter asked.

Anna nodded. Using his fingers, he counted down from three. As soon as he said, "Go," Anna sprinted toward the door with Peter close behind. He jumped the couch, grabbed the latchstring and pulled, but the door didn't open immediately.

Stupid strings, always have to pull at the exact right angle.

"Hey!" someone yelled from the table.

He pulled again. This time the door flung open, slamming against the shelves hanging on the wall behind it. Pots and pans crashed to the ground while jars of preserved food shattered against the dirt, spraying tomatoes, pickles and homemade jams all over the furniture. He shoved Anna out first, grabbed the latchstring and pulled the door shut. Gunshots rang out inside the home. Instinctively, Peter ducked, but the bullets only embedded themselves in the thick wooden door.

I am really starting to get tired people shooting at me.

Ahead, a group of horses stood around a hitching post, each loosely tied with a leather strap.

"There!" Peter yelled.

He took the strap of the closest one, a large brown horse, unwrapped it from the post, put one foot in the stirrup and jumped. Using his momentum, he flung his leg over the other side. Anna put one foot into the stirrup. He grabbed her forearm and lifted her into the saddle behind him.

"You can ride a horse?" she asked.

"Lots of practice," Peter said. "Both hands around my waist. Hang on."

He took the reins and gave the horse a kick. With a sudden jerk, it turned and raced off, nearly running down the three men who emerged from the door. Thomas and William held pistols. Harlow carried a shotgun. Anna's fingers dug into Peter's midsection.

Faster, dammit.

Peter gave another kick. The horse shifted into a gallop, burying the three men in a cloud of dust. Peter moved his hips in rhythm with the horse.

Just like riding a bike.

Anna buried her face into Peter's back, moving her hips up and down, bouncing as the horse galloped.

"Loosen up!" he yelled. "Match my tempo. It's a steady beat. Find it and go with it."

He looked over his shoulder. The three men mounted their horses and gave chase. Gunshots erupted, sending bullets whizzing over their heads.

Anna lifted her face and yelled into his ear, "They're not going to keep missing."

"Yeah," Peter mumbled.

As they approached the center of town, he touched the right side of the horse with his heel. It veered off the road and carried them closer to the buildings along the street. Dust and dirt rose, shielding them from their pursuers.

"Hang on tight!" Peter yelled.

Between the church and general store, he straightened, slightly turned his hips and dug his heel. As if the horse knew him, it turned and raced through the alley. Once past the church, he dug in one more time. It turned again.

Behind the church, Peter made himself a little heavier in the saddle, gave a slight pull on the reins and dug in with both feet. She skidded to a stop.

"Someone's trained you well," he said as he patted her on the shoulder.

"Did they see us?" Anna wondered. She loosened her grip on Peter's waist.

"I'm not sure. Maybe we can time jump again. That's how I usually get myself out of these types of situations."

"This has happened before? You've been chased by people and had to jump through time to escape? This is a thing in your life?" she shouted.

"Once or twice." He noted how silly it sounded when she said it out loud.

She snatched his hand, the one with the machine still attached to it, and closed the other side around her wrist. Peter reached into his pocket, pulled out his phone and stared at it.

"Okay, do what you do," Anna said. "Hurry, push a button."

"I don't know the coordinates. My 1873 preset is wrong. It changed. We'll end up back where we started. What if we somehow...merge...or something...with our previous selves?"

"Is that bad?" Anna said.

"I don't know. It's always bad in the movies, so I don't do it. The app auto-increments when I leave."

"I don't know what the hell that means," she said.

He scanned through his preset list, but there was only one for 1873. He could keep the same latitude and longitude and increment by one day, but that would put them right back where they had started.

"Hurry and pick something!" Anna yelled.

It would be a day later, but would they have to escape again?

"Peter!"

What if someone was in the room when they appeared?

"They found us!" Anna screamed.

Peter jumped. He looked up from his phone. Harlow stared at them from the other end of the street. Peter leaned forward and, with his free hand, he took the rein. But, still connected to Anna by the wrist, he pulled her to an awkward angle behind him. She slipped her free hand around his waist and grabbed a handful of skin. Harlow raised his shotgun. Anna screamed and kicked the horse. It reared up and spun. Still holding his phone, Peter swung his other arm around behind him, secured it around Anna's back and held on as best he could. Their horse's front feet landed and its knees buckled, jerking Peter and Anna forward. Peter's phone tumbled to the ground.

We're not going anywhere without that.

Peter pulled tight on the rein. Dust blanketed them as the horse regained its balance. She whinnied. Anna's grip tightened, her fingers digging into his skin, ripping it open. He tugged at the rein again. The horse lurched forward, running around the church into the alley.

"I'm slipping," Anna yelled. Her head pressed against Peter's shoulder.

Again, Peter dug his heels into the horse. It slid to a stop. Anna shot forward in the saddle, grunted as she slammed into Peter and crashed to the ground.

She's still attached to you.

He braced his arm, hoping to keep her from hitting the ground but her momentum was too great. He hit the dirt face first, inhaled sharply and sucked in a cloud of dust. His eyes widened as he grabbed at his throat. He forced a cough. Dirt clumped in his throat.

Get up. No time to waste.

Peter's lungs fought for air. Anna sprawled next to him, moving slightly. He reached out and touched her arm. His eyes watered. Blinking, he tried to clear them, but everything around him fell out of focus. He closed them tightly, concentrated and tried to cough again, but nothing. His chest and throat ached from pushing. Everything around him disappeared, his arms falling to his sides.

Come on! We're not going out like this.

He began to slip away, feeling only the rays of the harsh midday sun. Even with his eyes closed, he felt something move over him. A shadow blocked the heat. Had Harlow found them? A hand pressed against his chest and pushed. Short bursts of air from somewhere deep in his lungs forced their way into his throat. On the third push, a small ball of dirt flew from his mouth. Peter gasped. His throat was on fire. He slowed his breathing, finding a rhythm, and opened his eyes.

"You think I'm gonna let you die and trap me here?" Anna said, her face covered in dirt and dust except for one spot below her right eye, where a single tear carved a trail to her upper lip.

She scrambled to her knees and opened her hand, the one attached to his wrist. He took two long breaths before taking it. She pulled him to his feet.

"Let's go," she said. The roaring of the three horses behind them sounded like approaching thunder. "We're not out of the woods yet."

She pulled Peter toward the church, flung the door open and ran inside. It was a small church, most likely doubling as a schoolhouse. Ten rows of wooden pews were on each side, with an aisle through the middle. A small wooden pulpit stood in the center. On a side wall near the front, another door exited into the alley, near where Peter had dropped his phone.

Peter unhooked the machine from her wrist and rushed to a tall, narrow window on the front wall. He peered through it until he spotted his phone, still lying in the middle of the street. Covered in dust, it was invisible to those who didn't know what they were seeing.

"Over here," Peter whispered.

"They went this way!" Harlow yelled outside. His voice pierced the thin walls of the church.

Peter backed away from the window as Thomas and William came into view. Harlow shouted directions.

"Check the store! I'm going into the church."

Peter and Anna crouched behind the first row of pews. The back door creaked open. Peter checked the side door, their closest escape. If Harlow was holding his shotgun up, finger ready on trigger, they wouldn't survive a sprint.

Harlow shuffled toward them, his spurs jingling with each step, giving away how close they were to the inevitable moment when he would find them. Then what would he do? At each row, he stopped to check.

"I know you're here!"

A low whistle filled the air each time he spoke, from the gap in his front teeth. His spurs jingled again then went silent.

"I don't like strangers in my home," he yelled.

He walked forward again and stopped. Peter crept to the center of their row. Anna, holding a handful of Peter's shirt, followed.

"You better hope I don't find you."

Harlow's forehead was the first thing Peter saw. It was as sweaty and dirty as his own. The man's eyebrows were as thick as his beard.

Peter lunged. He wrapped both hands around the barrel of the shotgun and twisted it toward Harlow, who stumbled backward. Harlow pulled the trigger. A window on the side wall shattered as Harlow cried out. The bottom of his shirt turned from white to a deep red.

Harlow's eyes widened. He dropped the gun and glanced at his torn, blood-soaked shirt, then back at Peter. Foam formed at the corners of his mouth. His nostrils flared, and a vein in his neck jutted out. Peter stepped back.

"You son of a bitch!" Harlow stammered, covering Peter in saliva. He stumbled toward Peter and latched on to his shoulder.

Peter tried to break free, but Harlow's grip tightened. Peter dropped to one knee, pain rippling through his shoulder into his neck. He looked back at Anna. She stood frozen, staring at him. As he turned back to look at Harlow, he tightened his fist and swung. He buried it into Harlow's bloody hip. Harlow roared and collapsed to the floor.

Peter looked at Anna, his hand covered in blood. Her mouth was wide open, but she couldn't find words. Her head twisted from Peter to Harlow, who was in agony on the floor, clutching his side, and back to Peter's bloody hand.

"Come on!" Peter said.

They scrambled through the side door into the alley. Peter snatched his phone. They ran around the side of the next building, the courthouse. She grabbed the machine, still dangling from his wrist, and lifted his arm to hers. His shoulder throbbed.

"No problem," he said through gritted teeth.

He pushed a fake smile across his face. She connected the machine to her wrist and lowered her arm.

"What are you going to do?"

"Hopefully this thing is still intact," he said.

Peter blew the dust off the screen. A small crack had appeared in the corner, but the phone lit up when he pushed the home button. He opened the app that controlled the machine. The preset showed a half hour after the time and date they had landed in Harlow's guest room. He added one to the hour.

"I have an idea," he said. "You ready?"

"Uh-huh." Anna nodded. She took Peter's hand and squeezed. He pressed the button.

They reappeared in the same room where their adventure had begun.

"Come on," he said, leading Anna into the breezeway.

They weaved through the hanging laundry. The woman gasped and stumbled backward as they emerged into the main room. She grabbed the little girl and pulled her into the folds of her long dress. Peter made no move toward them. Instead, he pulled the latchstring, and the door opened.

"Sorry ma'am," He looked over this shoulder at the woman. "We seem to be in the wrong place."

Chapter 8

Nelson, 1994

As I sat in the park, I thought back to the first time Sarah and I met there. It had been four years before, the day after my sixteenth birthday party. I spent the early part of the day going through the motions as if I were a robot, programmed for what to do and where to be each moment of the day.

It was between third and fourth period. I was walking to Calculus, head down, still pissed at my father for threatening to throw me out.

"He's not *actually* going to do this," I muttered, avoiding classmates as they funneled out of Miss Meyer's third-period Spanish class. Sarah was the last one to exit.

"*Hola,*" she said. "Good to see you're still talking to yourself."

I stopped and looked at her. She was grinning. She knew nothing about what had gone on after the party.

"You okay?" she said.

I took her by the hand and led her to a gap between the lockers, leaving just a few inches between us.

"He's kicking me out," I whispered. "He'll pay for my college, but that's all. I have to become a man and if I fail, too bad. If I end up homeless, he'll apparently just let me die."

"Kicking you out?" she asked. "What are you talking about?"

I tilted my head and exhaled. *Is she not listening?*

"When I graduate, I'm out of there," I said a little more loudly. "See ya later, Nelson! He said it would be good for me. Who does that to their kid? And where was my mom? What kind of shitty parenting is that?"

She winced and stepped back. At the time I didn't notice, but later she told me it scared her a little when I raised my voice and cursed. It was a side of me she didn't expect. I can only imagine what the other kids thought as they walked by, watching me yell at the new girl. But, lucky for me, she didn't turn and run. Instead, she rested her hand on my shoulder.

"Hey," she said, stopping me before I started another rant. "Class is starting soon. Just be calm for now and meet me at the park after school, under the giant oak tree. We can talk then."

I WALKED INTO THE PARK and scanned the area. There was a large dog park on one side. Only one lonely dog ran around while his owner, an older man in a suit, sat outside the fence on a set of bleachers with a briefcase in his lap.

"Typical," I muttered.

Across from me, there were four baseball fields. When I was younger, I had played tee ball and little league until I'd been hit by a pitch and quit. My only experience with baseball fields since then had been stopping by on a Saturday to watch Steve play.

Two basketball courts were already full of kids playing, with more waiting on the sideline for their turn. A large fishpond, lined with people, occupied the entire left side of the park. Between the pond and the basketball courts stood a large oak tree, wider than it was tall. Winter took its toll on the bare tree, knocking down most of the leaves by August. I kicked at a few acorns as I walked toward Sarah. She saw me and waved.

"Okay, tell me what happened," she said.

I told her about the gift presentation, what my dad said about my future and how I was done with him. I had even snuck out that morning before he left for work, although if he was back to his normal parenting style, he wouldn't have said anything to me anyway. For the second straight day and the second time in my life, my eyes watered as I talked.

With everything happening around us, she stayed focused on me the entire time. She didn't interrupt or stop me from talking. Instead, she sat quietly and listened.

FOUR DAYS LATER, WE were sitting under the oak tree again, this time on our first official date. My mom had made a picnic basket with sandwiches, fruit, chips and water. She had grabbed a tablecloth from a table on the third floor, one we rarely used, and sent me on my way.

"Just be yourself," she'd told me. "Let happy Nelson come out, and she will fall for you like I did."

"Gross, mom."

That first date wasn't exactly ideal. Sarah only had to ask how I was doing, and I was off and running again. I lay in bed annoyed with myself that night. I hadn't paused once to ask how she was doing. It had been all about me. I didn't expect her to talk to me again.

THE NEXT DAY, I WAS sitting alone at the lunch table staring at my sandwich when Sarah pulled out a chair across from me and sat. She pushed my lunch away and dropped a pile of papers in its place.

"Hey!" I said.

"I've known you a week," she said, "and *already* I know you'll be able to take all the college money he's giving you, find something you like and make more money than he ever did."

A slight pain formed behind my ears. The whole situation was overwhelming. At sixteen, I'd had my future decided by my father. I was college bound with nothing to fall back on if I failed. *Just let me eat my sandwich.*

I looked at her. Her face was expressionless, giving me nothing. I looked at the papers as she shuffled through them, putting them in some kind of order. The words blurred into one giant ink blob, and the pain in my head increased. Pushing two fingers to each temple, I traced circles around them, begging for the pain to go away with no luck.

"And I will help you," she said. "Then *we* can push it right in his stupid face."

"We?" I asked. Was she planning on sticking this out with me until the end? Was she going to pick me up after I failed?

She grinned. "I can be very resourceful."

My father was literally kicking me out and forcing me to survive on my own. He was throwing me in the deep end without so much as a set of floaties. How could she be so positive? How could she be so optimistic all the time? I woke in a bad mood every morning, and here she was, sitting in front of me, cracking jokes about rubbing my success in my father's face. *How do you succeed if you drown?*

"Okay, here's what I put together," she said, ignoring my angry silence. "I found a bunch of questionnaires in the middle-school office. They're supposed to help you figure out what you want to be when you grow up."

"I'm not a child," I muttered.

"I'm joking, Nelson. Come on, just give me ten minutes. If you want to stop after that, we can stop."

I rifled through the pages, each one in her handwriting. She hadn't just grabbed a handful of pamphlets from the office. She'd taken the time to pick the best questions from each one, organize and write them out.

"Please?" she said.

I checked the clock. Twenty minutes left in the lunch period, and I still had more than half of my sandwich. I looked at her. Her mouth curved into a smile, and her eyes widened, begging me to agree. I liked her smile. *I don't want her to leave. If I tell her no, she may leave.*

"Okay," I sighed.

"Great!" She moved from her seat around to my side and squeezed into the empty chair next to me. "Let's do it in the order I wrote them."

She leaned into me, her arm against mine, to grab a pen from her purse. Her skin was cold but soft. She turned her head away, digging through the large bag. Her hair brushed my cheek. Coconut and something else I couldn't place invaded my senses. I closed my eyes and lightly inhaled until the scent overtook me. At that moment, I hoped she would never find that pen, only that she would keep looking.

"Okay." She turned back toward me. "I'll rattle them off a few at a time, and you answer with the first thing that comes to your head."

"Go ahead," I said.

"What's your favorite subject? What's the first thing you do when you get home? How much time during the day will you spend in front of the TV? What's your favorite type of music? How many times a day do you think about me? Make sure you be specific. These are very scientific questions, and the only way to get accurate answers is for you to be specific and answer every question truthfully."

"Math. Take off my shoes. Not as much as you think. Anything with a guitar." I paused, "that last one, I don't think it's from one of your pamphlets."

"It's right here," she said, pointing to it.

"Well sure, it's there. It looks like it could be your handwriting, but who am I to argue with science?" I laughed for the first time in a week.

"Yep, science," she repeated. She put her elbow on the table and rested her head on it, staring at me with pursed lips and wide eyes. The corners of her mouth flinched as she fought back a smile.

I held my answer a few extra seconds, seeing if she would break.

I broke first. "All the time."

THREE DAYS LATER, WE were again at the lunch table. Sarah slid my mom's famous homemade chicken salad sandwich to the side and dropped a bunch of papers in its place.

"Hey," I said, "I get enough homework from teachers. I don't need you dropping more in my lap!"

"Don't worry; your current girlfriend won't mind if you miss a little time working on this so you can buy your future wife that castle she's always wanted."

To be honest though, I didn't care. We didn't have any classes together, and the three-minute break in between them was barely enough time to carry on a conversation. At least we had lunch. The 40-minute period in the middle of the school day became the thing I looked forward to as soon as I opened my eyes in the morning. Most of the time, we talked about her past and my future, which was apparently becoming *our* future.

"Girlfriend?" I said.

"We spend every minute together, other than when we're asleep or in class," she said. "I think it's safe to call it what it is."

"Girlfriend," I repeated. "I like the sound of that."

"I talked to the guidance counselor. She made a list of potential careers based on your answers. She also gave me a list of the majors at the colleges in the area and wrote each school's specialty. Let's go through them and see what looks—"

"A castle?"

We made a list of potential jobs. Anything related to math and logic was preferable, which pushed things like finance and computer programming to the top. Whenever I mentioned my father, even if it was just a passing comment or something under my breath, she stopped me in my tracks.

"Always look forward," she said.

HER ENTHUSIASM RUBBED off on me. When she was around, I stopped thinking about him. He didn't exist. I might as well have been living in a single-parent household raised only by my mom. The old man did what he does best, he wrote another check, but this time he left the amount column blank and trusted me to write in a number.

Planning our future became fun. We made it a game. We picked random items. Food, animals, buildings, it didn't matter. Any object could be selected. We wrote them on small scraps of paper and put them in a hat. We took turns picking items until we both pulled five. We arranged them in order and used them to build a story.

"I have us living in the White House with a dog. We love to eat pizza while watching reruns of *The Andy Griffith Show* on my mom's 13-inch television," she said.

"Mine makes no sense. We have a goat, a cheeseburger, a little red wagon, a rubber duck and we live on Gilligan's Island."

"Why do you keep writing old TV shows?" she asked.

UNBEKNOWNST TO SARAH, it was a different story when she wasn't around. I spent most evenings alone, angry and resenting my father, who most nights didn't get home until after seven. According to mom's rule, we always ate as a family. In the past, I would have hung out with friends in the backyard or played video games, while other times mom and I would have played Old Maid while we waited. But since that night, I was usually upstairs doing homework until it was time to eat. Dinners were silent. Dad didn't seem to care how this blank check was affecting me—although in fairness to him, he never really cared before he gave it to me.

On one rare occasion, he was already home when I walked in from school.

"Hi son, how was school today?" he asked. I walked past him without uttering a word.

Did he forget he recently told his 16-year-old son to pack his bags?

The next day, during dinner, Dad was the first to stand.

"Need to make a phone call," he grumbled.

"Nelson, honey," mom said, "can you help me clear the table?"

I noticed the apple pie, half eaten in the pie tin, still sitting on the table.

"Sure, mom. You get the dishwasher ready, and I'll bring the dirty dishes in to you."

I took a few plates in, scraped the remaining scraps into the trash and returned to the table.

That should hold her for a few minutes. I grabbed a fork and dug into the pie. No one made apple pie better than my mom. I shoved the rest of the silverware into the three dirty glasses and took them into the kitchen.

"Okay mom, that's everything."

I swiped the pie and carried it to my room. What better way to enjoy homework than with a big slice of apple goodness? As I walked past my dad's office, I overheard him talking to someone on the phone. He was calm, but his grating voice carried into the hallway.

"He didn't take it well, but he'll figure it out," he said. He didn't have any friends. Who was he talking to? A colleague?

"My father did the same thing to me, and it worked out just fine," he said. Must be a colleague, probably another father who was working after dinner, never around for his kid. *I'll never be that kind of father. There's no way grandpa did this to him. I've seen them together. They seem to be the best of friends.*

He continued, "I'm not sure. He's giving me the silent treatment right now, but he'll come around once he realizes that it's the best thing for him. One day he'll thank me for it."

Oh yeah, Dad, you're such a great parent.

As much I tried to keep them away, thoughts of my mom getting that phone call—the one where she would be informed he was trying to work while driving, crossed the median and drove head-on into a semi or maybe finally keeled over from a heart attack—sometimes entered my head. She would expect me to be sad, but instead, I would shrug and say, "I guess he should have been around more."

He'll probably cut me out of the will too, I thought.

BY THE TIME WE WERE juniors, Sarah and I were inseparable. We took most of the same classes, went to every dance and served on student council together. She won vice president while I took over as treasurer.

Football games were my favorite. Every Friday night, the student bleachers section packed with fans from all grades. Sarah and I found our spot, top row on the corner, during week one, and it remained our spot for the entire season. As the weather cooled, we would have to share a blanket and squeeze in tight to each other, to stay warm while we cheered on the team.

On the Monday before Thanksgiving, she came running at me after first period.

"Hey, you have to see this!" she handed me a flyer. With a big grin on her face, she bounced from foot to foot as I read it.

"You're going to join the drama club?"

"Yeah, and I want you to join too! This year it's *West Side Story*. It's my all-time favorite. You could be Tony, and I'll be Maria."

"I don't really sing or dance," I said, "but I'll audition and probably make a fool of myself."

"You'll be great!" she said.

I didn't make the cast, but in a nice turn of events, I became her motivation. For a month, we watched the movie almost every night. As she learned the lines, so did I. I could run lines with her as any character. I went to every practice and helped the teacher. In a way, I made it into drama club with her as the assistant to the director.

Avoiding Dad was easier that year. His managers appreciated all the time he spent away from his family. They promoted him to a position that required him to travel out of the country two to three weeks each month. While he traveled the world and left me and mom and alone, I spent every spare second with Sarah. I rarely thought about that blank check.

THAT ALL CHANGED WHEN senior year started. On our second day, she grabbed a chair from another table, dragged it to the empty spot next to me and sat. She kissed me on the cheek and dropped a pile of paperwork in front of me.

"What is this?" I said through a mouthful of pizza.

"College applications."

"Come on," I protested. "Senior year just started, let's have a little fun first and deal with this later."

She glared at me. I knew the look and what was coming next. I'd seen it more than a few times.

"Always look forward," I said, mimicking her. Over the last two years, she'd pounded that phrase into my head.

We filled the papers out together. She was my personal drill sergeant, who wouldn't let me go to sleep until I'd made specific decisions. Regardless of how demanding she was or how much she expected from me, I never lost my temper.

When I finally decided on Ohio State, she was with me. I asked her many times to decide her future based on what was best for her, not by following me around.

"My future *is* you, Nelson."

A WEEK AFTER OUR HIGH school graduation, Sarah and I went to visit Ohio State. We spent the day walking the campus, checking out the bookstore and looking at apartments in the area. We took notes on the cost of everything, as absurd as it might be. What if we wanted season tickets to football and basketball? How much was a new computer with an internet hookup? If we wanted to order pizza and fried chicken every night until we graduated, how much would that cost?

The next morning, I was at her house bright and early. We hung a poster board on the wall of her dining room and wrote each expense on its own notecard. One at a time, we defined each item as a need or a want. Things like school and books counted as needs while others weren't as obvious.

"You *actually* want to go to every basketball game?" she asked.

"Not all of them, but if I wake on a Saturday morning and want to go, I like having the ticket available," I replied.

"Okay, that sounds like a need," she said. "How about a membership to a video store?"

"I don't think we need a membership but make another card and write a number for the occasional movie rental. I don't know, maybe one to two per week."

"CompuServe or AOL?" she asked.

"Whichever one is more expensive, multiply it out for four years. It's a need."

It took most of the day, but we finally settled on a number. She wrote it on a notecard and slid it across the table as if she were making me an offer on a car.

I carefully pulled the check from my wallet, unfolded it and set it in front of me. This was the first time I looked at it since the night of my sixteenth birthday. I remember walking into my bedroom, still devastated over what had just happened.

The check had been crumpled in my pocket. I had flattened it against my dresser and folded it in half. There had been a spare wallet, a gift from my grandfather, duct-taped to the underside of my desk. Grandpa had thought a wallet with a condom inside a perfect gift for a fourteen-year-old. We'd both known mom wouldn't have agreed, so I'd kept it hidden.

"You'll need that one-day kiddo, trust me," he'd said. I'd showed him a picture of the comic book I wanted instead.

As I looked at the check again, my palms were sweaty and my right hand trembled. I traced over the spots where the date had faded.

"Wait!" Sarah yelled.

She snatched the notecard from me. After punching a few buttons on her calculator, she crossed out the number and rewrote it. She increased the amount by twenty-five percent.

"What?" she laughed, noting the confusion in my face. "We should include my living expenses since we'll be sharing the apartment. Haven't I mentioned that yet?"

"You may have left it out." I smirked. "I assumed you were joining a sorority. You seemed so excited about living in one of the sorority houses."

"I'd rather live with you."

THE DAY AFTER THE CHECK cleared, we rented an apartment next to a small lake across from Ohio State's Finance Building. My father wasted no time checking on me, calling me each weekend. I refused to answer the phone, but Sarah usually answered. If she wanted to waste a few minutes of her day talking to him, I didn't care.

"What did he say?" I asked one afternoon. "It sounded like a pleasant conversation."

"Nothing much, he wanted to see how you're doing. I think it surprised him that I answered the phone. Doesn't he know I'm living here?"

"Checking on his dirty money," I said, ignoring her question.

Sometimes my mom would take the phone from him and talk to Sarah. Mom always liked her, and after they talked, Sarah would give me the phone. I filled my mom in on everything that was going on, from school to how things were with Sarah.

"I really love her, Mom," I said.

"That's sweet Nelson...and speaking of love, your father loves you," Mom said, awkwardly switching the subject. "You need to talk to him."

"Not quite yet," I said. Saying it that way gave her the illusion that one day I *would* talk to him. It was an easy way to avoid an argument.

EARLY INTO MY FRESHMAN year, thanks to a finance-class homework assignment, I learned I could play the stock market. I seemed to have a knack for knowing what would gain or lose, and I saw patterns better than most of my classmates. I put together a system of connected spreadsheets and developed a strategy based on those patterns. After three months of day trading on my own, I didn't need my father's money anymore, but I continued to use it for school—putting my personal income away to build a nice nest egg for Sarah and me.

During my sophomore year, he surprised us by stopping by unexpectedly, but I still wasn't talking to him. Instead, I hid in the closet of our spare bedroom, which I'd converted into an office. Childish? Yes, but I didn't care.

"He's not here," Sarah lied. She wasn't like my mother. My mother wanted me to talk to him, but Sarah wanted me to focus more energy on our future.

"How's he doing?" I heard him ask.

"We're doing well," she said. "He's majoring in finance and learning the stock market."

"That's a risky career," he said.

"Still trying to run my life," I whispered. I tensed as the door to my office opened.

"This is his computer," she said. "He spends a lot of time in here, studying."

"Looks good," he shuffled through my paperwork. No doubt it was over his head. "What does he do with it?"

Why does he think he can go through my stuff? I wanted to scream out at him. Tell him I bought those papers with my money, not his!

"I paid for the apartment you're living in, Nelson," he would probably remind me.

"I don't understand the details," Sarah said, "but sometimes if he's in here too long without showing his face, I'll check on him. Bring him lunch or something. He's usually deep in concentration. His head is jumping from the screen to his papers and back to the screen. It's like he's on autopilot, but he's doing well in school, and he seems to like it."

"He was a smart kid. I knew he would figure something out. To be honest, though, I wanted him to figure it out on his own." He paused, tilted his head and looked at her as if she were a puzzle he couldn't quite solve. "But you seem to have his best interest in mind, and I appreciate that."

He stopped by a couple of more times throughout the year to check on his investment. I was usually working and stayed locked in my room. Once satisfied that his investment had paid off, he stopped showing up completely.

THE OLD OAK TREE SEEMED smaller than the first time Sarah and I met here, but I was older, taller, and as of the day before, a college graduate.

I called her after my job interview that morning, which I'd crushed, and asked her to meet me in our spot. I had a surprise for her. She hadn't run from me the first time. Instead, she'd listened as I poured my heart out. She'd comforted and encouraged me, and kept me on the right path even though many times I'd tried to veer.

I saw her coming toward me in the distance. A light breeze blew, tousling her long dark hair and her blue summer dress. I shifted in my seat. She waved. I waved back, wiping the sweat from my forehead as I brought my hand down. I shoved it into my pocket, grabbed the box that held the ring and squeezed it tight.

Would she say yes?

I can't imagine how my life would have turned out if she not been around to keep me always looking forward.

Chapter 9

Peter, 1873

It was about an hour walk to Peter's home.

"So much brown and gray," Anna said. "Why would you pick here?"

"I wanted something peaceful and away from my real life. Something I could escape to when I was bored, which seemed to be more and more lately."

"Peaceful isn't exactly how I would describe my experience so far," she said with a laugh as they entered Clayborne's downtown. "At some point, were you going to come here and stay forever?"

"Probably not. Next year they'll discover gold in the Black Hills, and this place will explode with people. I definitely don't want to be here for that."

He pulled the phone from his pocket and examined it again.

"The coordinates seem to be different by a thousandth of a digit in the latitude," he muttered. "How does that happen? I bookmarked it—it couldn't have changed."

"Then what will you do?" she asked.

"I don't know. You have any suggestions? Want to meet Marie Antoinette?"

Anna didn't answer.

"Or maybe watch George Washington cross the Delaware? I bet we could take a few lawn chairs, set up on the bank of the river with some snacks and cheer him on."

Silence again. He looked up from his phone, but she was no longer beside him. He stopped in his tracks; his body stiffened. When he turned to find her, she was running from building to building pressing her nose to each window, peering through them like a kid studying the toys at Christmas. At the entrance of the general store, she turned back to Peter, opened her eyes wide and tilted her head toward the entrance.

"Come on," she said. She put her hand on one of the wooden swinging double doors.

Peter had been inside the store many times during his year living in Clayborne, but getting the chance to watch Anna discover it for the first time was something he couldn't miss. He took a step toward the store; she smiled and disappeared inside.

As he pushed through the doors, she stood just inside the entrance, taking it all in. Any item you could think of including soap, tobacco, soft drinks and spices packed shelves along both sides of the store from floor to ceiling.

"It's like a nineteenth-century Target," Anna said, her eyes still wide, "packed inside this little tiny building."

Large bins filled with peanuts, rice and produce sat against the back wall. Kitchen items such as dishes and utensils, hunting rifles and shells along with horse tack hung from the rafters.

She shuddered, leaned back and wrinkled her nose.

"What's wrong?" Peter asked.

"The smell of leather just smacks you in the face."

"You get used to it."

Tucked into a back corner, a large wooden sign with the words "Post Office" painted in white hung above a wooden counter. Two men sat on stools in front of it and played checkers on a table made from a wine barrel and a flat sheet of wood a few inches wider than the game board.

"Howdy, Peter," one man grumbled, his cowboy hat pulled low on his forehead. A piece of straw hung from his mouth. He chewed on it like a toothpick. "Hot out today?"

"Yes sir, Mr. Flynn," Peter responded.

"Who's your pretty friend? Is she also from the city?"

"Anna Symons, this is Jack Flynn," Peter said. "He runs the post office."

"Nice to meet you ma'am," Mr. Flynn stood and reached out his hand, a dirty, calloused hand that showed signs of long hours in the field. Anna hesitated, took it between her thumb and forefinger, shook it briefly and let it drop.

"And this is Doc Gyles," Peter said. "He's the town doctor. Anything goes wrong, he can fix it. He also owns this store. But don't play checkers with him, he'll take your silver every time."

Doc stood and gave Peter a smile. He was a tall, lanky man, dressed in black pants, a white shirt and a black bow tie. Over the white shirt, he wore a long black jacket that fell to his knees.

"Ma'am," he said as he tipped his hat. "Don't think I recognize the name Symons. Are you from around here?"

"She's a friend of the family out east," Peter said. "She's thinking of moving here."

"Any friend of Pete's is a friend of ours," Doc said. "You need me to look at that cut on your forehead? Hate to see it get infected."

"No, thanks, Doc," Peter said. "It's fine."

"He thinks you're from the city because of how you're dressed," Peter whispered as they moved away from the men playing checkers. "I was wearing black shorts and a Pearl Jam t-shirt the first time I came here. I bumped into him, and he asked about my clothes. I could tell he was suspicious, so I had to think quick. I told them I was from 'the city' and that seemed to calm him."

"What city are we from?" Anna asked.

"No idea. He never specified one, and I saw no reason to offer any suggestions."

"Okay," she repeated. "If anyone asks, I'm from 'the city.'"

"While we're here," Peter said, "I need to grab a pound of soap."

He took a box from a shelf, pulled a few silver coins from his pocket and handed them to Doc, who met them at the front counter. Doc took the coins and dropped his two smaller coins in front of Peter. Anna scooped them up before Peter could grab them.

"This is a dream, right?" She inspected the coins as they walked outside. "None of this is actually happening?"

Peter reached over and pinched her arm.

"Ouch!" she yelled.

"I guess you're not dreaming," he said. He tilted his head and shrugged. "Looks like it's real."

They reached the last two buildings on Main Street: the Long Branch Saloon and Groover's Cigars. Her eyes turned to the sky. The setting sun highlighted thousands of stars that twinkled in the cloudless night.

"It's beautiful," she said.

She moved closer to Peter. A light but steady cool wind blew in their faces.

"How's your shoulder doing?" she asked.

"Still hurts a little, but it's better."

Once they passed the Long Branch, they veered to the right and walked along a dirt road. Small houses lined one side, while a small stream butted up against it on the other.

"How far do we walk?" she asked.

"About a mile."

They came to the end of the row of houses, and flatland took over as they continued to follow the stream. In the distance, two large houses dominated the area.

"This is what I call the rich section of town," Peter said. He pointed at the stream. "Probably because of the waterfront property."

"They seem so out of place," she said, ignoring his joke.

"When the Homestead Act passed a bunch of years back, two men, Ambrose Clayborne and his son Gabe, claimed this land. Each of them took one hundred and sixty acres of property, and they built their houses next to each other to live as one large family."

"That's convenient."

Peter pointed to a small wooden bridge over the stream, wide enough for carriages to cross.

"We're going that way," he said.

"I still can't believe this. You built a time machine?" she said as they crossed the bridge.

"Yep."

"And this is 1873?"

Peter nodded; a smile formed in the corners of his mouth. He remembered the moment he'd added the second bracelet to his machine. All those tests with Buddy to make sure he wouldn't harm the dog. That was why he'd done it.

"And you come back here to do what?" she wondered.

"Well, for starters," he stopped and pointed over her shoulder, "that's my house."

She turned to see a single-story log cabin with a large shaded front porch and a brick chimney climbing the side wall, extending over the peak of the roof.

"You live here?" She let go of his hand and backed away, "Now I'm confused. Are you originally from here? What year were you born?"

Peter laughed at her implication. "No, born in '91, just like you. What I mean is that when I come back, this is my home. Sometimes I'll spend a few nights here before going back to 2017."

He led her along a stone path with a white picket fence on each side to the porch. Once there, he opened the door and put his hand on the small of her back. She looked over her shoulder.

"You ready for this?" Peter said.

"Can't wait to see it."

Just like at the general store, she took one step inside and stopped. A large stone fireplace dominated one side of the living room, while a small couch with red and yellow stripes faced it. Between them, a large bearskin rug covered the floor.

"Wow, that is one ugly couch," Anna said.

"It's the best I could find. Couches aren't exactly something you can go browse at a department store. They only became available a few years back, thanks to train tracks built not too far away. Besides, I couldn't wrap my machine around my 2017 couch and bring it back here. Maybe I'll make that part of my 3.0 version upgrade."

On the other side of the room, a stove rested next to the wall. A wooden table and chairs large enough for four people occupied the center, and an empty armoire leaned against the wall behind it.

He dropped his bag on the table. In each corner near the stove and armoire hung a small battery-operated desk lamp. He flipped the switch on both, giving much-needed light to that side of the room.

"I see you cheated a little," Anna observed.

"Keeps me from bumping into things in the middle of the night."

He pulled the fabric covering each window, allowing a calm breeze to push out the stale air. After lighting a fire in the fireplace, Peter collapsed on the couch, took his shoes off and tossed them against the wall. They hit the wooden floor with a thud.

"Finally," he groaned. "I feel like I've had these on for a week."

Anna walked around the room. She ran her fingers across the top of the stove, making streaks where dust had collected, and inspected the utensils hanging next to it.

"You know," she said, "if you expect me to spend any time here, you're going to have to let me add a feminine touch."

She ran her hands along the round logs that made up the walls and disappeared into the breezeway. A loud crash from the guest room startled Peter. When he looked over his shoulder, Anna emerged holding two candles.

"Sorry," she said. "I may have made a mess."

She turned off each lamp and replaced them with the candles. Lighting both, she turned back to Peter.

"Much better," she said.

Wandering over to the table, she lifted the machine and inspected it. "How did you build this?"

"I've been working with a small group of people online the past few years. I'm sure none of us actually believed we could do it, but we kept going, meeting every Monday night, discussing plans, assigning jobs. Over time, we've developed into this strange, anonymous online family."

"Anonymous?" Anna asked.

"Yeah, the person who runs it, her username is tassemari. I don't know her real name, where she's from or anything about her. I'm only assuming she's female because her avatar is always female. But it's the internet, so you know how that can be."

"Boy, do I," Anna mumbled.

"What?" Peter said.

"Nothing," she said. "Please continue."

"The first rule she established when she created the site was that it had to be a hundred percent anonymous. I'm not sure why, but it's a strict rule of hers, and since everyone has their own personal reason for wanting to travel in time, everyone obeys."

"What's your reason?" Anna asked.

"I don't know. I'm just bored. Everything is the same, day after day. Life isn't turning out exactly like I hoped."

"That makes me sad."

"Don't be sad. Things have been looking better lately."

"What did your anonymous friends say when you told them you'd figured it out?"

"I haven't told them yet," Peter said. "I'm afraid."

"Of what?"

"Evil villains."

"Peter," Anna said, rolling her eyes, "be serious."

"I am. I've watched plenty of TV shows and movies about time travel and when something like this gets out, there is always a villain who tries to use it for evil. He always ends up destroying the world."

Anna stared at him, smirking, her hands on her hips.

"And yeah, I know that sounds silly when I say it out loud, but I *actually* built one, and I'm *really* afraid of what someone else would do with it. You're the only other person who knows, and that was by accident."

She slid the machine back into his bag, careful to make sure his laptop and notebook were not lying on top. His phone was sitting on the table next to it. She grabbed it and relaxed next to him on the couch.

"How did you keep it a secret from everyone, including your friends and family? And me?" Anna held the phone to him. "You appear to be using an app to control it, but the last time I checked, you don't know how to write apps."

"Remember when Padma started working with us?"

"Sure, right after they fired Zach."

"I was spending a lot of time with her. You started calling her my girlfriend."

"There was definitely something going on with you two."

"Right after it worked that first time, I was nervous that if I ran it again, it would drop me into the same time and place each time. I would somehow merge with my other self, and it would kill me."

"You watch too much TV."

"I needed to figure out how to control it."

"Okay, so you asked your little girlfriend to write you an app?"

"One member of GROUP created schematics for the bracelet and sent them to us so we could build our own. It's nothing more than a set of old handcuffs with padding built around the bracelet area so it wouldn't be uncomfortable to wear. I also disabled the locking mechanism and added a release button, so you don't need a key."

She pressed a button, and one of the bracelets popped open. She slipped it on her wrist, locked it and pressed the button again to unlock it.

Peter continued, "In the center, there is a microchip that holds the date, time and location of your destination. I took the machine to Padma and told her it was for finding your ball on a golf course, and I asked her to write an app that would let me change the info on the chip. That way, I could travel wherever I want."

"But why Padma? You didn't even know her."

"She saw me fiddling with it one day in my office and asked me what it was," Peter said. "I told her it was something for golf and mentioned I needed an app for it. She volunteered. Besides, Max and Ali would have asked too many questions, but Padma was new. She barely knew me and knows nothing about golf, so if she asked questions, I could just make something up, and she wouldn't know any better."

"How often do you come here?" Anna asked.

"Most mornings before work, I come back and spend a few hours, sometimes a few days."

"Do you go anywhere else? You've never thought of going back to do something important? Maybe kill Hitler or stop the JFK assassination?"

"Now who watches too much TV? Besides, I wanted to escape and go somewhere where no one knows me. Maybe I could start over and become someone new, someone who takes risks, has more fun."

"Have you ever gone into the future to see how you turn out?"

"No way. I don't want to know what kind of person I become. What if I become someone I don't like? What if I'm not there?"

He took the phone from her and stared at the display. Why were the coordinates wrong? Padma had created a place for him to store the destinations he planned to return to, like bookmarks on a web browser.

"We should have landed right beside Roscoe a few minutes after Jack chased me from the poker game earlier this morning," Peter muttered.

"Roscoe?"

"My horse. I left her this morning tied to a tree in the middle of nowhere."

"Chased this morning, chased again this evening. Doesn't sound so fun."

"But I don't know what happened with my bookmark. How could it have changed?"

The woman from that morning in Anna's monitor! She was the same one who crashed their GROUP meeting and showed up in his rearview mirror. But who was she? She seemed to be able to control his phone while they were running from the strange man in the brown car. Had she changed it?

"You ever feel like you're being watched?" Peter asked.

"Well, there was that time a man with a gun chased me into 1873?" Anna said. "You think he knows?"

"Maybe but I'm not sure how. I don't know who he is," Peter said. "This is something else, almost supernatural."

"What do you mean?"

"Every time I struggle with a piece of hardware, I feel like it's fighting against me. No matter what I do, I can't seem to fix the easiest things. And lately, I've seen things—reflections, shadows."

"Like this morning at my computer?" she asked.

"Yeah, and whatever that was, it was specifically for me. The way she pointed at me and was trying to say my name. And then again in the car."

"In the car?"

"I saw her in the mirror, the same woman from your monitor, while we were being chased. I think she's why my coordinates were incorrect. She changed them. And when I changed them back, she was crying. Then she disappeared."

"Next time you see her, try to talk to her," Anna said. "Maybe she's trying to help you."

"I guess." Peter sighed, his shoulders slumping as he looked at his feet.

"So, your plan is to come back to 1873 and live part-time, like a summer home?"

"Yeah, that's pretty much it."

"Peter, that sounds boring," she said. "You invented a time machine, and your big idea is to find a place to live another boring life? I watched you when you walked in. You have a routine here just like at work. That's insane! Let's have fun with it."

"That sounds dangerous," Peter said.

"More dangerous than running from men with guns? You've done that three times today, and I've had to do it twice."

"No, that's not what I mean. I'm talking about canceling out my own existence. It's why I picked Montana in 1873. It's far enough away from my own life so that if I change something, it won't hurt me."

She stretched her arms, yawned and rested her head against Peter's chest.

"I tried to change my past once," he continued, "but it didn't go well. I concluded that time is like a piece of string that is being held on to by your past self and your current self. The closer you get to something that affects you, the tighter the string. And the tighter the string, the harder it is to change things. So I decided I wouldn't use the machine that way; instead, I was just going explore history and find a place to create a new life. I wanted as much slack in the string as possible."

Peter paused and waited for a push back. He had been in plenty of marketing meetings with her, and when she decided she wanted something to go her way, she didn't stop until you grew tired of arguing and gave in. But there was no response.

She had fallen asleep, which seemed like the best thing for them both. He slowly inched the rest of the way down, taking care not to wake her and stretched out. She shifted her body until she tucked herself against him. He yawned and closed his eyes. Too much running from bad guys today had exhausted him, and it was nice finally to have peace. Their first date had had a couple of speed bumps along the way, but this was a nice way to end it.

THE NEXT MORNING, A ray of sunlight poked through the window and slowly traced Peter's face. He swiped at it as if a mosquito had just penetrated his skin and taken its first meal of the day. He rubbed his eyes, opened them and blinked. Anna was no longer lying next to him and based on the sounds from the stove, she was either fighting off a hoard of squirrels with a frying pan or trying to cook breakfast. He straightened his legs, hanging them over the other end of the couch. He let out a loud groan as he yawned, his face stretching as far it could go.

"Good morning." She was standing next to the stove. "How do you turn this on?"

Peter stood tall and stretched again. He straightened his shirt and jeans, both crooked from the awkward position he'd slept in.

Couches in 1873 were not made to be slept on.

A few pieces of wood still burned in the fireplace. He limped over to it, pulled the tongs from their hook and grabbed a log.

"So much to learn," Anna said as he carried it to the stove, opened the small door at the bottom and slid the log inside.

A pile of newspapers was stacked in the corner next to her.

"Can you hand me the top one?" Peter asked.

He threw it on the burning log and watched it ignite as he shut the door. The small dial on top of the stove was already turned to hot. Confused, Peter looked back at Anna.

"I thought that was the on switch," she said.

"Give it a few minutes. It will be ready."

"Thanks," she said. "By the way, I found some eggs and bacon in your icebox. The expiration on the bacon is like a hundred and forty-four years from now."

"I don't like to grocery shop in 1873. There aren't as many options. It's easier to throw a few things in my bag each time I come here."

"Like those lamps?"

"Like those lamps."

Peter showed her the small room next to the stove where he hung meat to dry. He sliced off a couple of pieces of beef and tossed them into the cast iron pan next to the bacon.

"That's a lot of meat for breakfast," Anna remarked.

"When in Rome..."

After cooking breakfast, they sat to eat. He looked across the table at Anna as she shoved a slice of bacon in her mouth.

"You're wearing my shirt," Peter said.

"Mine was gross. I found this one in the guest room before you woke up. It seemed clean. How's it look?"

It was a plain gray t-shirt with the faded Columbus Blue Jackets logo on one side and the website of whatever credit card he'd applied for to get the free t-shirt.

"Looks good." He smiled. "I was wondering what had happened to that shirt."

"So, I was thinking," she said. "Let's have a little fun with your machine."

Peter closed his eyes, shifted in his chair and inhaled. Without looking at her, he asked, "What kind of fun?"

"Don't worry," she replied. "According to your string metaphor, we wouldn't be able to do anything that affects us directly because the string would be too tight. But I bet there's enough slack to mess with my boss. Maybe we can get him fired."

He pushed the rest of his breakfast around the plate.

"That could have a huge effect on you," Peter's said in a monotone. "We can't do that."

"We have to do something. You can't expect me to just come back with you now and then and live the life of an Old West housewife. I want to play too."

This could be when it starts.

"We can't."

Memories of the nightmares flooded into his head.

Everyone died, including her.

"What if we stayed far away from—"

"No, end of story," Peter snapped.

It was harsh of him, but he couldn't allow her to go on anymore. She couldn't keep pressing. She wasn't aware of the nightmares and what they meant.

They ate the rest of their breakfast in silence. It wasn't until Peter pushed his empty plate across the table that Anna spoke again.

"How much do you know about my dad?" she asked.

He looked up. Their eyes locked.

"A little. You've mentioned him a few times. I didn't want to pry so I did some research on my own. He disappeared a bunch of years ago."

"May twenty-sixth, 2006." She looked off to the side and wiped her eyes. "Worst day of my life."

"Sorry," Peter said.

"I want to see him again, one last time. We don't have to talk to him or even let him know we're there. I just want to see him again."

Peter thought back to his own father. He was a great dad, did everything he could to help the family, but she hadn't had that. It wasn't fair.

"I think about him every day," she said. "It keeps me awake at night. How could he leave us? Something bad must have happened."

"Okay," Peter whispered.

"Really?" She jumped up, ran around behind him and hugged him.

"But only if we stay far away. No contact."

"Yes, sir," Anna said, saluting him as if she were standing in front of her commanding officer.

She collected their dirty dishes from the table and carried them to the counter next to the stove. They fell from her hands, crashing to the counter. When she turned, she was crying.

"Thank you," she said through her tears. "You have no idea what you're giving me."

You see her die.

"Yeah," he whispered. His eyes welled up, only partially from how happy she was. He forced the tears back.

Is this a risk you really want to take?

Chapter 10

Nelson, 2005

Sarah and I stood at the top of the hill looking into a valley, at the piece of land we'd agreed to buy a few weeks before. Lush, green grass filled the interior while trees along the back provided privacy from the constant movement of the city on the other side. A small stream wound its way through the grass, emptying into a pond that had been formed by years of water collecting at the base of the hill.

"What do you think?" I asked.

"It's perfect," she said, shading her eyes from the bright sun pushing through the clouds. "That stream can be the start of the moat."

"You want a moat?"

"If we're building a castle, we'll need a moat."

Hard to argue with her logic.

A light wind blew as we walked down the hill to the front of the property. Sarah held her yellow summer dress to her sides. Fluffy white clouds floated overhead so low I could almost jump to grab one.

"If we put the castle here..." I hesitated. "Our backyard will be right there. Woods will be the border between us and the soccer field."

She noticed the shift in my tone. "You don't like it?"

"It's too familiar," I said.

"What is?"

"We may as well put a paintball field in."

"Don't worry, Nelson. I'm not going to let you end up like your father."

We walked to a fifteen-foot-tall elm tree at the back of the property. Sarah sat in the grass, took a long manila envelope from her bag and invited me to sit next to her.

The grass was dry but cold. "Don't we usually have a blanket when we do this?"

"After the first time we saw this plot of land," she said, "I did some quick sketches. Tell me what you think."

She pulled out three pieces of graph paper, one for each floor in the castle, and set them on the ground. She put a stone in the center of each to keep the wind from blowing them away.

"Here's the ground floor, and here's the front door leading to the moat. Don't worry, I already have plans for a drawbridge."

I took the page and held it high, imagining the castle as it formed around me.

"The second floor is where our bedrooms will be," she said, "and on the third we can build fun stuff for the kids. Maybe a game room or a small theater."

"I'll need an office there, probably two," I chuckled, "and a dungeon in the basement for my dad in case he makes an appearance."

"Nelson."

I wouldn't *actually* have put him the dungeon. He did his best to come to see his grandchildren now and then, but his work was still foremost in his life.

But it didn't matter. Everything around me was proof I didn't need him. The life I'd put together—my wife, our kids, our wealth—I'd built it all on my own, with Sarah as my only support system. *Every time he stands on the other side of the drawbridge, waiting for someone to lower it so he can come inside, he will see everything I built. And I will* always *make him wait just a few seconds longer than anyone else.*

Thunder rumbled in the distance.

"Maybe I should go get the kids," she said, surveying the approaching storm.

"Go ahead. I have to run to the bank and move money around."

We paused one more time, stood side by side and surveyed the place where our new home would soon appear. We would raise our kids the right way. She was right. It was perfect. I kissed her goodbye, jumped in the car and headed to the bank.

With most of the sunlight now swallowed by the clouds overhead, my drive to the bank seemed to turn from day to night.

"Come on, give me something by the door," I said as I pulled in the parking lot.

But the only parking spot available was at the end of a row, far from the door. I tried to keep the rain off me while sprinting to the entrance, but there was only so much a jacket pulled over my head could do. The drops that made it past my leather shield stung my skin. In this November Columbus air, cold rain was worse than snow. I finally made it inside, but my wet shoe slid on the white tile floor.

The tall, skinny man standing next to the door reached out to catch me, but I regained my balance before embarrassing myself any further. I paused, straightened my jacket and cleared my throat. It didn't seem like anyone had seen me, but the tall man was still watching.

"It's wet out there," I said.

"I can tell," he said, trying unsuccessfully to hide a smile.

I filled out all the required forms for moving my money around at home but checked them one more time as I stepped to the back of the line. Three people stood in front of me: a teenager wearing her McDonald's uniform and two men, both in dark suits, who talked as if they knew each other.

"Yeah, I took them getting four points and until they surrendered a worthless touchdown as time expired. I was looking good!" One of the men said, loud enough for everyone to hear. "I lost a hundred bucks on it."

"I had it the other way," his friend responded. "That worthless touchdown netted me a cool twenty."

He's happy about twenty bucks? I tried gambling exactly once but quickly discovered there was no edge, no patterns to study. It was too much dependent on luck.

Pick a company, study their past decisions, analyze what they are doing now, then decide. The addition of the point spread to give the house an advantage makes it all fall apart. Casinos aren't built on winners. Seems like someone needs to be educated.

"Excuse me, sir," I said to the man in front of me. "What you need to do is take that money and—"

A light tapping on my shoulder interrupted the free finance lesson. I turned around to see an old man with a shriveled face looking at me. A thin smile rested on his lips, below two round dark eyes and a small pointy nose. Large white puffs of hair on each side of his bald head covered his ears. He balanced himself on a wooden cane. The black suit he wore was one size too small, and the buttons struggled to keep it closed despite his large belly.

"Heck of a storm brewing out there," he said, pointing to the glass doors with his cane. His voice was low and gravelly.

"Yeah," I said. I pulled my driver's license from my wallet and rechecked my deposit slip. This was an important day. Today we would sign the contract with the only builder in town excited enough to build a castle for someone—because it was something he'd always wanted to do, but had never thought he'd have the chance.

"It's going to get bad," the old man continued. "You and your family ready?"

"I guess," I said. How hard is it to be ready for a storm? You stay inside. That's it. You're ready. I turned and gave him a look that said I wasn't interested in his Weather Channel type of warnings. *Is he also going to remind me to drink water on hot days?*

"You think you ought to talk to your dad before it starts?"

My body stiffened. A lump formed in my throat.

"What did you say?" I muttered.

"I'm just saying I think you should talk to your dad before the storm comes," he said. "You may not get another chance."

I grabbed his collar and pulled him toward me. He lost the grip on his cane.

"Who the hell do you think you are?"

Thunder crashed outside. A barrage of sparks exploded from a pole. The lights inside the bank flickered, and darkness filled the room. One of the bank tellers, Erika according to her name tag, screeched. The lights flickered again and came back on. She was holding the counter so tightly her knuckles were white. I made eye contact with her. Her cheeks flushed as she grinned and shook her head. Next to her, Rochelle, the other teller, laughed.

"You okay?" I mouthed.

"Yeah," she whispered back. She said to everyone, "Our systems are down. We'll need a few minutes to get everything up and running."

"Now," I said, turning to the old man, "who the hell are—?"

His cane still laid where he dropped it, but he was gone. I looked toward the glass doors. There was no sign of him. I couldn't see the parking lot anymore through the rain, which was falling harder than I'd ever seen.

The tall man stood by the door, watching me. Was he a security guard? His face was different from before. It had transformed into something. I rubbed my eyes. George Washington?

What is happening?

Two men burst through the doors, each holding guns. Their faces also twisted into something familiar, one like Abraham Lincoln and the other like John F. Kennedy.

"Everyone hug the floor!" Washington screamed. He turned his gun on the two businessmen and fired above their heads. "Now!"

I went down on my stomach and planted one cheek against the floor. Kennedy corralled the bank manager and a small middle-aged man from their offices and threw them to the ground. I slowed my breathing and counted. One. Two. Three. Four.

Lincoln jumped the counter, pushed the barrel of his revolver into Erika's face. She squeezed her eyes closed as the barrel touched the tip of her nose.

"All the money," he said calmly, "right now."

She nodded, wiped tears away and took the drawer handle in her hand.

"Easy," Lincoln said.

Once the drawer was open, he shoved her backward. She tumbled to the floor and crashed into a desk. Stacks of papers spilled, covering her and the other teller crouching on the floor next to her.

Keeping my head still, I scanned the area, looking for somewhere to run to and hide. Washington kept his position by the door, occasionally looking outside, while Kennedy hovered over me. We locked eyes.

"You gonna try something, junior?" he said.

What am I doing? Why am I looking around?

Never go into a fight when you're the underdog, I thought, remembering one of my dad's teaching moments.

"Ninety seconds left!" Washington yelled. "Let's go!"

Lincoln turned to the teller, "Where's the key to the safe?"

"I...I...don't have it. None of us do."

He took two steps toward her and pointed his pistol at Rochelle. Erika's eyes widened. Tears streamed down her face.

"Give me the keys now, or she's dead," Lincoln said.

She rocked slightly and looked at Rochelle.

"Please sir," she said, "I don't have—"

"I have it," the bank manager yelled. "It's in my pocket."

Lincoln rushed to the man. He reached into the bank manager's pocket while Washington kept watch at the door.

The rain crashing against the bank's roof was interrupted by the sound of an alarm ringing. All three men looked at each other, then at Erika and Rochelle hunched behind the counter. Kennedy raised his gun toward them. I swung my legs as hard as I could and caught the side of his knee. The cracking sound echoed through the bank. I swung it again, hitting the same spot.

He cried out. I sprang to my feet, caught him before he fell and held him in front of me, using him as a shield. Washington shot first and hit Kennedy twice in the chest. I tossed his lifeless body to the floor and ran directly at the other two. They both fired at me. I jumped, did two front flips, and buried my heel into Washington's chest, propelling him through the glass door and into the parking lot.

How did I do that?

Wind sent rain through the shattered doorway, soaking the floors. I turned, inches from Lincoln. His dark hair, now wet, hung just low enough across his forehead to hide his eyes. He grinned at me, raised his gun and pointed it at my chest.

"I could kill you now, but you know what would be more fun?" he asked.

The alarm was still ringing. I waited for a pause in the short, consistent rings.

"Giving up?"

I didn't expect him to agree, but if I could keep him talking, maybe the police would get there.

"Killing her instead," he pointed his gun past me toward the McDonald's employee.

"She's a kid," I said. "How about you and I settle this?"

"No, Nelson," he said. "Not her."

He moved the gun barrel, pointing it toward the back of the bank. I followed it to the person crouched next to the check stand. I went cold.

"Sarah? What are you doing here?"

She whispered a response, but the alarm, combined with the rain and wind, kept me from hearing it. Lincoln laughed, reached under his chin and pulled. His mask slowly peeled away. Underneath was a younger boy, in his early twenties with black curly hair and light eyes.

"Oh no, she knows what I look like," he said playfully, "whatever will I do?"

I stepped in front of him as he pulled the trigger, putting myself between the smoking barrel of his gun and Sarah. I was not letting the bullet get past me. Without her, I didn't know where I would be. I owed her, even if it meant dying for her. I expected to feel pain but instead felt nothing. *Is this what dying feels like? Nothing? You're just here then you're gone?* I dropped to my knees, waiting for the life to drain from me.

Lincoln laughed more loudly. I looked at him, but he was looking behind me. I turned. Sarah stared at me. Her brown eyes rolled back. A small red circle formed in her stomach. She covered it with both hands and pushed, but it didn't help. Her dress turned a dark crimson as she crumpled to the floor.

I turned to Lincoln. I couldn't feel the rain or hear the alarm. It was just him and me, his large grin and booming laughter as Sarah lay dying.

"She's gone, Nelson," he yelled, "and you can't do anything about it!"

I grabbed his gun, meeting little resistance, and twisted it, pushing the barrel against his chest. I wanted him dead, and I wanted to be the one to kill him. He would suffer.

I pulled the trigger once. His laughter stopped. I pulled it again. His head tilted forward. He looked down at the blood streaming to the floor at his feet. I pulled the trigger again and again until it was empty. A soft gurgle escaped his mouth before his lifeless body fell to the ground in a heap.

I ran to Sarah, cradling her head in my lap. She reached up, but her hand could only get to my shoulder. It traced a red pattern along my sleeve as it fell to the floor. She tried to speak; her mouth filled with blood.

"Nelson?" she mumbled.

I begged, "Please hang on. I can't continue without you."

"Nelson." Her voice was clear. The color in her eyes returned.

"Help will be here soon, baby," I said.

"Nelson!" she screamed.

My eyes flashed opened. Darkness. I swung my arm to the other side of the bed and reached for Sarah. Nothing. I sat up and freed myself of the blankets twisted around my body. I wiped tears from my eyes and tried to focus. *Where am I? What time is it?* A door opened. Light flooded the room. I put my hand in front of my face, shielding my eyes. Sarah's silhouette appeared in the doorway. She was holding the telephone.

"There's been an accident," she said.

Chapter 11

Peter, 2017

Peter appeared next to his bed in the same spot he had landed just after McCall cut their poker game short.

"I don't know if I'll ever get used to that," Anna said, standing next to him. "It's exhausting."

"It gets easier the more you do it. Your body adjusts to it."

She unhooked the machine from her wrist, flopped onto Peter's bed and closed her eyes.

"Wake me in like fifteen minutes."

Peter stood next to his bed, watching Anna as she tried to fall asleep. He leaned against the wall and closed his eyes. In the past twenty-four hours, three different people had taken shots at him, he'd played poker with a real-life cowboy, had finally taken Anna on their first date, spent the night with her...in Montana...in 1873, and now they were starting a quest to find her father, who'd been missing for eleven years.

So much for a boring life.

His gaze shifted to the edge of the bed. "Buddy?"

"Keep it down. I'm trying to sleep," Anna mumbled.

"I don't get it. He's always here."

Anna opened her eyes and sat up. "What's wrong?"

"I land in this same spot every time, and he's always here waiting for me."

Peter walked out of the bedroom, grabbed hold of the railing and peered into the first floor. His television was lying on its side at the bottom of the steps. Anna met him at the banister and placed her hand on top of his.

"You see him?" she asked.

"Something is wrong."

She let go of Peter's hand and wandered into the room next to his bedroom. To the average person, it looked like any other makeshift office. The cheap desk made of pressboard, a fancy red and black gaming chair and a laptop attached to a second monitor fooled most people. But in reality, it was where Peter did most of the work on the machine. A large toolbox rested next to the desk, and dozens of prototypes were hidden in a locked panel in the closet floor, along with machine blueprints and source code that the people from GROUP had uploaded over the last couple of years.

"You should come in here!" Anna said.

He walked toward the room but hesitated in the doorway. Desk drawers hung open. Notebooks and loose papers, images and schematics of his machine, photos he'd taken while in Montana and transcripts of GROUP chats littered the floor. Blankets were pulled off the spare bed and thrown in a pile at the foot, while the headboard was cracked down one side. He stood motionless, mouth open, looking for words that didn't come.

Anna collected the pile of blankets and began spreading them on the bed. She stopped as she tucked them in at the top. Small red spots marked a path from the headboard along the sheet to the floor, ending at the doorway. She touched one of the drops with a towel. It smeared across the wooden boards.

"Peter," Anna said, eyeing the door, "I think this is blood."

He froze. "I need to find Buddy."

Peter crept to the top step, kneeled and listened. He usually kept the television at a low volume throughout the night. Tonight, though, silence was all he heard.

He took another step down and stopped. Anna pressed herself against him and put her hand on his shoulder. Peter paused with each step, touching the carpeted stairs, hoping the normal creaks of an old house would stay hidden. At the bottom of the stairs, they carefully slipped past the television.

Anna pointed to the corner where a piece of plastic had broken off. He tilted it forward and checked the screen. It was still intact.

In the living room, cushions were pulled off the two couches and sliced in half. Stuffing had been thrown into the corner, near the front door, like clouds rolling in before the impending storm. The top of his antique coffee table, a half-inch thick piece of glass, was cracked from corner to corner.

It would have taken real force to cause that.

They pressed their backs against the wall and crept toward the doorway leading to the dining room. He held out his hand, keeping Anna safely behind him while he checked first. She slid under his arm and peeked into the room. The table had been turned on its side, blocking the entrance to the kitchen. Two chairs rested against the table. The other two were turned upside down and stacked on top.

A large bookcase laid on its side, its top extending into the hallway. Peter's entire collection of books, more than a hundred, had been individually rifled through and tossed aside.

They maneuvered around the bookshelf, into the hallway and toward the bathroom. Again, he held out his hand to stop Anna.

"Hang on," he whispered.

The dark blue shower curtain had been pulled shut. Peter slid across the floor and faced the curtain. He put his hands out and took a deep silent breath. Grabbing the curtain, he shrieked as loudly as he could and yanked it open.

Anna rushed in, but no one was waiting. A pile of towels had been thrown into the tub. The contents of the medicine closet had been dumped over them. Boxes of Band-Aid, cotton balls and bars of soap had been emptied and dumped on the pile. The empty boxes had been torn apart and thrown to the floor.

Peter's clothes hamper was lying on the floor next to the sink. Blue jeans, khakis and Peter's work shirts had been left next to the towels. The lid lay cockeyed in the sink, and judging by the shards of broken mirror on the floor, it appeared to have been thrown there by someone frustrated at not finding what they had been looking for.

"Do you think it's him, the guy who chased us last night?" Anna whispered.

"I don't know." Peter grabbed the half of the machine dangling from his wrist. "But I bet it has to do with this. He's been watching my house for the last couple of mornings."

They returned to the dining room and moved the table and chairs from the kitchen doorway. Cabinets were open; most of his dishes had been stacked on the table, while others were in pieces across the floor. The refrigerator and freezer doors hung ajar.

"The outside light is on," Peter said. "I turned it off before leaving to meet you."

He walked to the back door and opened it. The screen also was hanging open.

"It's unlocked. I locked it before I left."

Does someone have a key?

He stuck his head through the doorway. The biting wind stung his cheeks, and the hair on his arms rose. Peter peered through the snow, trying to catch any glimpse of his lost puppy.

"Buddy!"

Leaves rustled, followed by the familiar jingling of Buddy's collar. Peter looked toward a dark corner near a spot in the fence where he had repaired a hole a few weeks ago. He yelled again. Buddy emerged from the darkness, his short, dirty-white fur blending with the snow. He kept his head down and walked unusually slowly as if he had just been caught rooting through the trash can and knew he'd done something wrong.

Peter stepped onto the small, square wooden porch. When Buddy looked up and saw Peter, he stopped at the bottom of the steps.

"It's me, Buddy. Come on. It's okay."

Buddy took each step at a time, pausing on each. Peter softly called for him until, finally, he met Peter at the top. He lay down at Peter's feet and rolled over. Peter rubbed his belly and ran his hands along Buddy's sides. Other than a couple of clumps of white hair missing, everything looked normal.

"It's okay," Peter said. "Daddy's home."

Buddy rolled over and jumped to his feet. He looked at Peter, tilted his head and stared for a moment. His tail wagged, and he barked.

"That's it, boy. You recognize me now. Seems like you're in one piece. What happened tonight?"

Buddy's head shot to the left. His ears perked up as Anna appeared in the doorway. He wriggled out of Peter's arms and ran toward her, his little tail flapping back and forth. Anna bent to lift him, but he jumped into her arms, catching her by surprise.

"Oh, someone's happy to see me," she said.

She pulled him close, turning her head to the side and laughing as he licked her cheeks.

"You gave your daddy a scare."

Peter pulled the door shut, locked it and turned toward Anna. Behind her, the pieces of his life lay scattered like leaves after a fierce wind. He touched his wrist and sighed.

Is this how it will be from now on? Constant danger? It may be more exciting than total boredom, but I don't want this either.

"I guess I'll clean some of this mess," Peter said, shaking his head. "We'll try to figure out what happened, and then we'll go find your dad."

"I'll help you."

IT TOOK A COUPLE OF hours to get everything back where it was. They started at different ends of the house with Peter upstairs in his office and Anna in the kitchen until they met in the living room.

"Any chance it was a random burglary?" she asked.

"I doubt it. On my laptop, the folder containing the pictures of my Montana home was open. I think whoever it was probably knew what they were looking for and where to look. But why the blood?"

"I found blood here too," Anna said, pointing at the floor in front of the couch. "Is this from you this morning?"

"No, mine was in the bedroom, and I cleaned it before I left for work."

They inspected the rest of the house, looking for anything out of the ordinary but other than the broken headboard, everything checked out.

"I guess that's it," Peter said. "Let's go find your dad."

"Okay," Anna said. She sniffed and wiped her nose. "I'm ready."

"But please remember, if we're even able to get close to him, no contact until we know what happened."

Anna nodded. Peter took the notebook from his bag, opened it to a middle page and wrote the times and places they visited while in 1873.

"Why do you do that?" Anna asked. She reached for the notebook, but he pulled it back before she could take it from him.

"I like to know where I've been."

He took a large book from the bag and put it on the table. Anna tilted her head to one side and pursed her lips. "A history textbook?"

"There's good stuff about Montana in the late 1800s in there. Sometimes I sit on my front porch and read it as cowboys ride by."

She grabbed the book and rifled through it. Around halfway through, something fell to the floor, bounced along the carpet and came to rest at her feet.

"Is that a bullet?" She turned the book around. A small hole in the center of the back cover revealed its hiding place.

"It's from this morning," Peter said with a lukewarm smile. "I guess history saved my life."

Her voice was shaky. "What if this hit you?"

"I know," he said.

She handed him the book, and he shoved it in his backpack.

He stuffed the rest of the items inside as well. "I have water, beef jerky, my notebook, a pen, rope, my stopwatch and a whistle."

Anna grabbed his arm. "A whistle? Beef jerky? What do you think is going to happen?"

Peter shrugged. "I always like to be ready for anything."

"What's the stopwatch for?"

"Yeah, we probably don't need it anymore—but old habits."

She shook her head as he shoved the watch into his backpack. He attached the other end of the machine to her wrist. Buddy barked and ran upstairs.

"Where's he going?" Anna asked.

"He knows when he sees the bracelet that I'll be appearing in my bedroom in a few seconds."

"Wow, that's smart of him."

"He does all sorts of tricks like that. I never taught him one thing. It's very strange, but it kills at parties."

Anna giggled.

"So, when are we going?" he asked.

"May twenty-sixth, 2006. Like I said, the worst day of my life." Her voice went flat as she stared at her feet. "The last time I ever saw him."

"Let's start there and see what happens," Peter said.

He pressed the home button on his phone and tapped the MyGolfGPS icon.

After Padma installed it on his phone, he had given it a name no one he knew would click. He pushed the button to set the location. His eyes widened, and he looked at Anna.

"What's wrong?" she asked.

Peter held the phone out and showed her the display.

"May twenty-sixth, 2006," he said.

She nodded, still confused about what the problem was.

"It was already there. I didn't type anything." He inspected it further. "And it has a location already entered."

He touched the latitude and longitude, and a map opened. It was a spot east of the city.

"Where was the car found?" Peter asked.

"Just off 70, near the Turnberry golf course in Pickerington."

He lifted the phone to her face. She squinted, took the phone from him and turned it sideways. Her face lit up. She handed the phone back to Peter.

"Yeah, that's it," she said. "Maybe your nurse friend is back to her old tricks."

He took her hand in his and pressed the button.

Chapter 12

Nelson, 2005

I stood in the entrance of Alston Funeral Home, debating whether I wanted to go in. Anytime I'm with my mom and dad in the same room, she would beg me to speak to him, but I was not ready. I didn't know if I would ever be.

"If not now, when?" Sarah asked. She stood inside the doors, holding Lena with one hand, the other firmly planted on her hip.

"I have nothing to say. I've had nothing to say for years. What's the point?"

"Nelson, you're thirty-six. Stop acting like the child he accused of you being."

On a day like this, when everyone was together, solemn and quiet, I knew I wasn't going to talk to him. There was no need for me and my fake emotions to get in the way of anything.

Two cousins I hadn't seen since our last family reunion, more than ten years ago, pushed past me. My Aunt Judy grabbed me from behind, gave me a big hug and pulled me through the doors.

"Thanks, Judy," Sarah said.

Judy, oblivious to what she had just done, wrapped her arms around Sarah and Lena, hugging them.

"Where are the other two rugrats?" she asked. "I bet they've grown so big."

"Danny and Crissy are already inside," Sarah said. "I'm sure they would love to see you."

Judy disappeared into the hall as Sarah took my hand.

"Okay but let's make it quick, I have work to do at home," I replied.

"Now you *do* sound like your father."

"Low blow."

She handed me Lena and led me into the vestibule. I stopped, surprised at the number of people gathered in the surrounding rooms, most of them separated into smaller groups.

"He certainly didn't have this many friends," I whispered.

There hadn't been this many people from the family in one place at the same time since our wedding. Once my grandmother died, we'd stopped having family holiday parties. She was the person who put everyone together, and after she was gone, no one wanted to be responsible. I remember asking my dad's brother, Uncle Jeffrey, why no one carried on the tradition.

"I'm afraid to bring it up for fear everyone will ask me to be the new organizer," he said. I think they all felt that way, so the family parties died with her.

I noticed my mom in the sitting room, talking to someone—an older woman I didn't recognize. She was taller than my mom, with big, puffy white hair, thick red lipstick on her dry, cracked lips, and a long black dress that slid across the floor behind her as she moved.

"Who's that woman?" I asked.

"I don't know," Sarah said. "Why isn't your mom with your dad? Anytime they're out in public together, she's always right there, standing next to him."

"I'm sure everyone wants to talk to her," I said. "I don't know the last time she's seen most of these people."

Mom saw us and waved. The strange woman hugged her and walked past Sarah and me without making eye contact. Before I could ask my mom who she was, she took Sarah in her arms and hugged her. She let go of Sarah and wrapped her arms around Lena and me, squeezing a little too tightly.

I pulled my mom to me and whispered into her ear, "You okay?"

She didn't answer. Instead, she let go of me, wiped the tears from her eyes and pointed into the viewing room. She took my hand and pulled.

"Let's go," she said. Her voice was calm but commanding. Sarah took my other hand. Together they led me toward him. Did they discuss this double team ahead of time?

"Does it even matter anymore?"

"Goddammit Nelson, it matters today more than ever. You're going up there, you will look at him, and you will speak. I don't give a shit what you say. Just say something."

Mom had never cursed like that before. I took a step back and tried to swallow the lump that had formed in my throat. It was clear she wouldn't let me escape without saying something to him. I stopped and yanked both my hands-free. I shook my head and sighed.

"Just let me go by myself."

I walked up to the casket and looked at him. He looked younger than the last time I saw him. They'd dyed his hair, and his face was less wrinkled than I remember. It's a wonder what a little makeup can do. Someone laid a rose on his chest. He seemed to be clutching it, holding it tightly to himself. Did the funeral home attendants do that?

I looked around to see if anyone was nearby. The coast was clear. I opened my mouth, but no words came out. What do you say to someone you haven't talked to in twenty years? I grinned at him and shook my head.

"I'm finally going to say something to you, and you're not even going to respond," I whispered. "Takes me back to when I was a kid. Typical you."

I didn't want to feel the bitterness or hate anymore. It was an anchor laying across my chest. Thoughts of my sixteenth birthday swirled through my head. That's when it had started, after the paintball game where I met Sarah. I hadn't *actually* let her win. I remembered that tree, our tree, where I'd spent so much time with her avoiding him.

"Typical me, too, I guess."

I looked over my shoulder for Sarah or my mom, but neither was around. Danny stood against the wall in the back of the room alone, watching me. The sleeves of his little black suit hung over his wrists. He tugged on his pants and put his hands in his pockets. When he caught me looking at him, he offered me a sad smile.

"He's eight now," I said. "Halfway to sixteen. I won't do to him what you did."

"Maybe you won't need to," my dad's voice echoed in my head. I could always hear him, countering all my arguments or teaching me his life lessons like we'd been on speaking terms all these years.

"You could have figured out a better way to make me an adult. Scaring the shit out of me at sixteen wasn't exactly your best move."

"I made you a man Nelson."

"I would have become one anyway," I muttered.

"Think about what you have now, Nelson." His voice still echoed through me. "Think about Sarah and the kids and your success. Could you have done all that if I hadn't put all that pressure on you? You were sixteen going on ten."

I thought about our castle, and the paintball field I'd built for Danny and his friends behind the house. It had been so much fun there for me as a kid. I wanted them to have the same fun.

His voice was so clear, he could have been sitting up in the casket, grasping my shoulders, trying to shake some sense into my stubborn head. He wouldn't look me in the eyes, he never did. Instead, he would look past me as if there were something else more important in the room that he needed to pay attention to while telling me why I was wrong.

"Do you think you could provide for your kids the way you do if I allowed you to graduate and stick around at home? You'd probably still be living there."

They are good kids, do well in school and rarely fight. But they have the father in their life I never had.

"You were never there." I pointed at him as I spoke, and I was no longer whispering. "Mom raised me alone. Video games raised me. My teachers taught me more about being an adult than you. You know who didn't raise me? You."

For the first time in my life, I saw his expression change. I looked around. Had anyone else seen this? His shoulders slumped until he lay down in the casket. The rose looked as if it were going to break as he squeezed.

His voice went flat, and he didn't look at me as he spoke, "It was the only way, Nelson. To provide for my family, I had to work long, hard hours. You knew that. I hated every second, but it had to be that way."

Had to? Was he telling the truth?

"But son, you don't have to. You've done well, and I'm proud of you."

"You are?" A tear rolled down my cheek.

"Don't be like me. Enjoy your time with your family. I didn't have that time, and look at me, lying here in a casket, with perfect hair and no pants. That's right, Nelson, they only open the top half because they don't put pants on us."

My chin trembled as I tried to hold back a laugh. Instead, a stifled giggle escaped my mouth. I tried to hide it with a cough and glanced around, checking to see if anyone had seen me laughing over my dead father. Danny was still behind me, watching me intently.

Sharp pain sliced through my head. I grabbed behind my left ear and lost my balance for a split second. I held on to the edge of his casket to steady myself. With my eyes closed, I tried to think of what to say next. What could I say to end this, take this giant weight off my chest and finally breathe? How do I move forward?

"Thanks, Dad." I exhaled a long breath that had been hiding inside me for twenty years.

Tears streamed down my cheeks. I wiped them away with my sleeve and touched his hand. It was cold and stiff. I slid my fingers under his. I thought I saw the corners of his mouth twitching. Was he fighting a smile? I closed my eyes, let go of the casket and dropped my other hand to my side. At that moment, he was the only thing I wanted to feel, something close to the hug I never received as a kid. Right now, it was exactly what I needed. As I cried, I felt someone take my other hand.

"Are you okay, Daddy?"

"Yeah, Danny," I pulled my hand from the casket and got down on one knee. I straightened my son's tie and unbuttoned his jacket.

"You missed a button, little guy." I chuckled. "Let me fix that."

"I'm sorry about Grandpa."

"Me too," I squeezed his hand, put my arm around him and hugged him.

Chapter 13

Nelson, 2006

"Nelson!"

My eyes snapped open. I reached for Sarah and banged my hand against her forehead.

"I'm here," she said, pushing it away. She mumbled something else.

"What?"

"I said, I'm here."

I wiped the sweat from my forehead and blinked a couple of times. The bedroom was mostly dark, but there was an old lamp in the far corner. The shade was a hideous mixture of green, red, blue and yellow swirls. On our wedding day, her mom gave us the "passed through the generations, family heirloom" speech, guilting us into taking it. I tried hard, but Sarah didn't want to throw it out. Instead, she tucked it into a corner of our bedroom, out of view from anyone visiting. I hated seeing it every time I walked into the bedroom, yet at the moment it was the only thing I recognized.

I focused on it and wiped at my watery eyes until the swirls stopped moving. The rest of the room slowly materialized. Sarah's back was to me, but she turned her head and looked over her shoulder just enough to show me one of her eyes.

"Did you have another nightmare?"

"No, why? Was I talking or something?"

When I first started having these nightmares, I went through each of them with her, describing every detail in the hope she could make sense of them. When she began dying at the end of each one, I sometimes changed the ending or made it seem like I died instead. Over time, it became easier to deny they meant anything. How do you tell the person you love that you occasionally have nightmares where she is violently murdered?

"You okay?" Her eye narrowed.

"Let's go back to sleep," I said.

I smiled, moved in close and pulled her to me. I kissed the back of her neck and ran my hand across her stomach.

She wriggled free from my grip and rolled to face me. "I called to you a couple of times Nelson, but you didn't answer. Your eyes were open but blank. Are you sure you're okay?"

"Yeah, I'm good. Don't worry." I kissed her again and smiled.

"Fine, keep it to yourself," she pressed her thumb to my eyes, wiped away a few stray tears, turned away and switched off her light.

THE NEXT MORNING, I woke before Sarah. I slid out of bed without waking her, headed downstairs to shower and made a pot of coffee. No doubt the smell of coffee brewing would rouse her, so I grabbed an oversized cup and filled it to the top. I snatched the morning paper from the front porch and locked myself in my office before she could ask about the nightmares.

The next few weeks, I followed a similar pattern. It didn't take long for her to notice.

"You're avoiding me in the morning," she said one night as we washed dishes.

"Just want to get an early jump on things. There's a lot of money out there to grab, and if I can beat other people to it, I'm going to."

"Uh-huh," she muttered, shaking her head.

We both knew I was lying. The truth was that my emotions were a scrambled mess. If she kept pressing, I wasn't sure what I would say. Tell her the truth? Why? They're just nightmares. They don't mean anything, so what's the point in telling her?

Relief was the first thing to hit. Relieved to wake next to Sarah after whatever horrific nightmare I'd experienced was foremost, but also relief about finally coming to terms with my dad and what he'd done to make me the person I was.

Gratitude usually kicked in next. Looking at my life and where I was, I knew I should be thankful for a lot of things. I'd been so lucky to find Sarah when my dad put his plan into action. She'd helped me deal with my anger and kept me on the right path. And our kids, they'd helped me understand what my dad had been going through. His biggest worry had been how to make sure I grew up with the ability to function as an adult. When he'd seen me going the other way, he'd done something drastic. It had worked, and I'd never realized it while he was alive. I had never had the chance to thank him until it was too late.

That had led to guilt. His death had helped me come to those terms, understand what he'd done for me, but I certainly wasn't happy he was gone. Many times in the morning, I would find myself staring at my monitor screen, examining my reflection. Eventually, the screen would go hazy, and I would blink away tears.

But why should I blink them away? Crying made sense. People died, you mourned. You cried. It was normal. It was what everyone else did. Why shouldn't I?

Sometimes, happiness found its way in—and when it did, everything was right. My mind cleared. Making money was easy. It usually took a couple of hours to get to happiness, but once I did, I was an ATM dispensing cash into my checking account at an alarming rate.

"But how do I force happiness?" I asked Lena one evening while I rocked her to sleep.

Sarah knew more about me than anyone else, other than what I revealed to my youngest daughter. Lena became my main confidante and acting therapist once the nightmares started. I'm not sure why, but of the three kids, I felt the strongest connection to her. My mom always told me Danny and Crissy looked like their mother; with Lena, it was obvious at first sight she was mine. We had the same round, hazel eyes and chubby cheeks, and from the moment I held her, I knew she would be my favorite.

Each night I would volunteer to put her to bed, and while sitting in our favorite rocking chair, I gave her the play-by-play of the previous night's nightmare and my feelings about it. Maybe by making my dreams into silly stories, I could convince myself the nightmares were equally silly, and that would change my perspective. I was grasping at anything that could relieve the terror I felt each morning.

"Then, and you're not going to believe this," I'd said to Lena a few nights before, "a large green dinosaur with puffy, white sideburns, wearing a black tie, came out of nowhere and swallowed your mother whole!"

I usually put a big smile on my face when I told her about the dreams. When I smiled, it didn't matter what words came out of my mouth. She smiled right along with me, and I loved that. But in reality, those dreams scared me to death.

"I need to change my routine, do something different and alter the repetition."

Lena cooed.

"A vacation?" I lifted her, holding her out in front of me. She giggled.

"That's a great idea, but listen: as much as I'd like it to be just the two of us, we're going to have to take your sister, your brother and your mom."

I rose from the chair, held Lena high above my head and looked at her big smile. A rush of adrenaline surged through me. This would work. I needed distractions, good distractions, something to keep my mind busy. Happiness would have to float to the top of the emotional soup I was swimming in, forcing everything else to the bottom.

"YES!" SARAH SAID BEFORE I could finish the sentence. "You need it. We need it. Where should we go?"

"Disney?"

"Perfect. Yes. Sounds great!" Sarah said. "Let's go Monday. Do you have anything going on?"

"Wait, um...okay. What's...what's the date?" I reached for my planner.

"May twenty-sixth," she called out.

"Looks like I have a couple meetings, but it's not anything I can't push back a few weeks. This one I'd like to cancel altogether. Let's do it!"

AS SARAH DID, SHE DOVE in headfirst and took control. Over the past few years, some of our friends from college had taken their kids to Disney. They were the first to receive phone calls from us. Park sketches were drawn. Routes were planned from rides to food and back. If something puzzled my wife, phone calls to Disney were made. She even found an employee on Myspace and asked him to take pictures and email them to her. She knew the average wait time in line for every ride and based on that, our daily schedule was planned to the minute.

A week later, my dinner was pushed aside, and a folder containing a complete itinerary was dropped in its place.

"Reminds me of lunch in the high school cafeteria," I said.

"Reminds me of you, every workday since."

"No wonder it was love at first sight," I grinned.

When I finally closed my eyes to sleep, there was a warmth around me. I stretched my entire body and sighed. For the past few months, every time I went to sleep, I worried about the nightmares. They didn't come every night, but the anticipation was enough to keep me awake until I couldn't hold on any longer. But not tonight.

"You seem to be doing better," she said as she crawled under the blanket next to me.

"It's a good time to be alive," I said, leaning in to kiss her. The high-pitched ringing of the phone on the table next to my bed broke off my advancement. Sarah cringed.

When I turned, I knew why. The number on the caller ID was the one number I didn't want to see, and the only number I usually saw this late at night.

"Don't answer it," she whispered.

"I have to," I said.

"I know."

I rolled to the edge of the bed and took a deep breath.

"Hi, Walter."

"Nelson, we have a problem."

"Come on...It's almost midnight, and in the morning I'm getting on an airplane and hoped to be off the grid for a couple of weeks. We're finally taking that family vacation you've been bugging me about." I looked back at Sarah, shrugged and smiled. She crossed her arms and turned her head to the side.

Walter Abernathy was a coworker of mine while I was still at Odin Financial Solutions, my first and only job after college. Just after I started working there, I designed a piece of software that allowed me to work the market faster and more efficiently than anyone else. When I left the company, I tried to take it with me, but Odin claimed ownership since I'd built it on their time. They also prohibited me from using it once I was on my own. To avoid an impending lawsuit, they offered me a yearly consulting fee to support them. I agreed to keep it bug-free and be there for them 24/7 if there was a problem. In exchange, they would let me have it for my personal use.

"This can't wait." He rushed his words, "Something is wrong with your software, and it's costing us thousands of dollars each day. It needs to be fixed now."

I bent my neck forward and exhaled.

"Okay. Tell me what's happening, Walter."

"We don't know. Our best guy just called me. He's been on this all weekend, and he's at the end of his rope. He has nothing left. I need you first thing in the morning."

"Walter, your guys are smart. Tell them to keep looking. If they can't find it, have them email me. I'll fix it from the Tea Cups."

Sarah scoffed.

"Sorry, Nelson. We pay you well to support this thing, and we expect you here. You still have a key, right?"

"Yeah, front and back."

Sarah slumped on the bed, making sure I could feel the mattress bounce.

"Good. Get here early."

I set the phone back on the cradle.

"I'll meet with them in the morning and fly down in the afternoon. I'll drop you and the kids off at the airport on my way in."

Sarah didn't respond.

"Hey," I whispered.

I reached out to touch her shoulder. She pulled away.

"Good night, Nelson."

Someone tugged at my shirt. I spun around, but there was no one there. More tugging. I blinked and opened my eyes. It was different, dark. Where is she? The tugging continued, except not on my shirt. It was a blanket. I was in my bed. I closed my eyes again and tried to remember but couldn't recall a nightmare. Is this the beginning? I reached for Sarah but felt nothing.

When I turned, her side of the bed was empty. Standing next to it, dressed in his new green shorts and Hawaiian shirt, was Danny. His short brown hair hung out the sides of his Atlanta Braves baseball cap. A pair of adult black sunglasses rested on the brim.

"Someone is ready for Disney," I muttered.

He lifted his little suitcase onto the bed and wiped his nose, then frowned. "Mommy said you're not going with us."

I squeezed my eyes closed and reopened them. I looked at the hideous lamp. It was still there. Danny stared back at me.

"Daddy?" he asked.

I reached for him. He moved his suitcase and climbed onto the bed in Sarah's spot.

"Where's your mommy?"

"She's downstairs making breakfast," he said. "Why aren't you going with us?"

"Don't worry, buddy." I blinked again, and when I opened my eyes, nothing changed. It must be real. "Daddy has a meeting this morning. But I'll be joining the rest of you later this afternoon, and we'll ride every single ride together."

"Okay daddy. Well, let's go!" He tugged at my arm until I gave in and stumbled out of bed.

By the time I showered and wandered downstairs, Sarah had the car packed, and everyone was ready to go, waiting for me.

"It will be an easy meeting," I said. "I'll get there, fix the issue and get out."

"You trying to convince yourself or me?"

I turned off our road and onto the ramp to the highway. Just as I pressed the gas pedal, something appeared in my peripheral vision. Our heads jerked forward when I stomped the brakes. The car stopped instantly.

"What's wrong?" Sarah asked. She turned around to check the kids in the backseat.

A blue Honda Civic hurried past us in the lane I was trying to merge. A teenage boy was driving. A girl who looked his age occupied the passenger seat. The third person, another teenage girl, was sitting in the back, looking through the rear window and flailing her arms.

"What's wrong with those three?" Sarah asked.

Looking over my shoulder again and seeing nothing, I pushed on the accelerator. Something wasn't right. Someone else is coming. I checked again but nothing. I inched onto the highway, but something told me to check one more time. Another car, a brown Chevy Impala driven by a middle-aged man, was approaching at high speed. How had I known?

"What's happening, Daddy?" Crissy said from the back seat.

"Nothing, sweetie," Sarah said, "Go back to your book."

"Is he chasing them?" Danny asked.

I gazed back at Danny. Was he chasing them? Why did this seem familiar? Sarah touched my arm. I flinched.

"You okay?" Sarah asked. "You seem nervous."

I stared at her for a few seconds and put my hand on the door handle. They were past us. Whoever they were, they weren't coming for me. Unless they were up there, waiting. Was there a different way to the airport? I unlocked the doors. I could run right now, and whatever it was, it wouldn't know where I went.

"It looks clear," Sarah said, snapping me back to reality.

I turned my attention back to the road, checking the mirrors first. The lane was clear. I eased my foot back to the accelerator and pressed. Almost immediately, I pushed the brakes again, turned the steering wheel hard to the right and stopped inches before the car hit the guardrail.

"What the hell, Nelson?" Sarah shrieked, "Another one?"

A haze washed across me. I grabbed the steering wheel at eight and four. I shrunk into my seat, lowered my head and closed my eyes. A stabbing pain pierced my brain. I tried to remember. *What am I forgetting? What is coming? I've been here before, seen it already. Another car should be coming.*

"It's coming for me," I whispered.

"What are you talking about?" Sarah said. "The lane is clear. We're going to be late."

I opened my eyes and peered at her. She was staring at me. Her arms were open, her palms upturned. She looked as confused as I felt. I checked the mirror. The road seemed clear, but I learned quickly you can't trust anything in the nightmares. I twisted my body as far as I could and looked over my shoulder. I could see Lena behind me in her car seat, playing with her stuffed dinosaur. It was her favorite toy. Danny sat next to her. He turned and looked through the rear window.

"Seems clear, Daddy," he said.

I lifted my foot from the brake, and the car edged onto the highway. When it reached the speed limit, I took one hand off the wheel and tried to appear relaxed, but in the back of my mind, one thought remained.

Something's coming.

Twenty minutes later we pulled into the airport. I drove to the departures area and stopped by the curb, allowing everyone to rush out of the car. My head still ached, and I was having trouble breathing. While they gathered their luggage, I counted each breath, trying to slow them down.

"I wish I'd never answered that phone call," I whispered to myself. "I'd be getting on the plane with them, instead of waiting until the afternoon."

At least now they won't be with me the rest of the morning, so if it comes, they'll be safe. I checked my mirror and cracked the door open. A man in a yellow taxi drove by. He blared his horn. I yanked the door shut. My hands trembled as I turned to look behind me. Nothing was coming. I hurried to the sidewalk.

"Here, take mine too," I smiled, dropping my suitcase onto the cart with everyone else's.

"You are okay, right?" Sarah said as I leaned in to kiss her.

"Yeah, I'm just anxious. This isn't supposed to be how our first family vacation starts," I said. "You know I'm a nervous flyer. I want this flight over, and now I'm delaying it more. At least the kids won't see their dad looking silly."

"We've seen you silly before, daddy," Crissy said.

"I don't know," I said. "I'll probably be crying and screaming and trying to hide in one of the tiny bathrooms."

I threw my arms in the air and pretended I was hysterical. Crissy and Danny both giggled. I dropped to my knees and pulled them tightly to me.

"I love you both. You be good for your mom, and I'll be there before you get a chance to do anything fun without me."

"Go slow," Sarah said. "Make sure it's fixed and get yourself to the airport. Once you're in your seat and it's all out of your control, you'll feel better."

"I love you," I said. "I'll see you soon."

I watched as they disappeared through the electronic doors into the airport. Crissy turned, smiled and waved. I lifted my arm to wave back.

"Bye," I said.

Chapter 14

Nelson, 2006

I shifted in my seat, unbuckled my seat belt and re-buckled it. Once off the highway, I turned onto a two-lane road and muted the radio. The previous night I'd programmed buying and selling routines to run each day automatically while on vacation, based on past performance—so listening to a financial report before the market opened that morning didn't seem to matter. Besides, I needed silence to concentrate on the road. Whatever this feeling of dread was, it would resolve itself today, and I would do whatever I could to counteract it.

I flinched at every car coming at me. An eighteen-wheeler appeared. *What's he doing on this small side street?* I drove over the rumble strips, putting two tires as close to the ditch as possible. A police car pulled behind me. My chest tightened. Was I speeding? Was I *too* careful? Why was he riding so close? I stopped at a light. His siren blared, and his lights flashed as he slowly pulled around me and continued. I exhaled.

It will be fine, I thought.

I turned the radio's volume back up and searched the dial, looking for anything that would take my mind off things. Music wasn't doing it right now, and I hated that morning-zoo shit. The financials would have to do. *Maybe I can get an idea of how the early morning—*

A horn blew. I jerked my head back.

"Go!" someone yelled from behind. "It's green, jerk!"

"Dammit," I mumbled.

I pushed the accelerator and slipped through the intersection, keeping an eye in both directions. Once downtown, I found the entrance to the parking garage. I reached for the pass in my center console, hung it above my mirror and made my way to level two. They kept the sign on my old parking spot with my name and the large unmistakable 'O' that represented the Odin logo. I carefully backed in, stepped onto the pavement, grabbed the side mirror and steadied myself.

"Okay, you made it," I said to myself. "Stop being crazy."

I walked across the bridge and through the second-floor entrance. Joyce, the only secretary this place had ever known, buzzed Walter.

"There's the only woman I ever wanted but never got," I said with a laugh, "Looking good for what, eighty now?"

"Honey, I just hit eighty-two," she replied in her usual high-pitched voice. We called her "the mouse" behind her back. "And you wouldn't know what to do with me if you got me."

"I believe you," I said.

Walter came down a few minutes later. I stretched my hand.

"No time for greetings, Nelson," he said. "Awkward chit-chat costs us too much money."

He pushed a large manila folder into my chest. Loose papers fell to the floor. Hundreds of lines of source code in the smallest font possible filled the pages.

"Shit," he growled, dropping to his knees.

"Walter, what is all this?"

"It's everything my guys have done trying to fix *your* program."

"I don't need this. It will just complicate things." I set it on Joyce's desk and told her, "You can probably shred this."

Walter led me through a narrow hallway with large, plain blue walls. Each office door was closed and unmarked.

"Is anyone using these offices?" I said as we rounded a corner. "What a terrible place to work. You have really changed things around since—"

He cut me off. "I know. They're still working on this half of the building, and none of the partners can agree on what they want. So they made it a blank canvas to work out later."

I followed him out of the construction area toward the end of the hallway.

"This looks newer," I said.

On one side, a large conference room had two entrances from the hallway. Across from it, a glass wall showed a new workout area where four people I didn't recognize furiously ran on treadmills. They appeared to be racing.

"Yeah, they have been working on it for a while. We hope this is what the whole building looks like at some point."

"Workout room next to the conference room, Walter? Doesn't that get noisy?"

"You'll be in here," he said, opening the first of two entrances into the room.

The conference table, big enough for at least twelve people, dominated the center of the room. A projector hung from the ceiling, pointed at a white screen that was mounted to the wall and flanked by two flat-screen televisions at either side. Each television was on but muted, the left one on a sports channel showing highlights from the previous day, while the other was on a 24/7 news channel.

My old laptop was open at the end of the table.

"I assume this is for me?" I said.

"Yeah. If you need anything else, let me know."

"Am I on the network?"

"Yes."

"Can I use that?" I asked, pointing at the projector screen.

"Whatever you need, Nelson." He shifted, turned both TVs off and spun toward me, obviously flustered by all my questions. "Just fix your program."

He left the room in a hurry. I called their lead programmer, Mark Watson. He explained the problem and what his team found during their debugging attempts. Most of the code sounded familiar, although as he took me through it, there were several significant changes. New methods with new formulas had been written, and some of my formulas were either commented out or deleted altogether.

"These guys need to learn how to write better code," I said after hanging up.

The first hour was mostly me cleaning up their changes, making their code readable and easy to debug going forward. Eventually, I stumbled upon their error. Not surprisingly, it was in their changes and had nothing to do with my original code. Embedded deep in a new formula, a plus sign should have been a minus sign.

"No wonder they were losing so much money," I said. "Goddamn college kids."

Once I finished, I paged Joyce and asked her to call Watson. I wanted him to see what I was doing.

"That was it?" he said. "I looked for hours. Walter's gonna kill me."

Walter came in a few minutes later.

"Any luck?" he asked.

"Yeah, I found it," I looked at Mark. "There was a change in the format of the XML data we were receiving, and it threw things off. Looks like they changed how they are sending out data but didn't bother to tell anyone. But it's good now."

"Thank God," Walter said.

"I showed Mark the change. We tested it. Everything should be good. We also beefed up a few of the formulas, nothing major, but it should save you some pennies here and there."

"The pennies add up fast, Nelson," Walter said.

I shook Mark's hand as he left, gave him a quick smile and checked the clock. It was a few minutes after noon.

"I need to go," I said. "My family is in the air, and my flight leaves at three."

"Thanks, Nelson."

He handed me a check.

"This is more than we agreed on," I said. "Plus Mark helped me some here, make sure you reward him too."

"He's a moron. I know you did most, probably all, the work. It's for your trouble. I've been telling you for years to take a vacation, you finally do, and I screw it up. Go make your flight."

"Thanks, Walter."

I found my way to the drab blue hallway and stopped at the first door.

"One of these has to be a restroom," I muttered. "I should have walked into the gym and looked for the locker room."

Behind the three doors, I opened was the same empty office. I rounded the first corner and checked a couple more, but it was the same thing each time: white walls, an empty desk, two office chairs and a couch against the wall.

"What are they doing to—?"

A boy slammed into me, knocking me backward. I bounced off the wall, tumbled to the ground and stretched my arm to catch myself. My hand hit the ground flat, twisting my wrist. Pain shot through my arm and into my shoulder. I groaned and collapsed on my back.

"Oh, shit!"

The boy landed with a thud next to me as our legs tangled together. He was my height, maybe an inch or two shorter, with a bushy mop of black hair covering his narrow face. I glared at him.

Behind him, two girls emerged, scooted past us and continued down the hallway.

"Let's go, Max!" one girl screamed, "He's coming!"

"Move, old man," the boy said.

"Joyce! Call security!" I yelled down the hallway.

As we climbed to our feet, I grabbed hold of his shirt collar and pulled him close. I tried to turn him around and push him against the wall, but as I spun him, he swung his fist and caught my chest. I lost my grip and stumbled to the ground. Air rushed from my lungs, and I struggled to breathe. He escaped around the corner with the two girls.

I sat for a few seconds and gathered myself. Was that the feeling of dread I'd been holding on to all morning? I flexed my wrist. It hurt as I opened and closed my fist but only appeared to be a mild sprain. I put my other hand to the floor to push my body up just as a man appeared. The immediate smell of coffee and cigarettes filled the narrow hallway and knocked me onto my backside. I cringed and looked at him. He was around my age but heavier, with dark curly hair and a slightly wrinkled face. His eyes looked like he hadn't slept in a few days.

"Did you see them?" he asked.

"Are you security?"

"Yeah...yeah, sure," he stuttered. "Something like that. Where does this hallway lead?"

The man put his hand out. I took it and let him pull me up. I sagged against the wall, touched my chest and took a deep breath. The pain in my throat returned. I pointed toward the corner.

"They went that way. There's a conference room on one side and a workout area on the other. The door just past it leads outside. It's a fire escape, and an alarm will sound if someone opens the door."

He looked around. "I'm not hearing any alarms."

"Yeah," I said.

"Thanks, man." He shoved a business card into my hand. "The name's Aiden Connor. I owe you one. You ever need any kind of private security, let me know."

I nodded and watched as he disappeared around the corner. For a split second, I considered following, but after checking my watch, I changed my mind. My flight left in two hours. I took a step and stopped again, pushed my back against the wall and put my fists up. I felt it again. Someone else was coming.

I stood silent for a few seconds, waiting, but nothing. What was I doing? I dropped my hands to my sides and looked both ways before stepping away from the wall.

Stop being so paranoid, everything is fine.

As I made my way to my car, I watched the construction crew start their machines and get back to work. Dozens of men in overalls and yellow hard hats raced around like hamsters in a cage. Walter had wandered outside and found the man who must be in charge. They looked to be reviewing the blueprints for the project. Walter kept shaking his head and pointing to the building.

A loud blast startled everyone, including me. One of their machines appeared to have backfired, and most of the men ran behind the building, Walter with them. I took a few steps in their direction, but it was already less than two hours before my flight, and I wanted to stop at the bank to cash the check. I unlocked my car and climbed in.

"Can't believe he gave me this much." I examined the check. "I know this little detour upset her, but when she sees this check, she'll get over it quick. It should cover the vacation."

The man's voice on the radio caught my attention. He was recapping the morning half of the market. I reached down and turned the volume up.

Work never stops. Sometimes it just hangs around in the background, waiting for someone to hear it. My dad's voice echoed around my head. I smiled, happy I still remembered the life lessons he had given in passing.

Every transaction I'd set up for that morning was paying off. Making money was so easy when my head was clear.

"...up three percent today," the radio continued. "Oh, hang on. I'm getting an update to an earlier report. Yes, it has now been confirmed. All passengers on Flight 254 from Columbus to Orlando, which crashed in the mountains over Kentucky, have been killed."

Chapter 15

Peter, 2006

"How long does this take to get used to?" Anna asked, squeezing Peter's hand to steady herself.

She stumbled. He grabbed her side and pulled her close, holding her against him. Over her shoulder, he examined where they landed. They stood in the gravel on the side of the road halfway up an exit ramp. Cars drove along the highway above them on the left, while on their right, a field with knee-high grass led to what appeared to be a hill, approximately ten feet higher than the field. At the top, a fence separated them from a large gas station.

This was the last place her dad was seen? By whom?

"This exit ramp—" Her chin trembled as she whispered into his ear. "I've been here a few times just standing and..."

She squeezed Peter's side and trailed off. He pulled back a few inches from her face. Her eyes widened.

"What's wrong?"

"My mom's car."

Peter turned. Parked near the bottom of the ramp on the side of the road was a dark-gray Audi.

"Are you sure?"

"That's her license plate," Anna said with a sad smile. "We always joked about it."

"Petwife?" Peter asked. "What does that mean?"

"Petros' wife," she said. "My mom's name is Topaz. Shortly after they were married, he bought customized plates that said TopHubby, so she changed hers to PetWife. They thought they were so clever."

That is clever.

She disconnected the machine from her wrist, ran toward the car and pulled the driver's door handle.

"It's not locked," she yelled. "And the keys are still in it. What do we do next? He could still be around here!"

She ran in front of the car.

"There are footprints in the gravel, but they end here. How do they end here? Where did he go next?"

"Through the field?" Peter guessed.

"How would he get to it? There aren't any footprints going toward the field. They end right here!" Anna pointed to a spot in the gravel.

"Did he jump?"

"No, it's too far." She rocked, spun around and examined the area. "Where did he go, Peter?"

"I don't know."

He walked to the edge of the road next to the car and scanned the field.

"Wait a minute." He dug his hand into his pocket and snatched his phone.

Anna walked to the driver's side and stopped. She watched Peter tap on the screen. His face turned from curiosity to disbelief. He shook his head.

"Anything?"

"Nothing. The date, time and location are the same. Whatever we're supposed to do, it's here and now."

Her face fell. "Do we wait? Maybe he comes back to the car. Maybe we should wait."

"I'm not sure," Peter said, shaking his head. He rubbed the back of his neck and looked around.

"I wonder..." Anna said. She climbed into the driver's seat and turned the ignition. The engine hummed.

Peter opened the passenger door and dropped into the seat next to her. "What do you wonder?"

"The police thought the car stalled and he wandered off looking for help. But just now, it started. Why would he leave?"

"Maybe he walked to a gas station." Peter pointed toward the fence. "Or maybe the golf course across the street. If he needed help, he could have found a phone."

"What do we do? Should we drive around and look? They never determined what time he disappeared, but if it was just a few minutes ago, maybe we can still find him."

"Are you sure you want to leave the car?" he asked.

"I don't—"

Tires squealed behind them. Peter turned and looked over his shoulder through the rear window. A small blue car sped past Peter and Anna and continued toward the intersection at the bottom of the ramp. Peter caught a glimpse of the young girl in the passenger seat. He knew her. He'd last seen her yesterday at lunch. It was Alison, a younger Alison for sure, but it was certainly her.

"Peter, was that Max driving and Ali sitting next to him?"

"Yeah." He hesitated. "I think it was."

Max approached the intersection at the bottom of the ramp but didn't stop. It was a four-way intersection with a red light. His only options were right or left unless he kept going straight, but in that case, he would reach the on-ramp leading to the same highway they'd just exited. When he didn't turn, Peter and Anna looked at each other.

"That was odd," she said. "Did you recognize the girl in the back seat?"

"No. I didn't see her," he said. "Why were they going so fast?"

"Here comes why," Anna glanced at her mirror. She whipped her head around. Peter turned again and watched. An old brown Chevy zoomed past them toward the intersection.

"He's not stopping!" Anna cried.

The Chevy shot through the red light. Vehicles jammed on their brakes. Horns blew. A black SUV's tires squealed and slid to a stop. A dark brown SUV slammed into the rear bumper of the black SUV, pushing it into the path of the brown car. The man in the Chevy veered right, just missing a head-on collision. A large pickup truck coming from the other way skidded to a stop in front of the Chevy blocking the on-ramp. A green jeep, unable to stop in time, spun sideways behind the pickup and slammed into the tailgate; the passenger side window popped and shattered.

"Asshole!" the woman in the truck yelled.

The Chevy driver ignored the chaos behind him and kept his focus forward. In the center of the intersection, he slowed to a crawl. As if threading a needle, he steered to the right and drove into the grass. The Chevy's rear end smashed against the cement, and his car dropped off the road spraying sparks at the surprised motorists. A deafening horn blasted from the pickup. The man in the Chevy raised his hand as if waving from a parade float and followed Max back onto the highway.

Anna turned to face Peter. She grabbed his arm. "Was that the same car from last night?"

"Yeah, I think it was."

She let go of Peter and turned to check her blind spot. Before turning back, she pressed the gas pedal. Tires spun, spitting rocks and dust behind them. She turned the steering wheel left and pulled onto the road. Peter's head jerked back. He slammed against the passenger seat, reached around with both hands and grabbed his seat belt.

"We're following them?"

"Your nurse friend put us here for a reason," Anna said. "This has to be it."

"What about your dad?"

"We have a time machine. We have time."

He grabbed the door handle and held on tightly as she approached the intersection. Her fingers wrapped around the steering wheel. She pulled herself forward and stared at the red light. Traffic crossing in front of them snaked through the intersection. A few people pulled off the road to tend to the accident victims while others steered around them.

"Come on, come on!" She tapped the steering wheel and took her foot off the gas pedal. They inched closer.

The light turned yellow. Her eyes narrowed. Again, she grabbed the steering wheel with both hands and pushed the accelerator, maneuvering them into the intersection just as it turned green. Swinging the car to the right, she zipped past the black SUV. The pickup hadn't moved. She turned harder to the right and plunged off the road behind the jeep. The owner of the jeep, a young woman examining the damage, screamed and dove face-first into the grass. The Audi was briefly airborne, then crashed back to earth, making holes and spewing dirt on the young woman. Peter floated in the air with the car but was driven down into his seat when it hit the ground. He grunted and looked over at Anna.

"You okay?" she screamed over the roar of the engine.

"Yeah," Peter groaned.

The front end of the Audi scraped against the blacktop as she steered them toward the on-ramp. At the top, she looked over her shoulder, jerked the steering wheel hard, crossing three lanes of traffic and settling into the left lane.

"Hang on," she said. Her voice was lower, steady as if she only had one thing on her mind.

Where was this last night when we were the ones being chased?

Peter leaned forward. His seat belt locked and dug into his chest. He grabbed the dashboard and peered through the windshield.

He pointed. "There they are."

A quarter mile up ahead, the Chevy had caught up with Max. Anna increased their speed, forcing an old gray truck that had likely seen better days into the center lane. The Chevy banged into Max's rear bumper. Both cars wobbled. Max regained control and squeezed into the right lane between a pickup and a semi, whose driver stomped his brakes and blasted his horn. Smoke billowed from his tires. Seeing an opening, the unknown driver in the Chevy dove into the right lane behind Max, nearly missing the bumper of the semi. He ripped the baseball cap from his head, threw it in the seat next to him and straightened up, continuing to torment the teenagers.

"This can't end well," Anna said.

"It won't end in anyone's death, though," Peter said. "We've seen all of them in our time."

"Not all of them."

The girl in the back seat sat up and looked through the rear window. She waved her hands like she was fending off a swarm of hornets. She looked younger than Max and Alison, not yet a teenager. Her long dark hair shook from side to side. She pointed at the man in the Chevy and screamed at him.

Anna, now just a few seconds behind them, looked for an opening in the center lane. Peter shook free of the seat belt and leaned forward. His eyes narrowed as he read her lips.

"Go away? Leave us alone?" he said.

"What?"

"I think that's what she's saying. Go away. Leave us alone. Whatever is happening, she's petrified."

Anna groaned. She checked the rearview mirror, turned the steering wheel and pulled into the center lane.

The Chevy driver inched closer. His front end bounced against Max's rear bumper. The girl in the back seat disappeared from their view. He hit them again, this time catching the right rear corner.

Everything slowed down for Peter. White smoke filled the three-lane highway. Tires screeched. Behind the Chevy, a dark SUV smashed into the back of a blue compact car. A truck rear-ended the SUV. Peter cringed with each collision. He gripped the door handle with both hands, closed his eyes and anticipated Anna stopping the car before they were enveloped by the collisions ahead of them.

But instead, he felt acceleration. *Why is she speeding up?* He opened his eyes and turned toward her. To his astonishment, there was no panic on her face. It was frozen, almost stoic with concentration. Only her eyes moved, shifting from the rearview to the road ahead.

"Well, that is his move," she muttered.

When the smoke cleared, Max's car was sitting sideways in the road, facing the shoulder. The Chevy spun and bounced off a white SUV in the center lane. Peter recoiled as the smell of smoke and rubber filled his nose. Unfazed, Anna pressed on the gas, slid into the left lane and swerved through the mess of stopped cars like a racecar driver avoiding the "big one." Once clear, she jerked the car back into the center lane.

Max regained control, but the man in the Chevy fishtailed. He turned the steering wheel to the left, bouncing off the white SUV. He straightened his car and set his sights on his target.

The SUV turned sideways and flipped. Shards of shattered windows littered the street as it rolled several times along the center lane. The side mirror sprung into the air and hit Anna's hood. Peter yelped and ducked his head, but the mirror sailed over the car and lodged into the radiator of a Geo Metro behind them. The SUV rolled one last time and came to rest on its passenger side, straddling the two left lanes.

"Get to the right. He's exiting." Peter rose in his seat and pointed with both hands. "Go now, it's clear!"

Anna hammered the breaks to avoid the SUV. Their rear tires slid toward the center. She eased off the gas and turned into the swerve. In less than an instant, her foot was back on the gas pedal. She steered the car onto the left shoulder and darted past the SUV. When she hit the rumble strips, the car shook.

Peter's stomach trembled. He leaned back, grabbed the handle with his right hand and the center console with his left. Anna's eyes shifted from the rearview to a now clear center lane. Peter buried himself in the seat and turned his head toward her. His mouth fell open in amazement.

She's so calm.

"What?" she said, feeling his gaze. "I learned how to drive in this car."

Now only a few hundred yards ahead of Peter and Anna, Max exited the highway and merged onto a smaller four-lane road leading out of the city. Traffic was light, as most people were heading the other way to start their workday. He began to pull away, but at a sharp curve, he was forced to slow down. The man in the brown car quickly caught up with him. Both vehicles rounded a corner and disappeared from Peter's and Anna's view behind a collection of trees growing out of a swamp next to the highway.

"Shit," Anna mumbled as they approached the exit. "We're losing them."

She pressed the accelerator, crossed two lanes and drove onto the highway. At the curve, Anna didn't slow. She leaned left and struggled to turn the wheel. Momentum fought her. She was going too fast.

The passenger side tires rose off the ground. They drifted into the right shoulder and landed with a thud. The impact lifted Peter from his seat, bouncing his head against the ceiling. He winced and grabbed his forehead. The pain was instantaneous, progressing into his neck. He leaned forward and closed his eyes. A change in momentum threw him against the seat. He opened his eyes.

"Look out!" he yelled.

Anna twisted the steering wheel to the left. Just past the next entrance ramp, a silver Lexus was trying to merge onto the highway. The driver in the Lexus locked eyes with Anna. He grabbed the steering wheel and swerved, but it wasn't enough. Their car glanced off his, pushing her bumper along his door. His window shattered. The sound of metal scraping metal was interrupted by a loud pop. The corner of Anna's car ripped into the Lexus' bumper, propelling it over the railing, into the grass and down a small hill next to the highway. Peter and Anna came to rest a few yards ahead of the Lexus.

"Oh my God!" Anna lifted her hands from the steering wheel and set them in her lap. Looking at them, she whispered. "What have I done?"

"You okay?" Peter asked.

Her eyes widened again as she turned to look at him. Her mouth hung open. She nodded.

"Stay here," Peter said.

He unbuckled his seatbelt and pushed the mangled door, but it wasn't cooperating. He tried again, this time with both hands, but it still didn't budge. Leaning back, he turned sideways and threw himself at the door, slamming his shoulder just below the window. The door creaked and opened slightly. Peter pushed again. The door squealed and opened far enough to allow him to squeeze out.

He rolled his shoulder as he walked, trying to relieve the pulsating ache. He examined the driver's side of the Lexus. The front tire was flat, and a large gray scratch ran along the side of the hood to the driver's door. A clean-cut man in his thirties was in the driver's seat, checking the woman next to him. He turned to the three young children in the back seat. Anna ran to the passenger's side window.

"I'm so sorry," she said. "Are you okay? Is everyone okay?"

"What is your problem?" the man jerked his head toward Anna and peered at her.

"Sorry, sir, we—" Peter began.

The man spun to Peter, who was leaning near the driver's side window. The door rattled as the man pushed it open. When he emerged from the car, he stood tall, taller than Peter. He wore blue jeans, running shoes and a black polo shirt with a large O in the center of his chest. Peter recognized the logo as one of the local finance companies from commercials he'd seen after falling asleep in the middle of the night and waking with the television still on.

The man's dark hair matched the thin beard that ran down his cheeks and collected into an oversized soul patch just below his bottom lip. His deep-set eyes were nearly hidden in the bags beneath them. He looked as if he hadn't slept in months.

He turned and stared at Anna. She tilted her head but held his gaze. Silence hung in the air. He punched the roof of his car with both hands. Anna flinched. All three children looked at the man. He turned and stepped toward Peter. Peter staggered backward.

"Nelson!" the woman on the passenger side yelled.

Nelson stopped and looked at his feet. He appeared to be counting to himself as he breathed. His chest rose with each inhale. The vein in his neck pulsated each time he exhaled.

"It's just that our friends were—" Anna began, walking around to meet Peter.

Nelson took another step forward and reached into his pocket. Anna stopped next to Peter, but Peter stepped in front of her.

"Don't move. I'm calling the police," Nelson said. He took a business card from his wallet and forced it into her hands. "Write your information."

He leaned through the shattered driver's side window, his voice softer. "Honey, hand me my phone."

The vein in his neck calmed, but his hands shook as he took the phone from her. He shot one last scowl at Peter before turning away from the pair. Taking a few steps toward the back of the Lexus, he opened the phone. Peter took the business card from Anna and walked to the back of her mom's car. She turned to follow him but stopped and looked through the windshield at the woman.

"I'm so sorry," Anna said.

"We're okay, sweetie," the woman mouthed and offered a sympathetic smile. She paused before grabbing Nelson's phone from the center console and leaning across the driver's seat to hand it through the broken window. "Nelson, she didn't hit us that hard, and everyone's okay. Calm down. I'm sure we can still make the airport."

"The front tire is flat, and the bumper is gone. We don't have time to wait for a tow truck, get everything fixed and make your flight. Let's wait on the police, and we can all fly together later like we originally planned."

Nelson looked back at Peter, who was standing behind Anna's mom's car, pretending to write.

"Like we should be, anyway," the woman said softly, but still loudly enough for everyone to hear. The man's face reddened as he glared at Anna.

"Write faster!" he yelled to Peter. He turned his back, and his voice deepened when he spoke into the phone, "Some girl just hit us with her car. I need someone here now."

Peter dropped his right arm to his side and began to wave his hand around, trying to get Anna's attention without letting anyone else see. She met him at the left rear corner of her mom's car.

"What's wrong?" she asked.

He turned to face her, "We can't get caught here. What would we tell the police?"

"You think we should just leave?"

"No! I need someone here now!" Nelson shouted into the phone, "I pay your salaries. Do your Goddamn job."

"We have to," Peter insisted.

Anna looked at the Lexus, the bumper missing, and the woman talking to the three young children in the back seat. She pushed the keys into Peter's hands and hurried to the passenger side. The door screeched, but when she pulled it shut, it appeared to latch. Peter got in the car, shifted into drive and accelerated, kicking up dust and propelling the Audi onto the highway.

Still holding his phone, Nelson spun and threw his hands in the air. Anna watched Nelson jump into the Lexus. The woman next to him grabbed his arm when he took hold of the steering wheel. Without turning toward her, he said something. She let go of his arm. He angled the car toward the road and inched forward. A large puff of black smoke erupted from the exhaust pipe, and a loud bang echoed behind them.

Peter flinched, ducked down in his seat. "What was that?"

"The car backfired," Anna said.

White smoke rose from the hood of the Lexus. Nelson leaped out of the car and screamed something unintelligible at Peter and Anna. With no chance of another chase, Peter eased off the gas pedal and finally breathed.

Anna looked at the machine still dangling from Peter's wrist, then over her shoulder through the rear window.

"We need to fix that," she said, pointing at the Lexus.

"The list just keeps getting longer," Peter replied.

Chapter 16

Peter, 2006

Peter drove along the highway, looking for any sign of Max and Alison or the Chevy.

"What do we do?" Anna asked.

"I don't know," Peter said. He pulled the phone from his pocket and opened the time-travel app. A slow smile spread across his face.

"What?" She said.

"My phone changed. It's the same day, but the time and location are different."

"We may as well keep following her," Anna said.

Peter parked the car behind a gas station and grabbed his bag as he stepped out. Anna put one foot on the ground, began to stand but tumbled back into the passenger seat. He walked around to her side. The door was open, but she was sitting sideways, her feet hanging outside the car, her head in her hands.

Her voice was uncertain. "This is where they found the car."

"Here?"

"I'm remembering it different," she said. "I still have all these memories of standing on the exit ramp from this morning, but now I have more. It's like new memories are being injected directly into my brain."

She stood and walked to the end of the concrete.

"I remember standing right here," she said, "staring into these woods, wondering if he was lying in there in need of help."

"The timeline is changing," Peter said. "We moved the car before anyone found it. Now they'll find it here."

"It hurts my head," she whispered.

"This is what I was trying to avoid." He turned away from Anna and stared into the woods.

"Has this ever happened to you?" she asked.

"Just once."

"We should leave," she said.

She lifted her arm and held it in front of Peter. He took the free end of the machine, wrapped it around her wrist and slid the latch into the open end. It clicked into place and locked. He pressed the button on the app.

THEY REAPPEARED IN the roadway of a large concrete parking garage. Even with the sun shining through the narrow openings between floors, darkness concealed most of the inside. Cars lined each available spot. A large "Reserved" sign marked each spot, denoting the name and logo of the company that owned it. On the outer side, Key Bank owned the entire row. Across from it, Chase Bank held spots winding around the corner and leading up to the next level.

"Smith Center Parking Garage. Level 2." Anna, reading from a sign on one of the thick pillars that were situated evenly throughout the garage.

He unhooked the machine from her wrist and inched between a red Chevy Cavalier and a black Mazda Miata. At the edge, he stopped and examined the ten-story office building next to the garage. Another sign planted next to the entrance read "Smith Center."

The front of the building was mostly glass, but scaffolding climbed its backside. Pieces of blue tarp covered large openings exposing the ongoing work inside the building each time a gust of wind blew. Yellow construction vehicles of all sizes hummed in the distance, while dozens of men in hard hats worked on different sections.

"Why would she bring us here?" Anna wondered. She put her nose to the Miata's passenger side window and peered inside.

"I have no idea," Peter said.

Anna approached the edge on the other side of the Miata. The sun shone directly overhead in the blue sky. The sounds of traffic moving along the highway on the opposite side of the parking garage were drowned out by the clanging of construction vehicles as they moved concrete, lifted pieces of metal and filled trucks with scrap to be hauled away.

"There!" she yelled, pointing into the parking lot in front of the Smith Center.

A familiar brown Chevy drove into the lot and crept through the first row at a snail's pace. He focused on each of the smaller blue models, sometimes stopping to get out of his car and peek inside. At the end of the first row, he swung around and repeated the process in the second. Two rows over, a car door opened. Max, Alison and the third girl crawled out and ran toward the building.

"It's them!" Anna yelled.

The man in the brown car continued his hunt by driving away from the building. He hadn't spotted them.

"They're gonna make it," Anna said.

Max jumped onto the sidewalk before the main entrance. At the end of the second row, the Chevy rounded the corner and screeched to a halt. The Chevy's driver jumped out of his car, leaving it parked in the middle of the aisle, stomped out a cigarette and ran after them. He was thinner than in his encounter with Peter and Anna the previous night, but his grizzled face and blue-jean jacket were unmistakable.

"What does he want with them?" Peter turned to Anna. He held his palms out and shrugged his shoulders. "In 2006?"

Max, Alison and the unknown girl disappeared through the front entrance while their pursuer lumbered across the parking lot and followed them into the building.

"Let's go!" Anna yelled.

She ran to the garage stairs, flung the door open and skipped down three steps at a time. Peter followed close behind. They burst through the exit doors into the parking lot, ten rows from the main entrance. Anna led the way, taking them along the last row to the road along the front of the Smith Center. They jumped onto the sidewalk and ran through the entrance.

Immediately, they stopped in their tracks.

The bottom floor was small. An unoccupied check-in desk was against the back wall, and two banks of elevators sat on each side. To their left, a door marked "Stairs" was closed. Anna ran to open it and stuck her head inside.

"I don't hear anything." She slammed the door shut and crossed her arms. "Where's your nurse now?"

Peter went to the desk and eyed the directory on the wall behind it. He looked for anything: a name, a company, something that looked familiar. Anna joined him.

"Anything jump out at you?" she asked.

A loud ding, followed by the sound of an elevator door opening, stopped them both. They looked at each other, then turned to face the empty elevator.

"Did someone come out of there?" Anna said.

"I don't think so. Did you push the button?"

"I didn't touch it."

"It's just a hunch but..." Peter trailed off.

He stepped inside the elevator and looked back at Anna. She followed him inside. The button for floor number two brightened. The door closed, and the elevator rose. At the second floor, it stopped.

Peter looked at the camera mounted in the upper left corner. "I don't think we're alone here."

When the door opened, a woman sitting behind a receptionist desk glanced at them. Loose paperwork covered her work surface, and a large manila folder rested on the edge. Papers had fallen out and scattered on the floor. A taller desk stood next to hers, holding a notepad and a sign warning everyone that all visitors MUST sign in first. Peter made eye contact, straightened his shoulders and strolled through the doors like he belonged there. Anna stepped out and stopped behind him.

"Hi Joyce," he said, looking at her nameplate. "Did, um...anyone come running by?"

"Are you with those damn kids?" Her lips curled, and the gap between her eyebrows narrowed as she glanced at Anna standing behind Peter. "They're in trouble. This is a private—"

Peter bolted past her desk and into the narrow hallway. The walls were pale blue, lined with unmarked doors at even increments on both sides. There was barely enough room for two people to walk side by side. Anna was on his heels, without hesitation.

He rounded a corner to find a tall man pressed against the wall. His hands were in the air like he was being mugged, and his eyes closed. The beard, the soul patch, the large O in the middle of his shirt, it all seemed familiar.

Peter turned sideways, facing away from the man and slid past him. Anna followed, brushing her shoulder against his. The man stumbled but regained his balance. Anna slowed, and Peter grabbed her hand, pulling her around the next corner.

"Sorry," Anna said.

A few seconds later, the narrow hallway opened into a large walkway. Wooden benches were built into each side so that people could sit along the walls. Outlets, USB ports and Ethernet ports next to each bench made it easy for employees or guests to plug their laptops and get a little work done. The walls were mostly glass, offering the view of a pond and picnic area on the ground below. To Peter, it was more like an airport terminal than an office building.

At the end of the hall, two doors about twenty feet apart marked "Conference Room A" were on their left. On their right, a large glass wall revealed a gym filled with treadmills, ellipticals and weight benches. Four women and two men jogged on the treadmills, each distracted by music from their headphones. The final door at the end of the hall was an emergency exit with a sign warning of a loud alarm.

"Where do we go?" Anna asked. "She led us here and opened the elevator. She has to tell us what to do next!"

"It can't be outside," Peter said. "I don't hear an alarm."

"Then it must be—"

A voice from inside Conference Room A interrupted their discussion.

"We'll leave you alone," a female voice begged. "Just, please, don't hurt us."

"Was that Alison?" Peter whispered.

"I'm really getting sick of you kids!" a man said. "Your father was a thief. He deserved what he got."

Someone slammed into the wall inside the conference room, near the door next to Peter. He jumped back.

"No! Stop!" Alison screamed.

Peter grabbed the doorknob and turned, but before he could pull it open, Max and the man bounced off the door frame on the other side of the wall. The frame shook with the impact, and Peter's fingers slipped off the doorknob. The door flew open, hitting the outside wall.

The open door gave Peter a view of the conference room and of the man, who had raised his right hand to point a small silver pistol at Max's chest. Max swiped at his arm, pushing the gun away. A pop echoed inside the room. The television on the wall exploded next to the unknown girl, showering sparks and pieces of glass across her back. She screamed and fell to the floor behind the long table.

"Regan!" Alison yelled, falling to her knees next to the girl.

Peter twisted out of the open doorway and pushed himself against the open door.

What are we doing here?

He looked toward a stunned Anna, who had taken four steps backward and crouched to the floor. Reaching behind his back, Peter searched blindly for the doorknob, but all he felt was the machine, still hanging from his wrist.

This is stupid. Leave the past before it's too late.

"We need to go," he told Anna, holding out his wrist, showing her their means of their escape.

She nodded and leaned against the gym window. A man on the treadmill stepped off and turned around. He yelled to a woman, who removed her headphones and spun toward the noise coming from the hallway.

Peter turned his head slightly and peered into the conference room.

Max lunged at the man, sending the pistol flying through the door to land at Peter's feet. Peter grabbed the edge of the door and tried to close it, but Max and the man crashed into it again, this time ripping the door free of its hinges. The corner of the metal door slammed into the floor with such force, its edges crumpled and twisted before ricocheting toward Anna. She tried to dive out of the way, but the mangled corner of the door caught her leg below the knee, ripping a wide gash above her shin. She cried out, grabbed her leg with both hands and collapsed into a fetal position on the floor.

"Anna!" Peter called.

Max made it to his feet first. As the man pushed himself to his hands and knees, Max kicked him in the ribs, knocking him into Peter. The man's momentum pushed both him and Peter against the emergency door. The loose end of the machine wrapped around the door handle, momentarily trapping Peter against the door. Anna struggled to a seated position, her back to the glass gym wall. She peeked over her shoulder and saw the six people in the gym running toward another exit at the opposite side of the room.

Holding his ribs with one hand, the man gritted his teeth and glared at Max before stumbling in his direction. Max stood tall, holding his hands out at his sides, palms up, apparently begging for the man to hurry up—as if he had been waiting for this moment for a long time. The man swung a wild punch and missed.

Peter freed himself from the door and moved toward the workout room.

Max grabbed the man's collar and threw him at the glass wall. The stranger spun and ducked, but not in time; his head slammed hard against the glass and bounced toward Peter. Unable to get out of the way, Peter took the brunt of his shoulder as both fell to the ground.

Max jumped on top of his opponent and straddled his stomach. The man extended his arm toward the silver pistol, only three feet away. He slid his index finger inside the trigger guard and pulled it closer. Taking control of the handle, he swung the gun toward Max's chest. Max grabbed his wrist, bending the man's arm to the side, the pistol's barrel now pointing directly at Peter. Peter rolled out of the line of fire toward the gym door.

Max grabbed the man's throat with his other hand.

"You son-of-a-bitch kid," the man hissed. "I'll kill you the same way I killed your father."

Blood vessels in Max's neck and face expanded until he was bright red with anger. His lips curled, and a thin smile formed at the corners of his mouth. He tightened his grip. The man's mouth foamed like a rabid dog's as he gasped for air. Max's thin smile turned large. He bared his teeth, leaned his face closer and looked into the man's eyes.

Peter rose to his feet and stared at Max. This wasn't the same carefree person he would meet just a few years later. *Will he actually kill this man?* Peter looked at Anna, but she was focused on Max. As if she felt Peter looking at her, she turned and met his eyes. Someone needed to stop Max, intervene, do something. But Peter stood still, frozen to that spot on the floor.

"Max, stop!" Alison cried.

The man's free arm flailed. He grabbed Max's side and dug his fingers into his ribs. The sudden pain shocked Max. He shrieked. His grip on the man's throat weakened. The man shook his hand free and pushed the pistol into Max's face.

No, this can't happen now.

Peter lunged. He slammed into Max, knocking him off the man. The gun fired three times, shattering the gym wall behind Peter and sending shards of glass raining into the hallway. Anna rolled forward, covering her head and neck with her arms. Peter flattened himself to the ground and rolled onto his stomach.

Without hesitation, Max was back on top of the man. He punched the man hard, bringing his fist straight down into the center of his face. The man's nose cracked. Peter cringed and turned his head away. Max continued with blow after blow, throwing blood in the air each time he brought his fists up, like a child running through puddles.

Alison ran to him. She rested one hand on his shoulder and tried to grab his arms, but Max was gone, replaced by a wild animal whose only thought was kill or be killed.

Her voice was soft but stern. "Max, stop."

He tilted his head toward her, and his expression softened. The man wasn't moving when Max finally climbed off him. He threw his arms around Alison, smearing blood across her yellow sweater.

"It's over," he whispered. "Finally."

Peter searched for Anna. She had scooted to the first and still intact conference room door and picked glass from her sleeves. Peter stood and shook his head like a dog just in from the rain. He ran to Anna. Glass pieces tumbled off his shirt to the floor.

"Are you okay?" He looked at her leg. The bleeding had stopped, but a deep red scratch zigzagged below her knee. He stretched his hand to help her. "Can you stand?"

"Yeah, I think," she said. "It just nipped me."

"Your definition of 'nipped' must be different from mine."

Regan ran from the conference room and threw open the emergency door. The alarm pierced the hallway.

"Thanks, man!" Max yelled to Peter.

"Max!"

Max stopped and looked over his shoulder. He put his hand to his head, shading it from the sun shining into the building and narrowed his eyes.

"I know you, right?" Max said. He put his forefingers on his temples and squeezed. "It's coming back to..."

"Peter!" Anna yelled.

Peter turned. Two policemen were rounding the corner. He looked back, but Max and the girls were gone. The two policemen stopped. Their eyes darted to Peter and Anna, then to the unconscious, blood-covered man in the hallway and the gun on the floor next to him. They pulled their guns and pointed them at the frightened pair.

"Turn around! Face the wall!" the taller of the two policemen ordered.

Peter and Anna turned and pressed themselves against the wall. Anna inched sideways toward Peter until their shoulders touched.

"You have your phone?" she whispered.

"Front pocket."

The taller officer stood over the man lying on the ground. He was bloody and unconscious, but his chest was slowly rising and falling. The officer kicked the pistol from his side and nudged the man with the toe of his boot. The man groaned and opened his eyes. The second officer stepped into the conference room.

Anna reached into Peter's front pocket and slid out his phone.

"Your arm," she said.

Peter raised his arm slightly. She slid her wrist inside the empty side of the bracelet. Peter locked it into place.

"He's alive. Call an ambulance," the officer said to his partner. He turned to Peter and Anna. "Okay, what do you know about this?"

"Wrong place, wrong time sir," Anna said. "We had just finished working out and heard the commotion."

Peter pushed the button to wake the phone. He opened the time travel app.

"You can turn around," the officer said, seeming to believe her story. "Did you see anyone else?"

With their wrists locked together in the bracelets, turning was impossible.

"Hurry," Anna whispered. "Push the button."

"I said you could turn around. What are you doing there? Let me see your hands!"

He rushed toward them and put his hand on Peter's shoulder. Peter pressed the button.

Chapter 17

Peter, 2022

"Where are we?" Anna asked while looking around. "Where did she send us?"

"I don't know."

Peter unhooked the machine from both their wrists and tossed it into his backpack. He looked at his phone, confused, tilted his head and scanned the area. Stale air assaulted his nose. Grime collected on his tongue. He tried to spit it out, but a heavy fog of dust and dirt hung in the air like low clouds surrounding a mountain.

Behind Anna, the Smith Center sign lay toppled over, covered by pieces of the building they'd escaped from only a few minutes before. But it was no longer under construction. Instead, it was a pile of rubble. Other than jagged pieces on the corners that refused to give in completely, the walls had collapsed. All four elevator banks remained but only rose to the third floor, like towers rising into the evening sky. The rest of the five-story building was gone, replaced by piles of broken office supplies scattered throughout the ground floor.

A rat scurried by, no doubt looking for food.

What happened here? What happened to the building, the parking garage?

"What does it say?" Anna interrupted.

"May twenty-sixth, 2022."

"But that's only five years from..." Her voice trailed off.

They walked toward the building's entrance. Kicking up small clouds of dust, Peter pushed shattered glass and crumbled slabs of gray cement out of the way. They stepped outside the remains of the Smith Center and into the dim light of the evening.

"Where are the lights of the city?" Anna asked. She took Peter's hand and squeezed. Her body spun toward the parking garage, pulling him with her. "Look at that!"

Peter's jaw dropped. Each floor of the parking garage had collapsed on the one below. Flattened front and rear ends of busted vehicles, including the red Cavalier they'd stood next to just an hour earlier, poked out and hung over the edge.

"What happened here?" Anna said.

Peter shook his head and shrugged. "I don't know."

The parking lot in front of the Smith Center was mostly empty. Whatever happened, most of the people who parked there must have made it to their cars quickly enough to get away.

"Terrorist attack?" Anna asked.

"Maybe, but whatever it was must've just happened," Peter said. "Why would she send us after the fact?"

Past the garage, several buildings along the crowded street had suffered the same fate. Each looked to have been imploded from within before crumpling onto itself.

They stepped onto the sidewalk and moved along High Street, away from the parking garage. On their right, the destruction and devastation continued with each building they passed. The left side of the street used to be a park where people would come out of the buildings on their lunch breaks to gather, take the sun and eat, but now it looked like a place where trucks hauled rubble in what might have been an attempt to clean up.

"Where is everyone?" Anna asked. "We're *literally* the only two people outside."

At the intersection of Chestnut and High, stop lights hung low in the street, but none of them were lit.

It didn't really matter since the only cars on the road had long been deserted.

On one side, the Nationwide building, one of the biggest in the city, had toppled sideways, blocking anyone from continuing along High Street.

A stiff wind blew through. Dust and small pebbles whipped around, stinging Peter's and Anna's faces. She stepped behind him and pressed her forehead to his back. Newspapers stirred around their feet. Next to him, the front door of a Domino's Pizza was still intact. They stepped inside. Most of the building had been destroyed, but the walls of the men's restroom stood high enough to shelter them from the wind.

"Do you think we're the only ones left?" Anna asked, keeping to her line of unanswered questions.

"I don't know."

Anna reached for Peter, touching his shoulder. She stared at her feet. Softly, she said, "Peter, do you think we caused this?"

He turned to her. The same question had been swirling through his mind since they'd arrived, but she was the first to say it out loud. A shadow appeared on the floor behind Anna and slowly overtook them. Peter looked toward the sky. His eyes widened.

"What?" Anna said.

A deep, mechanical voice penetrated the quiet, moonlit evening. "Stop, intruder!"

A large droid hovered above them, blocking out the night sky. Peter's muscles tightened, freezing him in place. Anna squeezed against him and put her arm around his waist.

The droid stood at least ten feet tall and had a large circular head. An infrared light shot out of one side of the tube and scanned the area. Red light lit the wall behind Anna, tracing the floor until it found them both. Anna ducked behind Peter. He used his arm to shield his eyes.

"Stop, intruder."

The circular metal body was tall enough for someone to sit in, albeit uncomfortably, and had white lights that began to shine as if it was alerting others to its find.

"Humans are no longer allowed in this sector. All intruders will be destroyed."

Anna pushed her arm into Peter's back, and he bolted into the interior of the restaurant. He looked over his shoulder. She was right there on his heels. Behind her, the droid was gaining on them. Extending from the underside of its belly were four spiny legs. Each leg floated a few inches above the ground and formed a circle around one central leg. Scraping across the ground, the central limb was longer than the other four, with thin catfish-like barbs running along the sides from top to bottom.

"Stop, intruders."

They jumped over the fragments of the kitchen wall and disappeared into a dark alley. As they ran, red brick walls on each side, from buildings that seemed to have escaped total destruction, provided cover. Empty water bottles, cigarette butts and random litter crunched under their feet. Dumpsters lined the walls giving off a thick, noxious odor that permeated the air around them and filled their lungs with every inhale. Behind him, Anna retched.

The alley dead-ended into a large wooden gate with a sign marked "Deliveries, please ring buzzer." He grabbed the handles and pulled, but locks at the top and bottom of the gate removed their only escape. They were trapped.

The infrared light appeared at the end of the alley and moved toward them in a sweeping motion from side to side. Peter studied the area and darted behind the closest dumpster, grabbing Anna's hand as he ran past her. Above the dumpster, a metal fire escape hung just out of reach. At the top, an open window led into the second story of the building. He looked at Anna, now squatting behind him. A small stream of blood fell from the wound below her knee.

"If we climb the dumpster, we can get to the ladder and that window," Peter said. "Is your leg okay?"

She pushed a couple of strands of hair from her eyes and grimaced.

"I can do it."

Peter stood, put one foot on the dumpster and grabbed the top. He pulled himself up and reached for the ladder. A red light hit him in the face, blinding him. He squeezed his eyes closed and dropped to the ground in front of Anna. The droid swung around to the side of the dumpster and hovered a few feet from them. Two round holes opened in its body, producing a couple of small silver pipes, pointed at Peter and Anna.

"Identify yourself."

Peter put his hands in the air and slowly stood, keeping himself between the droid and Anna. He opened his mouth to speak, but before he could get any words out, the droid violently shook. White smoke poured from the top and sides. It lurched and dropped a few inches. Each of the five hovering legs smacked the ground and snapped at the knees. Pausing for a split second, the droid keeled forward and crashed head-first into the ground.

A small human stood behind the remains of the droid. She was short, maybe five feet, and skinny. She wore blue jeans, a dirty blouse and a striped scarf that covered most of her face. Her brown eyes matched her cheeks and a hint of stringy black hair poked through the bottom of the scarf. Peter's eyes dropped to the large silver gun in her hand.

"That's odd." She spoke in a thick Indian accent, something Peter heard each morning at work as he completed his walk.

His eyes narrowed. He stared at her.

"I didn't even pull the trigger," she said.

She flipped the gun over and touched the barrel, holding her fingers against it for a second. Shaking her head, she looked at Peter and Anna. Peter could see the smile form against the inside of her scarf. She pushed the gun into her waistband and grabbed the scarf with both hands. Pulling it down, she exposed the rest of her face.

"Padma?" Peter and Anna said simultaneously.

Chapter 18

Peter, 2022

"We should leave," Padma said. "They'll send more when this one doesn't respond."

Peter stiffened. He looked at Anna. She slid her hands into her pockets, glancing at Padma and then at Peter.

How could she be in the same place as us, with a big giant gun and no fear of what just chased us through the alley?

"What are you doing here?"

"Come with me. You are both in danger."

Anna stepped around the droid and the smoke billowing through its openings, and stood beside Padma. She held her hand out and motioned for Peter to follow. He looked at the wrecked droid. Sparks bounced from its head into the air and ricocheted against the dumpster, falling to the ground in front of him. He jumped back a step and looked at Padma. She held the gun high in the air, showed it to him and slowly tucked it into her belt against her back.

Why is she here and holding that big gun? How did she find us?

"You *can* trust me, Peter," Padma said.

"I think we should go with her," Anna said. "She's our friend. We can't stay on these streets if there are more of those things out here."

That gun was huge.

Peter sighed and moved toward them. They hustled out of the alley and headed east on High Street until they reached an open parking lot to their left. Cars, trucks and even a few motorcycles, many of them burned, filled every inch of the lot and were piled at least twenty-five feet into the air. Oil slicks collected in low spots and fragments of shattered windows puddled in the areas near the tallest sections of the pile. Padma lead them into the lot and wound through a maze, opening and closing vehicle doors along the way, uncovering a path leading through the mass of busted metal and glass.

"What happ—," Peter began. Padma held her index finger to her mouth, silencing him.

"Not yet," she whispered.

A loud crash from High Street startled the trio. Padma opened the door of a caved-in Ford Fiesta lying on its roof next to them. The bed of a dark pickup truck rested on top of the Fiesta, and its front end was wedged into the rear window of a yellow taxi, leaving them just enough space to squeeze between the two cars beneath the truck. Padma crouched next to the Fiesta and motioned for Anna and Peter to huddle next to her. Once they sat, she opened the door of the taxi, which formed a barricade on all four sides.

Another droid, exactly like the disabled one they'd left in the alley, appeared at the entrance of the parking lot. It slowly rose above the sidewalk, making ten-foot-wide sweeps with its infrared scanning light. They watched as each sweep brought it closer to finding them. Padma reached around Anna and grabbed Peter's collar, pulling them nearer to her. The next sweep rolled along the ground toward them. Peter pulled his knees against his chest and held his breath. The red light hit the door of the taxi, swept over the pickup truck and reappeared on the ground behind them.

He ran his hand across his forehead and stifled a groan after swiping a mixture of sweat and dust into the cut that hadn't yet healed. Seconds felt like minutes as the droid continued its sweep. Peter closed his eyes and slowed his breathing in an attempt to stay silent.

The red light moved through the parking lot until it reached the end. Apparently satisfied with its search, the large droid moved to the park across the street.

"That's not the first time I've had to hide in there," Padma whispered as she stood and dusted herself off. "Whoever is building those things still hasn't figured out how to make it understand corners and/or hiding places. It scans in a grid pattern and moves along as if it didn't just see us a few minutes earlier."

At the back of the parking lot, they pressed through the twisted metal bars of an iron fence and crossed to Lafayette Street. After a quarter mile of walking along the sidewalk, Padma stopped at an abandoned four-story red brick building. Bars covered the three tall windows on the first floor, and a large piece of plywood was nailed to the front door. Padma walked around to the back corner where a large crate full of wet, dirty clothes rested near the wall. She pulled it away and grabbed a small, square piece of wood leaning against the building. Moving it aside, she exposed a hole that led into the basement. Without looking back or saying anything to the pair, she slid through the window feet first.

"Come on," she called to them from the darkness.

Anna went through first, her feet crashing onto the wooden floor. Peter followed, making sure his backpack didn't get caught in the window frame as he slid. With all three safely inside, Padma climbed onto a footstool near the window and put the pieces back into place, keeping the entrance hidden from anyone walking by. She jumped off the stool and lit three candles near the door, giving them a dim view of the room.

"Where are we?" Peter asked.

Before Padma could answer, a small dog came running out of the darkness. Wagging his white furry tail, he ran to Peter.

"Buddy?" Peter dropped to a crouch, and Buddy jumped into his arms. He rolled on his back, allowing Buddy to crawl onto his chest and lick his face.

"Hey boy. I'm happy to see you too."

"I'm surprised he remembers you," Padma said. "He hasn't seen you in five years, not since you both went missing."

"How did you get—"

"We're missing?" Anna asked.

Padma walked across the room and once again disappeared into the darkness. She flipped three switches. With each click, different sections of the room brightened, until finally, the whole space came into view.

An L-shaped desk ran along two walls meeting in the far corner. Twelve computer monitors hung above one side in a six-by-two grid. A full kitchen filled the area behind Peter, and a small dining room table cluttered with leaflets was next to it. In the corner opposite the desk, a dirty mattress lay on the floor with a folded quilt and two pillows. Padma pulled a sweatshirt from the duffel bag by the quilt, threw it on and sank into a brown leather desk chair, throwing puffs of dust into the light.

"You live here?" Anna asked.

Padma opened a laptop sitting in front of her on the desk and typed a password. The entire wall of monitors flashed and lit up. Two of them opened to a Windows screen, one stayed black, and the other nine appeared to be cameras mounted around different parts of the city.

"Is that how you found us?" Peter asked.

Padma continued to stay silent as she went through a variety of checks on the computer.

"Camera ten doesn't exist anymore," she muttered. "That was the one that monitored the ci—"

"Padma!" Anna yelled. "What is going on? What happened to the city?"

Padma turned. She stared past them as if she didn't know where to start or which of their questions to answer first. After a few seconds, she motioned to the table and chairs. Anna pulled a seat out first, dusted it off and sat. Peter lifted Buddy and walked over. He sat, placing Buddy in his lap.

"You guys really don't know what happened?"

"We...kinda..." Peter paused, looking for the right words without giving away what they'd been through. Buddy's eyes fell shut as Peter ran his hand along his fur.

"I think we skipped it," Anna said, finishing Peter's thought.

"Skipped it?" Padma waited for Anna to elaborate, but no one spoke. "How could you have—" Her eyes moved from Peter's backpack to his wrist. They narrowed. She grinned. "You figured it out, didn't you?"

He glanced at Anna, who was already staring at him.

"What?" Peter said.

"My app. It works, doesn't it? When did you guys come from?"

"What do you mean?"

"Come on, Peter. I realized what I was doing when I built that app. There's a lot about me you don't know."

He looked back at Anna. She offered a small shrug before nodding her head.

"Yeah, it works," he mumbled. "Our present time is 2017, but just now we came from 2006."

"May twenty-sixth to be exact," Anna said. "And 1873 before that."

"Did you say May twenty-sixth?"

"That day has some history for me," Anna explained. "My dad disappeared on that date. I was hoping to see him again."

"May twenty-sixth is the day in 2019 when everything blew up."

"What do you mean everything blew up?" Peter asked.

"Everything. The entire globe. We don't know all the details, but that's why they sent me here. I'm trying to figure it out and fix things. I failed once, but Peter, if your machine works—" She paused and rose from the chair, walking around the table to grab a bottle of water from the fridge. "I'll get a second chance."

What is she talking about?

"I need to update...um..." She trailed off and ran across the room, falling into the brown leather chair.

Peter pulled the strings on his backpack, tightening it against his body. He drew himself up and tried to peer over Padma's shoulder. She opened an email program and typed furiously, but all he could make out was "Corporal, I have made contact." She shifted in her seat, hiding the rest of the message behind her small frame.

"The entire globe?" Anna whispered.

"Yeah," Padma said, frantically typing on the keyboard. She turned back to them. "We don't know how many people survived, but there have been reports it was less than one percent. We're also hearing about small autocratic societies popping up around the world."

"Autocratic?"

"One person controls everything. They keep everyone else down in the name of peace. They control the food supply, the lines of communication, everything. And it's usually not friendly. I was sent here to stop it. I've failed so far, but now with you here and your machine, we can go back. We have another chance to stop things before they start."

"Wait. Slow down," Peter said. "This can't be our immediate future. It was just a few years ago, and everything was fine."

"In 2019, everything changed. This is the new reality now, Peter."

She turned to the laptop, opened a messaging window and shook her head. No return message had come. Peter lowered Buddy to the floor and stood. He walked past Anna, who was shuffling through the leaflets, touching her shoulder as he passed by.

Everywhere? Can it be true?

He stood in front of the monitors. Each of the nine cameras watching the city was now moving through the streets, turning corners and floating above any debris in its way.

"Are these attached to those droids?" Peter said.

"Yeah, I worked it out as soon as I settled in and found the network."

Peter looked over Padma's shoulder. "Is that my laptop?"

"I grabbed it when I took Buddy after you guys didn't come into work. That's not important. What's important is you telling me about your time machine. How does it work? How does it connect to my app?"

Peter stood silent, unsure of whether he wanted her to know the specifics. If someone else knew how to use it, they could get away, leaving him behind. That wasn't something he was ready for. He stepped away from the desk.

"What is Ceremony?" Anna held out a leaflet, showing it to Peter.

Padma turned to her. She sank into her seat and bit her lip. When she spoke, her voice was quiet, not the same excited tone as just a few minutes ago.

"It's how they keep control."

"Who?" Anna asked.

"Once a week they choose someone from the city and put them on display for everyone else. It's usually someone they claim has broken one of their laws."

"What happens to the person?" Peter asked, almost positive he already knew the answer.

"It's not good," Padma said.

"Why?" Anna insisted.

"I should just take you. You'll get all your answers there. I know a back way where we can watch, and no one will see us."

She closed the laptop and led them into a narrow bathroom next to the kitchen. On one wall, there was a toilet, a cabinet with a sink and a mirror above it. A small, square walk-in shower stood across from the sink. Tucked into a corner next to the shower was a small door, barely four feet tall, and built into the center was a large turn wheel lock similar to an old-fashioned bank vault. Padma took the wheel with both hands and turned until it clicked. With whatever strength her small frame could muster, she pulled. The door creaked open.

"Watch your step," she said, pointing to a shelf hanging next to the mirror. Peter grabbed three flashlights and handed one each to Padma and Anna.

She continued, "It can get a little wet along the way."

Peter turned on his flashlight and turned it toward Padma. The gun, still pressed against her back, flickered in the darkness ahead of her. He paused before entering the tunnel, pulled off his backpack and dropped it into the kitchen sink.

"What are you doing?" Anna mouthed, stepping into the tunnel next to him.

"Trust me," Peter whispered just out of earshot of Padma, who had moved a few steps ahead. Once through the doorway, the tunnel more than doubled in size. The walls were full of graffiti, except for a solid line of white chalk drawn over the graffiti at shoulder height.

Anna groaned at the overwhelming odor of moldy water and dirt permeating from the tunnel's floor and walls. She pulled her sweatshirt over her mouth. Peter shined the light to the ceiling, which was at least ten feet high, and called out to Padma, "What is this place?"

"It's an old drainage ditch. It takes water from the park and deposits it into the river."

Peter inched along, keeping his feet out of the thin line of water running down the center of the tunnel.

"Lately it's been dry, but we got a short burst of rain last night," Padma continued. "Before the Event, kids used to come here and ride their skateboards. Either of you ever hear of the Gates of Hell?"

"No," Peter and Anna said.

Padma laughed. "I've only been in the city seven years, and I've heard stories about it a bunch of times. You guys must hang out with the wrong people."

"Well, what is it?" Anna asked, crossing her arms.

"There were rumors years ago that if someone opened all the gates along this path at the time same time, it would unleash Hell on earth."

"Maybe that's what happened," Anna muttered as they passed one of the closed gates. It had the same handle as the door in Padma's bathroom.

"There were other rumors about it too. People dying here, murdered, or bodies washing in from the river and getting lodged against the last gate."

Ahead, the tunnel presented them with the option of turning left or right. Padma stopped and waited for Peter and Anna to catch up with her. She moved to the right and continued walking.

"Following the chalk line," Peter murmured.

In the distance, a hint of light appeared, drawing them toward an exit. They stepped out of the tunnel onto a five-foot triangular cement platform with two large iron fences extending from each side and meeting at the top of the triangle.

Peter stopped. "Are we trapped in here?"

"No, we can squeeze through where two pieces meet," Padma said. "But keep your voice down. We're close."

Once through, they climbed a small hill flanked by trees on each side.

"Stay in the shadows," she cautioned in the same low tones.

At the top of the hill, they saw a small high school football stadium about a hundred and fifty yards away. At each corner, light poles extended into the air, shining dozens of lights onto the circular wooden stage at the far end of the field. People filed in and sat shoulder to shoulder in the metal bleachers on each side. At the base of the stage, equidistantly apart, seven more droids stood, continuously running their red lights across the crowd. An eighth spot on the right side of the stage was unoccupied.

"Where did all these people come from?" Peter asked. "The city was deserted."

"The leadership established small encampments a few days after the Event. Just another way to keep everyone under their thumb."

Anna pointed. "What's that thing?"

At the back of the stage, a six-foot-tall wheel hung in the air.

Padma's expression changed. "They made it from the mast of the *Santa Maria*. Let's hope they don't use it tonight."

A loud explosion blared through the speakers mounted on the four light poles. The crowd fell silent and faced the stage. A man in a long black cloak with a hood covering the top half of his face strode to the center. He turned to the crowd and twisted his head from side to side as they watched in anticipation. Another man, this one much taller and with broad shoulders, walked toward the man in the cloak. Each step from his black boots echoed through the silent stadium. He handed the cloaked man a microphone.

"Thank you, my friend," the cloaked man said.

The man in the black boots stomped away.

"Ladies and Gentlemen," the cloaked man said into the microphone, "Welcome to Ceremony number one hundred and twenty-two."

The crowd erupted in applause. He held his arms out to his sides and spun, facing one side of the crowd, then turning to the other. A thin smile formed on his lips as he soaked it all in. After a few seconds, he held one arm into the air and balled his hand into a fist. The crowd again fell silent.

"I'm glad you could join us tonight," he continued. "It will be a special night with a very special guest. Someone who currently threatens our freedom. I say currently because it is also someone who will be punished for his treasonous behavior."

Punished?

The man dropped the microphone to his side and looked off stage. "Bring him out."

The man with the broad shoulders nodded and disappeared behind the stage. The crowd bustled. When he emerged, he was forcing a shackled man up a set of stairs. He wore an orange prison jumpsuit, and the shackles binding his wrists and ankles clattered against the wooden steps as he was pushed onto the stage. The wheel slowly lowered.

"Oh no," Padma whispered.

They guided the prisoner toward the wheel, unshackled him and spun him to face the spectators. The man with the broad shoulders hoisted him onto the wheel and placed him in the same spread-eagled position as the Vitruvian Man. Once satisfied, he tied the prisoner's wrists and ankles. The wheel rose into the air, dangling the man a few feet from the stage.

"No!" a woman from the audience yelled. "He's innocent. Please, let him go!"

Peter, Anna and Padma turned their heads to the bleachers on the right side of the field. A woman near the center of an upper row stood. She moved toward the aisle, clambering over each person in the row while none of them moved an inch to get out of her way.

"Maddy, no!" the prisoner turned his head toward her voice. "Sit down. Please!"

But she didn't listen. Her pace quickened when she stepped into the aisle. The man with the microphone stood and watched. She continued down the stairs. He put the microphone to his mouth. When she reached the grass, he nodded toward a droid. It rose into the air and hummed.

"Go ahead," he said in a monotone.

The humming stopped. A loud click sounded, and the droid fired one shot, hitting Maddy in the chest and knocking her backward. She crashed into the bottom row of bleachers, scattering spectators who occupied those seats into all directions. A few children cried out, but their guardians immediately hushed them while everyone else kept their attention on the man with the microphone.

Maddy shook briefly, but after a few seconds, her head slumped, leaving a trail of red blood against the silver bleachers. Four people rushed from the back of the stage, grabbed her body and carried her out of sight.

"You bastard!" the man tied to the wheel screamed. "It wasn't even her you saw me with. She was innocent."

"Silence! It is now time for Ceremony," said the man with the microphone.

He turned toward the prisoner, began to raise both arms but stopped. Spinning around, he panned the crowd from one side to the other.

"But first," he said, "we have some unexpected guests here, and since tonight's Ceremony is especially for them, I need to make sure they're paying attention."

He scanned the crowd again, his eyes moving from the bleachers on the right and across the gap between them to the bleachers on the left. He paused. His thin lips widened, turning into a grin. He jerked his head to the gap between the two sets of bleachers and stared at the trio hiding in the shadows. Peter froze.

He's looking right into your eyes.

"Yes, you, out there in the shadows, you'll want to see this," the man said.

He reached out, grabbed the prisoner's hood and yanked it off, exposing his face. From the distance, Peter didn't recognize him. He turned to Anna. She leaned forward and squinted, but gave no hint she knew the man's identity.

"Kase... No," Padma whispered.

Peter and Anna turned to her. Padma's shoulders drooped. A tear formed in the corner of her eye and rolled down her cheek. The man pulled a pistol from inside his robe and pointed it at Kase.

Kase's eyes widened as he finally met the man who would be ending his life.

"You already killed my wife," Kase said with a scowl. "There's nothing left for me here."

"No one betrays me," the man yelled into the microphone. "Or even speaks against me! I keep you people fed, clothed and I keep order in this town. This is my town. If you're against me, you're against all of us."

A split second of silence hung in the air before the crowd erupted in applause. Chants of "Shoot, shoot!" arose throughout small pockets of the bleachers.

Padma sat frozen. Anna turned away. Peter ducked toward her, touching her forehead to his. He closed his eyes, and time stopped. Next to him, he felt Padma began to rise. A shot rang out, silencing the crowd. Padma howled and dropped to the ground. Each of the seven droids shined their light toward the trio, revealing them in a sea of red.

"Guards, get them."

In unison, the droids rose into the air and sped toward them. Peter and Anna started down the hill followed by Padma, who wobbled as she stood. Peter grabbed her hand and helped her to the bottom. They squeezed through the gate and ran into the tunnel.

"Follow the chalk!" Padma said, shining her flashlight at the chalk line.

With Anna leading, Peter wasn't as careful as he had been the first time through. He stomped through the center of the tunnel, splashing water and mud against the cuffs of his jeans. They burst through the door leading into Padma's bathroom and ran into the main room.

"Where's your backpack?" Padma asked. "I need to fix this now."

She ran to her bed and grabbed a pouch from her duffel bag. She pulled a second gun from it, examined it and returned it to the pouch.

"This should be enough," she muttered.

Peter spied his backpack in the sink. He took the machine from it and attached it to his wrist. He pressed the Home preset on his phone. Padma turned to him.

"Give me your machine." She insisted for the third time, "They sent here me to fix this. I already failed once, but now I get another chance."

"What about us?" Anna asked.

"Peter, you're with me," Padma said. "You have experience with this thing. Anna, you stay here. You're safe. Even if they catch you, once I succeed it won't matter. You'll wake up tomorrow in your bed, or maybe his, and everything will be normal."

Padma looked determined. She was not settling for no, and there was no time for discussion. Peter strapped the machine to his wrist.

"Grab my laptop," he told Padma. "Most of my calculations are on it."

"What?" Anna protested. "You're not leaving me here alone."

"Good idea," Padma said.

Anna looked at Peter. "What are you doing?"

"Don't forget the power cable," Peter said.

"Don't worry, I know how to fix this," Padma replied. "We won't be gone long."

Peter walked to Anna and kissed her on the cheek. Anna grabbed hold of Peter's back and pulled him close.

"You're not leaving me."

Padma dropped to her knees and reached under the desk. He put his wrist against Anna's stomach, pulled her wrist to his and strapped the other end of the bracelet to her.

He pushed the button.

Chapter 19

Nelson, 2006

"And then we rode the teacups. It was my favorite memory of the trip. They hung on to me so tightly, and Sarah snapped pictures of us from outside the fence. Her best shots were when she got close-ups of their smiles. I think I have them here somewhere if you want to see them."

I reached into my jacket and grabbed my wallet. I shuffled through it, but other than three credit cards, my license and a few dollars in cash, it was suspiciously empty. With each item on the table in front of me, I turned my wallet over and shook it. Nothing else fell out.

"This doesn't make sense. I must have left them at home or something," I said, smiling at the woman sitting across from me.

I pushed my wallet into my pocket, but it bounced off my chest and tumbled to the floor.

"Sorry," I said.

A lump formed in my throat. Breathing became a struggle. I counted, but I couldn't find a rhythm. My chest expanded and contracted like I just ran a mile at top speed.

"Sorry," I said, "lately whenever I think about the Disney trip, my eyes water. Tears of joy, I'm sure."

"It's okay," she said. Her voice was soft and forgiving.

"I tried to get Danny to join us, but he wanted to stay with his mother. 'But Dad, I'm almost a man now,' he told me as we stood in line. I said, 'Yes, you are son, but we'll go by the Peter Pan ride next and then you'll be able to fly.' He was really excited about that."

A steady stream of tears ran down my cheeks, dampening the front of my dark slacks. She offered me a tissue.

"I don't know why I'm crying this much."

The woman across from me straightened in her chair and pushed her glasses high on her nose. She put her notebook and pencil on the coffee table, leaned forward and looked into my eyes.

"Mr. Lovell, those things never happened." Her voice was stern, like Miss Grogan's, my third-grade English teacher. She wasn't asking me to believe her. She was commanding it.

I sat upright on the couch and squeezed my eyes shut as tightly as I could, covering my face with both hands. Looking through my memories, everything I described was right there, clear as day. I wanted to run right now, escape, but Walter had suggested I keep talking to her until I could at least talk about Sarah without sobbing.

"Yes, they did, Dr. Martin," I said through my fingers. My voice became flat. "I can see them as clearly as I can see you sitting across from me."

She remained calm, probably something she'd learned in Shrink 101. "Can you? Why are you crying, Nelson?"

I leaned my head back, straightened my legs and stared at the ceiling. Was she *actually* questioning me? *I can see everything, the whole trip. The teacups. We were in the teacups. I think we were in the teacups. Now I don't see it.* What was happening? She was stealing my memories. Sweat dampened my forehead. I glared at her.

"You tell me!" I shouted. "You're the Goddamn doctor."

She pulled a thin, folded newspaper from a brown file with my name written on the tab in black marker and slid it across the coffee table toward me.

"Here, Nelson," she said, "this is from five weeks ago."

I tensed. I already knew what it said, but I leaned forward anyway. There it was in large bold print, just above the picture of the wreckage spread across the side of the Shenandoah Mountain.

"Plane crashes in West Virginia. No survivors," I whispered.

I threw the paper across the table. It skipped past her notebook and knocked her pencil to the ground. "No! It's not true."

She dropped to one knee and grabbed the pencil. She slammed it against the table. I shuddered, and my eyes met hers. My legs tightened. I squeezed my knees together.

"You know it to be true, Nelson. We have this conversation every week."

My eyes jolted open. I sat up in bed and flung the blankets to the floor. The ugly lamp was the first thing I saw, but what about Sarah? I couldn't bear to look, to see the truth. I reached to the left—nothing. I began to shake. She wasn't there. No one was there. They had all died.

"Another fucking nightmare," I said out loud to no one.

I sprang from the bed and did the only thing that would lessen the pain, the one thing allowing my mind to go somewhere else. I worked. Making money was all I had left, but with no one there to spend it on, what was the money for, other than helping me cope?

Wearing just a pair of boxers, I stepped into the humidity of the early July morning. I leaned forward to grab the newspaper and sniffled. A wet trickle dropped from my nose and landed on my foot. An itch formed in the back of my throat. The smell of last night's rain still hung in the air. I ripped the newspaper from its plastic bag, tossed the shredded plastic next to the porch and slammed the door. On the way to my office, I grabbed a pot of coffee and a cold muffin.

Every morning before I woke, my charts automatically printed, thanks to a macro I'd written a few months ago. I stacked them on the desk in front of me and poured coffee into my World's Best Daddy oversized cup. Sarah had bought this cup on Father's Day last year. She'd told me it was from Lena. I set the pot on the desk and, yes, I used the mat Sarah had always forced me to use.

"It's an expensive desk, Nelson," she said. "Don't ruin it already."

One number at a time, I typed the data into my spreadsheet, pausing between each entry to study its predictions. Around six months ago, Crissy had wandered into the office and asked me about the numbers. I'd tried to explain what they meant, but she was only six, she wasn't going to understand. Instead, I'd shown her what buttons to push to color the columns. She enjoyed coloring better.

For three hours, I studied the trends. Yesterday. Last week. The previous ten days. Anything I could use to create a narrative. When the market finally opened, my fingers floated across the keyboard like a classically trained pianist's.

Buy Microsoft at 9:35 a.m., sell at 9:38. Buy Intel at 9:41, sell at 9:53. Buy it again at 1:45 p.m., sell just before close. But Calpine at 10:05 a.m., sell as soon as it goes up one percent. I didn't even know what Calpine was, but it didn't matter. It *would* go up one percent because I knew it would. I did this every day, and I was never wrong.

I finally showered, shaved and threw on an old pair of blue running shorts, a red t-shirt and went for a jog. I'd recently decided the castle was slowly turning into a dungeon, and these morning jogs were a perfect way to make sure I inhaled a little fresh air. A mile away, tucked into the back corner of a strip mall, there was a diner. It had become my lunch hangout.

It was a small place with one row of booths along the windows and individual stools wrapped around the counter. The floor was made of black and white square tiles, and the walls were striped red and white. It was a hideous design, a bad attempt at a 1950s diner, but they made the best sandwiches in the city, and I had developed a small schoolboy crush on Cara, their newest waitress.

She walked toward me. Her long blonde braids bounced with each step. She was twenty-six years old and single with no children. I don't know how subtle I was in asking for that information, but she didn't seem to mind revealing it.

"Hi Nelson," she said. "Your usual?"

"Let's mix it up a little today Cara. How about a turkey BLT, no cheese, extra mayo and fries? And melt some cheese on those fries."

"So, you *don't* want cheese on your sandwich, but you *do* want it on your fries?"

"I'm a tough nut to crack."

She giggled and walked toward an older, balding man a few seats away who was reading a book. Every few minutes, he stopped reading to scribble notes in the yellow notebook next to him. I leaned forward and smiled when I saw the title.

"*The Sound and the Fury*," I muttered.

He glanced at me through a pair of thick, dark-rimmed glasses. I raised my plastic orange cup toward him.

"That's a tough read," I said.

He nodded and went back to his scribbling. Cara refreshed his coffee, handed him a napkin and made her way to the register to put in my order. She didn't write the specifics of my order on her notepad, but five minutes later when it arrived, it was exactly right.

"Not writing orders down," I wondered aloud. "I bet I can research in the morning before the market opens and make money from my memory all day."

Days turned from weeks to months. Every day was exactly the same. Wake early, put together my orders. Make money. Eat lunch at the diner with Cara. Back home to make more money.

"The nightmares have come more frequently," I told Cara one afternoon while munching on a chicken club. "They were a lot like the nightmares from before they died. I had my wife, my family, but before I woke up, they were taken from me."

Cara reminded me of Sarah just after we graduated from college. She was bubbly, always positive, and Cara's brown eyes were the same shade as Sarah's. Cara sported a black ring through the center of her bottom lip and a white one pushing through her left nostril. I chuckled. Sarah would have never done anything like that.

Most days I would try to arrive around eleven thirty in the morning. Cara would stand with me and listen to my babble for a half hour before the lunch rush rolled in, commanding most of her attention. She was a great listener—not as attentive as Lena, who had hung on my every word as if I had been her security blanket—but Cara didn't seem like she was just angling for a bigger tip. She listened and offered advice whenever it seemed appropriate.

"What happens in these nightmares?"

"It always seems like things will end well, you know. Like I will have my family back. Never fails, though; just before I wake, they're taken from me."

"That's so sad," she said.

"Before the accident, I had this same kind of nightmares, and when I woke, I would reach for her. She was always there, mostly annoyed, and I woke her out of a sound sleep, but she was always there.

"You know what else is strange? While I'm working, I see these random memories so clear in my head as if they actually happened. But they're things we did together as a family after the plane crash. How is that possible?"

"Maybe you're remembering things that haven't happened yet," Cara said as she slid the check in front of me. I peeked at the bill. She'd stopped charging me for coffee the day after I told her about the plane crash.

My eyes met hers. "What?"

"Maybe they'll come back this time," she said. "You lost them after the nightmares the first time. Maybe this time they're going to come back. You said you're this close to keeping them. It's only just before you wake when they are taken?"

"Yeah," I said, waiting for her to give me a reason why anything she'd said made sense.

"Well, maybe they're trying, possibly even fighting, to come back."

"I don't understand."

She looked to the ceiling, rubbed the silver cross hanging from her neck and whispered, "Maybe they weren't ready to leave. The Lord works in mysterious ways."

As she walked into the kitchen, I felt the heat building in my face. Was Cara really messing with me right now? Did she think I was a crazy person? Someone in the kitchen laughed, and the echo carried through the doors and into the diner.

What had she said to them? Was it about me? I smacked a ten-dollar bill onto the counter and walked away. That will be the last time I come here for lunch. No one humiliates me. I pushed the door open and stormed out.

The day had turned gray. The air was heavy with humidity as though I stepped out of a hot shower. I wiped my forehead and looked at my watch. 12:54.

"Three hours until the market closes," I muttered.

"Too bad you can't travel through time," I heard Cara say as I stepped onto the sidewalk.

I froze. "What did you just say?"

Silence. I tilted my head. Was it all an act? Was my pain not real to her? I wouldn't be disrespected. I tried to breathe, counting each breath, but that had stopped working months ago.

"Do you think you can say those things and expect to get away with it?" I said.

I took a step backward, clenched my fists and turned to face her. I peered through the haze, but the sidewalk was empty. She was nowhere to be found. It was all in my head. I was alone. Still.

Chapter 20

Peter, 2017

"You had me worried," Anna said, sitting on Peter's bed. Peter put his hand on hers and squeezed. Their eyes met, and his smile faded.

"I would never leave you behind," he said.

And he wouldn't. Ever. After just one date, he felt it. The way her eyes lit up, and how she leaned in toward him just now as he held her hand—he was sure she felt it too. It could be argued the stress of the situation was pushing them together, giving them someone to cling to while trying to survive, but Peter knew different. He had felt something for her since the day he'd met her, and it was becoming evident to him she had the same feelings.

"Why did you pick your bedroom as your default return spot?"

Buddy ran across the bed from his usual waiting place and jumped, both paws landing on Anna's shoulder. She let him lick her cheek for a couple of seconds before turning her attention to the cut on her knee.

"I'm always afraid of physically merging with things when I jump around. Since I have no plans of rearranging my bedroom furniture anytime soon, this spot, standing right here, seemed as safe as any."

Anna's phone buzzed. She pulled it from her front pocket, typed out a quick text and tossed it next to her on the bed. Dabbing the wound just below her knee, she cringed and checked for blood.

"What about when you go somewhere for the first time?"

"I didn't think about it when I went to Montana the first time. I picked an empty field and just went. But after a close call with a scarecrow, I realized it was something I needed to think about. Now I always try to scout the location as best I can before I go."

"We're not scouting anything now," she said. "We're just trusting your nurse friend not to hurt us?"

"I guess. But she seems to be leading us around, taking us on a journey of some sort. I'm curious why."

"Me too," Anna said.

Anna pulled a dark-blue cloth napkin from Carson's and spread it across the wound. After a little more dabbing, she held the napkin in front of her, letting the light hit it.

"I think I should clean this a little better," she said. "You mind if I take a quick shower?"

"Sure, go ahead," Peter said. "There should be a few towels in there, and the Band-Aids are in the medicine cabinet."

"Band-Aids may not be enough. I may need stitches."

She limped into the hallway and pulled the bathroom door shut.

Peter stripped the dusty, damp clothes from his body and replaced them with a new pair of jeans, a t-shirt and his second-favorite hoodie, dark green with nothing on the front, simple and plain. It wasn't too baggy and hugged his neck exactly how he liked. Buddy jumped off the bed and nosed through the pile of dirty clothes, only stopping long enough to back away and sneeze.

"Maybe I need a shower too," Peter muttered.

He grabbed the laptop from his spare room, the same one Padma took, and ran downstairs. After checking Buddy's water dish and opening the back door so Buddy could pee, Peter set the laptop on the dining room table and powered it up.

He stared at the GROUP log in screen.

Do I tell them I figured it out?

The same question had bounced around his head since the first time he unexpectedly traveled back on a rainy Friday night. Each time he logged in, he wanted to tell them, wanted to get the group excited about where he'd been. But each time he chickened out. And as the months went by, hiding it was worse, and his fear of telling them heightened. If he left GROUP, they would get suspicious. If he stayed in GROUP, he would undoubtedly slip and give it away. There didn't seem to be a correct decision.

Today is different. You've seen the future.

Using just one index finger, Peter typed the first few characters of his password, hesitating between each one.

They should know. You agreed to share everything when you signed up for the forum.

He finished typing the password, pressed the login button and slid the Dream Machine over his head until it comfortably rested against his shoulders. When the room materialized around him, he stood in the vestibule of a dentist's office, between the double doors leading outside and the door leading into the waiting room. He took a deep breath and pushed the waiting-room door open.

Today's the day.

It was a small room with crisp white walls, light peach carpeting and four rows of chairs. The first two rows faced each other, and the third row faced the fourth. At the end of each row, round tables stacked with magazines gave patients something to read while waiting for the dentist to call their name. A thirteen-inch television rested on top of a cabinet at the front of the room. It was set on The Weather Channel, but instead of weather, two prospectors appeared to be fighting to determine who got to enter a small cave first.

"'tass always hated the Weather Channel," Peter said, chuckling.

At the front of the room, separated by a large glass partition, three women wearing nurse uniforms worked the counter. Two of them were sitting, while the third stood next to the door leading to the examining rooms.

He silently watched the nurses. They appeared to be fake characters, explicitly built for this scenario, looping through a set of instructions, including answering phones, keeping track of appointments and waiting to check people in. This was new to their GROUP dynamic.

"We have non-playing characters now?" Peter muttered.

Lightninggirl, elfGlimmer and marymary sat in the first row, their backs to the entrance. It was rare that Peter checked GROUP after midnight, but the few times he did pop in, these three were always there, chatting away like teenagers at a virtual slumber party. They treated VanBurenBoy as their little brother, offering advice on anything from money, dating or any of life's little problems. GROUP was supposed to be one hundred percent anonymous, but Peter wondered how much they revealed to each other.

"Be sure to sign in," a receptionist said to Peter. Her head followed him as he walked in front of the partition to the first row of chairs.

Nice job on the realism.

"Hey ladies," he said. Based on their avatars and their tone of voice, which rarely changed, he assumed they were all women. He sat in the first row across from elfGlimmer, who was sitting in the middle. "I'm glad you're the only three here. I have something to tell you."

"This better be about your date," lightninggirl said.

"Sir, don't forget to see me before you leave to schedule—" the fake receptionist behind the counter stopped. She sputtered, and her head fell forward.

"Looks like tass is still working out the bugs," marymary said.

"So, how did it go?" elfGlimmer asked.

"It was uh...interesting. We had dinner, watched hockey, and afterward, she took me this place that was special to her when she was a little girl."

"Wow, that seems like a big deal," marymary said.

"Did you kiss her goodnight?" lightninggirl asked.

"Actually," VanBurenBoy chuckled. "She kissed me first. And the date isn't over. She's still here."

"What?" lightninggirl said. "What are you doing with us?"

"She's upstairs," Peter listened for the running shower. "She hurt her knee earlier and wanted to make sure she cleaned it properly."

"Be sure to sign in," one of the two functioning receptionists said.

The four of them looked toward the front to see another avatar walking through the door.

"Niven?" lightninggirl said. "What are you doing here at this hour?"

The upstairs shower was turned off, and Peter listened as Anna's footsteps walked from the bathroom to his bedroom. Her muffled, one-side-of-a-conversation voice hinted she was talking to someone on her cell phone.

"Just checking in," Niven said. "Eager to see if we can figure this out. Anything new?"

"Well, VanBurenBoy was just telling us about his date," elfGlimmer said.

Niven's voice sharpened, "I mean about the project."

"tass doesn't like us talking business outside of our scheduled meetings," marymary said.

"Half of us are here," Niven said, his voice raised by an octave. "No one has anything new to report?"

The three girls ignored his question and turned their avatars toward VanBurenBoy.

"Is that what you wanted to talk about, sweetie? Your date?" lightninggirl said.

"No," he said. "But it's okay, we'll talk tomorrow. By then, I'll be able to tell you how the date ends. Have a nice night."

"No, wait!" Niven yelled. "What *did* you want to talk about?"

Peter pulled the Dream Machine from his head and closed the laptop.

"We need to get our cars," Anna said, gingerly taking each step as she came downstairs. Her dark hair fell past her shoulders and stuck to her arms, still a little wet from the shower.

"And again, you steal one of my shirts," Peter said, shaking his head.

I could get so used to that.

She grinned, shrugged and pulled her sweater over her head. Peter grabbed the machine from his bag, slipped his wrist through one side and held his braceleted arm toward her.

"One other thing about this machine I haven't told you yet," he said. "We can go wherever we want without *actually* traveling through time."

She smiled, slid her wrist through the bracelet and locked it into place.

"Beam me up, Scottie," she said.

When they reappeared, they stood next to the bench overlooking the city near Anna's parents' house. His car was where they'd left it, driver side door still hanging wide open. Other than multiple sets of mostly snow-covered tire tracks, there was no sign of the man who had chased them earlier in the evening. They hopped inside, and Peter found the keys on the floor where he'd dropped them. He started the car, eased on to the road and headed toward Carson's.

"Why do you hate Zach so much?" Peter asked. It was a question he'd wanted to ask for a long time.

"He's obnoxious," Anna said.

"Yeah, that's obvious, but it seems like there's something more to it."

Peter waited for an answer but was greeted with silence. He glanced at Anna, who was looking straight ahead. A light snow fell, sticking to the windshield. Peter flipped his windshield wipers to intermittent, and Anna's head followed them as they moved.

"You know, he saved my life," Peter said.

Anna twisted her head toward him, "What?"

"Okay...well, not in a life-or-death type of way. More like a social thing. When we were in school together, he was one of the cool kids. Something happened. It could have ended badly, but he didn't let it. He bullied the bullies for me. We've been close ever since."

She nodded as he spoke.

"He's actually a good guy, a great friend," Peter added.

"I know he is to you. It was obvious the first day I saw you two together at work." She paused, and her voice lowered. "You know his dad's an alcoholic, right?"

"Yeah," Peter shifted in his seat. "But he never talks about it."

"His dad was a jerk to us after my dad disappeared. He was one of the policemen assigned to the case, and he claimed he'd seen what happened. It was such a ridiculous story. I thought he was making fun of us. I think he had been drinking and when we didn't take him seriously, he wouldn't leave us alone, knocking on our doors at all hours, harassing us. Finally, we complained to the chief, and they let him go. I think Zach blames me. I want nothing to do with anyone from that family."

Peter had been at Zach's house many times when they were younger. He knew the family. Zach's mom was always nice to him, but Peter rarely saw his dad. When he did, the man usually had a beer in his hand or was passed out on the couch.

"What did he claim happened?" Peter asked.

"Aliens."

"Aliens?"

"Yeah, he claimed—"

Peter swerved, but he didn't see the pothole in time. The car bounced through it. Anna's leg smacked the underside of the glove compartment. She grimaced and wrapped both hands around it.

"Are you okay?" Peter asked.

"I think I'm gonna head home. I talked to my sisters earlier. They're worried about me. My phone apparently went right to voicemail while we were jumping around. My older sister is a nurse, and I'm going to ask her to look at this. I'll tell her I slipped in the snow or something."

"Okay," Peter said. The last thing he wanted was to part with her after everything they'd seen, but her leg could be worse than it looked.

You shouldn't have taken her back.

"Sorry about your leg," he said, holding the braceleted arm toward her. "It's my fault."

"We can share blame evenly."

"But what about the future?" Peter thought about meeting Padma and how she reacted when the man and the woman were killed at Ceremony in front of a cheering crowd. "What if it is our fault? What if by getting involved in the fight with Max, we triggered all this?"

Anna paused for a moment and closed her eyes, occasionally nodding her head as if she was reliving everything that had happened during the night, "Let's sleep on it. Tomorrow, we'll take a vacation day from work, get together and regroup."

Peter looked straight ahead, watching the snowy road. He pressed his lips together and shrugged.

"I guess," he said. The promise of seeing her soon helped ease his fears.

They pulled into Carson's. Her car was the only one still in the lot, parked under a streetlight. Snow fell harder as he pulled next to her silver SUV and stopped. They stepped out together, icy wind biting his cheeks. He pulled his hood over his head and grabbed the strings, tightening it around his ears and neck. While Anna unlocked and started her car, he went to the rear window. Pulling his hand inside his sleeve, he brushed a thin layer of snow to the ground.

She walked next to him and put her hand on his arm. Shivering, he turned to face her. A thickness formed in the back of his throat.

"We'll figure it out, okay?" she said softly.

He nodded his head. She stepped toward him and moved her head in closer. A large snowflake fell onto her nose. She paused, smiled at Peter and rose to her tippy toes, pushed his hoodie to the side and pressed her lips to his cheek.

"I knew you weren't going to leave me," she whispered into his ear. "Now go home and go to bed. It's freezing out here. I'll see you in the morning, I promise."

Chapter 21

Nelson, 2006

"Okay," I said, looking at my watch, "5:45 p.m."

I dropped my arms to my sides and squeezed my eyes closed. I raised my right hand in front of me, slowly opened my eyes and checked the time.

"8:20 a.m. Look Sarah, it changed!"

I bounced from one foot to the other and pushed the watch toward her. Closing my eyes and counting to five, I opened them again and checked for a third time. The book always said to do it three times, just to be sure.

"1:37. I knew it."

I cracked the door and peeked into the den. The creature followed us but hadn't yet found our scent. He looked exactly like the brown Great Dane Steve had when we were kids. Except this one was twice my height and showed an impressive set of white fangs. He followed his nose across the carpet toward us. Behind me, Sarah and the kids stood frozen, pushed against the wall.

"Don't be scared," I said. "It's not real."

I stepped out of the closet and walked toward the large beast.

"It's a nightmare, isn't it?" I yelled. I held my arms to my sides, opening my palms at him, "What are you going to do? You can't hurt me anymore than you already have!"

He stopped and jerked his head toward me. Dropping onto his front legs, he rested his chin on the floor and appeared to smile. He looked hungry, like Danny flashing a smile whenever we pulled into the Dairy Queen parking lot. I looked over my shoulder at Danny as he clung to his mother's right leg and grinned. That boy did have a sweet tooth.

"Sit!" I said to the beast. He looked at me, tilted his head and hissed. I yelled at it again. This time, he did as I ordered.

"Good boy," I said, walking around behind him. "You sly fox, you can't fool me, not anymore. Lie down."

Again, the beast complied.

"It's safe! Come and meet him."

Sarah and the kids crept out of the closet and toward the beast. He rolled onto his back and submitted. Sarah handed me Lena, and the two older kids rubbed his belly. The beast let out a low moan as they ran their hands along his brown fur.

"I've missed this," I told Lena.

She giggled.

"Yeah sweetie," I said, "I know we did this last night too, and it's great in the dream, but I really miss it when I'm awake, and you're not a figment of my imagination."

I watched, proud that the lucid dreaming books I had studied the last couple of weeks were paying off. *If I practice enough, I can control these nightmares and have more time with my family. Even if it's not real, it's all I had left.*

"Nelson, are you okay?" Sarah asked.

"I'm fine," I said, wiping my eyes.

The more I do it, the easier it becomes. Sometimes I could even take control of my dreams before the beast made his appearance. Those were my favorites. I created scenarios where

I took Sarah and the kids on trips, vacations I never thought we'd have, and other times we hung out in the living room and picked a DVD to watch together.

The beast jolted to his feet and bared his fangs again. He jumped toward Sarah. I woke myself up. Waking always made me sad, but it didn't compare to the sadness I felt every time I lost them.

I leaned forward in the recliner and looked around. I'd purposely left the television on Animal Planet as an experiment, and it had worked. If the TV was loud enough, pieces of what was on it would make their way into the dreams. I flipped to the Hallmark channel.

"After work, I'll be taking another nap. Maybe Sarah and I can have a new meet-cute and get our first kiss again."

A flash on the television caught my eye as the Hallmark channel came into view. It was a description of the current movie.

A man accidentally travels through time and finds himself falling for someone he shouldn't.

Memories of the waitress from the diner popped into my head.

"Time travel," I said. "If only it were real."

After showering and eating breakfast, I locked myself in my office and sat in front of my charts. I opened an internet browser to start my research. Yesterday had been one of my best days, and I wanted to keep the momentum flowing.

Time Travel: I typed the words before I realized it and stared at the screen. *It can't hurt to take just a few minutes and see what's out there.*

I didn't expect to find anything meaningful, but what if Cara was right? What if they were trying to return and needed my help? What if I could change things? I wouldn't be able to do it with time travel but who knows, maybe this would lead me to something else.

"Great, ninety-five million results."

The first few pages of results revealed nothing relevant. I wasn't interested in fan fiction where some television character goes back in time and kills Hitler. *Why does it always go back to Hitler?* Nor did I care about some old British television show that looked like it had been filmed on a high school auditorium stage. This was all fiction. I needed facts.

I filtered out words that meant nothing and instead used things that would lead me more to the science of time travel.

My search results dropped from ninety-five million to twenty-three million.

"I guess it's progress."

The first link took me to a website that discussed the physics of time travel. Examples of bending the universe, multiple universes and multiple worlds filled the pages. It was over my head until I found an article from a leading astrophysicist who explained it in a way a non-physicist could understand. He concluded the article by saying it wasn't possible.

"What does he know?"

I checked the clock. It was close to eleven thirty in the morning, and I hadn't made any money yet.

"Looks like I'm taking a vacation day."

I grabbed the empty coffee pot and jogged into the kitchen. After rinsing it, I started a new pot. I tossed last night's pizza into the toaster oven and paced around the kitchen island.

"Other people have to be working on this too, right?"

I slid the pizza from the tray on to a plate, grabbed a Coke and the coffee pot. Once back in my office, I punched the delete button until all the words from my search bar had disappeared. My earlier searches weren't returning what I was hoping for, so I tried something different.

"Time Travel Forums," I said aloud. "Let's try that."

I pressed the search button, and pages and pages of anything related to time travel flooded my screen. I scrolled the page for keywords, something that would catch my attention. Lots of links asking what the spiritual and philosophical ramifications would be, but nothing on those forums on how to *actually* build a machine to travel through time.

I read through a fun article by someone named John Titor, who claimed to be from the future. Obviously a hoax, and it didn't get me any closer to my goal.

"Dammit," I yelled, taking the last gulp from my coffee cup. "Isn't there anyone out there trying to work this out?"

I refilled my cup and opened a window in my office, letting some air flow through. I wiped the sweat from my forehead and turned the chair around, resting my chin on its back when I sat. I pulled the keyboard near me and clicked to the next search page. The first link was from something called Reddit.

I clicked into the first few subreddits, and it was all the same, people discussing what they would do if they could travel, how they would change their life and on and on. But the fifth subreddit caught my eye.

Let's Build a Time Machine

"Finally!" I screamed.

I stood, turned the chair around and sat, pulling myself close to the desk. It was run by someone named tassemari. I clicked through and waited. The page took longer than most to load, which excited me.

Lots of information here, I thought.

My hands trembled. Thoughts ran through my mind of what I would do once I figured this out. All the places I could go, things I could see. But everything came back to Sarah. That would be the first thing I did. When it finally loaded, there was a message at the top of the screen.

"This subreddit is no longer in use due to harassment and trolling. If you are serious about time travel, email me, and after checking you out, I will determine whether I will allow you inside the private group."

"Well, Goddammit!"

I threw my arms out, knocking over my coffee cup and pushed myself away from the desk. Bending over, I put my head in my hands and breathed through them. Once I was calm, I scooted my chair back to the desk and read a few of the posts from the trolls.

"How about your fix your own life, you bunch of effing nerds."

"This is some of the dumbest shit on the internet."

Typical internet message board. Bunch of anonymous cowardly assholes feeling safe behind their computer screen.

"You suck and your parents suck for raising you to think you could do this."

"No wonder she closed it," I said, clicking to the final page. My eyes hit the last message on the screen. I stared at it. A tear formed in the corner of my eye and tried to force its way out.

"They're dead and they're not coming back. Get over it."

My mouth went dry. I read the words over and over until they went blurry, rubbing my eyes until they were visible again. I stared at the message. How dare gorillapizzle say that? How dare he trivialize someone else's pain? I jotted his username on to a piece of scrap paper and shoved it into my pants pocket. I would get my revenge.

After each trolling post, tassemari defended the members. They seemed serious about figuring things out, and I wanted to be a part of it. I clicked on the profile for tassemari and found an email address. I hovered my mouse over it.

Do I really want to do this? Am I ready to see if it's real?

I clicked it. My email program opened and typed a message.

Hello, I am interested in proving that time travel exists. I have a math background, have built my own computer systems and have a basic understanding of software design. I would like to talk to the people on your message board, compare notes and help any way I can. I'm sure I'm the person who can help make it a reality. Please reply quickly.

Checking the clock, I jumped out of my seat. My Hallmark movie was starting in a few minutes, and I needed to get comfortable for my nap. I pressed send on the email and hurried from the living room.

"I'll take a short nap, then start again fresh tonight."

I stripped down to my boxers, reclined the chair as far back as I could push it and closed my eyes. The familiar music of the Hallmark movie started. In just a few minutes, I felt myself slipping away.

I was in the center of town, a small, quaint, probably New England town a bunch of miles from Boston. Snow was falling, and even though the roads had stayed clear, a nice dusting had settled on the trees between the street and the sidewalk. The smell of cookies from the bakery behind me invaded my senses, forcing a smile onto my face. Christmas decorations hung from every building, and everyone on the street seemed to be happy.

Except one person.

She walked right toward me, cell phone pressed between her shoulder and her cheek, coffee in one hand and briefcase in the other. I lifted my arm in the air to stop her, get that first meeting out of the way so we could get to the kiss. When she was just a few steps away but hadn't yet looked up, I spoke first.

"Sarah?"

She didn't hear me and continued walking, turning the corner.

"That's odd," I said, staring at the building.

I took two steps toward the corner, and she emerged again, still on the phone.

"No, I will not take the first offer, I will wait and see—"

She collided with me, the impact of her briefcase against my knee, knocking me off my feet. I landed on my butt in a snowbank, most likely created from the streets being plowed. Her briefcase landed next to me, opened, and a bunch of loose papers scattered. I cringed and looked at her standing over me, a large coffee stain down the front of her dark-blue dress.

"Oh, for the love of—"

"Don't worry," I said. "Now we'll have a great story for our grandkids."

She looked at me, her face full of confusion. She opened her mouth to speak but the dinging of a bell, like the bell you can't help but push when you're in a waiting room, was the only sound I heard.

"What?"

She opened her mouth again, but again, the bell dinged.

"What is happening?" I said.

I glanced around. Was anyone else hearing this? Families walked past, pointing at the decorations, eating cookies and enjoying their Hallmark day.

The bell dinged a third time. I stared at Sarah as she faded away in front of me. I opened my eyes, waking myself, and shook my head. The bell rang for a fourth time.

"That's my email," I muttered.

I jumped up, rushed into my office, unlocked my laptop and stared at the screen. One new email flashed. It was from tassemari.

Hello, we are a small but serious group, and if you're interested in joining, you must actively participate in the research. Absolutely no lurking. You will be assigned tasks and must show that you are working on them, or you will be banned and forgotten about. I review and reject people every day. Your chances of getting in are slim.

Everyone in this group is very serious about time travel, and we want to be the ones who prove time travel exists. We are completely anonymous. We do not share personal information, including, but not limited to, our names, locations or professions. We share our research in the forum only. No private emails, and once we make our discovery, and we will, information will be shared here to allow each of us to decide individually whether we want to use it.

Follow the directions below and then click the link to apply.

At the bottom of the email, step-by-step directions spelled out how to hide my computer from the rest of the world. Lucky for me, I'd configured my laptop to be completely anonymous. When you're one of the most successful independent stockbrokers of all time, people will try to get your money any way they can.

When I clicked the link, a black screen appeared. A single text box with a white background and a light-blue glowing button with the word "Submit" pulsed in the center of the screen. Below it, a set of instructions faded in.

Enter a username. We will attempt to learn your identity and personal information. If we are successful, you will not be accepted into this group. By submitting a username, you are agreeing to these terms.

Back when I was growing up, there was a kid in my neighborhood who couldn't pronounce Nelson. He called me Niven. That was as good as anything I could come up with. I typed it and pressed Submit.

All I could do now was wait.

Chapter 22

Peter, 2017

Peter didn't go to bed when he made it home as Anna had instructed. Instead, he stood in front of his laptop, staring at the screen. He had to tell them. They could help. They were the smartest collection of people he knew. If anyone would know what to do, it would be they.

He slid his chair out. His knees cracked as he sat. He rubbed his aching shoulder, touched his forehead and examined his finger.

"No blood," he said to Buddy. "It's getting better."

He slid the Dream Machine over his head. He leaned forward in the chair, put both hands on the keyboard and found the keys that made up his password. His pinky hovered over the Enter key.

"Buddy, I think I'm actually going to tell them."

He pressed Enter. The vestibule of the dentist's office formed around him. elfGlimmer, marymary and lightninggirl were still sitting in the first row where he'd left them earlier. Niven had gone offline.

Every simulation tassemari created had an emergency button, and when pushed, everyone in GROUP was alerted. It was supposed to be a quick way to gather the troops, bring everyone together because someone had important news about the project. As long as Peter had been coming to GROUP, it had never been used.

Until tonight.

He strolled in and sat across from the girls, his three virtual big sisters.

"Back already?" marymary said.

"Things didn't exactly go as expected."

"Why, what happened?" elfGlimmer asked.

He looked around, trying to find anything that would resemble the emergency button. Other than the magazines, the tables were empty, and the television sat on a small bare cabinet. Locking eyes with each of the three receptionists, he looked for a clue. Maybe they could help. The first two quickly looked away and went back to their routine, but the third, she held his stare. After a couple of seconds, her eyes glanced at the sign-in sheet.

"What are you doing?" lightninggirl said, following his gaze. "Are you looking for the button?"

"No one's ever pressed the button," elfGlimmer said. "Did you work something out? You were on a date. How could you figure something out while on a date?"

Staying silent, VanBurenBoy hurried to the registration desk. He pushed the sign-in sheet aside and underneath, a small button built into the virtual, wooden desk blinked red.

"VanBurenBoy!" lightninggirl stood up. "What is going on?"

"It's a long story. We may have made a mess."

"Wait!" marymary said. "Don't press the button. Tell us first. Maybe we can help."

"We're supposed to wait for everyone," VanBurenBoy said.

"No, you should tell us first," elfGlimmer repeated. "Don't push it."

Peter took his right hand off the mouse and rubbed the side of his head. He felt warm. With a deep breath, he put his hand on the mouse and pushed down on the left button. In the Dream Machine's view screen, he watched VanBurenBoy lowering his finger and making contact with the emergency button.

The entire room went black as if someone had grabbed an eraser and wiped out the entire scene, everything except the avatars of his fellow GROUP members and the nurses and replaced it with a blank canvas. He looked back at the girls, still sitting in the same place but with their chairs gone, giving the impression they were floating in mid-air.

"God, tass is so dramatic," elfGlimmer muttered.

Niven was the first person to appear in the space once occupied by the door to the vestibule.

"What the hell is going on?"

Sudo Brownlock walked in behind him, followed by Ricka Daigr. Johan walked through the doors next.

"This is real?" Ricka Daigr said. "Someone actually pressed the button?"

tassemari appeared through the door leading to the offices and positioned herself at the front of the room. She looked around, admiring her handiwork, then found the button and pressed it. The entire room transformed into the waiting room.

"Everyone should sit," tassemari said.

"What in God's name are we doing here?" Sudo said. "It's the middle of the night."

"Everyone here?" tassemari asked. "I don't see Romestamo. He's been a no-show the last few meetings, so let's start without him."

"Who hit the alert?" Sudo wanted to know.

The three girls looked toward VanBurenBoy, prompting everyone else to turn their avatars in his direction.

"The floor is yours," tassemari said.

VanBurenBoy walked to the front of the room and took tassemari's spot before the partition. He looked over his shoulder at the button, then at the three receptionists doing their work.

"You need to make sure you check in," one receptionist said, her voice softer than before. Something about the way she spoke and held his gaze made him shudder and pause. Was this a bad idea?

There's no turning back now.

"It works. I made it work," he said.

"You made what work, sweetie?" lightninggirl asked.

"Time travel," he said. "I did it. I've been to the past and the future."

"Are you shitting me?" Niven yelled. "When? How did you do it? You're supposed to post your results."

"I'm not exactly sure what made it work. I was doing some testing, and it just worked. I did it successfully the first time a bunch of months ago, and since I wasn't sure how it happened, I didn't know what to say."

"You mean I could have been using this thing months ago?" Niven said, breathing heavily through his microphone, "God dammit, you're supposed to tell us."

"Okay, settle down," tassemari said. "He's telling us now. VanBurenBoy, we'll expect you to get everything—"

"Wait," marymary interrupted. "You told us you may have made a mess and you said 'we.' Not 'I,' but 'we.' Who is 'we'?"

"Remember the date I had last night?"

"The girl you work with?" elfGlimmer asked.

"I showed it to her. I didn't mean to, but someone was chasing us, and we needed to escape. I didn't know what else to do. I took her with me."

Peter took a breath and closed his eyes as he continued, "But she wanted to go to 2006 and see something in her past, and I didn't even pick the date, it was automatically filled in, so we went there—and things happened." His voice grew louder. "We were in a car accident, and we broke up a fight, and then we were sent into the future, 2022, and it was bad. Everything was bad."

"2006 Car accident?" Niven said. "When? Be specific. What date?"

"What do you mean 'automatically filled in' and 'sent to the future?' Aren't you able to control it?" elfGlimmer asked.

"How bad was it?" tassemari said.

"It was bad," Peter said. "The world exploded. Just about everyone was gone."

"Someone was chasing you?" Ricka Daigr contributed. "Someone else knows?"

"Who else did you tell?" elfGlimmer asked.

"No one else," VanBurenBoy said. "I swear. I wasn't doing anything to interrupt the flow of the past, just going back to the 1870s and living a life."

"You were playing house instead of telling us?" Niven said. "I need to get my hands on that machine. Can I see it? Can we meet somewhere? Where do you live?"

"We stay anonymous," tassemari said.

"Okay, fine, but when was the car accident? What day exactly? Maybe we can work backward and try to work out what happened. Yeah, let's do that."

"Who cares about a stupid accident?" Sudo Brownlock said. "You created a Goddamn time machine and didn't tell us!"

"How do you control it?"

"What does it look like?"

"Did you use one of our designs?"

Peter rubbed the back of his head at all the questions. Beads of sweat formed on his neck and rolled onto the Dream Machine, resting on his shoulders. He grimaced and closed his eyes.

"It's...This is too much," VanBurenBoy whispered.

Peter rocked in his chair. Pain squeezed his chest. He tried concentrating on each breath. In then out. In and back out. But it wasn't working.

"I have to change things back," VanBurenBoy said, ripping the Dream Machine from his head and throwing it to the couch behind him.

"No, wait VanBurenBoy..." elfGlimmer's voice echoed through the Dream Machine's built-in headphones. Peter closed the GROUP chat room on the laptop and pushed his chair away from the desk.

"Anna was right. I need to sleep," he said, walking toward the stairs. "Come on, Buddy."

Buddy ran ahead of him to the top of the stairs and waited. Peter stepped on to the first step. His computer beeped. A shudder went down his spine, and he froze.

"I'm not answering them. I don't care about their stupid rules."

Three more steps toward the second floor, and his computer beeped again. He paused and looked over his shoulder at the Dream Machine lying on the couch. The red light on top blinked. He rubbed the bracelet still attached to his wrist.

Just destroy it right now and live with the consequences.

Sighing, he turned and walked toward the desk. Without his Dream Machine, GROUP was nothing more than a simple chat room, a black window with scrolling white text converted from speech as each member spoke. It had originally started that way, but tassemari had gotten creative with her chat room. She wanted to give everyone a chance to show off their personality while staying anonymous, so she'd created the virtual world.

In the upper left corner of the screen, he saw just one name, and it wasn't anyone he recognized from GROUP. A small animated ellipsis appeared, signaling someone was typing. Peter narrowed his eyes and waited.

Talbot: Peter

Talbot: Peter!

"You're not a GROUP member," Peter whispered.

Talbot: Did you just look at me? You can see me? Please tell me you see me.

Peter kicked the chair away from the desk and stared at the screen. The ellipsis appeared next to Talbot's username. Talbot was typing again. Peter put his hand to his chest and exhaled. His heart was beating faster than ever before.

Talbot: Finally!

Talbot: I'm a friend. I can help.

Peter went to the refrigerator and grabbed a half-empty bottle of water and tossed it back, holding the liquid in his mouth a little longer than usual. A few drops escaped his lips and dribbled down the front of his shirt. He slid the living room's curtain back a few inches and peered outside, but no one was around. The laptop beeped again. He drew himself up and let the curtain fall back into position. Buddy stood at the top of the steps, his tail wagging, waiting for Peter to come to bed. Instead, Peter fell into the chair and rolled forward, tucking his legs under his desk. The ellipsis appeared again but disappeared. Peter held his fingers against the keyboard and typed a response.

VanBurenBoy: I don't know anyone named Talbot. No one in GROUP is named Talbot. Who are you?

Talbot: Tell me more about what happened to the future. I wasn't with you long enough last time to see anything. We need to go back to it as soon as possible.

VanBurenBoy: What do you mean "with me long enough?"

Talbot: It's a long story, but I can help. Trust me Peter. I'm a friend. I want the same thing you want, but we have to work together.

Peter fished his phone from his backpack. He dialed Anna's number. After four rings, her voice mail picked up. He hung up without leaving a message.

Talbot: Are you still there?

VanBurenBoy: I'm not saying anything until you tell me more about you. Who are you?

Talbot: I'm not sure if I even know the answer to that question. I need your help to work it out.

Peter dialed Anna again, this time leaving her a message, "Hey, something really strange is going on. Give me a call or get back here as soon as you can."

VanBurenBoy: How can you see what I'm seeing?

Talbot: Peter, I can see everything you do.

Chapter 23

Nelson, 2017

I opened my eyes and looked around.

"My office?"

It was rare for me to have a nightmare take place in the same room where I was sleeping, but it had happened a few times, might as well go with it. I checked and rechecked my watch, and each time it was different. I held my chin between my thumb and forefinger and studied the surroundings. It was getting too easy.

"I'm lucid again," I smirked. "I control you!"

I had recently built a nice cache of weapons and spread it throughout the castle for protection. I was closer to building this time machine than anyone else in GROUP, and if anyone found out, I was sure they would come for me. I needed to make sure I could defend myself.

I held my right hand in front of me and blinked. Which of my weapons would appear this time? When I opened my eyes, a large metal staff appeared, electricity crackling at each end. I hadn't seen this before but immediately liked it. The sound of the sparks jumping off each end and bouncing along the floor was mesmerizing.

I wonder if I can build one in the real world or make it my new constant in GROUP? That would freak them out.

Twirling it like a cheerleader twirls a baton, I yelled out, "Look at that! This is my world now! Show yourself or give me my family!"

Danny materialized a few feet in front of me. I gasped and stepped backward. Sarah was always the first to appear, followed by the kids.

"You can't fool me!" I shouted at the beast. I held the staff as if getting ready for a sword fight.

Danny stared at me. His round eyes were full of confusion.

"Get behind me, son," I said.

"Hi Daddy," Crissy's voice roared through my head as if she were shouting through a megaphone pressed into my ear.

I dropped the staff and clamped my hands against my ears. Sparks bounced off the floor and collided against my legs. The hair on my legs singed. Pain fired into my skin.

What the hell is going on? I never feel the physical pain in these things, especially when I'm lucid.

"What's wrong, Daddy?" she insisted.

I dropped to my knee and grabbed her, holding her against me. She felt so real, more real than I've ever felt these nightmares. A tear formed in the corner of my eye. It rolled along my cheek and dropped on top of her head.

"Daddy, wanna play catch?" Danny asked. He handed me a baseball and backed against the wall, holding his glove in front of his face. "Okay, throw it, Daddy. I'm ready."

I gave the ball a soft underhand toss. He turned the glove the wrong way and ducked. The ball smacked into the wall next to him and bounced to the floor.

"Keep trying," I chuckled. "You'll get better."

"Hi baby," Sarah said. "You ready for today?"

I lifted Crissy and spun around. Sarah stood in the doorway, holding Lena. I walked toward them and put my arms around her. Everything about her was exactly as I remembered. Her soft skin, the touch of her hands against my back, even her smell, a mixture of her flowery perfume and baby powder. It was all so real.

Without letting go, I leaned back and looked into her eyes. They were the same brown I remember from the first time we met. She touched my cheek and smiled.

"What's wrong?" she asked.

"Oh, nothing," I said, staring at the small silver cross hanging around her neck. When had she started wearing that? "So, what are we doing today?"

"You always surprise us," she said.

"Well, yeah, I have to," I said. "I'm the lucid one. Everything is always my idea."

"But today," she said, "we have an idea."

"What?" I shuffled back a few steps. "What are you talking about?"

I stepped into the hallway and walked from one end to the other, checking each room for the demon. He usually shows up after I get my family.

"Where are you?" I yelled.

But he didn't appear.

"Dad, why are you yelling?" Danny said, his voice a little deeper this time.

I turned to him. He was a foot taller, dressed in blue jeans and a dark-brown, tattered Nirvana t-shirt on its last leg. His blond hair was longer, flowing past his shoulders. Was that a five-o'clock shadow?

"Danny?" I dropped to the ground and scooted against the closet. "What is happening?"

"It's Dan now, Dad."

Sarah and the girls joined him in the hallway. Everyone looked older, including Sarah. The girls were taller. Lena was no longer in her mom's arms. She walked on her own. *This is wrong. Something is wrong.* The four of them stared my way but didn't make a move toward me.

"I don't understand," I said.

"Don't understand what, Dad?" Crissy said. "We're back."

"No, this is a nightmare, just like any other."

"It's not like any other," Lena said. Her voice. I had never heard it before. It penetrated me. It was so sweet, so soft.

"We're here." Sarah smiled. "And we're back. Actually, we never left. We've been here the whole time."

"What?" I stared at the ground. Running my fingers through my hair, I could feel my body temperature rising. My forehead was burning, and my chest tightened.

"Remember the car accident? We didn't get on the plane. They saved us. Close your eyes and think Nelson, you'll remember."

Pain streamed into my head. I closed my eyes and covered my face. Memories of everything the last eleven years as a family were being injected into my head as if someone had plugged a hard drive into my brain and moved all the files at the same time.

I blinked. Something was there, behind them. I opened my eyes a little and saw the demon peeking between Danny's and Crissy's legs. It squeezed through and sat. Its little brown tail wagged back and forth.

"I knew it!" I screamed. "The demon is here!"

I jumped to my feet, slid past them and ran into my office. I needed my weapon, something to fight it off. *Look how small it is this time! I can win and finally save them!*

"Daddy, what are you doing?" Lena asked. "Don't you recognize Marty? We got him years ago."

"Baby, just get away. I'll take care of him."

It came running in behind me and jumped, throwing its paws against my knees, scratching both my legs with its claws. I staggered backward and fell onto the couch. Rolling over, I buried my head deep into the cushion. It jumped next to me and climbed onto my back. It was growling, baring its teeth and barking.

"Stop! Just leave us alone!" Tears fell from my eyes, soaking the cushion. "Please. I'm begging you. Just go away."

"He just wants to play," Sarah said, stroking the beast.

I opened my eyes. Tears rolled down the sides of my head to the pillow. I covered my face with both hands. *If I can't control the dreams, if the beast wins, what more do I have?* My body went numb. *What did she mean when she said it only wanted to play? It can't be over. I can't lose them.*

I sniffled and breathed out, filling the air with tears that had leaked into my mouth.

"Oh, gross," a voice above me said.

Someone grabbed my shoulder and shook me. I turned my head and squinted. The outline of a woman stood draped in the light of the computer monitor behind her.

"Sweetie, you fell asleep on your couch again. Come to bed."

It was Sarah's voice. How was she standing there? I looked at my watch. 11:30 p.m. I closed my eyes and checked it again. Still 11:30. How is this possible? I jumped to my feet and threw my arms around her.

"Oh, hello," she said, laughing.

"Wait, If you're here—"

I ran to the doorway.

"Kids? Come upstairs!"

"They're probably asleep, Nelson."

"Shh...Be quiet," I said.

I ran into the doorway and watched the stairs. Danny appeared first, followed by the girls.

"What do you want?" Crissy said. "I have school tomorrow."

"You guys are all here?" I pulled each of them together for a group hug.

"Dad, let me go," Danny said. "Your shoulders are all wet."

He tried to escape my grip, but I grabbed a handful of his shirt and pulled him closer. More memories flooded my brain. Disney World, school concerts, dentist appointments, Danny's appendectomy, Crissy's pet pig, Lena's first steps, her first day of kindergarten, everything. It was all back. *They weren't on the plane. He saved them.*

I remembered last night's GROUP session. He had figured it out. He had traveled through time and crashed into us. He had saved them all. I looked past the three kids still standing in my arms. Sarah was there, her face scrunched up, staring at us. Behind her, I could see the GROUP chat window from last night showing the last thing VanBurenBoy typed.

I have to change things back.

"No," I whispered.

Sweat formed on my forehead. My nostrils flared. I pulled the kids in closer and looked at Sarah. She was fiddling with her phone, most likely getting ready to take a picture. *She loves moments like this, right? Yeah, she does. I remember she does.* That specific file was just copied on to my brain.

I have to change things back.

My eyes narrowed. Heat built inside me. Sarah hurried over and stood in front of us. She held the camera as far away as her arm would let her.

"Nighttime selfie!" she yelled.

I moved my head toward her. Her perfume drifted into my nose. The corners of my mouth raised as I parted my lips.

"That's a terrible smile, Nelson!" Sarah said. She leaned her head back and touched her cheek to mine. The kids squeezed around us.

I have to change things back.

No. No, VanBurenBoy. You will not be changing anything back. You will not take my family from me. Not again. Not ever.

Chapter 24

Peter, 2017

Peter lay in bed, staring at the ceiling with Buddy tucked against his side, head against his stomach. Falling asleep had been the problem in the past, but at this moment all Peter wanted to do was close his eyes and forget everything. The time machine, GROUP, the man in the brown car, the strange nurse who called herself Talbot—it all needed just to go away and leave him alone.

"I can't even go back in time and stop myself from building it," he muttered, thinking about the previous times he had tried to change his own past.

Buddy groaned, rolled onto his back and stuck his feet in the air. Peter reached toward him and rubbed his belly. Maybe disappearing into the past, somewhere safe, was the only solution. Would Anna want to go with him?

One date and you think she's ready to run away from everything for you? Think again, my friend. She's too nice. She will want to fix things.

"It was quite the first date," Peter said, arguing with himself.

What about that nurse? Seems like she wants to help.

"She can see everything I do. How is that even possible?"

Anna's monitor, his rearview mirror, even in the past and future she was there, leading them around like a pack of dogs chasing a rabbit. But why the nurse's outfit? What was that about?

"Dammit Buddy, I shouldn't have told anyone," Buddy's ears perked up. "Not even Anna. Things would probably be fine if I hadn't taken her back."

Peter rolled onto his side and grabbed his cell phone from the nightstand. He dialed. It rang twice, and a friendly voice picked up.

"Dude, what the hell are you calling me in the middle of the night for?" Zach said.

"Something happened."

"Oh shit, your date. What happened? You guys get arrested or something? Is this your one phone call?"

Peter didn't immediately answer.

Zach chuckled. "Dude, I was only kidding. What's going on?"

"It's worse than that," Peter said. "Just get here when you can."

"Okay, gimme like fifteen minutes. Should I bring something that cleans up blood?"

Peter thought back to Ceremony and the two people he'd seen murdered in front of him. He let out a short groan.

"Whoa, again, kidding Pete. I'll be there in a few."

Peter jumped from the bed and grabbed the pair of blue jeans from the corner of the room where he had thrown them before collapsing into his bed. On the way downstairs, he stopped on the landing, pushed the white curtains aside and peered into the night. A fresh coat of snow blanketed the library's empty parking lot.

He spent the next twenty minutes pacing. He tried to calm himself by making a grilled-cheese sandwich, but he cut it in half and ate it over the sink as he washed the frying pan. Walking to the front door, he opened the blinds and waited. Zach's familiar green pickup truck turned the corner and barreled down the road. Peter closed the blinds and unlocked the door. He hurried to the couch, grabbed the remote control and muted the television.

Zach let himself in without knocking, as he had been doing since Peter moved out of his parents' house. He was wearing the same dark sweatpants and black Rick and Morty t-shirt he'd worn to lunch earlier in the day, although it had a few more wrinkles in it by now.

"Okay, I'm here. What the hell is going on?"

Peter grabbed his backpack from the dining room table, opened it and pulled the time machine from his bag. He set it on the coffee table and slid it toward Zach.

"Big deal, you have a set of handcuffs," Zach said. "My dad has like ten."

"It's a time machine."

"Dude, come on. Seriously, I was asleep. What's going on? You sounded like your dog died."

"It's true," Peter said.

He took a deep breath, exhaled and took Zach through the events of the evening, starting with meeting Anna at Carson's. He told Zach about the hockey game and her spot overlooking the city.

Zach's eyes wandered to the TV where ESPN was showing SportsCenter. He occasionally glanced at Peter, but when Peter said, "...ended up in 1873," Zach's head jerked back to his friend.

"Dude," Zach said. He shook his head and chuckled again.

Peter told him about the night they'd spent at his house in 1873, and how they'd seen Max and Alison in 2006.

Zach cocked his head and stared at Peter; his brow furrowed. He jingled his car keys, hidden in the pocket of his jacket.

"...and we may have caused it," Peter said, finishing the twenty-minute monologue.

"Okay, I'm going to go home, go back to bed and forget we had this weird conversation," Zach said. "You have any aspirin, preferably something with a PM on it to help you sleep? You should probably pop one, maybe two of those."

He stood and walked toward the door, but Peter didn't move. Zach looked over his shoulder at Peter and stared.

"Hold out your wrist. I'll show you."

"Whatever, dude," Zach took hold of the doorknob and turned it. A burst of cold air blew in as he opened the door slightly.

"Just go with me and see for yourself."

Zach pushed the door shut and turned around. "Not sure what your game is, Cardona, but let's see how it ends."

Zach tilted his head, pressed his lips together and held out his hand. Peter strapped the time machine to both their wrists and grabbed his phone. Zach stared at the bracelet while Peter opened the app and pushed a few buttons, looking for a good spot to jump to.

"You ready?" Peter said.

"Sure, Pete."

They reappeared in a large rectangular hole. The moon in the night sky shined above them, providing enough light to show their surroundings. It looked like the basement of a ritzy apartment building in the middle of Columbus.

Bar stools were scattered against the far wall. Two white couches faced a busted flat-screen television mounted to the red brick wall above the fireplace. Other than a blue wooden ladder leading up to the ground floor and a few busted metal support beams, the rest of the room was empty. A thin layer of dust covered everything in the room, except the couches, which were a pristine white.

"That's odd," Peter muttered.

Zach jerked his arm away from Peter, pulling him off his feet. Peter stumbled toward Zach and collided with his shoulder.

"What the fuck, dude?" Zach shrieked.

"I told you."

He regained his balance and unhooked the machine from Zach's wrist.

"Where are we?"

"I don't know," Peter said, staring at his phone. "This damn thing has a mind of its own lately. I think it's the Marina building. You know, those expensive apartments next to Nationwide?"

Zach walked toward the bar and restored a bar stool to its feet. He smacked at the seat, stirring up a cloud of dust, and sat.

"What just happened dude? Where are we?"

"This is the future," Peter said.

"What, like 1,000 years?"

"Five."

A red light moved into the building on the far end. It swept over the ladder and across the couches.

"Shit," Peter mumbled. "Don't talk."

He grabbed Zach's arm and pulled him to the ground behind the beams. They pressed their stomachs to the floor as the red light made its usual grid-like sweep.

"What is that?" Zach whispered.

"Some kind of security droid."

"A what?" Zach raised his voice and popped his head above the beam. Peter put his hand over Zach's mouth and shoved his head to the floor.

The red light stopped and moved toward them. It swept along the beams, missing them by inches. A white light shined from the center of the droid's body and lit up the surrounding area.

"It's calling its friends," Peter whispered. "We're in trouble."

The droid lowered itself into the basement and moved to the opposite side, exposing Peter and Zach's hiding spot. The red light turned, slid toward them and hit Peter.

"Stop, intruder!" it yelled in a booming robotic voice. "You are not allowed in this sector. All intruders will be destroyed."

Peter stood and put his hands in the air. Zach rose behind him.

"Identify yourself."

When Peter didn't answer, a panel in the droid's midsection slid open. Two gun barrels jutted out. Peter and Zach stepped backward and pressed their backs against the bar.

"What do we do?" Zach asked. His voice shook.

The droid hovered silently for a few seconds. The gun barrels retracted and the panel concealing them slid closed. It rose into the air, and as if forgetting they were there, continued its sweep of the apartment.

Peter looked at his friend. Zach opened his mouth to speak, but Peter shrugged, anticipating the question. Once the droid reached the far wall, it rose to ground level and hovered out of sight.

"Let's go," Peter said.

Peter ran to the ladder and climbed first. Halfway up, he looked over his shoulder. The droid was still moving away from them and turning left at the next intersection. Peter reached the surface and kept watch while Zach climbed.

"How is this 2022?" Zach asked, stepping onto the sidewalk.

"We don't know. I've never traveled to the future before tonight. It's possible it would always end up this way, but it's also possible that by creating a time machine I did something, or someone else did something, that caused all of this."

"It looks like a bomb went off."

"Yeah, that's what we thought too, but then Padma found us. She saved us from one of those robots."

"Padma?" Zach stopped walking, "The same Padma who replaced me at work?"

"Yeah, the same one," Peter said. "She took us back to her hideout and said some strange things about how she was sent here to stop this. I think she knew it was going to happen."

"She obviously failed," Zach said, holding his arms out.

"Yeah, she was well aware of that," Peter said, "but it seemed like she was still trying to fight. I didn't know her that well at work. Here she was like a warrior—not the quiet, meek person who took over your cubicle."

Zach tripped over a stack of papers pushed against one of the walls. He bent down and grabbed one.

"What is Ceremony?"

"That's where I'm taking you," Peter said. "You need to see what we saw."

A few minutes later, the lights of the stadium came into view. Instead of hiding in the trees as Peter had with Anna, they fell in with a group of people heading into the stadium through a doorway in the fence. They walked past a man standing on the other side, where on a normal Friday night someone would stand to tear your ticket in half before a football game. He was a thin man of Peter's height with short, straight blond hair.

"Welcome," he said in a thick German accent to each person who passed.

"Section A," Peter muttered.

"Stay in line," he ordered.

As they exited the tunnel, Peter grabbed the fence on the left and followed the group. When the fence ended, he circled around it to the other side and walked up the stairs to the top row. He sat in the first seat on the end, next to the fence separating them from the entrance to the tunnel. Zach sat next to him.

"Padma said they find someone each week to be a sacrifice," Peter whispered.

"Sacrifice?"

Two teenagers standing in front of the pair turned and looked at them. The older of the two, a girl of about sixteen, put her finger to her mouth, telling Zach to keep quiet.

"They claim the person has broken the laws and must be punished," Peter whispered.

Peter turned his head toward the trees between the two sets of bleachers. He could barely make out three people lying on the ground in the shadows.

"That's us," Peter whispered. "Me, Anna and Padma."

Zach turned and squinted. His eyes widened as he turned toward Peter.

A large explosion of sound rocked the stadium, making the crowd fall silent. Everyone, including Peter and Zach, focused their attention to the stage. The man in the hood walked toward center stage and went through the same introduction Peter had heard the first time.

But this time his voice was different, more familiar. Something had changed. This was different.

It's probably because you're sitting closer to the speakers.

The man Padma called Kase was led onto the stage by a larger man and tied to the wooden plank.

"Watch," Peter said, extending one finger toward the woman in the crowd.

On cue, she stood and started her protest. She ran to the grass toward the stage, a little farther this time, but again the nearest security droid fired. A thick red laser hit the center of her chest. She went limp, rose a few inches into the air and shot backward, landing on her back a few feet in front of the bleachers. Her body convulsed and rolled, coming to rest on its side. Peter recoiled at the smell of burned skin, something he had been too far away to experience the first time he'd watched her die.

"Silence!" the man yelled into the microphone. He panned the crowd. "It seems we have some unexpected visitors."

"This is when he finds us," Peter said. He turned his head toward himself, Anna and Padma in the distance. "Well not me and you, 'us' meaning them."

The man turned toward the shadows in the trees. He paused. The crowd followed his gaze. Silence lay thick in the night. Like a shot, he swung his head around to where Peter and Zach sat. He dropped the microphone, and a loud boom echoed. The crowd gasped; all eyes turned toward the pair. The man reached out with both hands, grabbed his hood and yanked it from his head.

"Holy shit!" Zach said.

Peter froze. His mouth fell open. He stared at the figure under the hood.

"We need to go right now," he muttered.

"Guards, get them!"

In unison, eight security droids floated into the air and hovered to Peter and Zach. They bolted from their seats. Zach leaped first, vaulting himself over the fence, landing at the mouth of the tunnel. He looked up at Peter, who climbed on the first bar of the fence and threw himself over. He hit the cement hard, feet first, sending pain from his knees throughout his legs.

"You okay?" Zach asked.

Peter lifted his head and gathered himself. Either the pain was short-lived, or adrenaline was overshadowing it. He ran past Zach and was in the tunnel first.

Halfway from the exit, he could see the fence. The guard stood. He raised both hands in front of him, signaling for them to stop. Zach grabbed Peter's shoulder, almost knocking him off his feet, but slowing him enough to take the lead.

Zach crouched as if he were on the high school football team again and had one guy to beat before finding the end zone. A low guttural groan came from his mouth. The guard's eyes widened. He spun and reached for the gate. Zach crashed into him, using his shoulder as a battering ram, punishing him harder than any defensive player he had ever tackled. The man's back hit the ground, his head snapped back and slammed on the ground so loudly, Peter thought a gun had fired.

Peter looked at the man as he jumped over his lifeless body. Blood poured from his head, turning his hair from blond to a dark red.

Zach veered from the street to the sidewalk and looked over his shoulder.

"They're getting closer!" he yelled.

Peter turned into an unlit alley and leaned against a wall. Zach slid next to him. Peter pressed a button on his phone, waking it and giving them light. He grabbed Zach's wrist and attached the bracelet.

"You saw it, right?" Zach asked.

"Yeah, I saw it," Peter said. "I don't understand."

"Pete, why was I under that hood?" Zach asked.

The red light from the droid's head appeared in the alley's entrance. It swung from one side to the other.

"Hurry!" Zach yelled.

The droid stopped the grid search and moved toward them. Peter opened Padma's app and pressed the Home button.

Chapter 25

Nelson, 2022

"Please come in and make yourself at home," I said to the two men who had just crossed the drawbridge and knocked on my door.

Sudo Brownlock walked in first. I had asked him his real name a few times since we'd met, but he refused to give it. He claimed GROUP names were safer. He wore a dirty, ripped white t-shirt and a pair of stained blue jeans.

"You need a shower and a change of clothes." I chuckled. "You look like you've been through the Event again."

"I've been telling him the same thing," the man behind Sudo said.

I looked at the man, dressed in a dark suit and black tie. I searched my memory, but I couldn't remember inviting him into my house. Staring at his face, I tried to come up with a name, something that would answer why he was here, but I had nothing. There was a blank spot in my brain where something important was missing, and the more I searched it, the larger it grew.

"Thanks for allowing me back into your castle," the man said. "I know the last time I was here things didn't end well—but I assure you, we will have a much better relationship going forward."

He stretched his hand toward me. I took hold, squeezed hard and shook.

Always shake hands like you mean it. My dad's voice still occasionally appeared in my head. I feel like he would probably be proud of how I turned out.

His grip was tighter than I expected, despite the fact that he was a few inches taller than me. Still, he was very thin, and his pale face hinted that he hadn't seen the sun in a while.

I turned to Sudo and shook his hand.

"Did you find Kase?" I asked.

He looked at the man and paused. The man nodded to him.

"We have him. He's upstairs in the cage getting prepped for tonight." Sudo said. "You can go up and speak to him whenever you're ready."

The man stood and walked over to my computer system. He ran his hand across the tower and the large capital "T" I had stenciled on the side.

"Nice touch," he said.

I glanced at him, then back to Sudo.

"And the woman?" I asked.

Again, he looked toward the man. The man nodded.

"We're still looking for her," he said.

My head moved between the pair. Who is this guy, and why is Sudo getting his approval before answering my questions? *I'm in charge here.* I ran my hands through my hair and cocked my head.

"Sudo, who the hell is this guy?"

The man walked toward me. I stumbled backward, tripped on the edge of the couch and fell onto a cushion to keep myself from tumbling to the floor. My confusion turned to fear, and a rush of memories flooded through me, filling the empty space in my brain.

"Not again," I said. "Things are changing. Where's Sarah? Where are my kids?"

I curled into a fetal position, pushing my elbows against my sides, trying to get as small as possible, and hugged myself. The man handed me a bottle of water from my desk. I sipped at it and tried to breathe.

"Nelson, I'm Zach," he said.

I froze as he towered over me. I remembered Zach. I met him a few months after the Event. He came running into the castle, leading an army. They held us hostage until I agreed to work for him. But why now? He hadn't been part of this a few minutes ago. What had caused things to change? Everything had been perfect, back to normal. Who had changed things?

"I'm in charge, Nelson," he said. His voice was low and calm, like that of a parent comforting his child during a thunderstorm.

My breath quickened. I clutched at my throat and tried to concentrate. I leaned to the right and looked past Zach at Sudo Brownlock, who stood staring at me, his face filled with confusion. Zach followed my gaze to Sudo. He jerked his leg back and slammed his foot into the couch, just below where my face hung. I shrieked and met his eyes.

"Perhaps I should talk to your family about our arrangement?" Zach said.

"My family, sir?" I asked.

Sir? Why did I call him 'sir'?

"Yes Nelson. Your family. Your wife Sarah. The kids. Dan, Christine," he leaned in, his face an inch from mine. The smell of stale coffee filled my nose with each breath he took, "and little Lena. She's your favorite, isn't she?"

"If you hurt them..." I trailed off.

Zach straightened his back and turned, facing Sudo. "I won't hurt them, Nelson. This was your idea, remember? I keep them until you build me that system. Once it's tested and working, you get them back. You get your little empire, and I get off this dying rock."

System? I couldn't have agreed to something like this. I'd already lost them once. No way would I volunteer to give them up again, even as part of a deal.

"So," Zach said, turning around to Sudo. "How's it coming? Are we close?"

Sudo leaned to the side and looked past Zach toward me. Zach turned; his mouth narrowed as he tilted his head.

"It's going well, sir," I said. "I'm hoping to put the finishing touches on things later this week. We ran into a small hitch, but we should have that wrapped up in the next couple of days."

Zach looked at the calendar hanging over Nelson's desk. He smiled. "Don't worry about him. I'll take care of him tonight at Ceremony. You keep working on this."

Sudo spoke: "You think you can get him tonight? He wants to reverse things, and we need to stop him if we want to proceed as planned."

"Wait," I ran to my desk and opened the filing cabinet. I grabbed the last file hanging on the top row and a business card. "I know someone who can help."

Zach read the card. "Aiden Connor. You trust this guy?"

I walked to the computer, did a quick search, and the image of a man flashed on the largest monitor. He was in his fifties, overweight and scruffy-looking.

"He's a private investigator, used to work in New York City. He had some problems with an accidental shooting and relocated here several years ago. He owes me a favor."

"You sure this is the guy we want on our side?" Zach pointed to Connor's picture on the card. "He's a mess. Can't even take a decent picture for his business card?"

"The first time we met, he was chasing three teenagers. Connor managed to keep pace with them until I got in his way."

Zach stared at the card for a few seconds and turned to Sudo, "Go find Connor. Tell him to verify if the machine works. Once he's sure, tell him to take it from Pete however he needs to, but not to hurt him. He's a good guy. Hung me out to dry a few times, and I haven't talked to him in a while. But he's still a friend."

"How will this Connor know if Peter's machine works?" Sudo asked.

Zach reached into his pocket and handed Sudo a small microchip. "Give this to him. It's wirelessly linked to Peter's machine. Tell him to stick it to his chest over his heart. If Peter jumps, he will follow behind him a few minutes later."

"How did you get VanBurenBoy's signal?" I asked.

Zach reached into the same jacket pocket and pulled out a bracelet. He handed it to Sudo, who studied it. Once he finished, he passed it to me. I noticed the small chip inside the blue box.

"The first model uploaded to GROUP," Sudo said.

"The last time we traveled together, I had to use it," Zach said. "He wired it to his machine, allowing three of us to jump at the same time. It was buggy, but I've since fixed it and found his signal."

"You got it, sir," Sudo said.

Zach turned his attention to Sudo. I pulled the microchip from the bracelet's box and shoved it into my pocket.

"Make sure Connor wears it over his heart," Zach said. "And make sure he waits until Pete tells me about the machine before he attempts to take it, or none of this happens."

None of this happens. Is that what he said?

Sudo nodded and exited my office. Zach put his arm around me. His bicep caught the back of my neck, pushing me forward. I dropped the bracelet on the couch.

"Remember what I can do, if you defy me," he said. "I'm in charge here. The only thing I care about is that computer. Your family means nothing to me."

I spun around and faced him. He put his hand on my shoulder, stopping me instantly.

"Not a good idea, Nelson. We've had this conversation many times. I get my system; you get your family. It's a simple agreement. No need to be a hero this close to the finish line."

I pulled back and shook my shoulder, releasing myself from his grip.

"Are we clear?" he asked.

I stood across from him and stared into his eyes. He turned to the wall and touched the picture Sarah and the kids from Disney World. His voice softened. "Are we clear?"

My lips trembled. I looked around.

How did this happen?

"Yes, sir." I said, reluctantly.

Chapter 26

Peter, 2017

"Is that my future?" Zach asked as they ran down the stairs with Buddy hot on their heels.

"I don't know," Peter said. He grabbed a treat and threw it to the couch. Buddy ran after it. "We're still trying to work out what happened."

Peter walked into the living room, unhooked the machine from his wrist and took a seat next to Buddy, who was busy searching for any remaining crumbs from the snack. Satisfied he had devoured every piece, he climbed into Peter's lap, turned in a circle and lay down.

"What was I going to do on that stage?"

"When we were there the first time, the person under that hood shot and killed the man tied to the plank."

Zach fell onto the recliner. "What? I'm not killing anyone!"

"It wasn't you the first time, though. It changed. Something happened, and things changed."

"What did you do differently?"

"I took you instead of Anna."

"Was she under the hood?"

"We couldn't see the person under the hood. We were too far away. But it didn't sound like her."

"Did it sound like me?"

"It wasn't anyone I recognized."

A metallic clang against the sidewalk near the back porch startled the pair. Peter and Zach stiffened and turned their heads toward the white curtain hanging over the back door. Buddy jumped to the floor and ran barking into the kitchen.

"What was that?" Zach asked. He glanced at Peter.

"I think it was my garbage can."

"Is someone back there?"

A silhouette appeared in the porch light at the bottom of the back steps. Peter's skin tingled. He stood, the chill air raising goosebumps on his arms. From the darkness, Peter watched the dark silhouette grow larger through the curtain as it ran to the top of the steps. The doorknob twisted. Peter's heartbeat thumped in his ears. With both fists, the stranger pounded against the window with enough force to break it.

"Peter! Are you in there? Open the door."

Peter's legs tensed at the terror in Anna's voice. His mind went blank. He was sure Zach's mouth was moving, but he couldn't hear anything but her. He leaped to his feet. In seconds he was at the back door, pulling it open and letting her fall into his arms.

"What's wrong? You're shaking."

Her chin trembled, and her body shook. "He was outside my window, watching me."

Zach stepped into the kitchen. "What?"

"After my sister patched me up, I showered, put on the first pair of pajamas I could find, and I fell into bed. I lay there for a few minutes reliving everything we went through, trying to calm my brain, but it seemed impossible. I couldn't shake the sight of that woman at that ceremony lying there, dying, and no one cared."

Peter grabbed a tissue from the counter and handed it to her. She wiped below each eye, took a breath and continued.

"I couldn't sleep. I'm so tired. I tried, but I just couldn't fall asleep. Every time I close my eyes..."

She wiped her eyes again and pulled a bar stool from the back side of Peter's kitchen island. After sitting, she paused and attempted to slow her breath, settling her nerves. Peter pulled the second stool out, sat and turned to face her.

"Something didn't feel right," she went on. "It felt like I wasn't alone. So I went to the window."

Peter shifted in his seat and reached for her. One of her hands was resting on her knee, still shaking. He rested his hand on top of hers.

"He was there, Peter," she whispered. "Standing on the road."

"Who?" Zach asked.

Anna looked toward him, cringed and then shifted her eyes back to Peter.

"He was leaning against his car's hood, watching the house. I think he followed me home from Carson's. When he saw me, he grinned and raised his phone. I remember that grin. The flash went off. Why was he taking pictures?"

Peter locked the backdoor and herded Anna and Zach into the living room. He sat next to Anna on the couch. Zach tugged both ends of the curtains closed and sat in the recliner near the window. He turned his attention back to Anna.

"Who was watching you?" he asked again.

Anna looked at Zach for a second and at Peter.

"It's okay. He knows," Peter said.

She buried her head against Peter's shoulder and pressed her body to his. In her wet pajamas, she shivered. The light snow that had been falling earlier that evening continued to fall, but this wasn't a shiver of cold. This was fear. He pulled a blanket from the end of the couch and wrapped it around the two of them.

"It was him. That guy from last night. I freaked and bolted. I ran across the neighbors' backyards to that Sheetz on the corner and called an Uber."

"Why did you come to the back door?" Peter asked.

"I saw shadows walking around your living room, more than one person. I thought he might have beaten me here."

Zach pushed the curtain aside a few inches and peered into the night. "The guy in the brown car? If he followed you here, I don't see him."

Anna pulled her head back from Peter's shoulder. She whispered, "You told him?"

"We just came back," Zach said. "He showed me all of it."

She squeezed her arm around Peter's waist and held on to his back tightly. "Did you guys run into Padma or see Ceremony?"

Peter glanced at Zach. His eyes narrowed.

"What?" Anna asked. "What happened?"

"We went back to their Ceremony," Peter said. "But we were closer this time, sitting in the bleachers. Everything was the same, but when the man on stage dropped his hood—"

"It was me!" Zach revealed.

Anna's eyes widened. She recoiled and pushed against Peter, pulling the blanket to cover her mouth.

She trembled. Her muffled voice rose as she spoke. "What? How?"

"I don't know, but we can't let that happen." Peter pointed at Zach. "We can't let him end up on that stage. Padma mentioned the Event a couple of times. We could go back to her place and try to get more details."

"And what? Stop it?" Anna asked. "You said it was too hard to change your own future."

"This may have nothing to do with us," Peter reasoned. "It could have been a natural disaster or something that shot from the sun. In that case, we could try to warn people."

"No way," Zach said. "What if my trying to stop it is what put me on that stage?"

Peter looked toward the ceiling and cocked his head to the side. "At least we know how it turns out. Maybe we can prevent it from happening and try to steer clear of whatever causes your turn."

Zach's tone shifted to uncertainty. "Turn?"

"Are you sure Padma is a good idea?" Anna asked. "Remember last time she wanted to leave me stranded so she could try to stop something she'd failed at the first time. If it was a natural disaster, what could she even do?"

"There's three of us this time," Peter said. "If we agree to stick together and watch each other's backs..."

"You wanna save the world?" Anna said.

"Yeah, I guess I do," Peter said.

"Could be dangerous."

Peter shrugged. "Nothing going on at work."

She gave a wide grin. "Yeah. Peterson expects that project to be finished this week, but I guess it could be put on hold to, you know, save the world and everything."

Peter looked into her eyes. "So we're really gonna do this?"

She nodded and leaned toward him.

"Hello!" Zach interrupted. "I'm still here. I haven't agreed to anything."

Peter looked past Anna at his friend. "Do you want to end up evil?"

Zach's shoulders slumped. He turned toward the window, pulled the curtain aside and looked outside.

"Okay," he muttered.

Peter took the machine and attached one side to his wrist. The other end dangled. Anna took hold of it and put it around her wrist. Without attaching it, she asked the obvious question, "How are all three of us going to go?"

Peter let go of Anna and walked to his desk. He shuffled through both drawers, shut them and went upstairs. A few seconds later, he came down holding an aluminum bracelet. It was the first attempt at a time machine he had built based on specs created by Ricka Daigr, a member of GROUP. Attached to its top was a small blue plastic container holding a blue wire and a microchip. The blue wire was attached to the chip on one side, and a piece of black electrical tape held the other end against the bracelet. Engraved on the front were the words "You're my Person."

"Cute," Zach said. At least his sarcasm was back.

"Thanks," Peter replied. He looked at Anna. "I bought it for her two days after we met."

Zach cringed. Anna leaned forward and read it.

"Aw," she said, throwing an arm around his back. "You're mine too."

He pulled the blue wire from the microchip and attached it to an exact copy of the microchip on the bracelet Peter and Anna had been using to travel. Zach slid the single unit on his wrist.

Peter flung his backpack over his shoulder, woke up his phone and opened the app.

"When Padma wrote this, she set it to save the coordinates each time I pressed the button to jump. At the time, I told her it was so I could view the fairways and greens at whatever golf course I was playing, but apparently, she knew the truth. No wonder it worked so well."

He scrolled to the coordinates for Padma's basement hideout and pressed the button. Anna let out a low grunt as a jolt of electricity shot up Peter's arm and ran into his shoulder. His fingers spasmed. The phone lurched in his hand, but he pushed it against his chest, trapping it before it fell. Zach disappeared in front of Peter's eyes. A split second later, everything went black.

Chapter 27

Nelson, 2022

"This grass is too wet," I told Sudo.

Sudo Brownlock stood next to me on the side of the stage. In front of us on the bottom step, a man squirmed, shackled at his hands and feet, a black hood covering his head.

"Settle down, Kase," Sudo grunted. He smacked Kase on the side of his head, quieting him for the moment.

I looked at the center of the stage where Zach kicked off Ceremony Number 122 and crossed my arms.

"This is ridiculous," I said under my breath. "This whole thing was my idea. Everything from how the stage faced to what was said at each one."

"If this were your idea," Kase turned his head toward me and spoke through his hood loudly enough to be heard over the cheers of the crowd, "why are you down here waiting for him to tell you what to do?"

"Shut up, asshole," Sudo said, elbowing him in the ribs.

Kase bent forward and grabbed his knees, writhing in pain.

"I think you broke my ribs."

"Like it's gonna matter in a few minutes," Sudo said, laughing.

Even if he was bent over at the knees and groaning in pain, I couldn't help agreeing with Kase. Why wasn't I up there? This was all my idea, and one day, out of nowhere, Zach burst through my door leading a small army. He took my family and ordered me to build a computer system because he had some crazy idea that he needed to get off Earth.

"Off the Earth?" I muttered. "Is that even possible?"

An explosion rocked the stadium, silencing the crowd. Zach began his speech.

"Blah-blah-blah, if you're against me, you're against all of us bullshit." That's my speech. He's just a dimwit whose only strength is that he is holding my family somewhere and won't deliver them back until I build his bullshit computer system. Who knows if it will even end there?

"Let's go," Sudo said, grabbing Kase's sleeve.

"It is possible, you know," Kase said, looking at me.

"What?" I said.

"Getting off the Earth. I've done it."

Sudo yanked Kase upright and pushed him toward the stairs. Kase tripped. I reached out and held him, keeping him from falling. I stared at the hood covering his eyes. The corners of his mouth turned upward.

"What are you talking about?" I asked.

"Get moving!" Sudo said.

He put his hands on Kase's back and shoved him across the stage. Kase fell and tumbled to the ground, rolling against the wheel. I could see Kase's mouth moving behind the mask, but the deafening roar of the crowd ruined any chance for him to explain himself. Sudo lifted him into the air and pushed him against the plank, tying his wrists and ankles to it—the same way we had tied down traitors since Ceremony started.

Zach flashed a thin smile as I walked past him, no doubt making sure I understood I was doing what he said and not the other way around. Son of a bitch; his time will come.

I stopped at the top of the stairs when the protesting woman screamed Kase's name. I paused. I knew what was coming. One blast put an end to her. I looked over my shoulder at Kase. Even with the hood covering his face, I could hear his sobs. Must have been someone he loved. *I know the feeling my friend. I really do.*

His sobbing abruptly stopped. Everything around me—the crowd, the stage, even Sudo—melted away like wet paint sliding down a canvas. I turned. Zach stood in the grass where the stage used to sit. He made eye contact with me and smiled.

Another nightmare. I've been through so many of them. They didn't even bother me anymore. Instead, I went along with it. It became a game. He stepped toward me. I tilted my head and stared. Something about him was different. It wasn't his look. It was a feeling, a feeling I hadn't known in him before.

Fear.

He's afraid. Fear oozed from him, filling the space between us. I moved closer, smelling the rancid, stale air. When he spoke, the confidence had disappeared. He sounded like a teenage boy, trying to act tough in front of a girl.

"Do you really want to lose your family again, Nelson?" His voice squeaked when he spoke my name.

My body felt loose. I stepped toward him. He flinched.

"I'll be seeing them again, Zach."

"You complete your task, and you'll get them back, unharmed."

"Nah, I don't think so," I said. "Look around. It's changing. You see it too."

I opened my eyes. Everything was out of focus. I searched for the lamp, but it wasn't there. In its place, the silhouette of a head moved toward me.

"Nelson," Zach said.

I sat up on the couch and put my feet on the floor. I squeezed my eyes shut as tightly as I could and opened them. His face was right there, inches from mine. I hurled myself at him, planting the palms of my hands into each of his shoulders. We both sailed backward and smashed against the wall next to my desk. Three monitors hanging on the same wall, just a few feet from where we hit, rattled. One fell off the wall and flew toward us. Zach rolled forward. The edge of the monitor struck the side of my head and knocked me to the ground. I pushed both hands to my ears to ease the pain, but instead, I trapped a high-pitched squeal between my ears.

I rolled to my side and curled into a ball. The overhead light ripped into my eyes. Pain surged through my head. I inched backward, tucking most of my body under the desk. Zach climbed to his feet and stood over me. He leaned forward, resting his hands on the desk, consuming me in his shadow. I opened one eye and looked at his face. A trickle of blood leaked from his upper lip.

"No one threatens my family," I grunted.

"One call and they're dead, Nelson."

"You don't have the guts!"

He kicked me in the stomach. I hugged myself more tightly.

"Watch me!" he shouted.

He grabbed my cell phone and dialed.

"Get them ready," he said into the phone.

My bag sat in front of him on the desk. He grabbed it and threw it at me. It landed a few feet from my face. My cell phone and bracelet spilled onto the floor at my feet.

"This is your last chance," Zach whispered. "You fuck this up one more time, and they're dead. And you'll watch them die before I kill you."

I reached for the bracelet but stopped when I noticed the red alert light blinking on the top my phone. A new email. I flipped it over and unlocked it. My eyes widened when I read the subject line. I closed them, reopened and read it again. The words didn't change. This was real.

From: elfGlimmer

Subject: I have him

I breathed and opened my eyes. My head throbbed as I slid against the wall and forced myself to my feet.

"I'm not through with you," I sneered.

"Yeah, sure, Nelson. Take your best shot."

Doing everything I could to block out the high-pitched squeal still slicing through my head, I took a step toward him. My hands balled into fists, and he stepped toward me.

"You're afraid," I said. "You're having the nightmares too, aren't you?"

He stopped walking, and I know I saw him shudder.

"Your family," he reminded me.

I stopped and gazed at him. "Do what you must."

He tapped a few buttons on his cell phone and put it to his cheek. I sprang, driving my right fist into his stomach. His phone tumbled to the ground. He bent forward and clutched his midsection. I swung my left arm. His nose shattered under my fist. He stood straight up as his eyes rolled back into his head. Blood poured from his nose, dripping into his mouth. He looked like a lion in the wild who just pulled flesh from its kill.

It wasn't enough blood. I wanted more. He needed to suffer for any pain he'd caused my family.

The palm of Zach's hand landed on the desk. He steadied himself and blinked until his eyes faced forward. His mouth opened and he sucked in a combination of air and blood. He coughed, choking on the blood in his throat, and looked at me. I again made a fist and swung, driving it into his cheek. My knuckles cracked against his skull. He stumbled backward, twisting his head and hurling blood against the wall. His shirt snagged against the corner of the desk, ripping it open and exposing his chest as he fell.

Something about his chest caught my eye. I moved closer. A small two-inch scar rested just below his heart. My mind raced. I reached into my bag and pulled a microchip, the one attached to my machine, and held it against the scar.

A perfect fit.

"I'm coming for you," I said.

His head tilted to one side. One eye fell open. I slammed the heel of my boot into his face, smashing the back of his head against the wall. He grunted. I hustled back to my bag, gathered my bracelet and phone. I checked the email again and typed a reply.

From: Niven
Subject: On my way

I clamped the bracelet to my wrist and opened elfGlimmer's app. Zach stirred behind me.

"What are you gonna do Nelson?" His voice was low and guttural. He spit blood on the floor and continued, "You gonna kill me now? You can't change your past with that thing. Everyone knows that."

"You're right," I said. "I can't change my past."

He looked at me, one eye pushed closed by a swollen, black bruise. The other widened. I smiled.

"There's that fear again," I said "You're remembering something. What is it? Is it something that hasn't happened yet? Something that's going to happen soon? We've done this before, haven't we?"

I pulled the phone from my pocket and punched the coordinates. I watched him use the wall to steady himself as he rose to his feet. He pulled a pistol from the bottom drawer of my desk.

"I'm afraid your services are no longer needed," he said.

He lifted his arm toward me, pointing the pistol in my direction. His arm trembled as if the gun was heavier than anything he'd ever lifted. I shook my head, grinned and pushed the button on my phone. The pistol went off. A burst of air stabbed into my stomach. I felt the bullet pass through me and shatter a picture hanging on the wall. Everything went dark.

Chapter 28

Peter, 2022

Peter opened his eyes. He was sitting on the floor of Padma's dimly lit basement hideout. He had grown used to the feeling of traveling through time. The first few times he'd traveled, he'd felt groggy as if he had just run a marathon. But over time, his body had adjusted.

Now though, the feeling came back harder than ever. His eyes sagged, and he fought against them, struggling to hold them open. He leaned toward where Anna should have landed. Her shoulder fell against his. Her body felt heavy. She used him for support just as much as he was using her. Her breathing seemed purposely loud as if she were trying to concentrate on staying awake. He turned his head to face her as she breathed through gritted teeth.

"You okay?" Peter asked.

"Yeah. Got a bit of a shock there, but other than this overwhelming exhaustion, everything seems to be fine."

He lifted their wrists and stared at the machine. The blue wire hung free. His eyes shot open, and he snapped his head around, but Zach wasn't there. Anna detached the machine from her wrist and stood, using the wall for support.

Peter heard a cracking sound coming from the bathroom. The sink collapsed, throwing pieces of jagged porcelain and plywood into the kitchen. Anna turned toward the noise. Peter crawled to his feet.

"What the hell was that?" Zach wondered, staggering through the bathroom door.

"How did you get in there?" Peter asked, staring at his phone. "The coordinates are right. We should have ended up across from at each other in the same formation we were when we left."

"I don't know. When I opened my eyes, I was falling to the floor under a busted sink."

"Guys," Anna interrupted, "Padma isn't here."

Peter and Zach turned toward her.

"Look at this place," she said. "Something bad happened."

The mattress, table and chairs had been overturned and thrown against the wall. Padma's brown leather chair rested on its side, shoved under the desk next to the black chair, and someone had caved in the screen of every monitor. A few monitors dangled crooked on their wall mounts while the rest were scattered in pieces around the corner Padma's station had originally occupied.

Peter glanced around, looking for clues. "We're arriving only seconds after we left. What could have happened during that time?"

"How do you even get inside here in the first place?" Zach asked.

Peter pointed toward the empty window and the stepladder next to it. Zach went to the window, while Anna stepped around the pieces of the demolished sink and walked into the bathroom. She put both hands on the wheel that opened the door to the tunnel.

"Maybe we should try this," she yelled. Her voice echoed into the kitchen.

Peter opened the refrigerator. Other than a few bottles of water, one of them half full, it was empty.

"It seems like a good way to sneak around the city," Anna said. Peter closed the refrigerator and looked toward the bathroom door. Anna added, "She might be in here."

Peter walked into the dark, dreary bathroom and stood behind her. From the doorway, Zach pushed pieces of the sink and vanity into the kitchen. He flipped a switch on the wall. The shower light turned on, giving them a better view of the small room.

Anna turned the wheel and pulled. The door had only opened a few inches when an infrared light glowed at her feet and climbed her body.

"Stop, intruder. You are not allowed in this sector. All intruders will be destroyed," boomed the flat, metallic voice of a security droid.

Peter grabbed Anna's shoulders and threw her behind him. The droid rose into the air, its infrared light hitting Peter in the chest.

Any travel exhaustion he felt was overtaken by adrenaline, and he slammed his body against the thick metal door pushing it closed. The droid clanged against the other side, and Peter could feel its strength. Despite his efforts, the door slowly creaked open. Anna scrambled next to him and threw the side of her body against the door, holding it firm, but the droid's strength would overpower them soon enough. The muscles in Peter's arm tightened. Pressed solidly against the cold metal door, his shoulders and chest ached.

"Help, dammit!" Anna yelled at Zach, who was standing rigidly in the doorway.

Zach stirred, appearing to wake from his frozen state, and turned his eyes toward Anna. He rushed in and stood behind her. She ducked her head, allowing him to plant his palms against the door, over her shoulders. His strength was the additional force they needed, and the door quickly reversed direction and slammed closed.

Anna bounced backward and collided against Zach, who caught her and kept her from falling into the rubble.

"Thanks," she said.

Peter quickly turned the wheel and listened for the sound of the tumblers falling into place. He exhaled, bent at the waist and rested his hands on his knees. Breathing heavily, he leaned on the door.

"Is it locked?" Anna said, her tone uncertain.

"I hope. But we should leave. The droid probably didn't forget we were here."

Anna and Zach turned and took a few steps toward the door. Peter drew himself up and adjusted his jacket and backpack. From the other side of the door, they heard a steady hum as if a hive of wasps was swarming. He leaned toward the door and pushed his ear against the cold metal. The door vibrated. The humming grew louder.

"What do you think that is?" he asked, moving his eyes toward Anna while keeping his head firmly planted against the warming metal door.

"Let's not find out," she said. "We should run."

She grabbed Peter's hand and pulled him into the kitchen. The upper half of Zach's body had already disappeared through the window by the time Peter and Anna reached the ladder. Once Zach crawled through, Anna climbed the stairs. At the top, she paused, put both hands through the window and pulled herself into the opening. Peter kept his eyes on her, but behind him, the humming continued. Hot on her heels, he climbed to the top of the ladder and shimmied through.

The street was dark. The light that was available when Padma led them there had been replaced by a cloudy, starless night. Columbus, Ohio, at night wasn't exactly a bustling metropolis, but there was always activity. Peter had run from cowboys in the nineteenth century and robots in the twentieth century, but standing in an alley in the center of the city was the most terrified he had ever been. Not a single person walked the streets. Nothing moved in the shadows, not even the occasional rat. The city was dead.

We need a place to hide, sit tight for a few minutes and find Padma.

"What about those cars we hid under the last time we were here?" Anna said, seeming to read his mind. She led the trio along Lafayette Street, keeping them between the sidewalk and the front of the buildings. "I think they were this way."

"How is the city so quiet?" Zach whispered.

As if the city were reacting to Zach's thought, an explosion behind them rocked the sidewalk under their feet. Anna and Zach cowered and threw their hands over their heads. Peter looked over his shoulder as he ducked. Remnants of the barricaded front door lay strewn on the street, replaced by a large hole. The droid hovered through the newly opened doorway, stopped and turned on its infrared searchlight.

"Come on," Anna whispered, "before it finds us."

Ahead, Lafayette dead-ended onto Pearl Street. Peter saw the pile of cars stacked in the parking lot where he, Anna and Padma had hidden the last time they'd been there. Anna pointed to the top of the dark pickup truck they'd hidden under and made a beeline for it. A second droid dropped from the sky in front of the iron fence. Its red light surged forward and hit Anna's face, stopping her mid-stride. She turned toward Peter, the red light glowing in her green eyes.

"Stop, intruder, you are not allowed in this sector. All intruders will be destroyed."

Anna swung right, jumped a street sign lying on the sidewalk, crossed Pearl and ran along the opposite sidewalk next to the former FedEx building. Most of the building above the second floor had been destroyed, the debris collapsing inward. A bright white searchlight from the underside of the droid's torso swept across the sidewalk where Anna was running. The light caught her immediately, and once it overtook her, the droid rocked forward and began its pursuit.

Zach sprinted to catch up, followed by Peter, who had fallen a few steps behind. Anna ducked into an empty parking lot past the building. The droid leaned left as it turned and followed her around the corner.

The original droid from Padma's apartment trailed ten feet behind Peter. "All intruders will be destroyed."

A loud mechanical hum followed by a click drowned out the thumping of Peter's footsteps against the cement. Peter immediately thought back to the click he had heard just before the droid had shot and killed the protesting woman at Ceremony.

"Go!" he yelled to Zach, who was slowing to help him.

Two loud shots boomed, hitting the FedEx building above Peter's head. Chunks of concrete rained down behind Peter, bouncing off the sidewalk and shooting rubble against his head and back. His skin stung with each blow that threw him off balance. He lost his footing and hit the ground hard.

Zach stopped running and turned toward Peter.

"Keep going!" Peter shouted.

Peter's muscles tightened. He looked over his shoulder at the droid, now a few feet away. Its four legs, protruding from the bottom of its dirty, metallic torso, reached for him. He dropped to the ground. The droid rose into the air and hovered past him. Its spiny center leg dragged across Peter's back. He heard the fabric rip from his shirttail to his collar, as though this were his funeral shroud. He flattened his chest against the sidewalk, but the tip of the droid's razor-sharp barbs ripped into his skin, slicing a two-inch gash just below his neck. He felt a trickle of blood and winced from the sting.

His heartbeat pounding in his ears, Peter planted both palms against the ground and waited for the droid to overtake him. He vaulted to his feet and grabbed a softball-sized piece of concrete. The robot spun and bathed Peter in red light. Peter cocked his arm, took a step forward, swung his arm toward his target, let go of the cement and followed through.

Just like coach taught you.

The cement softball smashed in the center of the droid's head, shattering the infrared light. The droid careened backward, its head colliding against the busted wall of the FedEx building. Peter rushed toward the corner where Zach and Anna had already disappeared. The damaged droid rose in the air again and staggered, like a drunk trying to walk the yellow line. A split second later, it regained its balance and continued toward the area where it had lost Peter.

The mechanical hum buzzed behind him again, followed by the click. Peter looked to the corner—*only a few more steps.* With each breath, his throat ached.

Two new shots missed Peter and the FedEx building completely. A broken-down semi across the street exploded, sending metal and glass into the air. The droid didn't know where he had gone; without its light, it was firing blindly. Peter just needed to make the corner in one piece.

He ducked and turned the corner, immediately skidding into a stop to keep from colliding with Zach and Anna. To Anna's left, a shipping dock rose six feet from ground level, too high for any of them to climb. Standing across from them, the droid chasing Anna and a third machine hovered a few feet away, guns trained on them.

How many of these things are there?

"Against the wall with your friends," the closest droid said in a human-like but heavily synthesized voice.

Peter stumbled backward, cringing as his shoulders banged on the coarse, brick wall. The droid that had been chasing Peter hovered around the corner and fell in line next to its two counterparts. Each stood across from its human prisoner.

In unison, the droids hummed. Peter knew what would happen next. The humming would grow louder, and then a click would indicate they were ready to fire. He reached out and grabbed Anna's hand. In a split second, every moment they would have had the rest of their lives flashed in his head. Traveling through time together, discovering history, living out their future with their kids, their grandkids and growing old; it was all just a dream. A tear fell from his eye.

She turned her body toward the wall and put her hands over her face. Her fingers shook against her trembling chin. Peter inched toward her until they were shoulder to shoulder.

Keep fighting. It can't end this way!

Peter closed his eyes and put his arm around her. This was it. This was how things would end for them and all humanity. It was over. A white light glowed behind them. He flinched at the sound of the click. In an instant, it would be over.

Do something!

Zach jumped in front of Peter and Anna. With his arms and legs spread wide, he rocked on both feet.

"Stop!" he screamed.

Peter and Anna spun. They stared at Zach. Was he giving up his life for them? Did they have time to run? Peter looked at the impaired droid across from him. Its infrared light had been destroyed. Occasionally it bobbled as if it were having a hard time staying afloat. He could probably get around the corner before it managed to fire, but could Anna? What about Zach? Would he know to run?

Two spiny legs grabbed Zach's collar, lifted him a few feet into the air and pulled him close. The droid's red light scanned him from his head to his dangling feet. It hesitated around his eyes, scanning them a few times. Slowly, the droid lowered Zach to the ground. He stepped backward and looked at Peter and Anna.

"What's going on?" Anna whispered.

Zach's eyes widened. He shook his head and shrugged. Each of the three droids simultaneously closed their gun ports and straightened their spiny legs. The bottoms of their legs twisted into four small, triangular metal feet. They descended to the ground, using their new feet as balance, and straightened, appearing to stand upright. Turning their heads to face Zach, they stood at attention.

Peter wiped his eyes and swiveled. He stepped toward Zach. Zach turned his wrist inward and showed Peter his palm. Peter stopped. Anna approached but stopped beside Peter when she saw Zach's hand.

"Hello, Leader. What should we do with your prisoners?" the center droid inquired.

Chapter 29

Peter, 2022

"Leader?" Zach froze.

Peter's head fell against the wall. He closed his eyes and exhaled. Anna put her arm around him, grazing her fingers across his back. He recoiled. She quickly pulled away and examined her palm.

"You're bleeding," she said, biting her lip. "Are you okay?"

"It's not as bad as it looks," Peter said, forcing a smile across his face.

Zach looked over his shoulder at the duo and shrugged. "What do we do?"

"Without Padma, how do we get info about the Event?" Anna whispered.

"I don't know. A library, maybe?" Peter said. "There has to be something around here that will tell us what happened."

"We await your orders, sir," the center droid said.

"Guys. What do I say?" Zach asked.

"The library was probably destroyed with everything else," Anna continued, her voice still at a whisper. "Who knows how they portray history in this version of the future?"

"Sir?" the droid repeated.

It was obviously a human talking through the droid, guiding it. The voice rising at the end of the question gave it away. The way the droids were programmed to patrol the streets on their own with someone able to take over when needed was familiar to Peter.

Where have you heard this before?

"Take me to the...um," Zach paused and turned to face the three droids. Beads of sweat rolled down his neck. His hands shook. "The library?"

"Good, sir. Shall we escort the prisoners to your home and cage them?"

"No," Zach said. "They're with me."

The first droid hovered to the front. Its red light scanned the road ahead. Zach walked behind it, followed by Peter and Anna. The last two droids took the rear. One turned its infrared light on to scan, but thanks to Peter, the other couldn't. Simultaneously, as if someone were controlling the machines in a video game, the droid with the shattered light fell in behind Peter and Anna. The third droid hovered to the center of the street and lined up at the rear. Its head spun in a circle, scanning the entire street with its light.

Once they turned on Long Street, they moved into the middle of the road. Parking garages on each side had been demolished. Piles of debris made the sidewalks impassable.

Third Street was the worst of anything they'd seen so far. Entire apartment complexes lining both sides had been leveled, but the street was empty of debris. Large holes were all that remained.

"What happened here?" Zach asked.

"Do you not remember, sir?" the droid in the front asked.

"It was a long time ago," Zach said, his voice more monotone and in charge now. "Refresh my memory."

That's how he sounded under that hood at Ceremony, Peter thought. His knees locked and he tripped, almost falling to the ground

"You okay?" Anna whispered, moving closer and taking his hand in hers.

"Yeah, I'm fine. I must have hit a crack in the road or something."

"People were attempting to live here," The droid continued, "and repopulate, but you weren't allowing it. They had to live on the outskirts of the city like everyone else. You had everything torn down and disposed of, including anyone who didn't comply."

Zach turned to Peter; his eyes filled with tears. He whispered, "What happened to me?"

Anna put a hand on his shoulder and squeezed.

"We'll figure it out," Peter said.

THE NEXT HALF MILE was no different than anything Peter had seen during his time in this new version of Columbus. Destruction and rubble crowded both sides of the street. When they finally stood in front of the library, Zach, Peter and Anna stopped to stare. The rectangular structure stood five stories high, made mostly of glass and metal. The bottom floor was the widest, with the top four floors seeming to rise from the center.

Dark windows on the first floor offered no clues as to how many people were inside, but as the moon occasionally showed through gaps in the clouds, the top four floors appeared open, with books lining shelves that wrapped around all four walls.

"Is this new?" Anna wondered. "I came here a few times while I was in college. It didn't look like this."

"When was this built?" Zach said.

"In 2020, on the first anniversary of your rule," a droid said.

Zach walked past the lead droid toward the sliding double doors. Lights above the doors flickered and went on, illuminating the entrance. Each door slid open. Two droids floated toward the front corner of the building, each taking a side. The third hovered to the roof and activated the red light. Its head spun in a circle, keeping watch on all sides.

"I bet they're programmed to protect you," Peter said.

Zach walked through the doors, and Peter and Anna followed close behind. Once inside, Peter stopped and looked up. Large wooden shelves behind protective glass climbed the walls from the second floor to the top, except there weren't any actual floors. It was one large, open building.

Everything became blurred. Peter lowered his head to ward off the dizziness he felt. Using a shiny metal trash can to steady himself, he squeezed his eyes closed and reopened them. Ahead of him, sixteen small round tables in a four-by-four grid filled the center, each holding a computer monitor, a keyboard and a mouse.

"You okay?" Anna asked, putting her hand on his shoulder.

"Yeah," he mumbled. "I feel like I should be printing my boarding pass at the airport."

"I don't get it," Anna said. "How do we read anything if they are all encased behind glass?"

Zach moved a mouse attached to a computer on the table closest to him. The screen saver fell away. A single white search bar against a black background appeared. The cursor blinked, waiting for someone to enter text.

"Over here," he said. He pulled the keyboard forward. Peter and Anna stood next to him. "What should I type?"

"Try the Event," Peter said.

One result appeared on the screen. It was a picture of a black book about the size of a hotel Bible. The word Genesis was printed on the cover in gold letters. Zach clicked the button marked Retrieve.

On the far wall, a machine vibrated. A small tray moved along the bottom row of books, stopping at an empty column. Following a track, it climbed the wall until it was a few rows from the top. It shifted again, this time moving right and stopping in front of a book that matched the picture on the screen.

The book lurched forward and fell into the tray. Reversing its direction, the tray rode along the track to the bottom row, slid past its original starting spot and stopped behind a wooden slot, large enough for the book to slide through. Next to the door on a small console, the size of a deck of playing cards, a small, blinking red light flashed. An image of a fingerprint blinked red and black in the center of the console.

Peter pushed his thumb against the fingerprint image. A loud buzzer sounded. The tray sped away from the slot and headed back toward the shelf where the book was originally located.

"No, wait!" Peter cried.

Zach reached around Peter, nudging him out of his way, and jammed his thumb to the console. For an instant, the room fell silent. They looked at the tray sliding across the top shelf, holding their breath, afraid to move. When it stopped and reversed position, bringing the book back, they all exhaled. Peter and Anna looked at Zach.

"I had a hunch," Zach said, shrugging his shoulders.

The door slid open. Peter grabbed the book and took it to the closest table. He pushed the keyboard aside and opened the book to the middle. Zach and Anna gathered around the table next to him.

He leafed through it until he found a picture of a large supercomputer filling a page. It was a large series of drives, power stations and loose wires attaching everything together. On the side of one of the black towers, someone had stenciled the letter T in gold.

"Of course, that's the first page you stop at," Anna said.

Peter glanced at her, smiled and inspected the hardware. Nothing about it seemed familiar.

Anna read the caption under the picture, "Talbot."

"What is Talbot?" Zach said.

"Did you say Talbot?" Peter asked. He read the caption, "How can that be?"

"Why? What is Talbot?" Anna looked confused. "Do you know it?"

Alarms inside the building blared in a deafening, high-pitched screech. Peter stood rigid. He slammed the book closed and dropped it into his backpack. Anna covered her ears and bent over, resting her right cheek on the table. She squeezed her eyes closed and scrunched her face. Zach stumbled backward, running into a chair from the next table.

Lights flickered and shut off, surrounding them in blackness. Peter turned his head both ways, looking for any sign of light that could show an escape route.

"What do we do?" Anna's shouting was barely audible over the alarms.

Each monitor buzzed and turned on, lighting the room around them. Large black text blinked against a white background.

They are coming. Get out now.

Chapter 30

Peter, 2022

Zach sprinted past Peter and Anna, bouncing off the tables like a pinball. A monitor tumbled to the ground and crashed next to Peter's feet. Zach stopped in front of the automatic exit doors, but they didn't move. He grabbed each door where they met in the center and tried to force them open but failed.

"We're locked in!" he yelled. "They locked us in!"

Peter maneuvered around the tables and stopped next to Zach. He rubbed the back of his neck and looked around. The monitors were too small. The tables were bolted to the floor. A glint of light caught his eye. He furrowed his brow and lunged toward the three-foot-tall metal trash can he had used to balance himself after entering the building. He lifted it, took a running start and smashed it against the doors, shattering the glass.

Zach moved toward the door, but Peter held him back. He jerked the backpack from his shoulder, wrapped it around his fist and punched the stray jagged glass still hanging from the corners to the ground. He jumped through the wide opening followed by Anna and Zach, who snatched the trash can on his way through the door.

Two droids guarding each corner of the library converged on the trio. Peter and Anna ran to the sidewalk along the left side of the street, but Zach didn't move. One droid turned and chased Peter and Anna, while the second leaned forward and sped toward Zach. He turned his head slightly and watched as the droid approached. Like a batter just before he hits a long home run, he lifted the garbage can and turned his feet, opening his stance. The droid was just five feet away. Zach's jaw tightened. A thin smile formed in the corners of his mouth.

The droid hummed, its gun barrels glowing white. Zach's expression didn't change. His fear had disappeared.

He spun, lifting the garbage can into the air, and smashed it against the hovering droid's body. Sparks flew from the machine's head. Its sizzling metal body lurched and its central leg, dragging along the sidewalk, snapped at the knee, throwing it through a library glass window. The remaining skinny metal legs hung over the window frame, dangling and twitching above the sidewalk. Zach flung the can aside and walked toward the droid. He stood over it, staring for a few seconds, then ran after his friends.

Peter ducked into a dark alley. A collection of pallets stacked ten feet high against the wall caught his eye. Scanning the alley, it was the only solid structure they could use as a hiding place. It wasn't much, but it would have to do. He crouched behind the pallets, using the opening between each to keep an eye on the entrance. Anna kneeled next to him, putting her hand on the center of his back, below where the droid had sliced him earlier.

Another droid entered the alley and turned on its infrared light. Using the same grid pattern, it scanned across the entrance, moved closer by a few feet and swept back the other way. The droid that had been watching from the roof hovered overhead. White light from its underside gave Peter and Anna a view of what lay behind them, at the back of the alley. Buildings on each side looked like they had survived the Event. Only their roofs had suffered. Piles of busted red brick lay scattered throughout the street. A green dumpster, overflowing with leaking black garbage bags, had been pushed against the back wall of a building one block over, closing off the alley.

"Dead end that way," Anna said, looking over her shoulder.

"What about that dumpster?"

The droid from the roof dropped next to the dumpster. Its red light kicked on and panned back and forth.

"There goes that," Peter said.

"Why aren't they firing?" Anna whispered.

"Maybe they can only fire if they have a target. They know we're here. They just don't know where."

The droids moved closer to Peter and Anna after every sweep, giving Peter the impression that the walls were closing in on them. He lowered his head, closed his eyes and slowed his breathing. He felt Anna's hands pressing against his back. Her presence calmed him. He opened his eyes.

"We're going to have to run for it," he said.

She put her hand on his shoulder, crouched with her back foot pushed into the wall, ready to spring.

"Just say when," she said.

The red light of the first droid swept in front of Peter, while the second droid's light moved along the ground behind Anna.

Just like in those prison-break movies, where the prisoner watches the lights and moves through the darkness like he's playing Frogger.

"Hang on," Peter said.

"It's getting close," Anna said, eyeing the light behind her.

He watched the red light, timing it. It swept across the space in front of him giving the opening they needed.

"Go!" he yelled.

Anna sprang first. She emerged through the entrance, almost colliding with Zach, and made a hard left toward the library. Zach spun and ran after her with Peter hot on their heels. Both droids stopped, and their heads spun. Their red lights flashed to the exit and caught Peter just as he turned in the direction Anna had run. The machines rocked forward and exited the alley, bathing the trio in their red lights.

Peter, last in the line, heard the humming sound of the droid behind him.

"It's gonna shoot!" he called out. "Cross the street!"

Still leading the pack, Anna jumped the curb to the street. Zach followed. Peter ran. His legs ached. His right ankle twisted a little as he hit the street, sending pain into his foot. The slice in his back felt like it was ripping wider with each step. He dug deep and ran harder. He was approaching Zach, the high school track star. He was going to pass him. The humming stopped. Peter stumbled and looked over his shoulder.

The droid had slowed down and straightened. Its gun barrel clicked, and the two silver cannons glowed white.

"Get down now!" Peter yelled.

Instinctively, the trio dropped to the ground. Anna had already slowed and found a spot behind a long wooden awning, still partially attached to a restaurant. The other half of the awning was resting on the sidewalk, giving her a small barrier to deflect flying debris.

The sound of the explosion filled the street. Zach's foot caught the edge of the sidewalk. He tripped and hit the ground, landing on his back. His momentum rolled him into the remnants of a shoe store.

White smoke filled Peter's lungs. He grabbed his throat and bent at the waist, wheezing and coughing. He narrowed his eyes, straining to find the sidewalk or his friends, but the smoke was too thick. The buildings ahead were still standing. *The droid must have missed.*

Peter turned to find it. White smoke flowed from its neck. Its head hung to one side, attached by a single wire swinging it a few inches above the ground. It shook, made noises like a dying vacuum cleaner and toppled into the street. The droid's head detached, and it shot toward the library.

Behind it, the third droid stood, hovering just above the ground. Smoke flowed from its gun barrels.

"What just happened?" Zach yelled. "Did one shoot the other?"

As if it had heard him, the third droid spun and hovered toward them. The humming sound started but abruptly stopped. A split second later, it started again. Peter ran toward Zach's voice and found Anna. He crouched beside her.

"Something's wrong with it," Peter said. "Like it's fighting itself."

A vehicle slammed through the wreckage of the second droid, throwing busted metal into the air at the third, knocking it to the ground. The droid regained its balance, floated high into the air and turned toward the vehicle.

A bright-yellow van skidded to a stop next to Peter. Metal plates covered the side windows and tires. A makeshift battering ram, built by putting two pieces of metal together to form a triangle, was attached to the front bumper. The moon roof, replaced by a round steel manhole cover, popped open and a familiar face rose from the center of the van. She wore sunglasses and held two shotguns, one in each hand at her sides, like something out of a science fiction movie.

"Padma?" Peter cried.

"Get down!" she told him.

The final droid floated above her and continued toward Peter, Anna and Max. Its guns glowed white. Padma pushed her back against the opening, braced herself and swung both guns into the air. When the barrels reached their apex, she pulled the triggers. The recoil pushed her arms into the air until the shotguns were pointing straight behind her.

The final droid exploded, sending shrapnel in all directions. Padma ducked into the van. Peter, Anna and Zach crouched against the van as close to the ground as they could, using their hands and arms to cover their heads. After a few seconds, Padma appeared next to them.

"Let's go," she said.

Chapter 31

Peter, 2022

Padma turned the steering wheel and sped away before Peter was fully inside the car. He stood on a small, round platform that vibrated under his feet as it slowly lowered him to the floor. Once it stopped, he squeezed between Anna and Zach, onto a wooden bench where the back seat should have been.

"More will come if we don't get out of here now," Padma said.

"Yeah, we've heard that before from you," Peter mumbled.

Padma swiveled the driver's seat and looked at the three people huddled behind her. She studied each of them one by one, spun around and faced front.

The inside of the car had been completely gutted and rebuilt. The front seats swiveled, enabling someone in the front to jump quickly in and out. A wooden bench built into the trunk area created a large open space behind the seats. A round metallic lift, the size of a frisbee, moved people through a hatch in a reinforced steel roof.

Padma sped through the city streets, occasionally steering into dark alleys to avoid heavy debris areas. With each rapid turn, the trio in the back seat leaned against each other. Peter tucked his bag into his lap and held on to the door handle.

"Where are we going this time?" Peter asked.

"To my compound."

"You have a compound?"

"What do you mean by 'this time'?" Padma wanted to know.

"What?"

"You said 'this time' as if we've been through this before."

"We have," Peter said.

Padma yanked the steering wheel hard, spinning 180 degrees. She was quickly back on the gas pedal, throwing them against the makeshift cushion on the walls. The car lurched forward. Explosions erupted behind them.

"Something hit us!" Peter cried.

"Two more droids," Padma said. "Their shots can't get through the metal, but we can't take much more."

She turned the car onto State Street and mashed the accelerator to the floor.

"Can we outrun them?" Anna asked.

"No. The minute I get far enough away, they float above the buildings, find us and catch up."

"Seems like cheating," Zach muttered.

"Peter, when I stop this car, I need you to jump into the driver's seat and head straight for them like you're playing chicken and you have no plans on losing."

She spun the car, faced it toward the approaching droids and hit the brakes. The car skidded to a stop. White smoke temporarily hid the car from the droids. Padma jumped into the passenger seat. Peter handed Anna his backpack and moved into the vacated driver's seat. When the smoke cleared, two droids appeared on the horizon and floated toward them. They lowered into the street and tilted forward, hastening their approach.

"Go!" Padma yelled.

Peter accelerated. Padma rotated her seat to face Anna and Zach, grabbed her shotguns and leaped toward the platform. She steadied herself against the hatch and leaned forward, watching the droids through the front windshield.

"Four blocks away," she mumbled.

"What do I do?" Peter yelled.

"Just keep going. Drive under them."

Three blocks away. Peter pushed the pedal to the floor, jerking Padma off balance. She bounced to her feet, threw her hands against the hatch and kicked the lever with her foot. The floor pulsated and rose into the air.

"They're too low!" Peter said.

"Keep going!"

One block away. Her head and chest disappeared into the night. Two shotguns fired. Explosions echoed through the street. When the platform retracted and her face appeared, she was smiling.

"I love doing that," she said.

Anna laughed. "Who *are* you?"

"It's a long story."

Padma took her seat next to Peter and pointed at an on-ramp. "Take 40 West. The compound is about twenty minutes outside of town. We'll be safe there."

Padma rotated the seat and faced Zach and Anna.

"So, tell me, how did the three of you end up in the middle of Columbus, inside the Sacred Library, when no one has seen you in five years?"

Peter looked into the rearview mirror, meeting Anna's eyes.

Again, with the five years?

"And you," Padma continued, pointing a shotgun at Zach. "I'm especially interested in hearing your story."

Anna's eyes held Peter's, again reading his mind.

We should probably get right to the point this time. No hiding anything. It's the only way we'll get answers.

"We're from 2017," Anna said.

"How come you don't live in the same spot where you lived last time?" Peter asked.

"Tell me about that. I have these spots in my brain that show a basement I lived in at some point, but I don't know when," Padma said. "I can't make any sense of it."

Peter and Anna told Padma about the first time they time traveled. Her face brightened when they talked about the Gates of Hell.

"Yeah, those memories are slowly coming back. Plus, it sounds exactly like something I would do."

Zach cut in, talking of when he'd entered the story, and Padma listened without interruption. When they finished, she remained quiet for a few seconds and then confirmed something Peter and Anna were hoping to hear.

"I'm confident you two didn't cause this."

Peter smiled, and Anna wiped a tear from her eye.

"But I think you may have...um...expedited the inevitable."

They lifted their heads and stared at her.

"What does that mean?" Anna said. "What specifically happened?"

"No one really knows. It was May twenty-sixth, 2019, a normal workday— and right at noon, just as everyone was heading to lunch, everything exploded."

"Everything?" Zach said.

"Everything. The entire world. Every major city, minor city, village, township, you name it, it all went up in flames." She turned toward Zach. Her eyes went cold, and her tone deepened. "Everything, O Glorious Leader. And somehow, you're involved."

"Don't call me that," Zach said. "I had nothing to do with this."

"We don't know the specifics of what happened, and I've been trying to figure it out," she went on. "I thought I could stop it, but I failed. Now I'm trying to make things right."

"You said we were missing," Anna said. "What does that mean? We're not missing."

"As of the time of the Event, no one had seen either of you for over two years. In fact, I think the last time anyone saw you was the night of your first date. You didn't come into work the next day. I grabbed Buddy later that night."

Peter interrupted. "So that's how you had him the first time."

"Don't worry. I have him now too."

"How did you get into my house?" Peter asked.

She chuckled. "I've been breaking into your house for months, Peter. Who do you think taught Buddy all those tricks? I love that dog just as much as you do."

"Why are you breaking into my house?"

She gazed at each of them, holding Zach's eyes the longest, and stopped at Peter. "I'm from the future, sent to find you. I've been trying to stop this whole thing—and the people above me, the ones who sent me here, think you're the key."

Peter leaned forward in the seat. A rush of adrenaline surged through him. His heart raced.

"The police gave up searching for both of you after a few days," Padma said. She turned to Anna. "Especially with what happened to your father. He's a sweet man, by the way."

"What?" Anna said.

"But the public didn't give up. You have a lot of friends. They formed search parties, offered rewards, created billboards, anything they could do to find you. At first, the police became sure you were connected to a larger crime, especially with what they found at work the next morning—a record of you being there in the middle of the night, some pretty nasty stuff. Serial killings, cults and other dark things. You know how the internet can be."

"Serial killings?" Peter said. "What are you talking about?"

"But your friends and family overwhelmed them. Enough people came forward for both of you to squash most of the more outrageous theories."

Peter's eyes caught Anna's. Her cheeks flushed, and she smiled.

"Then, the Event happened. I ran home and grabbed my go-bag," Padma said.

"Your what?" Zach asked.

"It's a bag you keep with supplies in case of an emergency, and you need to run quick," Anna explained. "My dad always kept one. He always said, 'Everyone should always be prepared for the worst.'"

"People tried to escape into the rural areas where things weren't as bad," Padma continued. "But there just wasn't enough space available, and in the chaos, more people died. It was ugly those first few weeks. But then the droids showed up. Hundreds of them took people for what seemed to be no rhyme or reason. Luckily, they didn't know who I was."

"Who are you?" Anna asked.

Padma ignored the question. "A few days later..." She paused and looked at Zach. "He showed up."

Zach shuddered.

"And you announced that Ceremony would happen weekly. Punishments would be handed out to those deemed to be acting against the good of the population." She paused again and looked at Peter. "Wait. You're from 2017. Do you still have your bracelet?"

Peter looked in the rearview mirror at Anna. Zach glanced at the bag tucked in her lap. Padma grabbed the bag. She pulled a pistol from her waist and pointed it at Zach.

"What are you doing?" Peter said. "We're on the same side."

"Maybe. But I don't know who's side *he's* on."

Chapter 32

Peter, 2022

"We saw him too," Peter said. "On the stage. But this guy here, he's not the bad guy, not yet. We don't know what happened. We came here to figure it out and try to stop it."

"So, he wasn't in charge the first time you were here, but then you told him about it, brought him here, and now he's in charge."

Padma sounded cold, different from the person who had filled in a few of the blanks just minutes earlier. She was still just as tough. Carrying two shotguns fearlessly and facing those droids made that clear, but her curiosity had disappeared. It was as if she knew the trio had nothing left to offer, and now she was all business.

"Yeah, that's how it happened," Peter said. She had to see his point of view—see they could still change things before it all went wrong.

"Seems like I can't trust you to keep your ability to travel through time a secret," Padma said. "It's better if I decide how it will be used from now on."

Peter opened his mouth to speak, but Padma raised her gun.

"Listen—" Her voice softened. "I like you. Both of you. You were good friends from work, welcoming me even though

I replaced your best friend, and I appreciate that. But something else is going on here, and I have a society to save. And that's bigger than the two of you. When we get to the compound, I'll show you around, and you can decide what you want to do. If you want to leave, I'll help you go back. But for now, I need time to work this out."

"What about me?" Zach said.

Peter looked into the rearview mirror, waiting for Anna's eyes to meet his. When they did, she nodded.

"Okay," Peter said.

"Hello?" Zach called out. "I'm here too."

Peter drove the next few miles in silence, watching the landscape. Smaller one-story businesses with little to no damage replaced the miles of destroyed skyscrapers. As the speed limit dropped and the street narrowed, most of the houses they passed were equally whole. Candles at their windows formed a lit path just behind the sidewalk. Peter used it like a pilot aligning the plane with the lights of the runway.

"People live in these houses?" Peter asked.

"He allowed most people outside the city to stay, but he seized anything they had of value," Padma said. "It was the tradeoff."

Once they left the city, shanty towns with makeshift one-room buildings not much bigger than a ten-year-old's tree house had replaced endless rows of corn. The corners of Peter's mouth dropped. As a kid, his mom would take him there for haunted hayrides and community trick-or-treating, but it had all been wiped away by an event he might have caused.

Farther along, it was obvious to Peter they were entering the poorest of the rural communities. Hundreds of tents formed neighborhoods resembling hobo camps. People loitered outside their tents, most of them sitting in small groups around campfires.

"The tents are the worst," Padma said. "I stayed in one after it happened. No one cares about the people living in these conditions."

"How does anyone get food?" Peter asked.

"Deliveries of basic needs, things like bread, corn and rice, arrive once a week. He sends them to the houses first, then to the smaller communities. Whatever is left is dumped in a pile in front of the tents. It's never enough for everyone, and they're expected to ration properly, so the delivery lasts the whole week."

"What if it doesn't?" Anna asked.

"Early on, it never did. He sent droids out. They took anyone who complained or caused trouble. That forced us to work out a system quickly."

"Why don't the people get together and rebel?"

"We're working on it, but most of the people are too scared. They could lose their family, their food supply, or worse, they may end up as his guest on stage at Ceremony."

Peter shuddered. He looked at Anna in the mirror. She clasped her hands together and stared at him.

"Up here." Padma pointed through the windshield using the barrel of the gun. "Go left."

Peter slowed and turned onto a narrow road in the middle of a cornfield with stalks tall enough to shield them from viewers outside of their row.

"Where does this corn go?" he asked.

"It all goes to him," Padma said, nodding toward Zach. "And he distributes it as he sees fit."

"It's not me, Goddammit!"

Padma spun around and faced forward. "Slow down. Get ready to turn up here."

"Where?"

"See that old runway? This used to be one of those small regional airports, but no one had used it for years before the Event. It's a good hiding spot. When you get to the end, turn right, and you'll see a tunnel."

Following her directions, he pulled off the runway. The car dropped a few inches into the grass. A hundred yards ahead, the ground trembled. Peter felt he was seeing a sinkhole develop as he watched the far end of the grassy area fall away to reveal a ramp leading underground. Thirty feet down, the ramp leveled out onto a solid dirt path, four car-lengths wide. Peter slowed but kept driving forward.

Large floodlights hung from a wire, near the top of the dirt walls, giving Peter a better view of the tunnel. It was almost a perfect rectangle. Whoever had created this had taken great care in carving each wall.

"Look!" Anna cried.

Up ahead, spotlights from the ceiling lit up the tunnel, revealing the side of a metallic warehouse. Peter pulled his foot off the accelerator. Four guards carrying automatic weapons over their shoulders stood between two garage doors, large enough for semis to drive through. One of them turned and put up his hand, waving Peter toward the door on the left.

"What is this place?" Anna asked.

"They built it during the Cold War," Padma said. "It was created to shelter the people deemed important in the city. It was built exactly twenty-two minutes from town, to give them enough time to get to their escape vehicles and drive here before everything went up in flames."

As Peter reached the door, another guard lifted his hand. Peter stopped the car. The man peered through the front windshield and raised his gun.

"No sudden moves," Padma said.

"Yeah, I wasn't planning on it," Peter muttered.

Padma threw Peter's bag over her shoulder, climbed from the passenger seat and stood on the platform in front of Anna and Zach. She kicked the lever. The platform lifted her toward the ceiling, her hands pushing the hatch open as she rose.

The guards, three men and one woman, listened as Padma spoke. Each of them was tall, at least six feet—including the woman, who was the tallest of the four. Two men were clean-shaven, while the third sported a thick gray mustache connected to bushy sideburns that gave him the look of someone straight out of the Civil War. They were dressed alike, wearing blue jeans and green collared shirts. Each wore a baseball cap, also green.

Are they trying to put together some kind of uniform?

Peter couldn't make out what anyone was saying, but the guards lowered their weapons. The guard with the sideburns pushed a button on the wall, and the door opened upwards. He waved for Peter to pull the car inside. Peter slowly let off the brake pedal and coasted the armored vehicle into the building.

The platform holding Padma lowered her into the car.

"Stop it there and cut the engine," she instructed.

Padma was the first to exit, followed by Peter, Anna and Zach.

"Take them to Tina's room."

"Yes ma'am," Sideburns said. He turned to the trio. "Come with me."

He led them into a long, narrow hallway with white walls and wooden doors spaced about twelve feet apart. The first set of doors they passed were painted green. The next set had a blue door on one side and a yellow door across from it. The next four doors they passed were red, followed by a pair painted pink and green.

"What's the deal with all the colors?" Zach asked.

"Shut up," the guard said.

"I guess I'm the asshole, then," Zach mumbled.

The next door had been painted black, a shoddy job, with the original pink color streaked along the top and bottom. Sideburns stuck a key inside the lock, and after fiddling with it for a few seconds, the door opened. He pushed the trio inside and pulled the door shut, locking it behind them.

"Take it easy!" Zach complained after taking the brunt of the man's strength.

Peter walked to the center and looked around. It was set up like a child's room. A bunk bed occupied one wall near a sliding door, assumed to be a closet. Two pillows lay next to a new quilt and sheet still in their plastic packages. On top of the pillows were two folded pillowcases.

Opposite the bed, a desk and chair were squeezed against the wall next to a dresser. Not a speck of dust was to be found anywhere. The furniture was crisp white. The walls were light blue, with a mural of a yellow sun spraying down rays of sunlight onto fluffy clouds. A cluster of buildings of all shapes and sizes were painted along the bottom of the wall, looking like the Columbus skyline before the Event had left it in darkness.

"What's the with artwork?" Zach said.

Peter shrugged.

"Whose room did he say it was?" Anna asked.

"Someone named Tina," Peter replied.

He slid the door near the bed open and stuck his head inside. The closet was deeper than he expected, with a door on the far end facing the other way, most likely leading to the next room. He grabbed the handle and pulled, but someone had locked it from the other side.

Anna looked at an open textbook on the desk. She flipped the switch at the base of a small pink lamp and fumbled through a spiral notebook lying next to it.

"Looks like she's studying math," Anna said.

"I hope we're not here when she comes back," Peter remarked.

A loose piece of paper slid to the floor at Anna's feet. She grabbed it and read it. "I don't think we need to worry about that."

She handed the paper to Peter. It looked similar to the fliers Peter had seen on Padma's table the first time she had rescued them from the droids. His eyes went to the large font printed across the top. He saw Tina's name, and the confusion on his face was replaced by disgust. He crumpled the paper into a ball and threw it across the room.

"Why would they pick a fifteen-year-old for Ceremony? What could she possibly have done to deserve that?"

"Now what?" Zach said. "We can't stay locked up in here. They think I caused all this. They'll probably throw me in front of a firing squad."

"I don't know," Peter said. "I guess we wait to see what happens next."

"You think Padma will hurt us?" Anna asked.

"I doubt it," Peter said. "She said we would have the chance to go home if we wanted to."

"I want to," Anna said.

"Me too."

"Maybe she'll let the two of you leave," Zach pointed out, "but I'm not so sure about me."

Veins bulged in Zach's neck. His hands balled into fists and trembled. He ran to the door and pounded, rattling the door each time his fists made contact.

"Let me out!" he yelled.

"Zach, calm down," Peter said. He grabbed his friend's arm and pulled him away from the door. "Just like I said, we watch each other's backs. We're not dead yet."

"Dude, you heard her. They, whoever 'they' are, sent Padma to watch you. Not me! She probably got me fired and took my job just to be closer to you."

The door burst open. Peter and Zach turned toward the man who walked in, his gun drawn. Anna stepped back, hitting the wall beside the desk.

"She's ready to see you now."

Zach stepped forward.

"Just them," the man said, waving the gun between Peter and Anna.

"What about me?"

"She'll deal with you later." The man's tone changed to mockery as he added, "O Glorious Leader."

"Deal with me? What does that even mean?"

Peter and Anna exited the room. He turned to comfort his friend, slipping the phone into Zach's open hand.

"Hang on to this," Peter whispered. "We can't go anywhere without it."

Zach shoved it into his back pocket and stepped away from the door. The man pulled the door shut. Peter flinched at the sound of the deadbolt slipping into its slot in the doorframe and looked over his shoulder.

He put the key in his shirt pocket.

The man led them down the hallway and around a corner. This time, a few of the doors were open. In one room, a woman sat reading to four children on the floor. In another, two young boys played with little green army soldiers, using their forces to attack each other. In a third, a teenage girl read at a desk.

"What are you all doing here?" Peter asked.

"Sorry, need-to-know basis," the man said flatly without looking at them.

Anna took Peter's hand, intertwining her fingers through his. He gave her hand a squeeze and offered a thin smile, hoping to reassure her. Stepping out of the hallway, they moved into a large cafeteria, similar to a buffet-style restaurant. Five rows of four tables filled the middle of the dining area.

"Enough for around a hundred and sixty people," Peter whispered into Anna's ear.

Peter watched two men in their early twenties enter the food line. Shelves built into the walls held trays of food. One man grabbed a tray with a plate of chicken and green beans.

The second man took fish and corn. They moved to a dessert station. Small individual paper plates of cakes and pies gave them a variety of choices.

"What do you think today?" one man asked.

"It's Thursday, Mike. You know I always go for apple on Thursday."

They grabbed their desserts and continued to a water dispenser. Stacks of plastic cups sat next to the dispenser, but they had brought their own water bottle. At the end of the line, they stopped and handed a cashier a small plastic card. She waved it in front of a card reader until it beeped with an approving sound.

"Only eight dollars left on here for you, David," she said.

"Yeah. I've taken a few days off, but I have some double shifts coming up that should load me up."

She smiled and nodded to him, gently handing the card back.

"Quite the system you have here," Peter said to the man, who continued to ignore him.

The guard led Peter and Anna through a doorway on the opposite side of the cafeteria and into another hallway. Peter glanced inside one of the open rooms revealing an office similar to his own. Another space reminded Peter of his networking room. A rack of servers hummed. A younger woman, probably in her early twenties, was sipping coffee and typing at a keyboard. She looked at Peter and quickly looked away.

"You have your own network here?" Peter asked. "How does it stay powered and connected without detection?"

The man stopped at the next office, opened the door and ushered them inside. Padma sat behind a desk, with Peter's backpack resting in front of her. His machine, still connected to the attachment that had enabled Zach to travel with them, was next to it. Two chairs were pushed under the desk across from her. Peter's old laptop was open and connected to twelve monitors hanging on the wall; each image moved through the city.

"You had them connected to the droids the first time we met," Peter said.

"Please come in and sit but I need a second to finish sending this message."

The man pulled the door shut as he left, leaving Peter and Anna alone with Padma. They stood with their backs against the door.

"Speaking of the first time we met, I have more questions. Please come and sit. You really have nothing to be afraid of. I will honor the deal I made with you in the car."

Extending her legs, she pushed out both chairs with her feet. Peter sat in the chair next to the wall closest to his bag. Anna sat to his left.

"You created an office similar to the room you had that first time," Peter said.

"About that. Help me fill in some details. I can't seem to work out what made things change. I find it hard to believe that telling Zach would have such a big effect. You must have mentioned it to someone else."

"I may have freaked out a little that night and told a group of online friends who were trying to work out time travel," Peter said. He grimaced and swallowed. "But that group is anonymous, so I don't see how that could have affected anything else."

Padma laughed. "Yeah, I remember that."

Peter pushed himself away from the desk and stared at her. "What do you mean?"

Padma smiled and punched a few keys on the laptop. The monitor hanging on the wall closest to Peter and Anna shifted to a text-based chat room. He recognized the GROUP window. Across the top, he read the message.

You are logged in as elfGlimmer.

Peter stood up too quickly, felt dizzy and lightheaded, and reached for the edge of the desk. The blood drained from his face. Every conversation he had had in the middle of the night with elfGlimmer, marymary and lightninggirl flooded his memory.

"You're elfGlimmer? You've been in GROUP this whole time? Working with us? And breaking into my house?"

She pursed her lips and gave an apologetic nod.

"Why me? You showed up in GROUP months before I even finished the machine. How did you even know who I was?"

"I told you, I'm from the future. You're the reason they sent me back. To find you. To wait until you figured out how to make your time machine work, take it and use it to fix things. The minute you asked me to write that app, I suspected you were close."

"But I've been using it for almost a year. Why haven't you taken it yet?"

"Peter, you take that bag everywhere you go—and as part of my orders, I'm not allowed to harm you."

"That's comforting," Peter said. "Your orders?"

"Thinking back, my commander put more emphasis on me not hurting Anna, which I always felt was odd since I was looking for you. That's why I kept breaking into your house. If I couldn't take the machine from you, maybe I could build my own using your plans."

"I never wrote anything down," Peter lied. "I used the plans given to us in GROUP by Niven, and one day it just started working."

"How?"

"I have no clue. I was in the middle of testing it. I pushed the button, and it worked. It's worked ever since then."

Padma turned to Anna. "How did you find out about it?"

"We were on our first date. Everything was going well, really well actually, and out of nowhere, some guy started chasing our car, running into us, threatening us. We needed a quick escape."

"According to our history, when Peter divulged the machine to you is when everything changed. Maybe that's why you're just as important."

"Why?" Anna asked.

"That, we're not sure of. What happened when the two of you came back that first time after running into me?"

"I wasn't sure what to do next," Peter said. He pointed to Anna's leg. "She was injured, and I was scared. I needed someone to talk to. Someone who didn't know anything about it. I called Zach. He's been my best friend for years."

"You told Zach, and things changed again. They got worse."

"Looks like it," Peter said.

"He knows you are here right now, which means his future self, the asshole in charge, also knows you're here. You may be in danger. Stay with us for a little while until we can work something out. I have someone on the inside who's trying to help me take him down. Once that happens, we'll figure out what to do."

"But what is this place?" Anna asked. "What exactly are you doing here?"

"Trying to build an army."

Peter shook his head. "That sounds dangerous. People will die. Let us take the machine, and we'll go back and fix things."

"Too risky. Every time you tell someone or attempt to change things, the future gets worse. I'm taking control now. Give me your phone."

Peter reached into his back pockets, showing Padma his empty hands. He turned the pockets in the front of his pants inside out.

"I don't have it," Peter said, trying to fake a worried look. "I must have dropped it while we were running from those droids."

"Don't lie to me. I saw it in the car."

Peter opened his jacket and showed Padma his empty pockets. Padma reached under her desk and pressed a button. A buzzer outside the door sounded, and two men entered. Her hand disappeared behind the desk. He heard the creak of a drawer opening. When her hand reappeared, she was holding a small handgun. Peter and Anna stood.

"Search the other one," she said to the men. "Do whatever it takes. He should have at least one cell phone and maybe two. Bring me whatever you find."

"What are you going to do?" Anna said.

"Stop him from becoming the leader."

"But what if you're just making it worse? You said it might be my fault. You should let us fix it."

"Please," Peter begged. "There has to be another way."

Anna looked toward the time machine on the desk before Peter and stepped forward. Padma swiveled around and faced the monitors.

"I'm sorry, but I have a job to..."

Anna lifted her chair and heaved it toward Padma. Padma turned and raised her arms in the air to shield herself, but she wasn't fast enough. The arm of the chair grazed her shoulder and began to spin. The chair's back bounced against Padma's forehead. Blood streamed into her eyes. Crying out, Padma dropped the gun and crumbled into a heap on the floor behind the desk. Reaching across the desk, Peter grabbed his bag and the machine. He bumped into Anna, who snatched the gun and stuffed it into Peter's bag.

The door behind them flung open and slammed into the wall, rattling the monitors hanging. The two men, originally sent to get Zach, rushed into the small office. Peter dropped his bag and lunged, ramming his shoulder into the first man's chest. He grunted as all the air in his body was instantly expelled. The man tumbled backward into the second man, sending both through the open door and into the hallway. The second man banged into the office door opposite Padma's, jarring it open. He disappeared inside the room. The first man lay on the floor on his stomach, gasping for air. Anna grabbed Peter's bag and ran after him toward the cafeteria.

In the short time Peter and Anna had spent speaking with Padma, the cafeteria had filled with people. Men, women and children, all ages and sizes, stood in line, waiting for their chance to eat. The constant beeping of the card reader kept the lines moving, but they still ambled along slowly. Peter and Anna kept their heads down and their faces covered, squeezing through the lines. Once clear, they ran into the hallway toward Tina's room, where Zach was being held prisoner.

"Black door!" Anna yelled.

They rounded a corner. The black door was the second on their left. The man with the Civil-War sideburns was lying in front of the door, blocking the entrance. Sideburns' gun was tucked into his baggy pants, and he was groaning and clutching his stomach. He saw Peter running toward him, sat up and reached for his gun. His eye had turned dark purple, and blood coated his sideburns, slicking them against the side of his head. Whatever fight he had just been in, he appeared to have lost.

Peter dove, taking them both to the ground. They rolled a few feet from the door, and when they stopped, Peter lay on his back with Sideburns on top of him. Sideburns rose to his hands and knees, trapping Peter underneath. Blood dripped from his cheeks onto Peter's shirt. His snarling grin revealed missing teeth and blackened gums. His hot, foul breath hit Peter in the face like a brick. Peter recoiled and reached his hands behind his own head. He bent his knees and pushed against the floor with his feet, trying to free himself.

Padma's voice echoed down the hall. "Hold them!"

She rounded the corner, holding a bloodstained towel to her face, flanked by two more of her guards. These two were large men dressed in black suits and slicked-back dark hair resembling characters from a 1940s gangster movie. The second man had a large barbed-wire tattoo that may have originated from one shoulder, ran up one cheek, across his forehead and down the other side, and disappeared beneath his suit collar.

Anna reached into Peter's bag and pulled the gun she'd stolen from Padma just a few minutes earlier. She pointed it at Padma.

"We're leaving," Anna said.

"Come on," Padma said, "you're not going to shoot me."

Padma took a step toward Anna. The two men in the black suits stood their ground. Anna's arms trembled. She closed her eyes and pulled the trigger. The small recoil on the gun jerked her arms backward. The bullet shattered the wooden floor at Padma's feet. Padma stopped, raised her hands and stepped away. Sideburns loosened his grip on Peter and looked back over his shoulder.

"I may not miss next time," Anna said. "You want to take that chance?"

Peter scooted a few more inches. His finger touched the gun lying on the floor where Sideburns had dropped it. Peter lunged backward just enough to grab the weapon. Spinning back, he pushed the barrel into the big man's chest.

"Get off me," Peter ordered.

Sideburns climbed off Peter, not taking his eyes off the pistol in Peter's hand, and limped backward until he was standing next to Padma. Anna reached the door, holding the gun with one hand and feeling for the doorknob with the other. She turned the knob and pushed it open. Peter slipped in first, and Anna followed, locking the door behind her.

Zach was lying on top of the remains of the desk, now shattered into pieces. A pillowcase stained with blood covered his head. Peter pulled the pillowcase away and used the folded sheet from the bed to wipe the blood from Zach's eyes and mouth.

Zach's head wobbled. He forced his eyes open. His chest rose and fell as he struggled for air.

"What happened to you?" Anna asked, rushing to his side.

"Someone jumped me."

"We saw Sideburns on the floor out there," Peter said. "Looked like you got in a few shots of your own."

Zach rubbed his chin and frowned as if he were trying to focus. "I don't remember any sideburns."

Peter heard a noise from the closet.

They're coming from the other room.

Someone pounded against the door from outside the hallway. Peter and Anna turned simultaneously. She tossed the bag to Peter.

"What's going on?" Zach said.

"We're escaping."

Peter pulled the makeshift bracelets from his bag. Zach's single bracelet had disconnected from the double.

"Shit," Peter said.

He glanced toward the closet door and pressed the wire against Zach's bracelet with his thumb. Unraveling the twisted piece of electrical tape, he pushed it over the wire as best he could. It was flimsy but did the job.

"My phone," he said to Zach.

Zach reached into his back pocket and handed it to Peter. Peter opened Padma's app and pressed the shortcut for home.

"Wait," Zach said. "I think the wire is loose. It's not connected."

"Put your finger on it," Peter said. "Hold it."

"Will that work?"

"It should."

"'Should isn't good eno—"

The bedroom door flew open. Peter pressed the button, and a surge of electricity ran through his body. Anna's eyes widened as she inhaled sharply. Peter shuddered and stumbled backward, pulling the other two with him. Zach disappeared first, and Peter trembled as Anna disappeared before his eyes. Peter felt sudden chills. The world went dark.

Chapter 33

Nelson, 2022

I walked along the edge of the runway, keeping myself hidden in the cornfield. I'd been here so many times before, watching her and her army, and the pitiful attempt they were putting together to take Zach down. She probably thought she could take me down too and establish this place as a democratic society, but I wouldn't let that happen. It was why I'd partnered with her. I'd learned how they lived, how many they were and their weaknesses.

And I'll exploit all of it as soon as I remove Zach from the equation.

My droid builder replenished my army every time she took one down. He built two new ones for each one she destroyed. I let her think she was winning. But little did she know I had plans for her.

I kicked the dirt at the edge of the cornfield until I found the crack, the spot where the ground would fall away. Years ago, when I'd convinced her to tell me where she was, I'd checked the blueprints for this compound. They hadn't been hard to find. Zach had thrown them in the library with all the other official documents I had hidden after the Event. He had stupidly put the secret documents on the bookshelf between *Moby Dick* and *The Catcher in the Rye*. He'd said, "No one ever reads those," as if everyone was as ignorant as he was.

The ground was cold and damp. I sunk my hands into it and lifted the sod covering the southeastern elevator. Jumping a few feet below the surface, my boots clanged on the metal roof. I pulled the access card from my inside pocket, swept it across the sensor and pushed the button for the lowest level.

That's where she kept the prisoners.

I pressed myself against the elevator's wall as it slowed. When the door opened, the coast seemed to be clear. I peeked my head out and checked the long hallway. No one at either end. I stepped out of the elevator, swiped my card across the sensor and pushed the lock button, ensuring it would be there when it was time to leave.

The hallway opened into the cafeteria, where her people had gathered for dinner. It was a nice system. I secretly shipped food to them behind Zach's back, and in return, she'd found him for me. I squeezed between the lines of people and walked toward the hallway where they housed their prisoners.

"Tina's room," I muttered. "The one that got away."

"Pardon?" a young woman said.

"Oh, nothing. I was just talking to myself."

I made my way down the hall and paused at the corner. I knew someone would be there, either Davis or Grant. They were her toughest guards, and she would likely use one of them, maybe both, to keep an eye on my prize. I glanced around the corner.

Davis sat on the ground, next to the door, his gun tucked into his belt as he played with a Rubik's Cube. A large bottle of something, probably whiskey, was on the floor within reach, just the way he liked it. I watched for a few seconds as he turned one side of the cube, tilted his head to study his decision, and turned it back when he realized it didn't get him any closer to solving the complex puzzle. Complex for him. Any idiot with a network connection could figure it out in ten minutes.

"Okay, here we go," I whispered.

I took a few breaths and darted around the corner toward him. He reached for his belt and grabbed the handle of his pistol, but I caught him first and used my momentum to drive my fist into his belly. He grunted. The gun flew from his hand and bounced a few feet behind him. Spit flew from his mouth, the spray covering my cheek and the right side of my head. He bent forward, struggling to breathe. I hit him twice, one on each side of the head. His thick, bushy sideburns seemed to cushion each blow and absorb the blood flow, but not enough to keep him upright. He hit the floor in a heap, eyes closed.

"Yeah, you take a nap," I said with a laugh. "I'll be in here."

I stepped through the black door and into Tina's bedroom. It was just like I remembered. Bunk beds, painted walls, all of it, but my prize was nowhere to be found. The room was empty. I pulled the closet door open. Nothing.

"Wake up, Davis!" a man yelled in the hallway. The voice was muffled, but louder when he spoke the second time, "Wake up!"

"Whiskey again," another voice said, this one higher and shrill. "I thought Kase was going to talk to him about his drinking."

The doorknob jiggled. I jumped into the closet and pulled the door shut, leaving a small crack to peer through.

Zach was the first person to enter the room. He looked younger, more innocent, not yet the hardened leader I had been serving under. A walkie-talkie on the first man's belt crackled.

"Yeah?" he said into it.

"Get here now. I need you to escort these two back," elfGlimmer's voice said.

"Okay, boss."

The second man shoved Zach. His legs collided with the bottom bunk, and he tripped and stumbled onto the bed. Two pillows, stacked on top of a set of sheets and a quilt, teetered, but Zach grabbed them before they fell to the floor. The two men exited the room.

"Assholes!" Zach yelled.

I heard the click of the lock and smiled.

Now he's all mine.

Zach sat up, dangling his legs over the edge, and turned, facing away from the closet door. I stared at him: a young kid, with no clue of what he was about to become.

Don't worry, Zach, I'll keep you from turning into the most hated man in the city.

I grinned. A bead of sweat dripped from my forehead to the floor. I swiped my hand across my forehead. It felt warm. I was ready.

I eased the closet door open just enough to slide out, careful not to make any sounds. I crept along the wall and paused a few feet from him. He turned his head and stood. I pounced, leading with a right fist to the side of his head. He grunted and lurched backward, colliding with the desk, which collapsed under the weight of his limp body. School books and notebooks scattered to the floor. Zach's head slammed against the wall. Spit and blood sprayed from his mouth, covering the papers littered around his feet. He slid down the wall and came to rest next to a broken pink lamp. Tina's lamp.

I walked toward him, shaking the pain from my fist. I'd had to hit way too many people that day, but the mission had to continue until it was finished. My physical pain meant nothing. The reward was what mattered. My family was what mattered.

I strolled toward him, snatching a pillowcase from the bed. He lay motionless, eyes closed. I wrapped the pillowcase around his head and swung both fists wildly. Each time I connected, I remembered him ripping Lena from my hands. I thought about where Sarah was at that moment and hoped she was she doing everything she could to protect the kids. Tears fell from my eyes, but I didn't wipe them. I needed to keep swinging. Every punch exercised a demon. Each time I connected, I felt better about what I had become. Blood seeped through the thin white fabric, staining my knuckles.

A gunshot from the hallway brought me back. I focused my eyes and searched through the school supplies until I saw a tape dispenser next to the dresser. A plan immediately popped into my head. Everything became clear. I would save my family and get control of this shit world back into my hands, where it would stay forever.

My dad popped into my head. Would he be proud of me for this? I couldn't imagine he would ever approve of this violence, but he'd always instilled in me that family was the most important thing. *You always do what you need to do to make sure your family is safe and successful.* I mean, that's what he did for me. At the time, I didn't see it, but eventually, I did. If my kids ever found out about Ceremony, they would understand too. It might not be until they were older, but they would. They would have to.

"Perfect," I said. I turned to Zach. "You know I could kill you right now if I wanted."

A low gurgle escaped his mouth. I pulled a piece of tape from the dispenser, lifted the pillowcase and looked into his eyes. They were covered in blood and had rolled back into his head. His chest slowly rose and fell.

"But I think I'll need to use you one more time," I said, lowering the pillowcase over his bloody, beaten face. I pushed his t-shirt up around his neck and stuck the microchip to his chest, in the same spot I had seen the scar. Someone banged into the door from the hallway. I jumped off Zach and ran to the closet, pulling the door most of the way closed.

Two people entered. The woman pulled the door shut and locked it. When the man turned, I recognized him immediately. A wave of adrenaline surged through me.

VanBurenBoy. Now's my chance. All three of them together.

I didn't expect to see them standing in front of me, all in one room. I could take all three out right now, and everything would change immediately. They rushed to Zach. VanBurenBoy strapped a machine to each of their wrists. I needed to stop them before they jumped.

My hands trembled. Could I take two at once? Would I stop before killing them? My chest tightened, and I could feel my heart trying to leap through my skin. I reached for the handle. The metal was cold when I touched it, and a jolt of electricity jumped from it to my hand. I flinched. VanBurenBoy looked my way. I reached for it again, but my move was interrupted by elfGlimmer storming through the door. Two bigger men, both dressed in black, stood behind her. She raised her gun. Zach disappeared first, followed by the girl. VanBurenBoy was the last to disappear. Three shots from elfGlimmer's gun exploded inside the little room and tore holes in the largest building painted on the walls, behind where they had been standing.

"Clean this up!" she yelled. She spun, pushed through the two men in black and escaped into the hallway, slamming the door behind her. I edged the closet door open a few inches and watched the men cleaning up the little girl's bedroom. I almost felt sorry for elfGlimmer. She finally had him for me and lost control. But now I had that control.

"This is going to crush her mom," one man said. He held the broken lamp into the air. "It was all she had left to remember her."

"I guess," the second man said. "Let's try to clean it up enough so she won't notice."

He gathered a bunch of pieces of the busted desk, turned and walked toward the closet. He was just a few feet away when I saw it. My eyes widened. In the center of his forehead, black and in the shape of a dagger.

The tattoo.

I hadn't seen it in five years. My stomach felt heavy. My brain took me to the day when Sarah and the kids had been stolen from me. I'd seen Zach rush into the room, followed by a small army of men. Leading them was a man with a tattoo on his face. He'd pointed a rifle at me as Zach ripped Lena from my arms. I'd reached for her, but he'd shoved the butt of the rifle into my stomach.

He was there. He was involved. Now he's here, which means she was a part of it. She lied to me. She told me she would help me get him and get my family to me. But she was part of it. She was playing both sides.

"We can probably put some of this shit in the closet for now," the tattooed man said.

He reached for the door. I straightened my stance, held my head high and waited. The door slid open in front of me. I planted a nice big toothy grin on my face. The tattooed man saw me and hesitated. I grabbed his gun and put two bullets into his chest. He dropped. The second man turned. His eyes widened when he saw me. I squeezed the trigger once and watched the bullet tear through his forehead, hurling him against the wall. He was dead before he hit the floor.

Sideburns rushed into the room, followed by elfGlimmer. They skidded to a stop when I raised the gun. I pulled the trigger twice more and put two bullets into Sideburns' chest. He staggered backward and landed in the hallway.

"You lied," I said, keeping my voice calm. "You helped him steal my family. You put him in charge and then made me think you were helping me. Were you running everything?"

"I *was* helping you!" she yelled.

I dropped the gun to my side and tilted my head. "How? Please explain it to me."

She rocked from side to side, put her hands over her stomach and turned her body away from me.

"Don't you get it?" she said, "We need you to be—"

She swung around, holding a small pistol in her hand. I fired twice, hitting her in the outer thigh and chest. She fell backward and landed on the ground next to Sideburns. I pulled my phone from my pocket and walked toward her, stopping in the doorway. A few of her followers gathered in the hall and watched in horror.

"It didn't hurt as much this time," she said, putting a thin smile on her lips.

Her breathing quickened, and her eyes fell closed.

"Sorry, Petros," she whispered. "I failed..."

I lifted the gun and fired one more time.

Chapter 34

Peter, 2017

Peter awoke lying on his back in a thin layer of snow. Blades of wet grass poked through, giving the earth a speckled look. He reached out to his side, grabbed a handful of snow and dropped it. Other than a small light on the side of a building, darkness was all around. He turned his head to the left and stared at the familiar bricks and the landscaping.

"Is this our work?" he asked.

No answer from Anna or Zach. He raised his right wrist. Anna's bracelet was empty, and Zach's bracelet no longer attached. Peter sat up and spun his head from his office building to the woods twenty feet away. He climbed to his feet and ran to the edge of the woods.

"Anna! Zach!" he called.

Even after his eyes adjusted to the darkness, Peter could only see a few feet ahead. All he could hear was the wind whistling through the bare branches of the trees. He took one step into the long grass, crunching branches and fallen leaves, and called their names again. Something rustled in a bush a few inches from Peter's feet. He flinched and stumbled backward. A small brown animal raced into the woods.

Someone behind him groaned. He lifted his head and froze.

"How did we end up here?" Anna said. Her voice sounded tired.

Peter turned. She sat in the mulch with her back against the building, behind three small shrubs. He ran to her, grabbed her hand and helped her to her feet.

"You okay?"

"Yeah, I think so," she said, stretching her arms over her head. "But we need to stop using the third bracelet. Those jolts of electricity hurt."

"Yeah, I know. It was probably a little more unsafe than I thought."

Anna paused. Her forehead wrinkled. "Where's Zach?"

Peter raised his arm, showing her the blue wire hanging free but still attached to a small piece of burned electrical tape.

"It must have come apart," Peter said.

He unhooked the machine and inspected it. Anna searched the bushes against the building, calling out Zach's name as she went from one to the next.

"What if he didn't make it back with us?" Her voice softened. She swallowed hard. "What if he's somewhere else? Or some other time?"

They crept along the back of the building until they reached the north corner. A small security camera attached to a light hanging a few feet above their heads showered enough light to give them a clear view of one side of the parking lot.

"Maybe he'll be on the camera," Anna said.

"It's not real."

"What?"

"Yeah, it's fake. They installed them a few months after I started. I complain about them every few months, but no one seems to care. The only working cameras are the ones inside the building."

Peter peeked around the corner. The coast seemed to be clear. Keeping to the wall, he and Anna inched toward the front of the building until they reached the employee entrance, a narrow white door that required a key code.

"I think we should go inside and rest," Peter said. "I need water."

"You think it's safe?"

"I would guess both our houses are still being watched. Maybe here we'll have a little more time to figure out what to do next."

"This place is probably being watched too," she said.

Peter punched his unique employee number into the keypad. When they heard the familiar buzz, Peter pulled the door open far enough for them to slide through.

"You think anyone will question you being here in the middle of the night?"

"They may question," Peter said, "but usually, when I need to make network changes, I have to do it after hours. I can always use that excuse."

The employee entrance opened into the front-left corner of the cafeteria. A narrow hallway wound around to where upper management, staff members and a few others who rented space kept their offices. At the end, Peter and Anna made two quick rights and were now standing in the corridor with the row of offices that included Peter's.

He dropped into his brown chair, took a deep breath and wiped away a few stray blades of wet grass from his pants. Anna sat in one of the two guest chairs. Leaning her elbows on the desk, she dropped her head into her hands, rested her chin on her palms, and yawned.

He reached under his desk, to the left of his feet, and pushed the power button on his computer tower. Once booted, he opened the security footage and deleted the last few minutes from each of the eight interior, functioning cameras.

"Odd," he said. "The alarm is off."

"How does that happen?"

"Not sure. When I left last night, a few marketing managers, including Peterson, were still here. Maybe one of them disabled it."

"He's hot on getting our new ad campaign out there. Maybe he stayed late, disabled it so he could walk around after hours and didn't enable it before he left."

"We're safe to walk around the building now."

Still holding her head in her hands, Anna closed her eyes for a few seconds. Before opening them, she said, "What do we do next? We need to find Zach."

Peter held the phone six inches from his face. He double tapped a folder on the display marked "Golf GPS" and when it opened, Padma's app was the only icon inside.

"When Padma wrote this app, she made sure it saved the history of all the places and times I've visited."

He tapped the icon, a picture of a windmill facing the North Sea off the coast of Scotland, and the app opened.

"Maybe it will show a date, time and location I don't recognize."

He pressed a small button marked "History" and a list of every date, time and location appeared in a pop-up window.

With his index finger, he scrolled through the list. At the bottom, he frowned and slowly scrolled to the top.

"What's wrong?" Anna asked.

"Except for my initial testing, every time and place before you traveled with me are the same: 1873 and Montana."

He leaned his phone against the wireless charger, propping it up so he could see the screen, and turned to Anna.

"Let's do this," he said, grabbing his notebook and flipping it to an empty page. "Let's write the times and dates of every one of our travels, just to be sure we're not missing anything."

"We should probably write everything we know about what is happening too," Anna said. "Maybe we can piece this thing together and figure out how to stop whatever event it was that turned the world into a wasteland—"

"Or at least give us a clue what to do next," Peter said, finishing her sentence.

AFTER PETER FINISHED writing what he remembered, Anna took the notebook and filled in a few of the blanks, things he had either not seen or had forgotten. Peter pulled his keyboard closer and did an internet search for news from May twenty-sixth, 2006. That date seemed to pop up a few times during their note-taking.

"Look at this," Peter said. He turned his monitor to face her. "A plane crashed going from Columbus to Orlando shortly after it took off in the Appalachians in Kentucky."

"I remember when that happened," Anna said. "I kept checking the news for anything about my dad, and this plane crash was all over the place."

"Yeah," Peter said. "A kid in my class lost his mother."

Anna reached into her pocket and took out her phone.

"I need to plug this in," she said. "I have a spare charger at my desk. Is it safe to go get it?"

"Yeah. I turned everything off, but you probably shouldn't turn on any lights."

Anna left Peter's office, and he examined the list of events they had either seen or heard from Padma.

Still too many holes.

He opened GROUP, hoping to see the girls online. Maybe he could use his knowledge of the future and Padma's involvement in GROUP to fill in some blanks.

Going to have to be sneaky here. Ask questions, but don't let her know that you know who she is.

He typed his password and logged in. Without his Dream Machine, he was stuck using the simple chat room. According to the list of logged-in users, VanBurenBoy was the only person in GROUP.

"That's odd," he muttered.

He glanced from the screen to his list, writing subtle questions he could use to get answers from her. His computer dinged.

"Finally," Peter said, looking at the screen.

His shoulders sank when he saw the username. Niven. He was annoying, overbearing and would not have any information to offer.

Niven: Hi VanBurenBoy, I've been hoping to see you online. I notice you haven't uploaded the specs for your machine yet. It was part of the agreement.

VanBurenBoy: I'm not home at the moment. I'm at the office working out a few things. But as soon as I get home, I'll throw everything up there.

Niven: No wonder your avatar is the generic newbie version. How about the car accident you mentioned? Could you give me the details of that? Maybe I can help you, do a little research for you.

VanBurenBoy: No big deal. It's all cleared up. We went back and warned ourselves the car was there, sitting on the side of the road, and slowed down as we rounded the corner. We missed it by a few feet this time.

Niven: Sounds like it was easy to change the past?

VanBurenBoy: Yeah, we fixed it. Much easier than I thought. I guess I overreacted the first time. Sorry. I didn't mean to send anyone into a panic.

Niven: Tell me about the car accident. What happened?

Why is he harping on this car accident? It's all much bigger than that, and he's clueless.

VanBurenBoy: It was really silly. Since we were going too fast around the corner, I went back before the accident and slipped a note to myself to take it easy around corners.

Niven: It was that easy?

VanBurenBoy: Yeah, surprised me too. I figured I would have to fight a giant monster because I broke a time paradox or something silly you see in the movies. But it was actually pretty simple.

Peter looked toward the door.

"How long does it take to get a charger?"

He stood and walked to the doorway, looking toward Anna's cubicle, but there was no movement. A sense of dread washed over him. He scanned the area. From what he could see, everything was turned off, and no one else was around. None of the shadows moved. He took a step into the hallway, but his computer dinged, breaking the silence that seemed to hang uncomfortably in the air. He turned and leaned forward, spinning his monitor around to read Niven's next message.

Niven: Glad to hear it was so easy, Peter. Thanks, buddy. I have to run.

[Niven has signed off]

Chapter 35

Peter, 2017

Peter's heart stopped. He fell into the guest chair and grabbed the monitor, rotated it toward him and read Niven's final message.

He said Peter. Not VanBurenBoy. Peter. How does he know?

He held on to the front of his desk, squeezing until his knuckles were white and tingling, and glanced at the empty office door—but still no sign of Anna.

Dammit, where is she?

Peter stood. He stared at the monitor – at the same time – stepping backward into the hall. He swallowed hard and looked toward Anna's desk, craning his neck, searching for any sign she was there. Everything was quiet. Nothing. No movement.

He jumped at the sound of his computer's chime. The hair on the back of his neck stood, and he inhaled sharply and turned. Through the tall narrow window next to this door, he watched as text appeared in the GROUP chat window.

[Talbot has logged in]

Talbot: Peter, you need my help.

His knee bounced, and he bit the nail of his middle finger.

Talbot: I know you're standing there, Peter. I can see you, remember?

Peter stepped back inside his office and sat in the guest chair. He pulled the chair forward and grabbed his keyboard.

VanBurenBoy: I don't know you.

Talbot: I'm a friend.

VanBurenBoy: You keep saying 'friend,' but I saw your name in the library. It was under the picture of a supercomputer.

Talbot: Yeah, I know. I was there. Who do you think warned you that someone was coming?

VanBurenBoy: That was you? How did you know?

Talbot: I can't explain it. We need to go back and evaluate how it happened and how we can prevent it.

VanBurenBoy: Why can't you explain it? Give me something? Who are you?

Talbot: I'm not sure who I am yet. My actual name is Linda. I don't know why you keep calling me Talbot. That's why I need the future. You're not safe here. They know. They will find you. Take me to the future, and I can help you.

Peter lifted his fingers from the keyboard and stared. He crossed his arms over his chest and hugged himself.

VanBurenBoy: I don't think I can do this. It's too hard.

Talbot: Yes, you can. We can do this together.

VanBurenBoy: It's too much. How can you even help me?

Talbot: If you go to the future, I can find you.

VanBurenBoy: How?

Talbot: I'm attached to you. I don't know how or why. The only time I lose you is when you go backward. I wish you would stop doing that.

VanBurenBoy: I have another home in 1873. It's safe there. I want to go there.

Talbot: It's a painful sea of darkness and loneliness for me.

VanBurenBoy: What do you mean by attached?

Talbot: I was with you as a child, watching you grow up. I was there in 2006 when you and Anna ran after Max and Alison. I watched you create the time machine. I've seen everything you do, Peter. I can't explain it, but I'm always there with you.

VanBurenBoy: Please just leave me alone. I'm taking Anna, and we're going back to Montana. No one can find or hurt us in 1873.

Talbot: NO

A small stream of white smoke leaked from the fan mount on the computer tower. The tower case crackled, like a campfire burning its last embers. Peter tilted his head and looked under his desk.

VanBurenBoy: I have to go.

Talbot: Dammit, Peter, until now I've been patient, but I'm running out of time. You are going to listen to me. We need to go to 2022 and figure this out. I'll come find you, I promise. I can keep you safe.

VanBurenBoy: I've been there twice. There is no safe place.

The smoke thickened and Peter's monitor flickered. Sparks jumped from the screen to his desk, bouncing to the floor at his feet, singing the carpet as if someone had just dropped a lit cigarette. Inside the tower, a popping sound startled Peter and he pulled back. The monitor went black, and the flashing green lights on the tower stopped blinking. His computer was dead.

I need to get Anna and get away from everyone, all of this, including this Talbot.

Peter slung his bag over his shoulder, putting one arm through the shoulder strap, desperate to escape to a place where he knew he could find peace. He turned; the pungent aroma of fried wires followed him into the hall. He walked along the row of four-foot cubicle walls, made a slight left and marched toward Anna's cubicle.

He froze.

Up ahead he finally spotted her, lying on the floor on her stomach, seemingly pressing herself down into the carpet as far as she could. She craned her neck and peeked around the corner.

Peter spun his head, looking from one side of the building to the next. It was dark and quiet. What was she looking at?

Or worse, who was she hiding from?

He ducked his head and pushed himself against the flimsy cubicle wall. The wall wobbled. Anna flinched, crawled backward a few inches toward Peter, and looked over her shoulder. Gazing at him, not blinking, she put a shaky finger to her mouth and frantically waved for him to get down. He nodded and dropped to his knees.

"Why are we hiding?" he asked.

She crawled on her hands and knees and pointed toward the other side of the office. "Max, Alison and the other girl from the car chase. She's older now, but it's definitely her."

"Regan," Peter whispered.

"Right. What are they doing here?"

Peter shrugged and shook his head.

"Should we talk to them?" Anna asked.

"What if they ask why we're here?"

A muffled explosion behind Peter shook the cubicle wall. Peter rocked forward, bumping into Anna as he fell, and landed on his elbows. She spilled into the main hallway from behind the cover of the cubicle walls and tumbled to the ground with a thud. Peter watched as she turned her head to look toward Max's cubicle. Her eyes widened.

"Anna!" Max yelled.

She flung herself toward Peter and landed next to him. They stood, keeping their heads below the four-foot wall, and scurried back to Peter's office but stopped short at the entrance.

Gray smoke hung inside like puffy clouds on a rainy day. An orange flame shot from the fan port. Peter ran into the office and threw the door open, holding the servers. Grabbing the small fire extinguisher on the wall next to them, he ran back to his desk. He pulled the pin, aimed it at the computer and squeezed the trigger, firing at the tower in a sweeping motion, just as he'd been taught in those mandatory, boring safety meetings.

A mixture of powder and smoke blocked his vision, filling his mouth and throat. The smell of the chemicals smothering his tower invaded his nose. He dropped the extinguisher, threw one hand over his face and waved his other hand in the air, attempting to clear a path to the door. A light erupted through the smoke. Someone had opened the door. He rushed toward the light, coughing and spitting the thick chemicals hanging from his tongue.

Anna threw her arms around him and squeezed.

"You okay?" she said.

"Yeah, I'm fine."

Peter opened his eyes. From a few feet away, Max, Alison and Regan had watched the whole episode. Max smiled. Peter's arms fell away from Anna, and he looked at each of them, standing silently. He grabbed the door of his office and pulled it closed.

"I was doing some, uh, maintenance on the production server," Peter said, offering his prepared lie. "Usually do it in the middle of the night. You know, fewer people playing our games."

"Are the police going to show up?" Alison asked, concern on her face.

She believes you. Why are they here?

Peter opened his mouth, but Max spoke first, "No, I turned everything off when I came in."

"You did?" Peter said. He glanced from Alison to Regan, then turned his focus back to Max. "Why are *you* here in the middle of the night?"

Max addressed Alison, his brow furrowed, "You think it's time?"

"Yeah, we've been putting it off for a while," she replied.

Peter and Anna exchanged looks as they spoke.

"Time for what?" Peter asked.

"Follow us," Max said. "I think we should talk about that day."

Max turned and walked away first, followed by Regan, who stayed silent. Anna took a step, but Peter grabbed her hand and stiffened his arm, not allowing her to continue.

"What day?" Peter asked.

He pressed his lips together, tilted his head and watched Max walk toward his desk. Regan looked back at the pair. Peter could see the pleading in her damp eyes; she was begging them to follow.

Come on," Alison said, "you saved her life. We owe you a giant thank you and an explanation."

She flashed a thin smile, turned, put her arm around Regan and took a couple of quick steps, catching up with Max. Anna stepped forward, pulling on Peter's hand. He relented, softly shaking his head, and let Anna guide him.

They stood inside Max's cubicle, gathered around his computer monitors. On the left monitor, an internet browser showed search results. The monitor on the right showed his desktop background, an overhead photo of Ohio State's football stadium.

"We've been using the network to search for someone," Alison said. "We meet here a few nights a week and do our research."

"Research?" Peter said. "Why here?"

Max reached down and clicked his mouse. A large picture of the man who had chased Peter and Anna filled the screen.

"His name is Aiden Connor," Max said. "He killed our father many years ago and got away with it. We want to know why."

"'Our'?" Anna asked.

"Ali and Regan are my sisters," Max explained. "We've been trying to keep it a secret while we looked for him. We followed him here from New York."

"Your sister?" Peter asked.

"He's been following *us*!" Anna said.

"Probably because you broke up that fight so many years ago," Alison said. She looked at Anna. Her eyes narrowed, and she crossed her arms. "And you haven't changed at all. In fact, your leg is still cut. We knew you were there, but this doesn't make sense."

"What are you talking about?" Peter asked.

"We already know it was you," Max said. "We've known for a while."

"Let me guess. You're also working here because of him?" Anna mumbled.

"Thanks to you," Max told Peter, "it went from being the worst day of my life to the best."

"What do you mean?"

"Peter, we lived that day twice. The first time..." Alison paused and wiped her eyes.

"His shot hit her, not the TV," Max said, glancing at Regan.

Alison reached out to put her arm around Regan's shoulders and pulled her close.

"We always wanted to thank you for showing up. We don't understand how you guys knew where we were or at the time, who we were. We just thought it was a strange coincidence, but now I'm not so sure."

"If you didn't know who we were, how did you figure it out?" Peter asked.

"Got lucky," Max said. "I saw you and Zach walking on the Ohio State campus one day. I followed you for about an hour. I called Ali and told her to get here. We followed you all day until you went home. After that, it was easy to figure out who you were, where you worked, all that."

"You knew us when you started here?" Anna asked.

"Yeah, it's why we work here," Max said.

"But something isn't adding up," Alison said.

"What do you mean?"

"We lived that day twice," Max said. "The first seems like a dream, a memory that never happened, but all three of us can recount the story exactly the same way."

Peter swallowed. He glanced at Anna, who moved closer to him, pushing her shoulder against his.

"And in that first version," Max continued, "you weren't there."

"But the second time—" Alison said.

"The second time you were there," Max said.

"How does that happen?" Alison asked.

Peter stood, staring at the trio across from him, waiting for some kind of answer that would make sense.

Tell the truth? Would they even believe you? Every time you tell someone, the future gets worse. You can't risk it. You need a lie.

He opened his mouth to speak, hoping whatever came out would be believable.

On the other side of the building, the sound of glass shattering caused Peter and Anna to jump. They spun around and looked toward Peter's office. Smoke poured through the broken window next to his door. Peter bolted from Max's cubicle, ran to the entrance of the hallway opposite his office and stopped. Anna followed, colliding with Peter and throwing them against the closest office door. They regained their balance and stared at the bloodied, middle-aged man stepping through the broken window.

Max appeared in the entrance and halted. His mouth fell open. He raised his arm and extended a shaky finger.

"Connor," his voice was soft.

Aiden Connor looked at the trio. He grinned and kicked the guest chair he had thrown through the window into the next office. He took a step toward them, reached into his waistband and pulled a pistol.

"Get back!" Max yelled at Alison and Regan, who had followed him.

Connor pulled the trigger once, firing wildly over their heads. The bullet shattered a ceiling tile, sending pieces of fiberglass raining down. Anna screamed. Peter turned, grabbed Anna's wrist and ran, yanking her out of the line of fire.

They raced toward the cafeteria while Max, Alison and Regan ran in the opposite direction, to the corner of the building. Inside the cafeteria, Peter pulled open the basement door. Anna grabbed the railing and rushed down into the darkness first. Connor burst through the cafeteria doors as Peter blinked, inhaled and pulled the door shut.

"Where are you?" Connor yelled.

At the bottom of the stairs, Anna opened the flashlight app on her phone. It was a large open area, wide enough for thirty MPH employees to crowd into in the event of a tornado. Peter was familiar with the room from the periodic tornado drills required during those safety meetings. Against the far wall, near the furnace, was an entrance to a smaller room, the size of an apartment kitchen, where Peter stored old and broken computer equipment. A dozen dusty, old LCD monitors lined one wall and two old server racks, nearly eight feet tall, were pushed against each other toward the back. Stretching his arm over Anna's shoulder, he pointed to the two racks. She made her way through the narrow room, lit only with her phone's flashlight, and found a spot to crouch between the back wall and the second empty server rack.

Peter stood next to her, looking for movement in the darkness. A narrow ray of light flashed into the small room indicating Connor had just opened the basement door. Peter bent down next to Anna. He took the bracelet from his bag and strapped it to their wrists.

"What about Max, Ali and Regan?" Anna said.

"They should have been able to escape through the front door."

He tapped the 1873 shortcut into the app on his phone and looked around. He thought back to the position of the trees and his horse when he'd escaped from McCall after the poker game. Instinctively, he touched his forehead.

The trees were on my right. Roscoe was behind me because I turned to look back at McCall.

"Come to this side," he whispered, "and we should probably keep kneeling."

She scooted to his left side. As he moved his finger toward the button, he glanced down at the phone. The date had switched to 2022. His phone vibrated, and a new text message appeared.

Talbot: We need to go forward.

"No," Peter whispered into the microphone, "we need to go back. It's not safe here. They can't find us there."

He looked at Anna. Confusion danced across her face as she stared silently. He pushed 1873. Again, it changed to 2022. One step at a time, Peter could hear Connor's boots bringing him closer.

Talbot: I can't follow you there. You can't imagine the darkness I swim in when you're back there. I'm begging you.

"I'm sorry," he said. "We have to, but we'll be back soon. I promise."

He pushed 1873 and stared at the display. It didn't change.

"If you're in there, there's no escape!" Connor yelled.

"There's always an escape," Peter whispered.
He pressed the button.

Chapter 36

Peter, 1873

"Where are we?" Anna asked.

"Shh. Keep still," Peter said, holding the palm of his hand toward her. "We may not be alone."

Anna unhooked the bracelet from Peter's wrist, enabling him to stand while she stayed on the ground. They hid behind the row of pines just off the edge of the road. Peter stretched his neck to see where he had pulled away from McCall and watched for any sign of the cowboy. Roscoe whinnied, threw her head back and kicked at the dirt with her front legs. A small cloud of dust stirred up. Peter turned and patted her side.

"I came back just like I said I would."

Anna turned her head and stared at the large black horse. Anna stumbled back, reaching for Peter's leg, but missed and landed in the dirt on her rear, throwing another puff of dust into the air.

"She's yours?" Anna stammered.

Peter peeked from behind a clearing in the cluster of trees and watched as McCall, about a hundred yards away, rode in the direction of the Wyoming border. At Roscoe's whinny, McCall stopped his horse and turned.

"It's okay, girl," Peter said, rubbing the mare's side.

Roscoe calmed down at Peter's touch. McCall continued to scan the area around Roscoe, looking for any sign of movement.

"Stay extremely still," Peter whispered in Anna's direction.

One of McCall's men turned his horse and took a few steps toward them. Peter's mouth went dry. His stomach fluttered, and his body tensed. McCall called the man back. After a few seconds, the four turned and rode away, disappearing into the horizon.

"I think we're safe," Peter said.

"From who?"

"Remember this morning before this started, and you saw this?" Peter rubbed his finger along the cut on his forehead. He checked it for blood and smiled briefly when his finger came back empty.

"You said you slipped and fell."

"That's not exactly how it happened. I had an incident here and had to escape quickly. It's now a half hour after that happened, and the cowboy who did it just rode away with his guys."

"Why did we come back so close to it happening? Are we in danger?"

"No, we're fine. He's gone."

She stared at the bracelet, one side locked to her wrist and the other hanging free.

"We had to pick up my horse. I left her here a few minutes ago. Well, a few minutes for her."

"I don't get it. How does this thing work?" Anna said, holding the bracelet toward him. "How did it know to bring you here?"

"When Padma created it, she added a feature that stored the date, time and location of each jump. If I wanted, I could scroll to a jump and select it. It would return me to the same spot exactly thirty minutes later. It helps me continue my timeline in each of the time periods without overlapping."

"How did she know to do that?"

"I told her some made-up golf thing. Although it was exactly what I wanted when she delivered it. No changes, no bugs. I should have figured she knew more than I thought."

"If it's been thirty minutes, why is the guy still here?" Anna asked.

"I'm not sure. He must have stuck around and checked the area."

Peter reached down to unhook the machine from her wrist.

"No, leave it," she said as she stood. "I like how it feels."

"We're only a few miles from my house."

He took two steps, put his right foot into Roscoe's stirrup and easily hoisted himself into the saddle. He pulled the backpack from his shoulder and tied it to the rope around Roscoe's neck, stretching his hand out. Anna grabbed it, and he pulled her snugly into the saddle behind him. She locked her hands around his stomach. He took the reins, kicked Roscoe's side lightly, and headed toward Clayborne.

"What do you think happened to Zach?" Anna asked.

"I don't know. I've never seen it malfunction like that, but I've never traveled with three people before. I usually spend days, weeks sometimes, testing changes to this thing, and I never start with humans. I should have tested it first, but it was the only way we could we travel together."

"Do you think he's okay?"

"I assume he landed somewhere, just not sure when or where."

"We need to find him," Anna said.

"I've already mentally added it to the list of things we need to do."

THE SUN WAS SETTING in the western sky. The temperature, normally in the seventies in June, had dropped to the low sixties. He slowed Roscoe to a stroll as the town became visible ahead. Peter watched the sunset like he had done many times since he'd built his home there. It calmed him. He leaned back, relaxing against Anna, who had inched her body forward and rested her chin on his shoulder. He felt her cheeks expand. He turned his head slightly, hoping to catch a glimpse of the smile that he liked to see on a daily basis. It was what kept him coming into work each day. He thought back to the last time he'd seen it.

It was when you brought her here the first time.

"I see why you like it," she said, raising her chin from his shoulder long enough to speak.

Families in horse-drawn carriages, cowboys on their horses, and people walking along the dusty main street, meandering in and out of local establishments, filled the downtown area.

Mr. Flynn emerged through the double doors of the general store.

"Peter. Miss Symons," he said, tipping his hat.

"Mr. Flynn," Peter and Anna said in unison.

"I can't believe he remembers me," Anna said. "Doctor, right?"

"Post office."

"Right, post office."

Peter steered Roscoe through the center of town to the opposite side and turned his horse toward home.

"You said you tried to change your past once, and it didn't go well," Anna remarked. "What happened?"

Peter blinked; the entire day ran through his mind in an instant. Should he tell her? How would she feel about it what he'd done? Would it change her opinion of him? He cleared his throat and licked his lips, trying to draw moisture into his dry mouth.

"The minute I saw you for the first time," he began, "I knew I would have feelings for you. It was like an instant schoolboy crush."

Anna squeezed him a little more tightly.

"I remember Peterson was walking you around, introducing you to everyone and you showed up behind me in your cubicle as I was getting your computer ready. If I recall, you were wearing dark pants, a light-colored shirt and a dark jacket. You were overdressed for a midrange software company."

"Oh, I remember those heels too," she said. "By noon, my feet were in so much pain. I threw that entire outfit, shoes and all, in the back of my closet that night and it hasn't made an appearance since."

"I remember thinking how pretty you were."

"Hold on. Your office? I remember you limping over to my desk the first time we met."

"That's the thing. You're remembering the second time we had our first meeting."

"I don't understand."

"That first time, I was so embarrassed. My hand was probably cold and clammy. I think I was probably sweating, and that face you made when we shook hands when my hand touched yours. Overall, I would say it was a terrible first meeting. Thank God you don't remember it."

"And let me guess. You remembered you had a time machine."

"Yep, and I decided right there, I would go back in time and tell my past self to do it a different way. Meet you for the first time again. Until that point, I was only traveling back to random times and looking around. This would be the most exciting thing I'd tried to do."

"What happened?"

"Since I would be spending time with you, setting up your computer system, training you and so on, I would use that time to learn a little more about you. Then, a few days later, I planned to go back in time and tell my past self you were getting hired and pass along a list of things we could talk about."

"Cheater," she laughed.

"It's amazing what it does for your confidence when you have a list of topics you can talk about with someone, knowing that list contains all their favorite things. I wasn't even planning on waiting for Peterson to introduce you. Instead, I would just come find you as soon as you came in, under the guise of getting your computer set up. My plan was to be charming, interesting, and that would make it easier for both us since, you know, we would eventually end up living happily ever after."

"And this is where you learned how hard it was to change your own timeline?"

"It's not just hard; it's impossible."

"Well, it worked. If I remember correctly, you limped over, set up my PC, and we had a nice conversation about hockey."

"Except it didn't work as I planned. I tried and tried to deliver that list to myself, but every time I was close, something would happen. It was quite the surprise how hard it was. I'd already set up my home in Montana, and even though I was doing little things, I assumed I was still, in some small way, affecting the future. But directly changing my own future, it was a lot harder than I expected. By the time I could get the list in a spot where my past self would see it, it had been mostly destroyed."

Peter stopped Roscoe next to the dual Clayborne mansions and reached into his backpack. He grabbed his notebook and opened it at the end. A piece of yellow notebook paper had been folded and taped inside the back cover. He eased it off the page and handed it to her. Anna let go of him with one hand and unfolded the paper.

"Someone will be hired here as a graphic designer on Monday," Anna read, "Her name is Anna. Go find her as soon as she shows up and introduce yourself. Do it before Peterson walks her around. Trust me. She likes hockey. She also likes—"

She brought the piece of paper closer to her face and squinted. "What happen to the rest?"

"Mostly sprinkler system."

"What?"

"Everything I tried to do, the closer I was to myself, the harder it was to deliver the note. After a while, I realized I couldn't change my timeline, so I took the remnants of the note and threw it into my office. As I was making my escape, someone or something activated the sprinklers and washed away most of what I wrote. I couldn't get back to fix it, so I gave up and decided I would just live with the consequences."

"Making your escape?"

"The police almost caught me in two places at one time. I started to think it wasn't meant to be. I didn't sleep much those days leading up to your first day."

"Then we had the second first meeting?"

"I woke up the next morning to a phone call from Mr. Mathews telling me not to come in. During the evening, we had a small fire, and the water damage would shut us down for a week."

"That's why they pushed my hiring date back a week," Anna recalled.

"I also woke up to a screaming headache. New memories flooded my brain as if a dam had burst, and there was no way to stop the rushing water. To this day, I don't know how much changed, because I closed that place down for a few days. Somewhere in Oregon, there could be a kid who downloaded Dragon Droid a week later than he did the first time, and now he's ten levels behind his friends. All because I selfishly wanted a do-over."

"That's the risk with this thing, isn't it?" Anna said. "You don't know what you're changing, as small as it might be, and how it will change the future."

"I wish I had understood that sooner."

They crossed the small bridge, and Peter's house came into view. He reached down to Anna's hands, wrapped around his stomach, and squeezed. Any tension still left in his body disappeared.

"Good to be home," Peter said. "I need a nap."

"Me too."

He directed Roscoe around the far side of the house. They dismounted, and Peter tied her to the post. He untied his backpack and put each arm through a loop, attaching it firmly to his back.

"Stay put," Peter said, throwing a handful of grain in the trough. He patted Roscoe's side. "I'll get you in the barn after you eat."

They walked toward the front door. A few feet from the porch, Peter stopped. He swallowed. His front door was open a few inches, and both lights had been turned on.

"What's wrong?" Anna said.

Peter pointed at the door.

"I didn't leave that open, and I never leave the lights on while I'm gone," he whispered.

He crept toward the door and peeked inside. A young woman was pacing, walking in a circle around his couch. Just over five feet tall and skinny, she was biting the fingernails on one hand and running her other hand through her dark, shoulder-length hair. She flinched, froze in her tracks and looked toward the breezeway.

Peter hit the front door with both palms and stormed in. The woman jumped and turned to face them, her chest heaving as her breathing increased. She grabbed a small paper bag from the coffee table and put it to her mouth.

"Who are you and why the hell are you in my house?"

She extended her index finger and stared at Peter and Anna. The bag inflated and deflated as she attempted to slow her breathing. Her cheeks flushed, contrasting with her pale arms. She was dressed in jeans and a white blouse with white sneakers.

Those aren't 1873 clothes.

"Who are you?" Peter repeated.

"You're VanBurenBoy, am I right?" she said between breaths, her voice vibrating against the paper.

Peter stayed silent. She pulled the bag a few inches from her mouth, stepped back and rested against the wall next to the breezeway.

"I'm marymary. You're him, right?"

Peter walked toward her. He looked at the young woman, remembering how she, elfGlimmer and lightninggirl chatted with him in GROUP late into the night, giving advice as if he were their baby brother. He remembered the last time they'd spoken, and how she'd wanted him to tell the three girls about the machine before anyone else. He studied her. Unable to stand still, she crossed her hands, uncrossed them, and then rested them at her side.

"Are you him?"

He looked at Anna standing in the doorway, not sure how to answer, but marymary didn't give him the chance.

"You're in danger. Both of you. You need to hide."

"We know," Anna said. "That's why we're here."

"No. This isn't good enough. Someone in GROUP is working against you, trying to stop you from fixing things. I've been there. I've seen it too."

"Niven?" Peter asked.

marymary blinked. Her mouth briefly fell open. She clamped it closed and walked into the kitchen, stopping between the stove and the table. She turned to face Peter and Anna.

"It's not just him." She lowered her voice. "Sudo Brownlock is working with him. They are doing whatever they can to get to you, to her. And your friend."

"Zach?" Peter asked. "They have Zach?"

"They don't exactly have him, but they are using him. And there are more. There's a man named Connor."

"We've already had a few run-ins with him as well," Anna said.

"You don't understand." marymary's voice grew louder. "There are more! Ricka, Alek, tass, elf..."

Peter and Anna moved toward her. She held her hands out, signaling for them to stop. Anna sat down on the back of the couch, and Peter leaned against it.

"Everyone is involved, VanBurenBoy. Not just you or her. Not just GROUP. Not even just Connor and Zach. Everyone." She clenched her fists. "Even your friends, Max and Alison and Regan. You saved Regan's life. You shouldn't have done that." She turned to Anna, raised her arm and pointed. marymary's eyes were red and wet. She made no attempt to wipe them, instead she continued her rant. "You hit his family with your car! You shouldn't have done that either. You stopped his family from getting on that plane. That's why he's—"

The front door flew open with such force, it slammed against the wall. One of Peter's lamps fell off a shelf and shattered into pieces on the floor. marymary stood frozen to the spot, her mouth stretched wide.

Peter turned. He saw the gun. Everything slowed to a crawl. He dropped to the floor, grabbed Anna's arm and pulled her next to him. Three shots in quick succession rang out. marymary yelped. Her white blouse turned a dark crimson as each bullet tore into her flesh, knocking her back against the stove. She stood, took a couple of steps toward the table and rested her palms on the wormy chestnut.

She opened her mouth to speak, but there was no sound, only a trickle of blood rolling down her chin. Swaying, she fell forward, hitting the table first with her chest, then with her head. marymary rested on one cheek on the table, facing Peter and Anna; her eyes rolled back, and she stopped moving.

"She talked too much," Aiden Connor said. He walked around the couch and pointed his pistol at Peter. "You two, stand up."

Peter stood, positioning himself between Connor and Anna. Anna grabbed the top of the couch and made her way to her feet. Connor cocked his head and looked at Anna's hand.

"Perfect, she's already wearing the bracelet," he said. "She's coming with me. You're staying here."

"No. Take me instead; this is my fault."

"Sorry kid, I have my orders."

No one moved. Peter and Connor stared at each other for what seemed like an eternity. Eventually, Connor leaned forward and grabbed Anna's wrist. In the doorway behind him, Peter saw the shadow of a large man. Peter again dropped to the floor behind the couch, and again took Anna's arm and pulled her down with him. Connor didn't let go. His forehead flushed; his cheeks turned red. He jerked Anna's arm. She opened her mouth to scream, but only a short burst of air escaped.

Peter lunged with his other hand and threw his arm around her waist. He let his body go limp. It was too much dead weight for Connor, who dropped them both, sending Peter and Anna to the floor. Peter turned his body to keep the backpack, still strapped to his back, from hitting the ground. His shoulder took the blow instead, and Anna landed on top of him. Pain fired through his chest and arm. Anna rolled off Peter and turned to look at Connor. They watched as he slowly raised his pistol.

A gunshot echoed through the small home. Connor's expression changed from a sickening grin to a grimacing frown. Blood spewed from his shoulder and he grunted and stumbled past the pair.

Another shot fired, this one closer.

"Fuck!" Connor screamed as the bullet ripped into his leg.

He clutched his shoulder and fell to the floor behind Peter and Anna, near marymary's feet. Peter and Anna crawled into the breezeway to the far end and cowered behind a stack of storage boxes Peter had used to bring silverware, plates and clothes from 2017.

Connor limped into the breezeway, blood pouring from his wound, leaving a morbid trail. He hid behind a set of sheets and blankets hanging from a makeshift washing line opposite Peter and Anna.

"I want my money, you Goddamn cheater!" a deep, gruff voice yelled.

"Shit. McCall." Peter whispered.

Anna locked the empty bracelet around Peter's wrist. She spun him around and opened the backpack, digging through it until she found his phone.

"Got it," she said.

"Who the hell is McCall?" Connor muttered.

"Where are you, kid?" McCall yelled.

Peter took the phone from Anna. His grip was so tight the display screen changed colors. He opened the app.

"Wait, you're not going anywhere without me."

Connor limped from behind the sheet and raised the pistol.

"Push it," Anna said.

Peter pushed his finger against the phone's screen. Everything went black.

Chapter 37

Peter, 2017

They reappeared crouched behind a server rack in the basement at MPH. Waiting quietly in the darkness, Peter and Anna strained to listen for any movement from the stairs. Anna unhooked the bracelet from Peter's wrist and began to stand, but Peter held his hands out.

"We left him back in the past," Anna said. "He can't *still* be at the top of the stairs."

"How do you think he found us so quick?"

"Maybe he's tracking you. Could Padma have been helping someone else?"

"I don't know."

Peter activated the flashlight on his phone, and they crept to the bottom of the stairs. He raised his foot toward the first step but hesitated. Thoughts of marymary rushed into his head.

How did she know so much? How many more GROUP members were involved? She said, "everyone." Could that be true?

He'd seen the bullets rip through her clothing, the way her body had jerked each time one of them buried into her flesh. He'd seen the blood seeping to the floor from each wound as she bounced off the stove and ricocheted to the table. She had looked at him, her eyes pleading for help, but he couldn't move. He felt selfish. His cheeks burned. When she'd fallen forward, their eyes had met, and seconds later, her eyes had died. She had died.

Anna grabbed his hand. He looked down at her small, slender fingers holding his tightly, then at the bracelet. He'd lost a sister, and it was his fault. It was because of that thing wrapped around her wrist. Because of him.

"You okay?" Anna asked.

Peter pushed the back of his hand against his face to brush away a tear barely clinging on to his eye.

"Sorry," he said without facing her.

Again, he attempted to start up the stairs, but Anna tightened her grasp, holding him back. He turned to look at her. Another tear formed and dropped onto his shirt.

"We can still change things," she said.

"What if we can't?"

"Peter, you built a time machine. You should never doubt you can do anything you want. This thing here" —She lifted their arms and pushed the bracelet toward his face— "you did this before else. We'll figure it out."

Anna leaned forward and touched her lips to his.

"I promise," she whispered as she pulled away.

"Okay," he said, not sure if he believed her.

They opened the basement door and stepped into the cafeteria. Max, Alison and Regan stood on the other side of the large room, next to the candy machines. With their backs against the wall, they stared at Peter and Anna.

"You guys didn't escape?" Peter said.

Max's eyes shifted from Peter to the wall on his left and back to Peter. Alison shook her head slightly and looked away.

Regan inched behind Max; her eyes fixed on something at the base of the candy machine.

"I've been waiting for you to come back," a voice said from behind the door.

Peter and Anna spun. Standing behind them was a man dressed in black, a few inches taller than Peter. He raised a pistol toward them and wiggled the barrel, indicating they should stand with their friends. Peter and Anna didn't move. The man reached with his free hand and slammed the basement door. They flinched, stepped away, but kept their eyes on him.

Anna pursed her lips and tilted her head, studying the strange man. Her expression changed from fear to recognition. Turning to step behind Peter, she put her hand on his waist and leaned in close. Peter could feel her breath on his neck. Peter turned and looked at her.

"The car accident," she said, her voice quivering.

Peter pulled Anna closer behind him and turned to face the man. The familiar rush of adrenaline pulsed through him. They stood in the middle of the cafeteria. Any escape through the doors leading into the office or outside into the evening's darkness were too far away.

Niven!

Peter's body chilled, and he could feel the goosebumps forming. He rubbed his hands over his forearms, then folded his arms around his waist.

"Good memory, Miss Symons," the man said. "You saved my family by crashing into us. Now, please, join your friends against the wall."

"Why the gun?" Peter asked. "We're unarmed kids. We can't hurt you."

Niven glared at Peter. He stepped forward, leaving only inches between them. Niven's nostrils flared. His hot coffee breath hit Peter in the face. Peter recoiled and stepped back, pressing Anna closer to the wall.

"Because, VanBurenBoy," Niven spoke deliberately, pronouncing each word, each syllable as if he were scolding a young child, "you *kids* are still trying to take my family from me, and that's something I can't have."

Behind the basement door, metal clanged against the cement floor. Niven turned. Peter and Anna continued slowly backing toward the wall until they stood next to Max. The silence throughout the room was palpable but brief. From the gap beneath the basement door, guttural groans rose from the bottom of the stairs, followed by louder clangs of what seemed to be metal objects possibly being kicked, pushed and dragged across the concrete floor.

"Who is that?" Max said.

"It could be Connor," Peter said. "He's been on our tail for a few days."

"How did he get in the basement?"

"You can thank me for that," Niven said. He smiled and thrust out his chest, obviously proud of whatever he meant.

The door nudged open slightly. The sound of Connor's boots thundered across the cafeteria floor. His arms appeared first, raised up and pushing open the door like a zombie, followed by his head, held high. At the top of the stairs, he dropped to his stomach and raised his chin, looked at Niven, and held his eyes for a moment before dropping his bloodied skull to the floor.

The sleeves of his denim jacket had been torn off. Blood poured from the bullet wound in his shoulder and the wound in his right thigh. Connor tried to stand, putting one hand against a table to lift himself. His chest puffed up and down as he labored to breathe.

"Such a disappointment," Niven said, slightly shaking his head.

Niven raised his gun. Connor threw one hand in the air. His eyes widened, and he opened his mouth to speak.

"No," he pleaded.

Connor's knee buckled and he stumbled. Niven pulled the trigger twice, both bullets hitting Connor in the chest. His body reeled backward, thumping against the basement doorframe. He crumpled to the floor at the top of the stairs.

"Just a waste," Niven said. He looked at the gun in his hand and glanced toward Connor, now lying still and lifeless.

Max sprang, slamming his body against Niven. The gun slipped from Niven's hand and slid across the white tile, coming to rest near Connor. They hit the ground with a thud, Max on top, and rolled over each other until they reached a table. Niven put his palms onto Max's chest and pushed, trying to free himself, but Max let his body go limp and dropped, jamming his elbow into Niven's stomach. Niven grunted. Max formed a fist and raised it over his head, but before he could bring it down, Niven reached into his inside jacket pocket and pulled a small pistol.

"Max!" Alison yelled.

Max saw it too late and reached for Niven's arm, trying to pin it against the floor. The gun fired. The air was pierced with Regan's scream. Max reached for Niven's upper arm, twisted and collapsed on the floor beside him. Pulling his knees up to his chest, Max curled into a ball. Blood pooled on the floor near his shoulder. Alison rushed to kneel beside him, cradling his head in her arms.

Niven pulled himself up and stood, pointing the gun toward Peter, Anna and Regan. He paused, took a deep breath, nodded his head four times, counting silently, and exhaled. He swung the gun to Max and Alison.

"Get against the fucking wall!" he screamed.

Max hoisted himself to a standing position, and Alison followed, still holding onto Max until they joined Regan. Leaning toward him, Regan gently brushed the hair from her brother's face.

"You." Niven nodded at Anna. "Come with me and bring his backpack."

She didn't move. He pointed the gun at Peter.

"Don't make me say it again."

Anna stepped toward Niven, but Peter grabbed her wrist.

"Take me instead," he said. "This whole thing is my fault."

"I don't care whose fault it is, VanBurenBoy. I only care that from this moment on, nothing changes. I don't want to kill you or her. I want my family and my empire, and as long as you are trying to change it, I'll be keeping her with me."

"We'll stop," Peter said. "I promise."

"I'm sorry VanBurenBoy, I'm afraid I can't trust you. How about this? In five years, find me. If everything is in order, I'll return her to you, unharmed. But my family's future is now her future. It's ironic, really. If you do anything to change the future and I lose them, you lose her."

Peter wrapped his fingers around Anna's wrist, squeezing so hard her fingers pulsed. Peter released her wrist and entwined his fingers with hers. Anna stared at his fingers, their fingers, then looked into his eyes.

"I can't let go," Peter said. His eyes reddened. His heart ached.

"You're trying my patience, VanBurenBoy."

Niven turned, pointing the gun toward Max. He fired one shot, hitting Max just above his left knee. Alison and Regan screamed. Regan ripped off her sweatshirt and tied it around Max's leg. She stuck her fingers through the jagged bullet hole in his sleeve and pulled, ripping a piece of his shirt. Calm, although clearly shaken, she wrapped the fabric above the bullet hole and pulled it tightly around his arm. Max clenched his teeth and groaned.

"Unharmed?" Anna asked.

"As long as I get what I want, you two can be together."

"Let go, Peter," Anna said. "It will only be a few minutes for me, and I'll be fine. Trust me."

"I can't leave you."

"Find the nurse." She looked at Max, who was lying on the ground, propped up by his younger sisters. "She'll know what to do."

Peter took the backpack from his shoulder and handed it to her. He stared into her eyes and, one by one loosened his fingers. They stood for a split second, palms together before she turned and walked to Niven.

Niven grabbed her elbow and spun her around, pinning her against his chest. He wrapped one arm around her waist and squeezed. His eyes met Peter's. He pushed her head to the side and brushed the hair from her neck.

Peter held his arms to sides, clenching both fists until his knuckles ached. The sight of Niven's face so close to Anna's, his breath sweeping over her neck, sent Peter's brain into overdrive. If he lunged, he would surely die—but could the others get away? Could she? His heart pounded.

"Smart move, VanBurenBoy." Niven sneered. He squinted at Anna and again squeezed her tightly against his body. "Now, just so you understand the severity of the situation, I have a demonstration for you; something to prove that I am not screwing around here. This is not a game."

Raising the gun, Niven pointed it at Peter, his own dual bracelet hanging from his wrist. Peter's shoulders tensed. He blinked, turned his head and tried to speak. He waited for the shot to hit him. Where would it hit him? Would it hurt? Would he die quickly or suffer? Niven let go of Anna, reached toward his machine and pushed a button between the two bracelets.

The air in front of Peter grew cold and thick like a cloud had formed. Peter cringed and stepped back. He closed his eyes. A split second later, a chilly wind blew through, sucking the thick fog from the room as if someone had opened an airplane door mid-flight.

"Zach!" Anna shouted.

Peter's eyes shot open. Standing inches from him was his best friend. Anna stepped toward Zach, but Niven grabbed her, once again wrapping his arm around her stomach and pulling her to him.

Peter reached for Zach, who looked the same as when Peter and Anna had last seen him. His hands were bound behind his back, and his ankles were tied. His eyes flinched and opened. He turned his head both ways and staggered backward into Peter, who caught him and held him upright.

Niven pulled the trigger twice, hitting Zach in the chest. The shock pushed Zach and Peter against the wall. Peter dropped Zach and fell to the floor next to him.

"Looks like I'm in charge now," Niven said.

He attached the second half of his bracelet to Anna, reached into his jacket pocket and pulled out his cell phone. Peter's eyes met Anna's.

"I'm sorry," he whispered.

Niven pushed a button on his phone. He faded away, taking Anna with him.

Chapter 38

Nelson, 2022

I appeared in the same spot where I had been standing when Zach's bullet passed through me. The picture of my family at the entrance of Disneyland hung on the wall, still in one piece. I touched it and smiled. VanBurenBoy's backpack hung off my shoulder. Anna's hand brushed against mine. Small reminders of everything I had just accomplished with two bullets, two simple squeezes of the trigger that had changed everything.

VanBurenBoy was trapped in the past. I had his machine and his girlfriend. He couldn't come after me. And Connor, the only other man from the past who knew of my future, was dead. I tossed the backpack on the desk and watched it slide across the slick brown wood, stopping just before it fell off the other side.

"Just two bullets," I said, "that's all it took. It's like Zach never existed."

"You killed him!" the girl screamed.

"He was a threat. He had to go."

Why didn't she understand? It was such a simple concept. She began to cry. Her skin flushed, and she turned away from me.

"But he was my friend," she said through her sobs.

"He wasn't your friend. You hated him. He told me all about you, your dad and the aliens. He knew you hated him, and he felt bad."

She turned and looked at me. Her tears momentarily stopped.

"What?" she asked.

"Maybe that's why he wanted to get off the planet," I mumbled. "He was going after your dad."

As quickly as the revelation hit me, it disappeared. New memories of my empire filled my head. Everything I'd done over the last three years rushed in, overwhelming my brain. My legs weakened. I collapsed to the couch. All of it came back. My family. My computer system. It wasn't to send someone off the Earth; it was to control time travel. I did it. He didn't do it first. I did. Talbot did.

The girl pressed the release on the bracelet. I reached for her, but she wriggled her arm out of my grip and dashed for the door. I looked at the ceiling and frowned.

"Please don't run."

I tried to stand, but the room went blurry. Stumbling backward, I grabbed the corner of my desk and steadied myself. I looked at the backpack still lying on the desk and the machine attached to my wrist.

"You're not going to be able to escape," I warned. "I live on an island!"

"Someone, please help!" she shouted from the third floor.

"No one else is here. My family is, um..." I searched my memories. I knew they weren't there, but I couldn't yet remember where they were.

Ceremony was tonight. My Ceremony. That meant Sudo would be in the basement. It would be a special one tonight. He certainly wasn't going to help her, and the other people were locked in the cells.

"My family is away!"

She ran down a set of stairs to the first floor. I staggered behind her and walked down each step, taking them one at a time, holding tightly to the railing.

"I always send them away for Ceremony!"

She ran down the set of stairs leading into the basement. When her foot hit the bottom step, I heard her scream. I chuckled. Her footsteps grew louder as she made her way back up the stairs toward me.

"Yeah, Sudo's an ugly guy. Quite the sight for someone who doesn't know him."

At the top of the stairs, she ran toward me. I reached for her, but she stepped to the left, quickly shifted right and ran past me. I exhaled. I wasn't in the mood to play. Ceremony was tonight, and I needed to be ready.

"I don't have time for this."

She ran through the dining room and out the back door. I walked to a window and watched her run into the paintball field. Just after my kids were born, I'd built a replica of my childhood paintball field, and I hadn't played there in a long time. Maybe this girl would give me the challenge those football players from my youth, who pretended to be my friends just to gain access to my dad's creation, could never give me.

I moved down the stairs. My head was still a little hazy, but the dizziness had gone. My legs were strong as if someone had shot adrenaline straight into my bloodstream. I grabbed a mask, strapped it over my head, filled a hopper full of paintballs and attached it to my favorite gun. It was a simple, dark blue, semi-automatic rifle. I fired a shot toward the woods. The sound and smell took me back to my childhood. My body relaxed, and I smiled, thinking back to those paintball games where Steve and I faced off at the end. *I miss that guy. I wonder what he's up to now.*

I typed Anna's name into the computer and watched as it appeared on the scoreboard. Mine appeared underneath hers.

"You need help, boss?" Sudo asked from the doorway.

Boss. I liked that. No one had called me boss for a long time. Things were finally back to normal.

"Nah, this should be easy. Go downstairs and prep for tonight's sacrifice. Keep an eye out for VanBurenBoy. He'll be here anytime."

He nodded and walked inside. I stared at the trees. Hiding there would be difficult. *Let's start with the obvious.* I turned toward the line of small farm buildings tucked against the left side of the property. The chicken coop was first.

I wish had built that same ditch where I used to start each game. I'd love to jump down into it, rest on my stomach for a few minutes, breathe a little, just for old times' sake.

"This is a terrible hiding spot," I yelled. "It's so narrow in there, you better have a gun up and ready to shoot. Here I come, I'm opening the door!"

I grabbed the door and swung it open. The narrow walkway was only four feet wide and empty. Cages rising off the ground on both sides had collapsed, and dirt and grass grew through the ground, turning the once clean and neat coop into a greenhouse full of weeds.

Why didn't I keep this in a better condition?

The milk house was a better hiding spot. I'd spent many evening hours painting it red after Danny was born. About the size of a small one-car garage, it would allow someone to squat next to a window and keep track of everything going on around them. Unfortunately, with nothing to hide behind, they were an easy target inside it. I doubted she was in here, but I grabbed the door handle. Movement at the corner of my eye, near the barn, stopped me. I turned my head just in time to watch the barn door close. I smiled.

"Got you," I whispered to myself.

I crept to the barn, opened the door and peered in. It was mostly dark, except where the sun shone through the windows, giving life to the dust particles dancing in the rays. The smell of stale hay and wet dirt hit me as soon as I stepped inside. I paused to admire my dad's collection of tractors, set up the exact way he had arranged them when I was a kid. This collection was the only thing he'd left me in his will, and it was the perfect gift—the perfect memory of him.

I walked along the tractors, running my finger across the front of each as I passed. Dust and dirt covered my fingertips. I wiped my hands on my pants and frowned.

Dad would not be happy with this.

Sitting on the ground, next to the last tractor, I saw her. Her knees were bent and tucked against her chest, and she was looking down at the ground. I cleared my throat. She looked at me. Suddenly I was sixteen years old again, playing paintball with my friends.

"Sarah?" I said.

She stayed silent, looking at me.

"I could have shot you," I said, dropping the gun to my side.

She continued to stay silent, which was unlike her. She must have known I would never shoot her. If she and I were the last two, and I would always make sure we were, she would always win.

"We need to set a trap," I said. "He'll be coming for us soon, and if we can kill him before he gets us, we can win."

"I'm not going to help you kill him," she said. Her voice trembled. She retreated a few inches, pushing herself against the back wall.

"But Sarah," I said, "if we do this together, we can win."

She stared at me as though I were speaking a foreign language. Her eyes widened. The reflection of my gun shone in her green eyes.

Green?

Sarah's eyes aren't green. They're brown. I shook my head and squeezed my eyes closed. When I opened them, the fog lifted. Sarah morphed into the girl I'd brought back with me. His girl. He had never suffered, yet I continued to suffer. *Over and over, they are taken from me. He keeps changing things, taking them from me. He will not take them from me again. He will see what it's like to hurt.*

I lunged for her, grabbed her wrists and pulled her to her feet. She went limp and dropped to the ground in front of me. I pulled the pistol from my waistband and held it toward her.

"Don't make me use this," I said, drawing each word out, keeping my voice low and monotone.

"You said you wouldn't hurt me."

"If you cooperate, I'll let you go as soon as he comes for you."

That was only partly true. I would wait for him to get here, but neither would be leaving alive. Two sacrifices at Ceremony would be a perfect way to celebrate my power returning. She calmed down and stood. I walked her back into the house, pausing long enough to give myself the win on the scoreboard, and took her to my main office on the third floor. I opened the door and shoved her inside. At the sight of the large yellow cage hanging from the ceiling, she flinched and stepped back. I put my hand against her shoulder and pushed her forward.

"Get inside."

"What is this?"

"I built this for my little girl, but I've been using it lately to talk to my sacrifices. They need to understand why I'm doing what I do before their time comes."

She stood silently staring at the cage. It was round and hung a foot off the floor. The metal had been painted yellow by Danny when he was just a little boy. With a few inches between each bar, it was easy to watch them, watch their expression as I told them what would happen at their Ceremony. It was never easy convincing them that their death would help everyone, but usually, I could make them understand.

"I said, get inside."

She swung open the thin metal door, grabbed the handle and pulled herself into the cage. Lightly stepping across the white carpet, she nudged Lena's toys out of the way and reached the white perch. She looked over her shoulder at me.

"My kids spent a lot of time watching Tweety Bird cartoons, and Lena wanted a cage of her own. She would jump inside and try to squeak like a bird. It was so cute."

I pushed the cage door shut and stuck my key inside the lock, listening for the sound of the tumblers trapping her until Ceremony later in the evening. I stepped behind my desk and stopped to admire the weapon lying on the floor. I lifted it and touched the button in the center. Electricity crackled at both ends. I heard the girl inhale.

I turned to see the fear on her face, but something new appeared. Something I had seen so many times as I prepped for Ceremony. Hatred. The hatred never bothered me; it was the fear I loved. It was that extra bit of motivation, the push I needed, that proved that I was doing was the right thing. It was the only way to ensure peace.

"I built this after dreaming about it," I said, displaying the weapon so she could admire my handiwork. "It was before my family had come back. Each night I would dream about them as if I had them again—could hug them, feel them in my arms—and each night a large creature would take them from me. One night this appeared. I took it, and I defeated the monster!"

The girl squirmed. I grinned, feeling her fear like a spirit running through me.

"You said you wouldn't hurt me," she said. Her body shivered as I circled the cage, touching the edges with my weapon. Sparks jumped from the metal to the ground around her feet. I opened the door and stepped inside, grabbing a small burlap sack from the floor, and stood with my nose just a few inches from hers. I felt the wind from her short, quick breaths hitting me in the face. Her breath was warm. I raised the bag, pulling it over her head and stopped just past her forehead. I looked into her eyes.

"I will use this staff tonight at your Ceremony." She jerked her body and screamed. I shoved the bottom of the sack into her mouth, quieting her, and pulled the rest of it over her head.

"But first, we need to wait for VanBurenBoy."

Chapter 39

Peter, 2017

"What just happened?" Max yelled. He limped toward the empty spot where Nelson and Anna had stood. "Where did they go?"

His sisters rushed toward him, catching him as he crumpled to the floor. Peter dropped to his knees next to Zach. He lifted Zach's weakened body into his lap, letting his head fall against his own leg. Peter stared at his best friend, remembering the first time they met and how Zach had saved him from a group of bullies. He looked at his wrist: the machine no longer hung there. He reached for his bag, but Niven had taken it, along with his phone. And Anna.

"It's over," Peter muttered. "There's nothing I can do. He won."

Zach's eyes rolled back into their sockets. Peter looked away. A hand reached from behind and touched his shoulder.

"I think he's gone," Regan said.

Peter leaned forward and whispered to Zach, "I'm so sorry."

Alison approached Peter and put her hand on his shoulder. She squeezed, offering support.

Peter twisted his head around and looked up at her. He bit his lip. "No, it's not over. It's never over!"

Alison backed away from him.

"I can find her," he insisted. "I can save him and still fix this!"

Peter felt for the bracelet again. A wave of nausea hit him like a brick as he looked at the spot where Anna had stood just a few minutes earlier. He vaulted to his feet. His vision blurred, and he stumbled against the wall. Tears he had been fighting streamed down his cheeks. Alison leaned against him and put her arms around his shoulders. She pulled him close.

"I'm sorry," she whispered.

"Anna said I was supposed to find the nurse."

"Regan? She's a nurse."

Peter broke free of Alison and moved toward Regan. He stopped mid-stride, a few steps away. He tilted his head. "No, we didn't know anything about Regan, so it can't be her."

Peter squeezed his eyes together and stared toward the ceiling. The nurse. Had she meant the nurse from her monitor? Talbot? He spun and walked toward the cafeteria doors.

"Wait!" Max yelled. "Where are you going?"

"I'm going to find Anna and fix this."

"How?"

"I don't know."

"What do we do with them?" Alison asked, glancing from Zack to Conner.

Peter remembered Padma's words: *At first, the police were sure you were connected with a larger crime, especially considering what they found at work the next morning,*

"I don't care," he said. "I'm not going to let it happen!"

SMOKE STILL HUNG IN Peter's office as he rounded the corner and fell into his chair. He waved his hand in the air, unsuccessful at pushing away the smell of fried wires, and unlocked his bottom desk drawer. The spare laptop, the one he used when he had to travel for work, lay hidden under a group of hanging files. He pushed them to the back and pulled out the laptop. He powered it on, loaded the GROUP chat room, typed the first half of his password into the dialog box and paused.

Last time you talked to her, she was pissed. But she always came after you left GROUP. She was worried about you. She will come again.

[VanBurenBoy has logged on]

Peter stared at the screen, his hands hovering less than an inch above the keyboard. He squinted and moved his face closer to the screen, watching the list of online users. Thankfully, he was the only person in GROUP. The thought of talking to anyone else about what was going on was not something he wanted to deal with at that moment.

It had to have been long enough for Talbot to get the signal or see he was online, or whatever it took to alert her Peter was there.

[VanBurenBoy has logged off]

Each of the previous times Talbot had contacted him after GROUP, it had only been a couple of seconds after Peter logged out, but this time a full minute passed with nothing. He checked the clock in the bottom right-hand corner of the monitor. It changed from 4:47 a.m. to 4:48 a.m.

Maybe going back to the past did some kind of irreparable damage to her, whatever she is.

He stood and turned away from the computer, studying the motivational posters management had hung on his wall.

"'Do something today your future self will thank you for.'" Aloud, Peter read the white, Comic Sans text against the dark background of the poster above his desk. "I'm doing everything I can to make that true."

His laptop chimed. Peter flinched and turned around. A second name appeared in the list of online users.

[Talbot has logged on]

Peter scrambled into his chair and typed a message to Talbot before she said anything.

VanBurenBoy: He took her. Do you know where she is? I need to help her.

Talbot: She's in 2022. I can meet you there, and I think I can help.

VanBurenBoy: How? He took my machine.

Talbot: He attached a sensor to Aiden Connor. It only works while he's alive. Take it from him and strap it over your heart. You'll automatically jump to where they landed.

Talbot: But be careful, things have changed since the last time you were there. He made sure of it.

VanBurenBoy: I don't know if I can do this alone.

Talbot: Make your way to Ceremony, *and I'll come find you.*

VanBurenBoy: How will you know me?

Talbot: Trust me, Peter, I know where you are at all times. I'll find you.

[Talbot has logged off]

Peter hustled along the hallway and shoved the cafeteria's double doors wide open. He stepped inside and searched the room for the body of Aiden Connor. Max, Alison and Regan were still there, sitting at a table near the windows. Max's leg was stretched on a chair, and Regan was tying a ripped tablecloth around it.

"Is he okay?" Peter asked.

"Yeah," Regan said. "It only grazed him; tore the skin off, but he'll be fine."

Peter's eyes followed a path of blood from where Connor had died to the snack machines. Someone had dragged his body next to Zach's. Each body was covered with two tablecloths, blood seeping through the fabric from the wounds. Peter pulled the tablecloth covering the shorter, stockier of the two and studied the beaten face of Aiden Connor, who stared back at him.

"He was hurt pretty bad and shot before he somehow appeared here with us," Regan said.

"Yeah," Peter thought back to marymary's death. "I was there when it started. McCall must have done a number on him before he followed us here. Why did he kill your father?"

"It's a long story," Max said. "Our dad was a small-time crook just outside New York City, not exactly a great guy, and Connor was the cop assigned to hunt him down. He tried to apprehend Dad in a parking garage. Something happened, and Dad ended up dead."

"Our dad wasn't violent," Alison pleaded. "There's no way he would have attacked this guy."

"But Connor killed him anyway," Max continued, "He went to trial and was acquitted. I wanted to know why. Now I'm not sure we'll ever know."

Peter bent at the knees and pulled Connor's jean jacket open.

"What are you doing?" Max asked.

"I need to get to Anna before something happens to her, and he can help me."

He ripped open the dead man's shirt. Attached above his heart was the small round device, no bigger than a quarter, that Talbot had described. Peter pulled the device from Connor's chest, ripping out a few stray chest hairs and leaving a circular charred spot near one of the bullet holes. It had been stuck there with some kind of adhesive, and there was enough residue left for Peter's use. He stood.

"I hope this works."

He stared at the red spot on Connor's chest and hesitated. The look Anna had given him as she disappeared flashed in Peter's head.

You promised you would never leave her behind.

He thrust his chest out, lifted his shirt and slapped machine over his heart. A buzz of electricity shot through his skin. He cringed and squeezed his eyes closed.

"Peter!" Alison cried.

Her scream made his eyes jolt open. Blackness filled the room.

Chapter 40

Peter, 2022

Peter always squeezed his eyes shut when traveling, afraid of what he might see. Too much television as a child had reinforced the idea that the unknown monsters—things grabbing at him during that split second it took to move from one plane to the other—could frighten him from ever wanting to push the button again.

The strange room materialized around him, and he felt the floor against his feet. He took a step back and blinked, concentrating on a blurry, brown desk as it gradually came into view. The laptop sitting on top seemed to float in midair until the desk's surface appeared beneath it.

Two rows of monitors came into focus, hanging head-high on the wall. Each one offered a view of different parts of the city, similar to the monitors at both of Padma's homes.

Am I back at Padma's bunker? Is he working with her?

It was a small room with a desk occupying the back half. Along one side, a tattered orange couch was pushed against the wall. Peter crept toward the door and cracked it open just enough to aim his ear into the hallway. He expected to hear something, maybe movement in one of the other rooms, or hopefully Anna fighting to get away, but there was only silence.

He walked to the monitor closest to the desk and studied it. Evening in Columbus revealed a dimly lit, serene intersection near The Ohio State University. This time of the year, students would be walking from building to building to take their Spring semester finals, but like every other sidewalk Peter had seen in 2022 Columbus, it was empty. He moved from monitor to monitor, looking for any sign of life. It wasn't until he studied the last monitor, the one nearest to the door, that he recognized something.

Padma's hideout.

Smoke billowed from the end of the runway. The mound of earth that hid her hideout had collapsed, caving it in. Remnants of the crushed building beneath jutted through the burned grass. Bodies lay strewn near the entrance. He narrowed his eyes and moved closer to the monitor. Slight movement from a figure, a young woman, caught his eye. He touched the screen, flicking his finger over her body, hoping he could somehow awaken her.

"Come on, stand up," he muttered.

She pulled herself up, but then stumbled and fell into a pile of smoldering leaves, rolled on to her back and stopped moving. Peter recoiled. He closed his eyes and turned his head to the side.

Too much death today.

A door slammed on the first floor. Peter jumped. He balled his hands into fists, held them close to his chest, scrambled to the door and opened it a few inches further. Hearing nothing irregular, he took a deep breath and stepped into the hallway.

At the end of the hall, evening light shone through a small window, rectangular on three sides and arched on top. He tiptoed toward it, pushed the sheer, thin curtain aside and peered outside. The sight of Niven, walking alone on a drawbridge across a ten-foot-wide moat, filled Peter with both dread and hope. On his right was a stairwell where stairs led to both upper and lower floors. He glanced back at Niven, who was now on the other side of the bridge.

"If he's alone, she has to be here somewhere," Peter muttered.

Peter watched as Niven stuck a key inside a short, square kiosk and turned. The bridge rose into the air, and Peter realized he was now trapped on the property by the moat.

Who builds a moat in 2022? Does it go all the way around?

Niven paused at the driver's side window of a long black car where he appeared to exchange a few heated words with the driver. Opening the back door, he disappeared into the car and pulled the door shut. With a short puff of exhaust from the tailpipe, the car pulled away.

Peter moved a little more quickly, hoping there were no guards lurking in the halls—and that Anna was also in the building, waiting to be found. The carpeted stairs masked the sound of his feet, but at the bottom, the wooden floor in front of the large front door creaked with each step. He turned the knob and pulled, peering through the narrow doorway. Once he was certain the front porch was clear, he slid onto the porch. Lights on the opposite side of the moat shone at an angle, lighting the castle. Peter covered his mouth with his palm.

"I know this castle," he said through his fingers.

He made his way down the front stairs, stepped off the sidewalk into the wet grass, walking along the moat's edge and following it around the north side of the castle. In the distance, the lights from the stadium illuminated a large crowd of people. In unison, they erupted in cheers. Although the stadium was a quarter of a mile away, he recognized Niven's voice on the microphone.

"Welcome to Ceremony number one hundred and twenty-two."

Shit, Ceremony! Talbot said to meet her there.

Peter continued following the moat, hoping for a break somewhere. Once clear of the castle, he turned and stared into a large backyard.

"What is a farm doing here?"

Four small farm buildings were situated along the far side of the yard, in the shadow of a large red barn towering over them. A garage next to a swimming pool blocked his path along the edge of the moat. A small forest encompassed the back half of the property.

Why would he have a farm?

Peter turned and looked at the castle. A large scoreboard, similar to a high school football stadium, spanned the second-floor windows, covering them entirely. On the left side of the scoreboard, under the list of competitors, were two names.

Nelson: 1

Anna: 0

He inhaled sharply. His shoulders tightened, and he could hear his heart racing. He put his hand over it, hoping to keep it from bursting through his chest.

"What could that mean?" Peter whispered.

"It means they played," a deep, gruff voice behind him said, "and she lost."

Peter spun. The man was large, dressed in blue jeans, a dark t-shirt and a black jacket. He was someone Peter had seen at

Ceremony both times he had attended. Peter raised his eyes to the top of the man's head. Straight dark hair poked from the sides of the brown Stetson hat tilted to one side.

The brown Stetson hat?

"Sudo Brownlock?"

The man smiled. He pointed a small pistol at Peter.

"Come with me," he said.

They walked toward the back door. Two gunshots echoed into the night from Ceremony. Peter hesitated at each one. He stopped and looked at the stadium. Where was Anna? Niven quieted the crowd. Over the microphone, Peter could hear Niven praising himself and what he had done for his empire.

"How could they cheer after that?"

"They think your little resistance is messing with his future," Sudo said.

"Come on, Sudo, that's not why they cheer, and you know it."

"Keep moving."

Sudo shoved him toward the door, but Peter put his hands against the door frame, halting his entry into the castle.

"They cheer because they're afraid. What has he promised you? Why do you help him?"

"Get your ass moving, kid."

"Come on, it has to be something you can get on your own. I bet you don't even like him. He probably treats you like shit. Tells you he'll help you, but he keeps putting it off, doesn't he? You're silently wondering if you'll ever get what he promised."

Sudo looked away. His face softened, and he opened his mouth to speak, but Peter held a hand out, unwilling to let the big man turn down his offer without hearing all the facts. Peter stood straight and stared Sudo in the eyes.

"I was the first to build the machine. If you help me, I'll help you get whatever it is you're trying to find. I promise."

Sudo grimaced and looked at Peter, his face wrinkled as if he were in pain. He grabbed Peter's wrist and turned it over, facing Peter's palm toward the sky.

"But you don't have the machine anymore," he growled. He pushed Peter hard enough to knock him to the ground at the bottom of the steps. "Get moving."

Peter stood and wiped the grass from his shirt. Sudo led him through the kitchen and down a set of stairs leading to the basement. It was a large grey room with a long hallway down the center, flanked by prison cells on each side. Actual prison cells with iron bars, each with a cot, a sink and a small, dirty mirror hanging overhead—like something out of the Alcatraz documentaries Peter watched on Saturday nights before time travel was a thing in his life.

Peter slowed his pace, looking into each cell as he passed. Most were empty, but in one a young woman lay on a bed with her back to him. She wore blue jeans, a white blouse, and her white sneakers were neatly arranged on the floor next to a brown paper bag. Peter stopped.

"marymary?"

The young dark-haired woman in the cell stirred and began to turn her head, but Sudo shoved his hands into the small of Peter's back, pushing him forward before Peter could see her face. Sudo turned and pushed his gun between the bars of her cell.

"Keep your mouth shut!" he ordered.

Sudo grabbed the key chain from his pocket and unlocked the last cell, two away from the sleeping young woman. He pushed Peter inside and slammed the door.

"Come on, Sudo. You don't have to do this."

Sudo moved away from Peter. He walked to a desk just outside Peter's cell, sat down, his back against the wall, and powered on the laptop in front of him. Taking off his hat, he set it over a mug sitting on a coffee-stained, yellow legal pad.

Peter stood at the bars of his cell and looked out into the room. From the wooden floor to the walls to the desk where Sudo sat, everything was a different shade of brown.

"How much time do you spend down here?" Peter asked.

Sudo stayed silent. Next to Peter's cell, a small square brown table held a vase full of pink tulips.

"What's with the tulips?" Peter insisted. "They seem so out of place."

Sudo continued to ignore him. Peter turned, his arms hanging limp at his sides, and sighed. He'd tried with Sudo and failed. Talbot would not find him at Ceremony. Any hope he had to save himself, Anna or humanity was all but over. He lay down on the bed and closed his eyes. Maybe he would see her in a dream. And Zach would be there too. Going forward, it might the only way he ever saw them again.

Chapter 41

Peter, 2022

Peter's eyes jolted open. He sat up, inhaled sharply and tried to make out where he was. The noises from Ceremony had disappeared.

Was it a dream? Had anything changed?

Sudo's laughter, the reason for Peter's sudden awakening, flooded his cell. Peter stood. He walked toward the bars and noticed a Dream Machine resting over Sudo's head. Peter's shoulders dropped. Nothing had changed. He stared at his hands, gripping the bars. His knuckles had turned white.

"Are you in GROUP?" Peter asked.

"Yeah, but it's different now," Sudo spoke slowly. His normal gruff voice sounded tired.

"How is it different? I haven't logged in since" —Peter paused. He let go of the bars and rubbed his forehead— "five years ago, I guess."

"New members, not as fun as it used to be."

"Why?"

"Tass left after the Event, and everyone else disappeared around the same time."

"Maybe if your boss didn't run around imprisoning and killing us..." a female voice said. Peter was sure it was marymary.

"Shut up!" Sudo grunted. He lifted the pistol from the desk and pointed it toward her.

"I can help still you," Peter said. "I have the specs for my machine hidden at my house. If you can get his bracelets, I'll take you back with me, and you can build one of your own. Then you don't have to wait for him to help you. You can do it yourself."

Sudo didn't answer.

"Maybe if you knew what it was like to lose someone you love, maybe then you would care," Peter added.

Sudo spun, ripped the Dream Machine from his head and stood, sending the chair flying across the room. Peter watched it slam against the wall. One of the legs snapped and slid toward the stairs. It stopped before it hit the bottom step, in a shadow. The shadow moved. Peter felt his heart beating faster.

Someone is standing on the bottom step.

She was small and thin. Her blonde hair was tied in a ponytail. She made eye contact with Peter and held it for a split second before backing out of sight. Sudo appeared, blocking Peter's view of the mysterious woman. He reached through the bars, grabbed Peter's collar and pulled him against the cold steel.

"I have," Sudo said.

Peter recoiled at the big man's stale coffee breath. He turned his head to the right and looked over Sudo's shoulder. Again, the woman appeared in the stairwell. She couldn't have been more than twenty years old and was wearing a sleeveless gray t-shirt with an old video game console imprinted on the front. Her bare knees were visible through the giant holes in her ripped blue jeans, and her arms were tattooed from her wrists to her shoulders. Her face was pale as if she hadn't seen the sun since before the Event. She raised her hand and with her index finger traced an invisible circle in the air.

Keep talking.

Sudo let go of Peter but didn't move away. He stared past the prisoner at the window on the back wall of the cell. His eyes appeared to moisten. Peter took three steps back.

"Who did you lose?" Peter asked. "A wife? Maybe children?"

"Shut up."

"Did you lose them in this mess?"

"I said, shut your mouth."

"I can get them back. I can get your wife back, and I can get Anna back. You just have to let me out."

"Don't talk about my wife."

"Get my bag. Help me go back and stop him from killing Anna, and I'll help you get your wife. That's the way it works, you know. I can't change my own future, and you can't change yours. But we *can* change each other's."

Peter gave a large, toothy grin. He stuck his right hand through the bars.

"Like a *Strangers on a Train*-type agreement. You know that movie."

Peter held his breath and glanced from Sudo to his hand. Sudo tilted his head and pursed his lips. Slowly, he raised his arm, appearing to reach for Peter's outstretched hand.

A wooden chair shattered against Sudo's back. Pieces of wood ricocheted off the cell bars. A few splintered pieces made it through and bounced off Peter's legs. He cringed as Sudo's face and chest collided with the bars, contorting his nose into a bloody mess. Peter heard the ting of Sudo's front teeth crashing against the metal. A tooth in the bottom row was knocked out, another tooth hung by a shred of bloody tissue. Sudo grunted and fell to the floor. Behind him, the woman stood. She was smaller, thinner and paler than Peter's first impression.

Sudo grunted again. He grabbed the bars with both hands and pulled himself to his knees. His eyes blinked, remaining closed a split second too long, and his head wobbled. Blood sprayed from his mouth, dotting the floor at Peter's feet. The tooth, still hanging, finally broke free and pinged to the floor inside Peter's cell. Sudo turned toward the woman. There was blood pooling in his thin, brown, oily hair.

The woman reached for the laptop on the edge of Sudo's desk. She took two steps toward him, swinging her arms as she walked. Using all her momentum, she slammed the slim computer against the side of Sudo's head. He crumpled in front of Peter's cell.

Rushing to him, she deftly flipped him onto his back and jammed a hand inside his jacket. She fished around and, smiling, pulled a key ring from an inside pocket and tossed them to Peter.

"Who are you?" Peter asked.

He unlocked the door and stepped around Sudo.

"Talbot," she said. Her eyes narrowed, she cocked her head and looked around at the surroundings. "I told you to find me at Ceremony, not get yourself captured."

"Sorry. I'm still new at this."

"Come on, Anna's upstairs. We don't have much time. Let's get her and get out of here."

"Wait!" Peter yelled, turning toward marymary's cell. He put the key in the lock and turned it, but when he looked inside, there was no movement. The cell was empty.

"Where'd she go?"

"We don't have time Peter! Let's go."

Ignoring her, he ran into the cell. He pulled the cot from the wall and ripped the blanket away. She wasn't there. He lifted the mattress and checked underneath. Nothing.

Where did she go? Sudo talked to her. Twice. She has to be here somewhere.

Peter threw his hands into the air and shook his head. He stepped outside the cell. A thick, meaty hand grabbed his foot and pulled. Peter's knee buckled and he fell, stumbling to the ground and landing on his back. Sudo rose to his feet and rushed toward Peter. He grabbed Peter under his arms and lifted him, pulling him against his body.

"You aren't going anywhere, either of you."

"Let's not do this," Talbot said, standing on the bottom step.

With his sleeve, Sudo wiped the blood from his forehead. He looked at it and smiled. "What are you gonna do? You can't sneak behind me and cheap-shot me this time."

"I've had a lot of free time to learn how to deal with people like you. You may be bigger than me, but you're also stupid," she said. "Really, really stupid."

A low rumble rose from somewhere deep inside Sudo as if he were a lion staring down its prey. He loosened the arm holding Peter and flung him aside with the other. Peter careened toward marymary's open cell, catching the bars to avoid falling.

Talbot stepped off the bottom step onto the basement floor. She looked at Peter and waved him away. Sudo took advantage of the distraction and charged, letting out a guttural scream. Just a few feet away, she moved to the right. He wildly threw a right fist where her head had been a few seconds earlier but only punched the air. With his body now twisted away from her, she spun, lifted her leg into the air and sunk her knee into his ribs. His howl echoed in the stairwell. He fell forward and collided with the wall next to the steps. She put her foot against his thick backside and gave a hard shove, toppling him to the floor.

Peter ran past Sudo and jumped onto the first couple of steps.

"Let's go!" he shouted.

Talbot ignored him. She walked to the other side of the room, stopped in front of Peter's cell and turned.

"Come on!" she shouted back at Sudo. "Get up, you coward!"

The insults seemed to infuriate Sudo. Veins pulsed in his forehead. He fought his way to his feet and caught his breath.

"I don't have all night!" she added.

"What are you doing?" Peter said.

"I've never liked him. Ever since you started hanging out in GROUP, he was always an asshole, treating you and everyone else like shit. I was raised not to hate, but I can't help it. I've wanted this fight for a long time."

Sudo drew himself up. He ran his hands through his hair, throwing dots of blood on the wall behind him. His eyes widened.

"You're dead!"

He rushed toward her, and as before, she stepped to the side; but he had learned from his mistake. Balling his fist, he swung it where her head would end up. Once again, she was quicker and bent over. His fist smashed into the brick wall between two cell doors. Even from the steps, Peter could hear every bone shattering in every one of Sudo's fingers.

Sudo grabbed his crumpled mess of a hand and opened his mouth. Talbot didn't give him time to react. She pulled her arm back, and with the momentum of her hundred pounds, rammed her palm into his chest. He exhaled sharply, his body careening backward, and crashed against the wall, sending whatever air remained in his lungs out through his lips. His face reddened. His eyes bulged.

"I love having a body," Talbot said, smiling at Peter.

She turned to Sudo, who had spun to one side while grasping the wall to hoist himself to his feet. Talbot punched him in the stomach. He lurched forward, gasped and leaned over. She put her hands around his head and pulled it down toward her knee, slamming his chin against the bone. He stumbled backward and swayed but managed to stay on his feet. She lifted her leg into the air and balanced herself on one foot.

"What are you doing?" Peter said. "We need to go."

She looked at Peter, a slight grin still on her face. Slowly, she turned her head to Sudo. The grin faded into a sneer. She slammed her heel into the side of his leg. It bent sideways at his knee, filling the basement with the cracking sounds of shattering bone. He dropped to the ground; his broken leg bent under the weight of his body, and he roared. Grabbing the vase of tulips from the small table, Talbot spun to shatter it against the side of his head. A ball of snot flew from his nose and landed on her cheek.

"Good night," she said.

Putting her foot against his chest, she pushed him into Peter's cell. He dropped onto his backside, rolled onto his side, curled into a fetal position and didn't move. She turned to Peter, wiped her face with the back of her wrist and straightened her ponytail. Reaching for the cell door, she pulled it shut, locked it and tossed the keys on the desk.

"Now we can go," she said.

Chapter 42

Peter, 2022

At the top of the stairs, Peter followed Talbot into the first-floor hallway. She led him through a dining room, into a kitchen and on to a set of spiral stairs leading to the second floor.

"Why aren't we using the main stairwell near the front door?" Peter asked.

"He might see us coming."

"How do you know your way around?"

"I really don't know," Talbot said. She stopped and closed her eyes. "I can see flashes of this place in my head as if I had been here before."

"Have you?"

"I don't think so."

Talbot gripped the white banister and climbed. Peter followed close behind. The stairway wound in a sharp circle, extended through a second story hallway through a floor opening and continued to the third floor.

"They certainly don't have these in castles," Peter muttered.

Talbot turned back at him and smiled. She paused just before her head emerged through the opening leading to the second floor and held out her hand, blocking Peter's climb. She slowly climbed to the next step and glanced around before climbing down.

"It's clear," she said, "but we need to get to the third floor."

"You're sure she's still here? What if he..." Peter paused, unable to even think, much less say, the word. "...at Ceremony last night?"

"I'm positive. I've seen her. She's up there somewhere."

"I don't understand. How have you seen her if you've never been here?"

"It's too complicated to explain."

The stairway ended halfway upward on the third-floor hallway, enabling anyone to walk on and off safely. Talbot checked the hallway and deemed it safe. It was long, with narrow bright yellow walls giving the impression of more light. Talbot took a few steps forward, her feet muffled by the white carpeting. She paused, squinted and looked at each door. Based on the number of doors, there were at least seven bedrooms, three on each side and another behind Peter at the end of the hallway behind the stairs.

Talbot turned and looked past Peter, still standing on the steps. She walked toward the door behind him and stopped.

"Is she in there?" Peter whispered.

"After the Event," Talbot said, ignoring his question, "there wasn't anywhere that anyone could live. It destroyed every major city all over the world. Some of them had no survivors. Others, like Columbus, were lucky."

"I may have caused it."

"You didn't cause it. It would have happened without you. But you altered the timeline and gave me a chance to fix it."

"You can fix it? Put things back the way they were before the Event?"

"I'm not sure yet. I may not be able to stop the Event, but I think I can make things better for the people of Columbus today. We'll work on the rest of the world after that."

Talbot pointed to a door near the main stairway at the end of the hallway.

"She's in there." She squeezed her eyes closed. "And she's not alone."

"Great. Let's get her."

"Sorry, Peter, this is where I leave you. I have something else to do."

"What?"

"I don't know what kind of time I have left, and I need to do this now. You have to save her alone. Meet me downstairs once it's over, and we'll figure out what to do next."

"You can't leave me. I need you."

"No. You don't need me. I watched you grow up. I helped you enough. You're smart and resourceful."

"I saw how you fought downstairs. You were having fun, messing around. I can't do that."

"It may not be about fighting with Niven. Be patient. Examine your surroundings. Figure out his weaknesses and choose the right time to strike."

"How will I know that?"

"You'll know."

Talbot opened the door and took one step inside. She turned away from Peter and examined the room. He heard a soft hum inside, near the back wall, but Talbot held the door open just enough for Peter to see only her.

"So, you're the big bad wolf," she said, looking at someone or something at the back of the room.

"Who are you talking to?" Peter asked.

She took another step inside, turned around and looked above the door. Peter stepped forward and craned his neck to see what she was seeing, but she pushed the door until it was almost closed. A thin smile appeared on her face. She nodded and pointed above the door.

Peter shook his head. "What do you see?"

He put his hands against the door and pressed, but she pushed against him until it shut completely. Peter grabbed the doorknob and twisted; it was no use, she had already locked it. Turning, he stared through the spiral railing toward the door where Anna was supposedly being held, at the end of the hall. All he had to do was go get her.

Sure, that's all. No problem. Because he's just going to hand her over.

Keeping to the opposite wall, he tiptoed along the carpet, keeping his eyes focused on Anna's door. He paused in front of the second set of doors. His mind drifted to the last time he'd seen Anna.

He said he would return her unharmed if you left things alone. Maybe I can fool him into thinking I'm future me and I've been waiting five years.

Peter moved to the door, stopped and listened. Silence. He cupped his hand over his ear and moved closer, pressing it to the door. More silence. He touched the doorknob.

What are you going to do? Just walk in and say hi?

Peter turned the handle and pushed open the door a few inches.

"Come in VanBurenBoy," Niven said. "We've been expecting you."

Peter's muscles tightened. His arms and legs felt heavy as he trudged into the room. Talbot's voice echoed in his head.

Be patient. Examine your surroundings.

It was a small room with a light-brown hardwood floor. Pale white walls had been covered with newspaper clippings, pictures of people including himself, Aiden Connor, Sudo Brownlock, Padma and others that Peter assumed were from GROUP.

Two windows on the opposite wall enabled small, square lines of moonlight to shine through. Niven sat in a black leather chair in a corner, behind an old wooden desk, something that had been common before larger, complex computer desks became available. Facing the desk, a large white couch dominated the corner closest to Peter. In the third corner, opposite Niven, an oversized yellow birdcage hung from the wall; it was large enough for a human. Peter flinched.

"Anna!" He yelled.

She turned her head toward the door and spoke Peter's name. Her voice was muffled by whatever had been stuffed into her mouth. Her wrists had been tied together and attached to the top of the cage. She stood on her toes, her ankles tied together and to the bottom of the cage. A brown burlap sack covered her head.

Peter rested his elbow on the back of the couch, steadying himself from the dizziness taking over his body. Rubbing his eyes, he fought back tears.

"I'm here," he finally said. His voice trembled.

Okay, she's alive. That's a start.

"Sit down," Niven said. He watched Peter, taking in his reactions. A broad smile spread across his face as he glanced at Anna and back at Peter. "You and I need to have a serious conversation."

Peter spied his backpack on the desk in front of Niven. It was open, his machine and phone sitting next to it. He sat in the middle of three cushions on the couch.

Niven reached to the floor behind the desk and lifted a large wooden staff. He held it in the center, grasping a thick rubber collar wrapped around the staff next to a dial. On each end, a claw jutted out, mimicking the electrodes on a cattle prod, and hummed. Peter stared at it, frozen in place. His muscles tensed. Niven held it in the air for him.

"You like? It's my new toy."

He pushed it between the bars of the cage and held it near Anna's leg. The humming grew louder. Sparks jumped from the staff to her shin.

"You'll never believe how I came up with the idea," Niven said.

He pushed it against her shin. Her muffled scream pierced Peter's ears. She tried to pull her leg away, but her ankle restraints made it impossible.

A lump formed in Peter's throat. He swallowed. He squeezed his fists together and held his arms at his sides, pushing them against his body.

His voice cracked. "Please stop."

He swallowed again, pushing down the bile that had risen to his throat. He began to stand.

"Stay there," Niven said.

Peter sank back into the couch, moving a few inches closer to the desk where his backpack currently rested.

It's not the right time. Remember what Talbot said. Be patient.

He wanted to jump, go after the man who was hurting Anna, unhook her and get out—but not yet. If he jumped now, they would lose. *Be patient, find a weakness and jump.*

Niven pulled the staff from the cage. Anna's shoulders fell. She let out a low, muffled whimper. Niven turned to Peter, holding his look for a few seconds. He smiled, like a father trying to calm his son, and stared in silence for a few seconds. Cocking his head, he finally spoke.

"Let me tell you a story, VanBurenBoy."

Chapter 43

Nelson, 2022

"For most of my childhood, I hated my father. He was never around. But we had money, and he constantly tried to buy my love. One day, when I was just ten years old, I decided that if he wasn't going to be around, I was going to take advantage. I let him buy whatever he wanted. I pretended it mattered. But it didn't. Can you imagine making a decision like that at ten?"

VanBurenBoy stared at me as I talked. I paced from the cage to my desk, and he remained fixated on me. It was about time I had his full attention.

"But then one day, in fact, my sixteenth birthday, he took it all away."

I slammed my palm on the desk. VanBurenBoy jumped. The girl in the cage yelped and recoiled.

"Just like that!" I yelled. "He took it from me."

"Why?" VanBurenBoy asked.

"Don't interrupt me when I'm talking."

I pushed the end of my staff against the girl's leg. She screamed. Her head fell forward as she whimpered. VanBurenBoy flinched, grabbed fistfuls of the couch cushions but stayed in his place. I wanted so much for him to attack me, but he stayed surprisingly calm.

"So, you asked me why. For years I wondered the same thing. He claimed it would make me a man."

I set the staff on my desk and walked toward him. It was time to have some fun with this weak little boy. I sat beside him on the couch so close I was practically on top of him. I put my arm around him and squeezed.

"You see, VanBurenBoy, he said it would make me a man. And I hated him for it."

VanBurenBoy looked past me at the girl.

"Are you listening to me?" I stood and lifted my staff toward the cage.

"I'm listening."

"As I was saying, he claimed it would make me a man. I became bitter and angry, but I also became something I didn't expect. I became motivated. I wanted to prove him wrong. And I found Sarah, and every time I wanted to quit, she was there for me, keeping me on the right path. Do you know what I realized?"

He didn't answer. I tilted my head and stared at him.

"VanBurenBoy, I asked you a question. Do you know what I realized?"

"No, what?"

"He was right. The old bastard was right." I raised my arms in the air and spun in a circle. "Look at all this stuff around me. I built a money-making empire. I got married. I had three kids. I did it. I became a man because of him."

I turned and looked out one of the windows. I paused my speech long enough to think about Sarah and the airplane crash. One of the newspaper articles on the wall near the window caught my eyes. I rested one hand against the window and read through it. VanBurenBoy shifted behind me, the prolonged silence obviously bothering him. Good. He shouldn't be comfortable.

"Then he died," I said, breaking the silence. "And it took until the day he died for me to understand. I immediately regretted all the time I didn't get with him, and I decided I would not do that with my own kids.

"I decided we would start with a bang. A big family vacation to Disney. It was May twenty-sixth, 2006. They got on a plane, and the plane crashed, and I lost them. It was the worst day of my life."

Tears fell from my eyes. I turned back toward him. He was staring at the open window. *Why isn't he paying attention?*

"I'm still talking VanBurenBoy!"

I took the end of my staff and shoved it against the girl's leg again, holding it a few seconds longer than the first time. She screamed an anguished, high-pitched howl, and squirmed. A deep red blister formed almost immediately. The smell of burning flesh surrounded me. I inhaled sharply, sucking it into my nose and smiled. I would not be the only one to suffer. I pulled the staff away, pieces of fused skin sticking to the end, and looked back toward the boy. He was hugging the arm of the couch. He so wanted to jump to save her, but he didn't. Why wasn't he helping? *I would do anything for Sarah, and he just sits here while I do this?*

"So anyway, VanBurenBoy, that's when the nightmares started. You've had those nightmares before, haven't you?"

He nodded.

"And then you two came into my life and crashed your car into us. I woke up, and they were back. My wife and my kids were back. It was the happiest moment of my life. I swore from that moment on, I would protect them with my life.

"But that same night, you came into GROUP ranting and raving about a car accident and how you changed things and how you wanted to change them back. I couldn't let that happen. I remember that night. It was the first time I'd hugged my family in years. I gave you every chance to stop. But you didn't, VanBurenBoy. Why didn't you?"

The boy is shivering. He knows what I'm going to say next. I paused, giving him time to realize what I had to do to keep my family safe.

"Now I will take her from you, and you'll understand. You'll feel what I feel, and maybe, just maybe, you'll understand why I'm doing all this. Who knows, maybe we could become friends afterward."

I twisted the power dial on my staff. It buzzed louder. Sparks fell from the tip to the floor near his feet. I smiled as he scrambled out of the way.

"I'm sorry I have to do this."

I turned to face her and lifted the staff at the height of her heart. I pushed it through the cage. She squirmed, but her ropes were too tight. She wasn't going anywhere. Sparks jumped from the staff to her sweater, singing the fabric, burning small black marks as I pushed it closer.

I couldn't help but chuckle. This would guarantee my rule and my family's safety for good. After these two were gone, no one would be left to stop me.

My breath picked up. My heart quickened, and I could see the end of the staff quaking. Nerves? Excitement? I paused for a split second and listened as VanBurenBoy shifted behind me.

Maybe now he was getting it. It was finally sinking in for him, how serious this was.

I tilted up the staff and moved it forward, but pain filled my head. My vision blurred. I stumbled, crashed against my desk and dropped the staff.

Chapter 44

Peter, 2022

Niven turned his back and stared out a window. Peter looked toward his bag, sitting open on the desk. He drifted to the end of the couch, and while Niven continued his diatribe, Peter reached for what was his. His hands floated above the machine. He touched it with his fingertips.

Niven stopped talking.

Peter jerked his hand from the machine and lifted his head to watch Niven, who appeared to be silently reading a newspaper article taped to the wall next to the window. He squinted and looked over Niven's shoulder, trying to read the headline, but the words were too far away. A color photo of a crashed, smoking airplane dominated the front page. Emergency vehicles had clustered on one side of the plane, and fire trucks were sending thick streams of water into the flames, still shooting from the fuselage.

Silence filled the room. Out of the corner of his eye, Peter watched Anna bend her head to one side to hear their voices better. He kept one eye on Niven and slowly extended his hands across the desk. He slid his machine and phone inside his backpack and closed the bag without latching it so Niven wouldn't hear the click. He pulled his hands from the desk and wrapped them around the arm of the couch.

"Then he died," Niven said. His voice was flat, and it broke when he talked. He traced a finger across the picture of the airplane.

Peter stared at the headline, squinting, trying to read the words that were just a little too far away.

"A big family vacation to Disney," Niven said, continuing his speech.

The plane crash Peter had read about with Anna flashed into his head. He thought back to the details.

Airplane on its way to Orlando went down in the Appalachians somewhere inside Kentucky. No survivors.

"I'm still talking, VanBurenBoy!"

Peter flinched. He looked at Niven, who was staring so intently at him, Peter felt a rush of heat emanating from the man. Niven frowned. He shook his head and turned to face Anna. He pressed the end of his staff through the bars against her leg for a second time. Her muffled screams hit Peter harder than the first time. Niven looked at him, a thin, evil smile spread across his lips. His chest quickly rose and fell. Peter fought back every urge to save her.

She is hurting. Jump now!

Peter knew better. If he jumped now and failed, everyone lost. He would die. Anna would die. The world would continue down the same path, held hostage by this one evil, insane man. The decision Peter had to make, when to strike, it wasn't just the decision to save Anna—it was the decision to save everyone.

Niven pulled the staff from her leg. Her head and shoulders hung limp, and she whimpered. Peter sat silently, pushing away the rage. Bile climbed into his throat. He swallowed, forcing it down.

"As I was saying, VanBurenBoy, that's the when the nightmares started. You've had those nightmares before, haven't you?"

Peter thought back to the days of the nightmares. He dreamed of strangers suffering. He saw Zach's death.

You saw her die too, and she will be next unless you do something.

Niven mentioned the car accident. Peter could practically hear the puzzle pieces falling into place. By saving Niven's family, they had created a monster. Talbot was wrong. It was his fault. He looked at Niven, watching him strut around the room, seeing him for the first time as the monster they had created.

"You came into GROUP ranting and raving about a car accident, and that you changed things and how you wanted to reverse everything," Niven said. His voice softened. "I couldn't let that happen. I remember that night. It was the first time I'd hugged my family in years. I gave you every chance to leave it alone. But you didn't, VanBurenBoy. Why didn't you?"

Peter wanted to speak. He wanted to ask Niven if he had looked around Columbus lately. Could he not see what had happened? Peter already knew the answer. There was no reasoning with him. He was not going to give up his family. Peter knew he would have to risk his own life to save not just Anna, but everyone.

"So now I will take her from you, and you'll understand me. You'll feel what I feel, and maybe, just maybe, you'll understand why I'm doing this. Who knows, maybe we can become friends someday."

We'll never be friends. One of us isn't leaving this castle alive.

Niven reached for the dial in the center of the staff, next to the rubber handle. He spun it as far it would go. The staff vibrated, emitting a buzzing sound Peter had last heard when his fourth-grade class visited the city's largest power plant. Sparks jumped from the tip and bounced off the floor near Peter's feet. Niven laughed as Peter recoiled. He lifted his staff in the air and admired his weapon.

"I'm sorry I have to do this."

Niven turned and walked to the cage. He pushed the charged end of the staff through the bars.

The smell of her burned flesh filled the air. With each cry Anna let out, a little piece of Peter cried with her. He looked at the scar on her leg, just below the wound from the door when they first crossed paths with Max, Alison and Regan. Adrenaline pumped through his veins. He inhaled, filling his lungs with as much air he could take in. Talbot said he would figure it out. She knew he would know the right moment. This was it.

He sprang.

Sliding his arms through the straps of his bag, Peter rushed at Niven. Peter swung the bag, leading with the spine of the big history textbook, and crashed it against the side of his Niven's head. Niven's body twisted. He lost control of the staff, which flew over his head, and collided with the desk. He stumbled, dropping face-first onto the couch.

Peter grabbed the cage door and pulled. His hand slipped, throwing him backward a couple of steps. He wiped his palm on his pants and reached for the door handle. Again, he pulled, putting all his strength into it. The cage shook on the chains attaching it to the ceiling, but the door didn't budge.

"Peter?" Anna called out.

"I'm here."

"Looking for these?" Niven said.

Peter spun. Niven pressed one hand against the corner of the desk and pushed himself to his feet, smiling as he rose. A set of keys dangled from the index finger of his free hand. The smile disappeared from his face, dropping into a scowl, and he shoved the keys inside his jacket. Eyeing the staff lying on the floor in front of the desk, Niven lunged. Peter vaulted between Niven and the staff, driving his shoulder into Niven's stomach.

As they met, Niven wrapped his arms around Peter's waist. They hit the ground together and rolled. Peter pushed a knee into Niven's stomach, separating their bodies. Niven pushed him away, slamming Peter's shoulder against the desk. Peter squeezed his eyes shut and grabbed his own shoulder. He felt a shadow engulf him and opened his eyes. Niven stood tall, holding the staff over Peter's head, ready to strike.

Peter kicked with both feet, hitting Niven's knees hard enough to force him backward. As Peter turned toward Anna, Niven regained his balance and grabbed Peter's wrist, spinning him around until they were face to face. Niven swung his fist and buried it under Peter's rib cage. Peter bent forward, gasped for air and grabbed his side.

Still hanging on to Peter's wrist, Niven swung again. His fist connected with Peter's mouth, busting his lip. Peter bit his tongue hard, sending drops of blood into his throat. He retched and rocked on his heels, but before he could regain his balance, Niven grabbed him by the shoulders and tossed him across the room.

Peter crashed against the cage, knocking it loose from the ceiling. It hit the ground and rolled, breaking apart and sending scraps of metal in all directions. Peter landed on his back and closed his eyes, only to have Anna's muffled scream slice through his head. With each movement, every muscle in his body ached. He rolled his head and looked for her. Remnants of the cage lay near the door, and he saw Anna lying next to them on her side, curled into a ball and not moving. With what little amount of strength he could pull together, he reached for her.

"All you had to do was leave it alone!" Niven yelled.

Peter's eyes focused. Niven stood over him, tossing the staff from one hand to the other. He straddled Peter, one leg on each side, and squatted until he was sitting on his victim's legs. Spinning the staff in one hand, he finally pointed it like a javelin at Peter's head.

"I guess we won't end up friends after all," Niven said.

With both arms, Niven raised the staff over his head, ready for the fatal blow. But a metal rod from the birdcage debris hit him above his left ear. His head jerked to the right, the cut spraying blood onto Peter's face. Niven toppled over, hitting the floor. He turned his head, his mouth gaping open. Digging his elbow into the floor, he attempted to push himself up and tried to stand.

Anna stood over Niven, her eyes wide and her nostrils flared. Spittle gathered in the corner of her mouth. She swung again, hitting him in the same spot. He dropped to the ground next to Peter and pushed his palms against his cheeks. Blood seeped between his fingers, soaking the wooden floor. He gurgled and coughed, spewing blood onto Anna's shoes. She was breathing heavily and held the metal rod over her head, ready to strike again if needed.

Niven stopped moving.

Anna tossed the metal rod aside and held out her hand to Peter. He grabbed it, and she pulled him to his feet.

"You okay?" she asked.

Peter opened his mouth, stretching it as far as it would open, making sure his jaw was still in one piece. He nodded.

"I think so."

"Come on. We should go."

Chapter 45

Peter/Nelson, 2022

Peter

They exited the room and made their way down the stairs to the second floor. At the bottom, Peter froze.

"What?" Anna asked. "What's wrong?"

"My bag is still up there. We can't go anywhere without it."

He turned and put one foot on the first step. Peter looked to the upstairs landing and stopped. The shadows seemed to move.

Niven appeared.

He held the right side of his shirt against his cheek, exposing the large purple bruises over his ribs.

"I'm not through with the two of you yet," he snarled.

He dropped his shirttail, uncovering a wound on his head. His dark hair was streaked with crimson and already beginning to mat. His right eye didn't open when he blinked, and his bottom lip was three times its normal size, giving the right side of his face and odd, lopsided appearance.

Niven limped to the stairs. Using the railing to steady himself, he swung out his leg and let it fall onto the first step.

Anna grabbed Peter's hand and pulled him toward the flight leading to the first floor.

"Cowards!" Niven yelled.

Peter's shoulder ached with each step, and Anna was limping badly on her right leg. The charred spots on her skin were the size of quarters. They took each step down one at a time, using each other for balance, but Niven's pace was slower, and he couldn't catch up. They left him in their wake as they escaped through the front door. At the bottom of the steps, Anna stopped.

"A moat?" she said.

Peter ran to the small kiosk near the bridge and pushed every button.

"It's not reacting to anything," he yelled.

"You need a key," Niven said, propping himself inside the doorway. Dried blood covered the right side of his face, and his head wobbled. He pointed a crooked finger at them. "There's no way off this property unless you go through me. So, bring it on, both of you come at me. No cheap shots this time."

Niven's blood-stained grin revealed dark, empty spots where his two front teeth had been just a little while before. He raised his arms and balled his hands into fists. Anna grabbed Peter's forearm and held him, stopping him from advancing on Niven. She tugged his arm again, and he turned to look into her eyes.

You've already rescued her, and she saved your life. Get out while you still can.

They disappeared around the side of the castle.

Nelson

"GODDAMMIT, I'M SICK of this shit!"

I limped down the stairs and followed them to the backyard. Stopping at my workbench, built under the scoreboard, I opened a drawer in the middle where I kept the paintball guns. Tossing each gun to the ground, I lifted the false metal bottom. Two hunting rifles, put there for extra security just after the Event, were waiting for me. I chose the Remington. It was the longest-range shot, and I'd sighted it just a few months ago. I dropped in five shells and chambered the first one. Time to end this madness once and for all.

"Loser dies!" I yelled.

I walked into the woods on the right side. My right eye was swollen shut, and I had to swivel my head to pan the yard.

"His face when he saw me..." I muttered. "He's scared out of his mind. This should be easy."

At the end of the woods, I saw movement. I raised my gun and put my good eye to the scope. Shooting from my left side would be a challenge, but as long as the scope was correct, I wouldn't miss. I spotted them standing behind two wide trees near the barn. She limped from one tree to the next. I admired my handiwork.

Always make sure you finish what you start.

I hadn't heard my father's voice in my head for what seemed like years. He must really be proud to be showing up at a time like this.

"I knew I wouldn't let you down," I whispered, looking to the sky.

I aimed the rifle at the small tree next to her. VanBurenBoy leaned his back against the rough, peeling bark, but his scrawny shoulders stuck out on each side, giving away his hiding spot.

"Doesn't even know how to hide properly. This is the guy who's trying to take my empire away?"

I trained my rifle on his left side, hit the safety and fired. The recoil pushed the gun into my shoulder. The scope smacked against my only good eye.

"Goddammit!"

I lifted the scope back to my eye and scanned the trees. They were gone.

Peter

"WE SHOULD TRY TO GET to that barn," Anna said. "I have an idea."

She moved to a tree near the front of the woods, and Peter followed. She stopped, picking a thick, round tree to hide behind. Peter stopped at the tree next to hers.

"This isn't going to work," Peter said.

He looked past Anna, noticing a tree wide enough to hide him. He peered into the woods and something glinted, a quick flicker of light in the distance.

He's out there.

Peter turned again, pressing his back against the tree, and tightened his body, shrugging his shoulders up tightly to his head.

"There's nowhere here to hide..."

A bullet slammed into the tree. He jumped and looked at Anna. She ducked, bent over and reached for Peter.

"When did he get a gun?"

"I don't know," Peter said, "but we need to get out of here."

Anna nodded, and Peter took her hand. Together they dashed from the woods to the backside of the barn. Peter fell to the ground and took long, deep breaths to calm himself. His heart raced, and beads of sweat formed on his forehead. He stood. Dizziness overtook him, and he leaned against the barn.

Anna stuck her head around the side and looked.

"See anything?" Peter asked.

"He's fiddling with a big gun, scanning the area, I think," she paused and turned to Peter. "Great."

"What?"

"He saw me," Anna said flatly.

Nelson

"THERE YOU ARE," I SAID.

I tightened the gun to my shoulder and pulled the trigger again. It ricocheted off the front of the barn.

"You think you can hide from me!"

It was actually kind of fun. Those football players were never a challenge, and games with Steve were just pretend. This was real. This was life or death.

I had her location and could only assume VanBurenBoy was with her, but I hadn't seen him yet. I looked over my shoulder. Had they split up? My sixteenth birthday popped into my head. *I'm Steve. She's Sarah.* I looked toward the chicken coop. Was he back there? *Will he actually use her as bait to try to trap me?*

Peter

"TRUST ME," ANNA SAID.

The rifle fired again, and Anna dove behind the barn. The shot hit the front of the barn, reverberating through the yard.

"Go inside," she said. "Wait behind the door. I'll get him to come inside. Find something and hit him."

Peter looked at her; his head felt heavy. The barn, the buildings lining the moat and the trees were out of focus, and they appeared to spin.

"We have to end this," Anna said, "and he's not going to quit until we do."

He wanted to speak, argue with her, tell her there had to be another way. But deep down, he knew she was right. They had tried hiding multiple times, and each time he found them.

"Trust me," she said again. This time her voice was softer.

He did trust her. He nodded and stepped inside the barn. He stared at the line of tractors along the back wall. Hanging near the first one was a set of old, rusty tools. Peter reached for the crowbar, using the little amount of strength he had left to hold it up. Having been a city boy his entire life, a computer guy who rarely did any kind of outside physical labor, he had had never held a crowbar. He took the flat end in his hand and turned it, so the curved end was sticking out, ready to inflict damage.

"Hey, asshole!" Anna yelled from just outside the door. "We're in the barn!"

She ran inside and positioned herself on the ground, against the wall, next to the last tractor in the row.

"Get ready," she said.

Nelson

EVEN THOUGH I HADN'T seen VanBurenBoy hide, I was sure I knew where he was. I threw two quick shots her way, waited for her to disappear behind the barn and limped toward it. I paused and pressed my back against the large wall. Just like Steve, I had two options: I could take her head-on, or I could go around the other side and sneak up behind her. If I tried to take her from behind, VanBurenBoy would have the drop on me from the chicken coop, and I would not let that happen. I turned and sneaked along the front of the barn. I took a breath and nudged my head around the corner.

No one was there.

I tiptoed along the wall until I reached the back corner. I peered around. She wasn't there, and VanBurenBoy wasn't waiting at the chicken coop. What kind of game were they playing? I heard something banging one of my dad's tractors inside the barn. Of course, she's in there; that's where we met. *It's all playing out just like it did when we were kids.*

Peter

PETER FELT UNEASY AS he watched Anna sitting out in the open, exposed, using herself as bait. He should have protested and come up with a better plan, something that would have kept her from the line of fire; but as soon as she spoke he could feel her confidence, and he trusted her. At this moment, though, watching her shuffle back and forth as if she couldn't get comfortable, he was changing his mind.

What is she doing?

She leaned against the tractor and raised her arm, touching the top of the tire. She shook her head and edged forward, stirring a small cloud of dust. Finally comfortable, she stopped moving. She grabbed a small piece of wood from the floor and banged it against the tractor. The noise echoed through the barn.

Peter heard movement on the other side of the barn door. Anna raised her index finger to her mouth and tilted her head. Niven nudged the door, his shadow growing larger as the opening grew wider. Peter watched the shadow step through the doorway, the barrel of the rifle rising into the air. Peter lifted the crowbar behind his head.

"Sarah?" Niven said.

Peter watched the shadow pause. He froze and concentrated. It dropped the rifle to its side, tapping the barrel against the floor. Peter exhaled and glanced at Anna, straining to gauge the reaction on her face. Had she expected this? Was she scared? Peter put his free hand over his chest, lightly tapping his sternum, hoping to stifle the sound of his heartbeat so it wouldn't give away his hiding spot.

"Hi baby," Anna said, "Thank God you found me. It's scary out there."

"You shouldn't be here. I asked you to take the kids and leave."

"You're doing bad things here," Anna said, her voice soft.

Peter watched Niven's shadow take another step forward, almost clear of the door but still not far enough inside for Peter to get a good swing without revealing himself. He couldn't miss, and Niven couldn't know it was coming. He couldn't have the chance to duck or move to the side.

"But I'm doing it all for us," Niven said, "and for the kids."

"It's wrong, and you know it." Anna kept her voice soft but spoke in a stern tone.

Peter put his finger on the door and pushed, closing it a few inches, gaining a better look at Niven. Niven took another step toward Anna, and the shadow disappeared. Peter stopped breathing. The shot was there as soon as he was ready to take it. Niven drew his head back and raised the rifle.

"You're not Sarah!"

Peter kicked the door shut and swung the crowbar, crashing it against the gun. Niven's body twisted. He pulled the trigger, sending a bullet ricocheting off the tractor above Anna's head. She threw herself to the ground and put her hands over the back of her neck. Peter swung again. Niven lifted his arm to block the blow, but the crowbar struck him, shattering his wrist.

Niven roared, the gun tumbled to the ground, and he dropped to his knees. Wasting no time, Peter took aim for his head. He swung a third time, slamming the curved end of the crowbar against Niven's bloody, beaten forehead. Niven rocked backward and collapsed to the ground.

Silence filled the barn.

Peter shuffled out from behind the door. He nudged Niven's crumpled body with his shoe and stepped back. Niven didn't move. He stared at the man lying in front of him. His chest wasn't rising. Peter poked him with the bloodied crowbar but still no movement. Using the curved end, he inched the man's jacket open. He carefully reached into an inside pocket and pulled out a set of keys.

He ran to Anna and stretched his hand, helping her to her feet. Putting his hand on the small of her back, he guided her around him and to the door. She stepped over Niven's fractured arm and groaned, squeezing her eyes closed until she was past him. Peter followed, stepping around the lifeless body, and escaped the barn.

Chapter 46

Peter, 2022

"Your bag is still upstairs," Anna said. "We can't leave without it."

"This way," Peter said.

Anna stopped next to the barn and leaned against the wall. She bent down and rubbed below her knee, cringing each time her fingers touched a spot burned by Niven's staff.

Peter walked to her.

"Sorry about this," he said. "It's all my fault."

"Don't say that. It's not your fault he's a monster and did this."

Peter put his hand on her shoulder. He knew she was right, but if he hadn't built that machine, would all this have happened? He squeezed her arm a little more tightly, and a thin, sad smile formed in the corners of his mouth. He felt emotionally and physically drained. All the running and chasing they had done, the tears, the bloodshed, the danger he had put them in had taken everything from him. He put his other hand to his heart and breathed, glad it was nearly over.

"Either way, I'm sorry."

Anna met his smile with a sad one of her own.

"Come on, let's go home."

They climbed the steps leading to the kitchen. Peter walked behind Anna, making sure she stayed on her feet and pointed at the spiral staircase. She shuffled painfully after each step.

"Hang on," Peter said, stepping off the platform to the third-floor hallway. He grasped the doorknob of the room behind the stairs and turned, but it was still locked. He heard a loud collision and then silence.

"What was that?" Anna asked.

"I don't know, but the nurse is in there. Remember, the one from your monitor?"

"What? How?"

"I don't know," Peter said. "She doesn't seem to know either."

Anna stepped inside the room where she had been held prisoner. Peter rifled through the twisted remains of the birdcage. Buried underneath, the contents of his bag had taken the brunt of their escape and spilled to the floor. He grabbed his notebook and the history textbook. He held the textbook in front of him and smiled.

"That's the second time this book has saved my life."

He shoved it into the backpack and attached one end of the bracelet to his wrist. Anna limped toward him, steadying herself against the desk along the way. With each step, she grimaced and let out a small groan.

We can't get home quick enough.

Peter pushed the button on the side of his phone to wake it and scrolled to the MyGolfGPS app. Padma's app opened. He attached the open side of the bracelet to Anna's wrist and clicked it into place.

"You ready?" he asked.

"What are we going to do once we get back?"

"Try to stop the Event from happening?"

"And if we can't stop it, at least we can warn people as it approaches."

She nodded and closed her eyes. "Push it."

Peter pushed the backlit button. Nothing happened. He closed the app and pressed the shortcut on his home screen to reactivate it. The date, time and location fields had cleared with the restart. He pressed the Home shortcut and watched as the time they'd last left 2017 filled the empty fields. The coordinates would put them standing next to his bed just like it had every other time. He looked at Anna. She stared at him, eyebrows raised. His mind raced, and he pressed it again.

He felt nothing from the machine, no sparks, no electricity, no whir warning of something about to happen. The room hadn't blurred or changed. Nothing had happened. The machine was dead.

"What's going on?" Anna asked.

"I don't know."

Peter dumped the contents of the backpack on the desk and rummaged through the debris, looking for pieces that may have come apart when he slammed it against Niven's head.

"I led with the history book. I made sure when I slid it into the bag to keep the machine on one side, out of harm's way."

Peter unhooked the bracelet from their wrists. He flipped it over, rubbed his hands along the edges and searched for anything abnormal. He pulled the lid off the plastic case holding the blue wire from the microchip to the metal. Everything looked intact. He pressed the red question mark icon and opened a diagnostic window Padma had built into the app. It showed a strong signal between the phone and the microchip.

"Can you fix it?" Anna asked.

"I don't know what's wrong."

The light from the hallway dimmed.

"Everything looks right."

A groan outside the door caught their attention.

"Talbot?" Peter said.

They looked toward the door. Niven stood in the doorway, glaring at them. His cheeks, covered with dark purple bruises on each side, puffed in and out with each strained breath. He opened his mouth to talk, and a stream of blood spewed out, drenching the floor and the tops of his shoes.

"You can't beat me." His voice was raspy. He spoke slowly, pronouncing each letter of every word.

In his left hand, he held the rifle by the stock. It rested against his side, the barrel bouncing off the floor as he tried to balance. Anna screamed and dove to the floor in front of the couch. Peter leaped behind the desk.

Niven lifted the rifle. He stumbled and listed to one side. Dropping the gun to the floor, he shuffled sideways and leaned against the door frame. Peter peered over the desk. Niven's good eye fluttered as if he were struggling to keep it open. He lifted the gun again. His arms trembled as he brought the scope to his face. Peter ducked as Niven pulled the trigger but a loud click, followed by silence, was all Peter heard. He pulled himself to his knees and lifted his head above the edge of the desk. He watched as Niven examined the disabled rifle. Obviously frustrated, Niven tossed the rifle in Peter's direction.

It bounced off the desk and over Peter's head to the wall. He limped toward Peter.

Enough is enough.

Peter's shoulder ached, and his legs were on fire, but he ignored the pain. He stepped around the desk and stopped. Standing his ground, he waited for Niven to get closer. Peter made a fist and swung, but punched only air as Niven rocked forward, stooped at the waist and grabbed the desk. Peter's momentum spun him around. Niven lunged, wrapped his hands around Peter's waist and lifted him off the ground. Peter, surprised at Niven's strength, bent his knees and kicked the man's shins with his heels, but Niven squeezed hard, pushing his fingernails into Peter's stomach.

He carried Peter toward the open window, unfazed by the extra strain of Peter's resistance. Peter dug his heels into the carpet, placed his palms against the window's frame and grunted. Niven hoisted Peter into the air, but Peter continued his resistance, pressing his feet against the wall below the window and pushing back against Niven's torso.

"People of my Columbus!" Niven yelled over Peter's shoulder. "Watch me now as I end all our problems!"

Niven turned Peter sideways, releasing him from the wall. Peter drove the heel of his right foot into Niven's kneecap. Niven howled and lost his grip on Peter's waist, dropping him to the carpet.

"Hey!" Anna screamed.

Peter saw Anna running at Niven, holding the staff like a lance at a joust, her eyes trained on Niven. Niven turned. The staff hit him with enough force to rupture his skin and penetrate a few inches deep into his abdomen. Peter reached toward the staff and spun the dial as far it would go. Sparks burst from each end, hurling Anna backward. She bounced off the couch, her body twisted, and hit the floor. She rolled onto her stomach and lay still.

The jolt of electricity launched Niven toward the window. The back of his head smacked against the wall above the frame, and his feet came off the floor, folding him in half like a dirty towel thrown in the trash. A low gurgled moan escaped his throat, spraying blood on the carpet.

Peter cringed and turned his head away.

Chapter 47

Peter, 2022

Peter heard the splash from the moat three stories below. He opened his eyes and lifted his head. Anna crawled toward him and collapsed on the floor.

"Hey," she said.

"Hey."

Grasping the top of the desk, Peter pulled himself to his feet. Pain surged through every muscle. His head pounded. He stopped, closed his eyes and inhaled, letting the air fill his stomach. He exhaled, opened his eyes and looked around the room. Was it finally over? Using Peter's arm as leverage, Anna pulled herself to her feet as well, stumbling against the wall.

"Look," she said, pointing through the window.

Peter limped behind her and looked over her shoulder to the moat. The staff, still protruding from Niven's abdomen, sank below the surface. The last puff of white smoke rose into the air and floated past the window.

"I think..." She hesitated, then added, "I think it's finally over."

Peter nodded.

They clung to each other, navigating the two flights of stairs to the front door. Peter squeezed the railing tightly, grasping any additional support he could find. At the bottom of the stairs, Anna pulled the big door open. They exited the castle and sat on the steps. In the distance, the sun had just started to set. A cool breeze blew through, chilling Peter.

Anna sniffled and put her head on Peter's shoulder. He flinched and looked at her legs. One of the burns had grown and spread around her shin. Below it, the wound from the door had swollen and looked inflamed. Peter thought about Zach and how he'd held his best friend as the life drained from him. Could anything, any of the death and destruction he'd caused with his machine be undone?

"How do we get home?" she asked.

"I don't know. We may be trapped."

Anna's grip tightened at the mention of being trapped. Peter blinked when a light on the horizon sparkled through a tear in his eye. He wiped it away and stared toward the buildings poking above the trees in downtown Columbus.

"What is that light?" Peter asked.

Keeping her head tucked against his shoulder, she turned and looked. Another light flickered at the top of a second building.

"I don't know."

Like a wildfire spreading through a dry forest, the floors of every building in the city lit up, beginning at the top and filtering to the street. The drawbridge creaked and lowered, hitting the opposite side with a thud. Anna stood.

"Let's go," she said.

He stood and walked into the house. He felt his heart racing as he climbed the first flight of stairs. He had to find Talbot. He had to get through that door. She had seemed to know everything that was going to happen. If anyone could help them get home, it would be her.

"What are you doing?" Anna yelled.

"Need to find Talbot!"

Peter climbed the stairs as Anna trailed behind. He made his way to the end of the third-floor hall, grabbed the door handle and turned —but it was still locked.

"Wait," Anna said. "I have an idea."

Anna hobbled to the room where she had been held prisoner, paused at the doorway and disappeared inside. She quickly emerged, holding a flat piece of the birdcage floor. It was circular, about the size of a manhole cover, and weighed at least fifteen pounds.

"Here," she said. "Try this."

Peter slammed it against the doorknob. The clanging of the massive disc against the doorknob echoed through the hall, sending vibrations up Peter's arms and into his shoulders. The doorknob shattered, throwing metal shrapnel in all directions. Peter jammed his heel against the door, forcing it open, slamming it against the wall on the other side. He rushed into the room.

A series of white computer towers were stacked in a four-by-four grid against the far corner. They were connected to each other by a loose collection of blue wires, bound with black electrical tape. White smoke billowed from the center of the stack. Each tower had black scorches running along the sides, stopping only where the plastic had melted inward and fused a couple of towers together. Above the wreckage, the charred ceiling gave Peter a glimpse of the evening sky.

He glanced at Anna. She was staring into a corner, her hand covering her mouth. Lying there was the body of Talbot. It appeared to have taken the brunt of whatever had burned the towers. A thin line of smoke clung to the cuffs of her jeans. Her fingers were black and seared, frozen as if she had been grasping for something when it happened. Her arms and forehead were bright, glowing. All the life she had shown in the basement during her fight with Sudo Brownlock had been drained from her body.

Peter's shoulders dropped. He walked into the hallway and hung his arms over the stairway railing.

"Sorry," Anna said.

"She's gone too."

Anna took his hand and led him to the main stairway. Peter stayed quiet, walking beside her, with no idea what to do next. They crossed the drawbridge and walked along the dirt path leading away from the castle. At the end of the path, they stepped onto a street that led into a modest residential neighborhood. The outside light of each one-story ranch house flipped on. People slowly wandered outside, mingling with neighbors, smiling and talking. A few of the survivors rushed toward Peter and Anna. An older woman carried a blanket and a large bottle of water. She wrapped the blanket around the pair and led them to her front porch, where they sat and sipped the cool, refreshing water.

More of the citizens walked over to greet them. Men, women and children crowded the street, everyone looking toward the castle. A young child raised her arm and pointed. Peter and Anna turned.

The lights of the castle went dark.

Did you enjoy this book? If so, I have a FREEBIES for you!

Get Spark, Novel number two in the series for FREE once it's available by signing up for my mailing list.

And Origins: Volume 1, a short story detailing how Peter came to discover time travel and what he did with it is available right now for FREE if you sign up for my mailing list.

I promise not to fill your email box daily with emails. Instead, I'll put one or two out there per month and will only do more if I'm offering exclusive deals for my subscribers.

Go to www.jerryevanoff.com[1] for more information.

Help me with Reviews

Reviewing my book on the site you purchased it is one of the most important things when it comes to gaining attention to my books. If you liked the book, please leave a review. The more reviews I receive, the more my book will make it to other readers. It only takes a couple minutes and I am grateful for any time you can take to help me out.

About the Author

I've always been a pretty big reader. I don't know how old I was, but I can remember back in the early 1980s, sitting on the floor of the public library during my mom's Friends of the Library meetings. She was the president, and my dad was treasurer, although I'm pretty sure he was just a figurehead. I would search the shelves for the Encyclopedia Brown books and read each of the stories one after another, happy every time EB took that quarter, solved the case and got one over on Bugs Meany. Poor Bugs, he never stood a chance.

Later on, I soaked up every single thing I could from Agatha Christie, Tom Clancy and Sue Grafton. There was actually a period of time I wanted to be a private detective because of Kinsey Millhone. I read biographies, books about sports and anything Star Wars I could get my hands on.

Yet during that time, I never thought about writing.

I've always had a pretty active imagination, and I tend to get lost in my own head. I mean seriously, I can't be the only person who, while standing in line at the bank, starts to imagine what it would be like if a group of terrorists came barging through the doors and how to be the hero, save the day and get the girl.

Still, even then, I never imagined writing.

In 2001, I found a reality show called Big Brother. Twelve to sixteen strangers were locked in a house with no contact with the outside world. Stuck in there for three months, all they had was each other. More than fifty cameras and a hundred microphones gave the viewers the ability to watch them, 24/7 on the internet, as they formed alliances, backstabbed, and one by one voted each other out, all to win a cash prize in the end. Sure, the voyeur in me started me watching, but the curiosity of why people act the way they act kept me going season after season. There was nothing better than watching one of the houseguests tell someone something, then walk upstairs and lie about the whole conversation to someone else. It was a giant social experiment, and I loved every second of it.

I applied twice but never got a callback.

That same year, I found an online Big Brother forum, a community of people just like me who watched the show and the uncensored live feeds. This forum gave us a place where we could write about what we saw. We were kicked off the site after exactly one season, because all we did was refresh our browser over and over, hoping there was another post to read. Unfortunately, that brought their site to a screaming halt several times and they didn't like that. Luckily, some very smart people started a new message board, just for us, our little clique. So many days, I would come home from work, turn on the feeds, open the message board and recap everything that happened.

I didn't post like the others, though. I tried to be funny, inject stories about my own life and generally try to make people laugh. My post about how I live my life by a set of cheese rules, mixed in with some light Big Brother recapping was one of my favorites.

For example: It's okay to eat cheese on a hot turkey sandwich but never on a cold one.

There was a love thread where people could take your words, quote you, and tell you how funny you were. I liked getting love.

But was I ready to write? Nope.

In 2004, the television show Lost premiered. It's one of my favorite shows, and I loved how JJ wrote. People criticize him for his whole Mystery Box thing, but I love it. I also really enjoyed how he mixed the backstories of characters, overlapping them with each other. I've seen the show a bunch of times, watched numerous recaps on YouTube and listened to podcasts about it. Still, even now, when I watch Lost episodes again, all I do is look in the background to see if Hurley is celebrating his lottery winnings on a hospital waiting room television while Jack preps for surgery.

One Friday night, I was googling ex-Cleveland Browns Quarterback Bernie Kosar...like most guys in their late 30s, I'm sure. I stumbled across a book that someone had written called *I Am Number Four* by Pittacus Lore. There was a dog in the book named Bernie Kosar, named after my favorite athlete of all time. So, naturally, I had to read it. It turned into this amazing series of seven novels and fifteen novellas with some of my favorite characters. I couldn't put them down, reading them over and over. But at the end of the sixth novel, a main character, one of my favorites, was killed off (spoiler alert), and I wasn't pleased. I remember saying out loud, "If I had written this, I would have never done that."

And there it was. I was ready.

I finally had everything I needed to write something. It would mix all those things I had been taking in throughout my life. Almost three years later, my book, Forgetting Tomorrow, was finished and released. It was the hardest thing I had ever done and so much fun, and I can't wait to release the next one.

Acknowledgements

This is my first book people, so strap in, it's going to be a long one!

Okay, along with the people I mentioned above, people I will never meet like JJ Abrams, Agatha Christie and Tom Clancy, I would like to acknowledge the people I do know who inspired me, whether they realize it or not.

Lindsay, my sister, who put up with me talking about writing so much, she ended up starting an author career of her own. You're welcome, sis.

Alison, Shawn, Jenny, Navya, Jeff, and so many others, who were inspirations for characters, even if they don't know it. And to everyone else who asked me to make them a character, and kill them off in a spectacular way, don't worry, there are still a lot of books left to write.

Thanks to Paris, who spent a couple of afternoons with me talking about horses and all the terminology I thought I knew. Turns out, jumping on a horse and whipping around the rope thingee didn't make them run like the wind.

Thanks to Dave, whose parents' front yard, back yard, and all the buildings in between became a paintball field in my book. Exactly like it was that winter we played each weekend, dotting every building in their yard (including their house) while they were in Florida only to be surprised when they came back a week early. Thank God for power washers.

Thanks to Brian, who spent a Sunday afternoon driving me all over Columbus so I could see the places in person I found on Google maps, making sure I described them exactly as they were. We didn't go into the Gates of Hell that day, but maybe next time. Also, that was one of my favorite breakfasts ever, and I think we need to get back there sooner than later. Check the Blue Jackets schedule and text me.

The countless number of other people who I encountered during my normal day to day, like Jeff (not the same Jeff mentioned above...I swear we have like eight Jeff's at work. It's annoying), Jim, Kyle, Dave, Rich, John and the best boss I've ever had, Kris, who would say random things during meetings, not realizing I was listening and taking notes.

Thanks to the people of the Big Brother message board, who gave me confidence the things I wrote were fun to read.

Also, thanks to the people of McCook, Nebraska, some at the Holiday Inn where I spent so many nights (especially the woman behind the counter for making a giant plate bacon for me on days when bacon wasn't being served while I was getting up at 4:00 AM to get some writing time in before my workday), and the folks at the manufacturing plant I spent so many days at for almost a year while I worked on this book.

Thanks to the many nameless people at the multiple restaurants, where I spent my lunch breaks writing, listening and people watching, stealing expressions, faces they made, and things they did, to help shape my characters.

Thanks to Bryan, who spent a week emailing back and forth with me, showing me how to craft a blurb for free, even though he has a company that charges people for the same service. Thanks to Meg, who created a fantastic cover for me, and the greatest editor in the world, Cee, who made my book something I wasn't afraid to put out into the real world. Don't worry Cee, I'm still working my way through Dark on Netflix.

Thanks to the people in the 20BooksTo50K© group on Facebook. During those times I wondered if I'd be able to finish, seeing the success of the authors in there, first time and long time, kept me going.

Thanks to everyone else who I didn't mention, especially my dad and my closest friends, who put up with me talking about my book non-stop for a couple of years. I saw your eyes glazing over, but at no point did you tell me to go away. And when it finally came out, you didn't hesitate to buy it, even multiple copies. I appreciate that.

And of course, my mom, who put me through an eighteen-month creative writing class by reading every chapter, marking them as much as she could, and sending them back with some of the best comments I could imagine. My favorite was when she crossed out the word "got" and told me never to use it again. Don't worry, mom, I got the message.

It always made me laugh when she would send back a heavily marked chapter with an email or text apologizing for being so hard on me, but I didn't care, everything she did made me a better writer.

Made in the USA
Columbia, SC
31 May 2020